# BEC MCMASTER

# The Hero Within

## THE BURNED LAND SERIES

# ALSO AVAILABLE BY BEC MCMASTER

## LONDON STEAMPUNK SERIES
Kiss Of Steel

Heart Of Iron

My Lady Quicksilver

Forged By Desire

Of Silk And Steam

*Novellas in same series:*

Tarnished Knight

The Curious Case Of The Clockwork Menace

## THE BLUEBLOOD CONSPIRACY SERIES
Mission: Improper

The Mech Who Loved Me

You Only Love Twice

To Catch A Rogue

Dukes are Forever

## LEGENDS OF THE STORM
Heart of Fire

Storm of Desire

Clash of Storms

## DARK ARTS SERIES
Shadowbound

Hexbound

Soulbound

**BURNED LANDS SERIES**
Nobody's Hero
The Last True Hero
*The Hero Within*

**OTHER**
The Many Lives Of Hadley Monroe

# The Hero Within

## THE BURNED LANDS SERIES

As the only healer in a war-stained town, Eden McClain is devastated when the salt plague sweeps through the wastelands she calls home. Suddenly she's racing against time to save her people—and her niece—before it's too late. When she hears whispers of a cure, she knows she can't cross the dangerous Wastelands by herself to get it. She needs a guide. And she's just desperate enough to turn to a man who once betrayed her.

### Redemption comes at a price...

After years living on the leash of a dangerous psychopath, Johnny Colton is finally free, but that doesn't mean he can wash the blood off his hands. The easiest way to deal with the past? Just stop caring. Which is working perfectly for the rugged outlaw, until a beautiful ghost from the past rigs a trap for him.

The last person he wants to see is the woman who haunts his dreams, but as Eden points out, he owes her one. The only problem? This plague is man-made. Someone unleashed it. Are they walking into a dangerous trap? And can two past enemies learn to trust each other enough to survive?

*Wastelands, 2149*

"We've got another case of plague," Meredith Hammerstein called.

Eden McClain's heart sank through the bottom of her chest. "Give me a moment," she said to Billy, trying to feign a smile. Dragging the stethoscope down around her neck and moving away from the teenager on the trundle, she shoved aside the flaps of the tent she was working in. Two of Absolution's men were holding a stretcher with a limp body slumped on it beneath a blanket. It could be anyone. Friend, neighbor, or enemy....

"Who?"

"Ian Carver," Meredith said.

*Jesus.* Ian had been with the town since the beginning, when Eden's brother forged Absolution out of virtually nothing. Ian had dandled her on his knee when she was a little girl and followed her brother here after the bloodied night that tore her family—and her village—apart when she was eighteen. In this violent wasteland she called home, all the townsfolk were practically family, but Ian was the grandfather she'd never had.

Eden twitched aside the blanket, revealing his gaunt face. He was sixty if he was a day, and though the red rash across his cheeks and dry, cracked lips looked like they'd only come through in the last couple of hours, he wouldn't last the usual course of infection by the look of it.

"Ian," she whispered, her heart breaking.

Delirious eyes met hers. He frowned, and then sucked at his dry mouth. "Edie...."

"I've got you," she said, the doctor in her taking over, even when her heart squeezed like it was about to send her into cardiac arrest. "Joe and Connor, set him up in the next tent over. I want an IV rigged into his arm, and start him on fluids. Make sure you set the containment up properly and disinfect yourselves, then find HAZMAT suits. You're both drafted."

The two men looked at each other. Grown men who quaked at the signs of plague, and the threat they could be next.

"Now," she stressed, setting her hands on her hips. "Before this gets loose in the general population."

*Too late for that.* But she didn't know what else to do.

She was a healer, damn it. Her duties ran the gamut of broken limbs, herbal remedies, births, and minor surgeries. The people of the Wastelands didn't have access to the fancy hospitals she'd heard the Eastern Confederacy used—sterile buildings created specifically for medicine, or so she could only dream—so she was it.

But everyone was looking to her as if she would have the answers to this, and Eden didn't have a clue.

The salt plague, some of them had taken to calling it.

Or the sweats.

"That's twelve cases." Meredith met her eyes.

"I'm well aware of that, thanks," she shot back, slipping out of the battered old HAZMAT suit she'd taken to wearing. Nobody knew what caused the salt plague. Not yet, anyway. It was bacterial in nature, but she didn't know how it spread. In the absence of that information, she'd taken to using all the precautions she could, including dosing herself with a prophylactic antibiotic. She'd felt guilty about wasting the medication when it could have been used on actual plague victims, but the council who ruled Absolution had ordered all medical staff start treating themselves, and she understood the precaution.

If her medical team went down, they were all dead.

Most of the infection cases had occurred in those who worked on the farms, and it hadn't hit the actual town until now. Infected body fluids were definitely a no-go zone, but from her questioning there'd been isolated incidences where patients *hadn't* come into contact with any body fluids or dead animals. One of the outrangers hadn't even come across a human until he roared into town on his motorbike and promptly collapsed in the dirt, begging for water.

Which left a damned mystery she needed to solve.

Something was spreading the disease.

But what?

"What are we going to do, Eden?" Meredith asked.

"I'm working on it."

The problem was, with her limited resources out here in the Wastelands there wasn't a damned lot she could do. Tugging off her plastic gloves, Eden threw them at the medical waste—which was a fancy way of saying the trash can someone would burn the contents of later. Then she washed her hands before she brushed her hair out of her eyes.

She had nothing.

No, she had less than nothing.

And she was down to her last box of antibiotics. She'd been expecting a truckload of oral antibiotics a week ago, but there was no sign of the regular smuggler.

*Maybe Absolution's not the only place that's hard up at the moment....*

Whispers kept coming north from the slaver towns down along the southern border with New Mérida of the plague running rife through the local populations down there. Entire slaver cities were burning as they tried to contain the spread. The thought of slavers dying didn't bother her—healing oath or not—but her heart ached for the slaves.

"We have to quarantine the town," Meredith said, folding her arms across her chest.

"And what about the outriders?" Not all of them had made it back to Absolution, despite the recall.

Meredith looked uncomfortable.

"No," Eden said sharply. She agreed with quarantine and had set up this facility in the outskirts of Absolution, but to lock down the entire town? Leave the rest of their people out there among the monstrous wargs and reivers that stalked the Wastelands? Not acceptable. "You're not just going to leave them out there. They'll be better off taking their chances with the plague."

"The council is meeting later this afternoon," the councilor warned. "Something needs to be done. We've all heard the rumors coming from the south. This could impact upon everyone. If we move too slowly...."

Eden turned on her. "What do you mean they're meeting?" She was part of that council, damn it. "Who called it?"

"Bart."

Of course. The bastard thought he ran the place. "Why am I only just hearing about this? And what time? I've been trying to get in contact with the Confederacy enclave. Our scheduled radio contact is this afternoon."

She needed to warn them. The secretive Eastern Confederacy had started making overtures toward the Wastelands and its people of late, and while Bart had shot down the deal she'd been trying to make with them—the mining rights to the old abandoned Copperplate mine nearby in exchange for vital medicines, food, gasoline, and technology—they were still surveying in the area.

Bart was practically rubbing his hands together at the thought of driving the deal up, but Eden had met with the enclave. Miles Wentworth, the man in charge of the surveying team, didn't strike her as someone who kowtowed to Wastelander scum. His words, not hers.

The last time Bart tried to add conditions to the exchange, Miles simply gave her a thin smile and told her he'd be in touch.

That had been three weeks ago.

"Meeting's at three."

"Which is exactly when I'm scheduled to radio them." Eden seethed. "How convenient."

Meredith had the good grace to look embarrassed.

What was more important? "I have to call in with the Confederacy." It was ethically irresponsible to not warn them, despite the fact their medical team had advances and technology she could only dream of. "Tell Bart if he makes any preemptive moves I won't like, he'd better damned well hope he doesn't get the plague. Remind him he might be at my mercy in the next week or two."

As far as threats went it was weak—Eden couldn't turn someone away who needed medical attention—but Bart had always been a little scared of her.

He might believe it.

"Eden!" someone called from several tents over. "I need you urgently."

Maggie Carpenter, if she wasn't mistaken.

Eden glared at Meredith. "Don't make any rapid decisions. We can still lock this down. We just need to work out how the plague's being spread. I'll discuss this with you later."

"What do you mean we've got an urgent case that needs my review?" Eden asked as she strode along in Maggie's wake. "I've got to radio in to the enclave. Can't Lou-Ann look at it?"

Diagnosing the plague was well within Lou-Ann's capabilities, after all.

Maggie led her toward the tent at the end, glancing over her shoulder. "I didn't want to say anything in front of Meredith, because she'll run straight back to Bart."

Maggie might have been Bart's younger sister, and a town councilor, but she and her brother were as different as night and day. Barely a year apart, she and Eden had become fast friends over a decade ago.

"What do you mean?" Eden's voice lowered. "What's going on?"

"We had a rider come in. He's got an unusual case of the plague, and his timeline doesn't match up. Asked to speak to you, and you alone."

Curiouser and curiouser.

Her interest zeroed in on the intriguing part of the sentence. "Unusual case of the plague?"

The first sign of the plague was the rash. Large reddish lumps around the lymph nodes and across the chest, which she was calling phase one. Onset seemed to occur between two and seven days after initial infection, though her case study was small and precise estimates difficult to lock down.

Phase two involved fever and intense sweating, which followed the rash by a couple of days.

Roughly twenty-four hours into the fever, the vomiting and diarrhea started, and this was where everything started to go downhill. In combination with the intense sweating, it caused hypernatremia; low fluid volumes with a high sodium serum concentration in the patient's plasma. Hence why they were so damned thirsty and confused. She'd been trying to cautiously treat the electrolyte imbalance, but the onset was often acute, and from there the diagnosis led to twitching, seizures, coma... and then, in the two cases that had progressed so far, death.

Only one of her patients had recovered, and he'd been a healthy young man with a strong immune system.

Maggie shrugged helplessly. "I don't know the details. He won't speak to me or any of the others on your team, he just kept insisting on speaking to you. He's in here."

Eden gloved up, dragged a surgical mask down over her mouth and nose, and then entered the tent Maggie had led her to.

A man sat on the trundle in the corner, his knees pressed together. A rash bloomed across his forehead and down his throat, though the olive color of his skin made it appear more of a ruddy brown in color.

She'd never seen him in her life.

"Hi," she said, "I'm Eden McClain. Maggie said you'd asked for me personally?"

"Eden McClain?" he asked, his eyes darting suspiciously. "Can you prove that?"

*Uh, what?* "Prove who I am?"

"Please."

Definitely weird. "I'm sorry, but I don't even know you."

"Henry Chin," he said politely.

Still not ringing any bells, but the flash of his perfect teeth momentarily transfixed her. White, straight, not a hint of decay or a single snaggle tooth. No Wastelander she'd ever seen had teeth like that. It finally dawned on her. "You're with the Confederacy."

Instantly he looked nervous.

She held her hands up to soothe him. "We don't exactly carry any means to identify ourselves here in the Wastelands, but I *am* Eden McClain. I've been dealing with Miles Wentworth, the Confederacy's chief surveyor."

"I know."

"I... see. Is everything all right in the survey camp? I was going to radio in this afternoon and warn them about the plague. I'd have expected you to have a medical team to see to your rash and—"

"Unfortunately, we know about the plague. I can't say any more until I've been assured of my safety." He looked uncomfortable. "I'm not supposed to be here. I want a promise of asylum before I continue."

"Asylum? From... the Confederacy?" What was going on? "You *want* to stay in the Wastelands?"

Who in their right mind would give up their advanced levels of society in exchange for a barren desert full of monsters trying to rip your throat out?

She pressed her gloved fingertips to his forehead. "Have you been feeling unwell? Hot? Sweating?" Maybe the confusion had gotten to him early? But his skin felt only mildly warm.

Mr. Chin grabbed her wrist. "Please. You don't know what you're dealing with. You'll let me stay? You won't let them take me back?"

"Of course you can stay. You'll have to volunteer on the settlement roster a minimum of fifteen hours a week, but housing can be found for you, and food."

The breath eased out of him. "Thank you."

"Describe your symptoms for me," she said, flipping open the data pad she'd practically sold her soul for.

"Is that Confederacy issue?" he asked.

She looked up over the edge of the data pad. "Yes. Mr. Wentworth gifted it to me."

"I wouldn't use that," he said, his gaze dropping. "They can hack your data from hundreds of miles away."

"I've been assured it's out of range of their data stations. Wentworth complained about Absolution being in a 'blackspot.' I think that was the term he used." She used the stylus to tap in a small note under symptoms: *Paranoia.* But was it merely a measure of Mr. Chin's personality? Or something more insidious? "And it's not as though I have anything on this of import."

Eden took his vitals. "You said the Confederacy know about the plague? How long have you been feeling like this? When did the rash first appear?"

He answered her questions tersely. *Yes, they knew. Two weeks. Eight days.*

Hmm. Pulse regular, limited signs of fluid turgidity when she pinched his skin. Taking the small torch she'd been given by the Confederacy during the opening negotiations, she peered into his eyes, and then insisted upon examining his chest and taking his temperature.

"You have a mild case of plague," she announced, stepping back. Maggie was right. The timeline was unusual. Phase two turned swiftly into phase three, and Mr. Chin's rash had appeared *eight* days ago. "You should consider yourself lucky."

"I shouldn't have any signs of it at all," he said tersely.

"I'm sure—"

"Wentworth promised the vaccination we received last month would protect us," Mr. Chin insisted.

Eden slowly lifted her head. "Vaccination?" She'd read about the theory in old pre-Darkening manuals she'd salvaged over the years.

When she'd been a little girl, she even remembered a smuggler injecting her with a combination of needles for a small fortune, though Eden had no clue what they'd been for. That was the year measles killed five people in their town, including her mom.

Her family had only had enough money to protect her and her brother, Adam, and Eden had known then she wanted to become a healer, so nobody else would lose their mom.

"Wait. Wentworth and the Confederacy expected the plague to hit?" And they hadn't breathed a word during the negotiations? Granted, they'd been stalled in the last month, but... it was common courtesy.

"He knew there were cases of it. I'm a geologist by trade, so I wasn't involved in most meetings, but I saw a disease outburst map displayed on the map table when I was checking in one night. Wentworth swiftly downsized the map, which made me wonder at the time. Not my area though, and it doesn't pay to be too curious. He evacuated the survey camp last week," Chin replied. "The reivers were starting to get restless, and there was talk of dead bodies being found out in the ranges. Wentworth wanted to clear the area until the mayhem died down, and considering there'd been no progress with the settlement agreement, he was feeling restless for home. Wanted to get back to Cortez City."

Eden had radioed in two weeks ago, as usual, and Wentworth hadn't breathed a word of it. That was the day Emily started complaining of a rash.

"How'd you end up being left behind?"

Chin looked down at his clasped hands. "I hid in the mines during the evac. Wentworth was on a strict timetable, so I knew he'd have to leave without me."

Guy was definitely crazy. "I would kill to have half the resources the Confederacy has."

"I would risk my life to have half the freedom you Wastelanders have," he replied simply.

Eden slowly nodded. She'd heard living in the Confederacy city-states was almost as dangerous as living outside their walls. No privacy. The military in charge of everything. Citizens encouraged to report dissidents. Enormous prison facilities where people vanished.

And that was only what she'd heard from traders.

"Tell me more about this vaccination," she said. "I've only been able to discover the disease is bacterial in nature, and seems to be responding to the antibiotics I have."

Antibiotics she was about to run out of. There were limited supplies of dextrose and saline solution too. Limited supplies of damned near everything. If she didn't get another shipment through from a Confederacy smuggler in the next day or two, she'd be shit out of luck.

"That's the problem," Mr. Chin said. "The salt plague isn't natural. Your antibiotics will seem to work. Initially. Your patients will start to feel better, their fever will break, and then all of a sudden you'll notice the bacteria seems to retaliate. Within twenty-four hours you'll lose them."

Eden's throat went dry. "*What?*"

Mr. Chin opened his mouth, clearly trying to work out the right words. "I don't know to how to say this, but this plague has been genetically tampered with. It's been designed to be resistant to most strains of antibiotics. Last year there were rumors of one of the Confederacy generals running a top-secret project that tested on human subjects. He set up a private laboratory in Cortez City, and a corporation called the Radisson-Meyers Syndicate.

"A whistle-blower broke the news to the military; General Radisson was buying Wastelanders from the slavers down south and using them in certain medical experiments. He used his military access to smuggle them into Cortez City." Chin swallowed, and glanced down at his lap. "My wife, Megan, worked as an attaché to Lieutenant Bligh, who exposed Radisson. They kept it out of the docu-feeds, but she spoke of it to me when she was home. Said there was enough salt plague created to wipe out millions. Radisson was planning on a coup; he was the only one with the cure. It bothered her how they kept it quiet, and then Megan was killed on her way to work one day. Someone planted a bomb under her car. I couldn't stay there any longer, so I put my hand up for the Copperplate Mine Expedition."

"Eden?" Maggie burst into the tent breathlessly.

Eden held up her hand, staring into Chin's eyes. This couldn't be happening. Most of her plague cases *had been* getting better. "How do I cure them then?"

"You can't," he said simply. "The only ones who might have that cure are what's left of Radisson-Meyers. Lieutenant Bligh locked down everything when he became general."

"Eden!"

*Damn it.* "Not now, Maggie," she shot, swiveling to face the other councilor as Maggie held the tent flaps open.

"It's Haven," Maggie said, her face drawn and pale.

That punched the breath from Eden's lungs. "What do you mean, *'It's Haven'*?"

"Luc Wade's on the radio. Said he needs you there. Now. He thinks they've got a plague case."

"Adam?" She straightened abruptly. Her brother lived there, but he was supposed to be in the north.

"No." Maggie shook her head. "Luc said he wasn't there. Adam and Mia left last week to visit her sister. There's been no word from them since."

Could be a good sign. Maybe they left before the first victims started coming down with plague.

Haven was a small nearby settlement that had been decimated by reivers a few years back. When her brother was outed as a warg and thrown out of Absolution, he'd eventually wound his way back there and settled. Only a couple dozen people lived there now, and she knew all of them intimately. Half of them were what she considered family.

The heat drained from her face. "Who?"

Maggie shook her head. "It's Lily."

Eden's adopted niece.

Eden kicked the stand out on the bike, and slung her leg over it as dust settled. She'd come as quickly as possible, but her heart was still racing, certain it was too late.

*Fourteen days,* she told herself, running facts through her mind. *You've got roughly twelve to fourteen days from the time symptoms appear.*

And then Lily would die an agonizing death....

Henry Chin's revelation had destroyed her equilibrium. She'd run all the way to the council chambers and slammed into the room, startling the other six councilors. *"Lock it down. Now!"*

Meredith and Maggie were starting to sort out who might have been in contact with those patients in the quarantine camp. Bart had warned her if she left the settlement, then they might not let her back in, and Eden had stared him in the eye. *"So be it."*

Family was family, and she'd trained her team well. She couldn't do anything more than they could to save her patients. Not against a maliciously designed disease that would ignore anything she could throw at it.

Eden dragged the helmet off her head and unzipped her leather jacket. She barely paused to sling them on the seat, grabbing her medical bag and heading for the main house in Haven.

Haven still bore the brunt of the reivers' attack from several years ago. Nestled in a canyon, the sleek stone cliffs at its back created a natural barrier to protect the town, and what was left of the perimeter wall had been repaired and painstakingly rebuilt with granite. Palm trees nodded lazily in the breeze, circling the main water source—a natural spring that bubbled out of the ground.

"Hello?" Eden called, leaping up onto the timber deck that surrounded the main house, where her friend Riley lived. She rapped her knuckles on the door, then pushed her way inside.

Riley looked up from where she was nursing the baby against her chest. Her long blonde hair tangled over her shoulders, and her eyes were red and raw. The baby's shock of black hair stood upright and he blinked big blue eyes at Eden, eyes that stole her heart in a second.

"How is he?" Eden whispered.

Riley's smile trembled for a moment as she curled her shoulder to allow Eden to have a look. She'd delivered Thomas Wade three months ago, and he was a fat and happy baby. It had been a harrowing birth as they all waited to see whether the baby would be infected with his father's warg curse.

"Tommy's fine," Riley said.

A flush of heat swept through Eden's heart; he was beautiful. "Hey there, little man," Eden whispered, tucking her finger into his curled fist as he blinked up at her through blue eyes. "Are you being good for your mama?"

"Always." Riley cleared her throat, determination gleaming in her brown eyes. "Eden, what have you heard? Do you know what this is?"

"I know a little. They're calling it the salt plague down south. Absolution was hit about two weeks ago, and I've been quarantining the patients. The second we realized it was contagious, we set up sterile tents, but now they're talking about quarantining the town and shutting the gates to all newcomers."

"How many?"

She reluctantly took her finger back from the little boy and met Riley's gaze. "How many plague victims?"

"How many have survived?" Riley corrected.

Eden shook her head, feeling sick to the stomach. Riley was not the sort of woman who wanted false comfort. "I've got twelve victims, and only seven still alive." She settled her bag on her shoulder. No point scaring Riley with the details Henry Chin had given her. Riley needed hope, not a nightmare. "The ones that are still breathing won't be by the end of a week, if the fever runs its course."

Silence fell, broken only by the baby's gurgle. A single silent tear slid down Riley's cheek. "How long?"

"How long since—"

The door to Lily's bedchamber opened, and Luc Wade stared out at her. Eden stopped speaking. As a warg, with his enhanced senses he'd have heard her. There was no hiding the truth. But when she met the raw grief in his eyes, she wanted to.

He closed the door behind him. "Riley, you're not supposed to be in here."

"The baby was fussing," Riley shot back, then shushed little Tommy, despite the fact he hadn't made a sound.

"Better that than—" Luc broke off, unable to say it. Energy boiled off him, as if he wanted to explode into violence, but restrained himself. "I want her and the baby away from here," he said, looking to Eden. "I can't catch this, but she can. And so can he."

Eden hated to agree, but she turned to Riley. "You can't help Lily," she said, taking her best friend's hand. "Do as Luc says. Keep Tommy healthy and isolated. Is there someplace else you can be staying?"

Riley swallowed. "Adam took Mia to visit her sister, so their house is empty."

*Thank God.* "Stay at Adam's place. It won't be a bother, and you'll be better off. Luc and I will look after Lily. Take all the precautions you can. I don't know how this spreads, though I suspect it's via body fluids, coughing, or sneezing. But it wouldn't hurt to boil your water and not let anyone else in the house. Don't touch anyone's hand, don't let them sneeze on you. Bleach all your blankets and clothes, and air-dry them in the sunlight to try and kill any bed lice or fleas." She continued through the list until Riley was safely on her way.

Then she turned to Luc.

"How's Lily?" It had been easier to control her fear when she was in doctor mode, but now Riley was gone....

"Tired," he replied bluntly. "Thirsty. Complaining of muscle aches."

Still in phase one then. Eden ran the timeline through her head. Maybe fourteen days, if they'd caught it early enough.

But then what?

Ever since Chin told her the truth, she'd had this hollow pit in her abdomen, like a black hole that just kept sucking at her.

"How long since the rash first started?" Eden asked, slipping the face mask over her mouth and nose and tugging on a pair of gloves. She'd been forced to leave the HAZMAT suit behind. Absolution only had three suits, and the others who were working in the isolation tents needed them.

"A couple of hours," Luc replied. He raked a tired hand through his hair. "Lil was complaining of being thirsty yesterday, but we assumed it was a sore throat, nothing else. Then she started coming down with a headache last night. Riley and the baby had been out all day, so I sat up with her."

"Who do you think she caught it off?"

"There was a pair of travelers come through Haven five days ago. They had a daughter around Lily's age, so the pair of them played together." His face looked stricken, and she reached over and squeezed his hand.

"It's not your fault. You couldn't know. Nobody could have known. There are no symptoms during the incubation period. Was she around the baby yesterday?"

Eden kept asking questions softly, trying to work out how far this might have spread.

No, she hadn't been around the baby or Riley yesterday. She'd been out riding with Luc, and the baby had been fussing, so Riley had been sleeping in the spare room with Tommy for the last two nights. Thank God. Fingers crossed Tommy hadn't picked it up.

Inside the room, the girl on the bed tossed and turned, stinking of stale sweat. A young man sat by her bed holding her hand, and Eden was about to tell him to get out when she saw the amulet around his throat.

Cole Jackson. Or CJ, as she knew him. The young man who'd been turned into a warg by Luc.

Just like Luc, he couldn't catch the plague, but she was surprised to see him here, near the man who'd torn his life asunder.

"She wants more water," CJ murmured, looking to Luc, and suddenly Eden realized the past didn't matter. Lily was the one thing that tied the pair of them together. Lily and CJ had always been close, even though five years separated them.

Luc fetched it, giving Eden a chance to examine Lily. She stroked a hand through the girl's silky blonde hair. She and Adam had raised the girl like their own for three years, until Luc came riding back into town. If anything happened to her....

"It's her birthday in a week," Luc muttered, and heartbreak echoed in his voice. He paused for such a long time Eden wondered if he was going to say anything else. "I want her to live to see sixteen, Eden. Please. Please tell me you have something."

Not enough to grant him much hope.

He saw it in her eyes.

"What do I do?" Luc's eyes gleamed with unshed tears, his voice roughening. "I only just got her back. Do I turn her?"

An instant wave of revulsion swept through Eden, even though she understood why he asked. Wargs were immune to sickness, and could heal from almost anything, apart from a silver bullet. But they were also monsters. Without another amulet to control the beast within, Lily would be prey to the creature inside her. She'd go on bloody rampages across the deserts, killing and tearing apart anything that lived before feasting upon it.

"I'd give her mine," Luc said, seeing the look on her face. He pressed both hands together, and dug his clasped fingers against his lips. "She could live an almost normal life—"

"And what happens to you?" CJ muttered.

Their eyes met. Luc wouldn't be able to hold back the monster he kept hidden within. "You get to finally take revenge for what I did to you years ago."

Once it had been all the boy dreamed of, but he reared back from the promise, shaking his head. "No. *No.*" His gaze slid to Lily's. The girl would never forgive him for killing her father—they all knew it.

"Then I'll do it myself," Luc said in a hollow voice, scraping a weary hand over his face.

It made Eden feel sick. Her brother had faced the same dilemma for years. It had always been the way Wastelanders dealt with the warg curse, before they realized there might be another way.

"And what about Riley?" she whispered hoarsely. "And Tommy? What about Lily? You're going to leave them behind to fend for themselves? You don't even know if turning Lily will save her. A full-fledged warg is immune to any disease, but what if the turning kills her?"

"Then you find me an answer, Eden," Luc snapped, shoving to his feet and glaring down at her. "What do I do? She's my little girl. She's already seen far too much suffering. I can't just sit here. How do I save her, damn it—"

"I don't know!" And there lay the crux of the problem. "I don't have more antibiotics. We're dangerously short of them. And this strain might be resistant, according to Chin. We're in the middle of the goddamned Wastelands and—"

"Then find something," he snapped, the muscle in his jaw shifting almost inhumanly, a ripple of muscle moving behind his stubble. "I can't just watch her die. Or pray the antibiotics work this time round."

Eden took a subconscious step back. If Luc was this close to the edge, then she couldn't afford to push him.

"Easy." CJ came to the rescue, stepping between them and slamming a hand to Luc's chest.

The men looked at each other, and Luc's nostrils flared.

*"Dad...."*

The hoarse whisper stopped him in his tracks. He groaned and turned back to the bed, sinking onto the covers to capture Lily's hand. "Hey, sweetheart."

"Why... are you shouting at... Aunt Edie?" Lily rasped.

"Sorry." He brought her hand up to his forehead and then kissed her knuckles. "It's all right. Everything's going to be all right. Eden's here now."

It was a knife to the chest, for what if she couldn't do anything?

"Hey, Lily Bell." Eden eased onto the bed, wishing she could hug her. "How are you feeling?"

"Horrible," Lily rasped.

"I want you to take these," she said, handing over the prophylactic antibiotics she'd been given for herself. It was breaking protocol, and maybe they wouldn't help, but she couldn't do nothing. "One every eight hours, with food." She met Luc's eyes. "You'll have to wake her. She can't miss a dose."

"Done."

Eden checked the girl's vital signs, making sure she washed down the first round of medication. When Lily's eyelids started growing heavy, she took her leave.

The pair of them withdrew into the kitchen, though she could still see CJ sitting on the edge of Lily's bed, talking to her as he stroked her hair.

"There might be... something I could do." It had been mulling in the back of her brain ever since she spoke to Henry Chin, and she'd made him write down the details for her before she left.

Luc looked up hopefully.

"I said antibiotics wouldn't work. A general in the Confederacy manufactured this plague a year ago. I don't know how it got out here in the Wastelands, but I do know there's a cure."

His gaze sharpened. "Where?"

"That's the problem." She scraped one hand through her hair. "If there's anything left of the research, it's in Cortez City. And this is not a guarantee, but it's all I have."

Thoughts raced behind his dangerous blue eyes. "We could contact the survey camp. Force them to take a helicopter ride back to Cortez, and bring us back—"

"They're not there. One of their team members defected. He said the survey team pulled out and evacuated a week ago."

"That sounds awfully fucking convenient. They knew. They knew this was about to hit, and they didn't even send an, 'Oh, by the way....'"

"Not important," she said sharply. "The fact is, they have a cure. I can't contact them as our two-way radios only have a fifty-mile range, and I have no idea how to work their data towers with their... Fednet, or whatever they call it.

"I can go to Cortez City. I have a contact there, Miles Wentworth. He might be able to assist me." *If she gave Wentworth what he wanted.* "I'm not doing anything here one of my medical team can't do. All I can offer is palliative care and quarantine advice. I've got nothing else." She crossed her arms over her chest. "You've got fourteen days, roughly. Give me that time to see if there's anything in this story of a cure."

"Cortez City's right on the edge of the Confederate territory."

"I know. It will take me at least five days to get there. Five back, maybe. That gives me four days in the city to track down a cure."

"You can't go by yourself. You'll be crossing right through reiver territory."

Eden took a shuddering breath. "I could speak to the council. Ask for an escort."

"Fuck your council, Eden. You know what they'll say. Absolution likes to sit on its hands when they might have to do anything risky." He looked torn. "I could—"

"No. You're needed here."

"I'm a warg, an ex-bounty hunter," he said bluntly. "I can get you to Cortez."

"And who's going to look after Lily? Or Riley and the baby?"

"I'll go with her."

The words came from behind.

CJ. For a moment she'd forgotten he was even capable of listening to hushed whispers. Eden looked at him hesitantly. He'd filled out in the past few years, but she couldn't forget the fact he'd only just celebrated his twenty-first birthday. She'd offered to make his cake, but Riley wouldn't let her.

"Don't look at me like that," he said gruffly. "I'm a warg too. And your brother trained me when he went into exile for a year. He taught me how to hunt bounties, kill reivers, and avoid other wargs. There's nobody better at killing than Adam."

"I beg to differ," Luc muttered.

"I can keep you safe, Eden," CJ continued, taking a step toward her. "You need someone to watch your back, and Luc's right. I doubt you'll get any volunteers from Absolution. If you go back there the council won't let you leave. Let me do this. Please. I can't just sit here and watch her die. I can't."

He was barely an adult.

He might also be the only option she had.

And every moment counted. There was a ticking bomb in her head now, and it had fourteen days on it at the absolute maximum.

"Adam's not—"

"Wasn't planning on getting back anytime soon," Luc said curtly. "You could send a message through the radio chain, but I daresay he's days away."

Eden released a slow breath. There was nothing worse than being unable to control her circumstances. She could react to any situation, but she hated the feeling. She preferred a plan. Control.

"We've got five more hours of daylight left in us." Then they'd be out there alone in the dark, where the monsters lurked. "I need supplies; gasoline, food, water, ammunition. Anything you can give me."

"You can have everything." Luc's shoulders slumped in relief. "I can mark out the route you'll need to take. You'll have to cross the Rim and the Great Divide, which means going via Rimside."

"Don't make any rushed decisions in the meantime," she said, patting his arm. "I need to make a radio call to Absolution. Let them know what's going on."

"Understood." His head swiveled toward her. "But if you're not back by the end of fourteen days, then I will do what I have to do to save my daughter."

"Fourteen days," she whispered.

"Fourteen days."

# three

"Excuse me," said a firm voice. "I want to hire a guide to take me across the Great Divide."

*How polite*, was the first thought that went through Johnny Colton's head.

It was the sort of female voice that stroked through him, enticing him with long-lost thoughts of community, when he'd stalked the edges of civilization and hungered to be a part of the human world. The sort of voice that turned a man's head out here along the edges of the Rim, where only the very desperate rode—bounty hunters searching for warg or reiver scalps; salvagers looking for scraps out here in the barren Wastelands; the odd Nomad biker turned smuggler; and those like him, who were trying to stay lost.

The sort of voice that conjured thoughts of a pair of well-shaped lips wrapping around the precise consonants, and leading directly to the idea of what else those lips might be able to wrap themselves around.

*Fuck.* Trouble had walked into the bar he'd chosen to dwell in for the past week. He just knew it.

Laughter exploded behind him as Johnny lifted his forehead off his arms. His blurry gaze locked on the slim figure standing in front of the bar.

"You've got to be fucking kidding me," said the bartender, even as one of the other patrons whistled at her. "Nobody crosses the Divide. It's full of shadow cats and wargs. Not even the reivers go there and they're borderline psychopaths *with* a death wish."

"I don't have a choice." There was definitely frustration in the young woman's voice now. "And I'm sure there's somebody who'll do it... for the right price."

*Son of a bitch.* Johnny was cursing her for walking into his bar when the woman turned and he caught just a glimpse of the side of her face and the stubborn jut of her chin.

Everything stopped.

For a second the world froze, dust motes hovering in the air as Johnny's gaze narrowed in upon her, his heartbeat pounding thickly in his ears.

A tangle of golden-brown curls. A firm ass clad in a pair of no-nonsense jeans. Knuckles resting on a set of generous hips as she glared at the bartender.

He had to be dreaming, but that looked like Eden McClain. He even had the knot in his gut to go along with it.

Hell, no. His memory must be playing tricks on him.

Johnny reached inside his leather riding bag—or the one he'd appropriated from his old enemy, Adam McClain—and withdrew the faded photo of McClain's baby sister from inside it.

A sunny-faced girl smiled out at him, her mess of chestnut hair snagging in unruly curls around her face, and her green eyes reminding him of McClain's.

Sweat sprang up along his spine. Memory swept him into the past—

*Johnny hauled the skinny young woman toward the hut his uncle, Bartholomew Cane, had picked out.*

*"What are you doing?" Eden McClain screamed, kicking out at him with her boot. "Adam! Adam, help—"*

*"You leave her alone!" McClain roared.*

Johnny looked up at the woman in front of him. She'd turned away from the bar with a scowl, chewing on her knuckle. She was at least fifteen years older than the girl in the photo. Far more serious of expression, with a small crease between her brows as if she frowned often— or needed glasses, perhaps.

But there were the messy curls, knotted back in a loose bun on top of her head, and there were those dangerous green eyes, and there were— Holy fuck, Eden McClain had grown one hell of a set of tits.

It *was* her.

Had to be. He'd been staring at that bloody photo for two years, ever since he stole the bag from McClain and found it within, just another memento to haunt him.

Panic knotted within him. He was shit out of luck these days. Johnny drained the last inch out of the bottle of whiskey that had been sitting in front of him, and then tugged the black hat down over his eyes. Looked like it was time to move on, before she spotted him. That was one ghost from the past he was better off avoiding.

"I'll take you," called a husky voice.

Johnny froze.

Eden turned toward the stranger at the back of the bar, her black tank straining over those generous tits, and Johnny suddenly realized what every other man in the bar was thinking.

Fresh meat. A gorgeous, slightly vulnerable woman who'd just proclaimed to the world she was carrying enough money to make a desperate man cross the Divide.

"And who are you?" Eden demanded.

"Tom Agoura." The stranger grinned through his black beard as he pushed away from the table. "But you can call me Black Tom."

"Black Tom," she repeated dubiously. "And you can guide me and my friend across the Divide? We need to get to Cortez City in a hurry."

Black Tom's expression tightened at the mention of a companion, but then he smiled, all slow and lazy enough to make Johnny's fists twitch.

"Sure." Tom gestured toward the door. "Why don't we go meet your *friend* and discuss this matter in a more private setting? Then we can talk about price and what you're willing to pay. The Divide's a dangerous place for a pretty girl like you."

*Don't get involved.*

*She won't thank you for it.*

And neither of them had noticed him, here in the shadows of the bar. Johnny could let her walk out of here, let her walk right out of his life.

She'd never even know he was there.

Eden smiled. "Sure. But you'd best walk in front of me. My *friend* is a little twitchy with his trigger finger, and he's got ideas about the right way to talk to a lady."

Johnny held his breath. Maybe she didn't need his help. Maybe she would stroll right on out of his life, and her friend would keep her safe.

But Black Tom's smile held all kinds of sins, and Johnny's pulse kicked hard as something shifted *beneath* his skin.

He flinched and looked at the thick veins in his forearm. *What the hell?* The warg within him rarely flexed its muscles—he'd had control over it for over twenty years.

All the hairs on the back of Johnny's neck lifted as Black Tom headed for the exit. "After me, then."

Tom strode through the bar doors, sending them swinging. Eden didn't even look around as she followed him out.

And then she was gone, vanishing like the remnants of a beautiful dream, where Johnny could almost recall the details, but not quite.

A bullet dodged.

A collision avoided.

But if he let her walk out of here with Black Tom, then he knew he'd never forget this moment—the moment when his one last chance of redemption slipped through his fingers.

*Sure it's got to do with redemption?*

Johnny's eyes narrowed. His fingernails started to itch, as if they were trying to turn into claws.

Getting involved with Eden McClain was the worst idea he'd ever had. Her brother, Adam, might have forgiven him for his role in inflicting Adam with the warg curse, but she wouldn't have.

Not when she'd been the bargaining chip used to condemn her brother to hell.

"Fuck." He snatched his bag with a growl. "Of all the shitholes left in the world, she had to walk into mine...."

"I need a guide to Cortez City," Eden said, striding along in the wake of Black Tom. The Rim-side town was more shanty than actual civilization, and she couldn't stop her heart from rabbiting in her chest.

*Two days down.*

*Twelve to go.*

She just had to surmount this first hurdle. Once they found a guide, they'd be one step closer to a cure.

Even if Creepy Pants in front of her was giving her vibes. Bad vibes.

*CJ will protect you. And if he can't, then you can make Black Tom realize you don't just know how to set bones.*

Thanks to a certain protective older brother who'd taught her how to punch and shoot.

"My friend's waiting for me at the Blue Moon." CJ had wanted to come, but the whole damned town was rife with warg dogs. The enormous brindled beasts were bred for hunting the wargs and shadow cats that lurked in the Rim, and despite the fact CJ wore his amulet, they could smell the warg on him. The second they entered the town, the dogs had started barking and she didn't want anyone growing too curious about why.

Plus, she'd gotten a flat on her bike, and someone had to fix it.

"So why Cortez City? You trading with the Confederacy?" Black Tom sounded interested.

*Sure, buddy. All the better for you to rob us when we try to cross back?* The more he opened his mouth, the more he gave her the creeps.

But she'd spent two hours trawling this godforsaken town looking for a guide, and Black Tom was the only one who'd volunteered.

CJ could decide.

"Not exactly." Eden brushed a strand of hair behind her ear. "They have something I want."

"Something you want...." Black Tom paused at an intersection, his murky green eyes raking the small shanties that surrounded them. "This way, sweet cakes. It's a shortcut to your friend."

*Sweet cakes?* Her eyes popped out of her head. No way. "It's Eden. Eden McClain. I'd prefer it if you used my name." She propped her hands on her hips. "And I think I'd rather stick to the main street."

Black Tom's grin seemed oily, but he held his hands up. "Sure. Sure. Just thought you was in a hurry."

*I am.*

He turned and strode on. Despite the name—Main Street—she couldn't help growing aware of how few people were out and about in the heat of the afternoon. A wizened old woman watched them with wary eyes as she clipped faded washing to a line, but there was no one else out. And if she cried out, Eden had the feeling no one would come running.

Eden's fingers grew damp, as she brushed them against the Taser at her hip. "So how much experience do you have? Have you ridden the Divide before?"

"Once or twice." He slammed to a halt as a pair of warg dogs burst into the street, fighting viciously over a bone.

The commotion caught her attention. Eden's head turned, tracking the dogs, and suddenly she was staggering back as Black Tom muscled her into a shadowy alley.

*Shit.* She staggered back into a wall—barely three sheets of tin nailed to a building—and reached for her hip, but Black Tom snatched her wrist.

He slammed his other hand against the wall beside her head, trapping her between his fleshy body and the hard tin. "I'm real fuckin' experienced, sugar tits, but the price suddenly changed." His gaze slid down to her cleavage. "I want the money *and* you can warm me up of a night...."

Eden took a slow breath.

No point screaming.

No one was coming to help her.

Slipping the Taser from her belt with her other hand, she pressed it against his gut and smiled up at him sweetly. "I am not in the mood, trust me. I'm dealing with a town full of dying people, a niece who's just come down with the plague, and I got a flat on my bike just outside of town." She pushed the Taser in nice and hard, gritting her teeth unpleasantly. "My friends are dying. My *niece* is going to die, unless I get to Cortez City and find a cure, and so you wasting my time? That's really, *really* irritating. The last thing I would do is even look at your disgusting penis, so back off before I make you pee your pants. Deal's off the table."

Black Tom paled, glancing down at the Taser. Holding his hands in the air, he took a step back. "You fucking little bitch."

"And," she said, a little louder, taking a step forward, "if you call me sugar tits or sweet cakes or *bitch* one more time, then I think I might just zap you for the hell of it."

An enormous hand came up, backhanding her across the face.

White exploded across her vision and Eden lost the Taser and the bag hanging from her shoulder. Her ears rang and she had a moment of disorientation before pain suddenly flooded through her jaw.

A hand wrapped around her upper arm.

The only thing that saved her was years of training.

Eden ducked under the grip, turning and disengaging as he reached for her. A punch directly to the solar plexus made the breath slam out of him. *Ow.* Eden stomped on his instep, fueled by adrenaline. It burst through her veins like rocket fuel.

She'd clearly taken him by surprise. Black Tom was a big, heavyset man.

But she was used to big. She was used to heavy. Adam had wrestled with her more times over the years than she could count, and her brother had at least two inches on Tom.

That didn't mean she was stupid.

A woman her size was better off with the element of surprise—and a weapon. And her ears were still ringing.

Eden scrambled for the Taser in the dirt, knowing there'd be no time to grab the pistol out of her bag.

Heavy weight came down over her back, and an *oomph* of breath slammed out of her lungs. A hand between her shoulder blades forced her face-first into the ground. Real fear began to bloom within her as she found herself coughing dirt in surprise. He'd recovered quicker than she'd expected.

"Get off me!"

A knee drove between her thighs, shoving them wide. Eden yelped, grabbing a handful of dust and flinging it back into his face. Black Tom swore, and his weight let up off her. She swiveled forward in the dirt, her fingers brushing against the grip of the Taser.

A hand around her belt hauled her back, and then a brutal knee drove into the back of her thigh. "Fucking... bitch."

He slapped her across the back of the head, catching her cheek a glancing blow.

Again.

"*Help!*" she screamed, flinching away. *CJ!* Would he even hear her at this distance?

"Deal's off," Black Tom snarled. "No money, no guide, but just for that, I'm going to take my pound of flesh."

Hands flipped her over onto her back and tugged at her belt. Eden tried to claw at his eyes, but another blow to the face made her sway. Fire bloomed across her cheek.

The world grew distant.

Noise subsided.

There were fingers unsnapping her jeans and she *had to stop him*, but her body wouldn't obey her. She could just make out a dark blur moving over Black Tom's shoulder as the bastard tried to tug her jeans open.

The heavy weight of him suddenly vanished.

Sound exploded back into the world, as if her body knew it was now or never. Eden rolled onto her side and somehow got the top button of her jeans done up. There was a scream trapped in her throat, her heart galloping a mile a minute as she realized just how close she'd come to being overwhelmed.

Someone squealed, and Eden scrambled for the Taser, needing to feel it in her hands. She rolled onto her back, Taser held out and giving that little electric whine as she aimed.

She'd been expecting CJ, but a massive man dressed in strict black stood over her, his face shadowed by his hat, and Black Tom a crumpled heap in the dirt.

"Are you okay?" the stranger rasped.

Eden took stock of the situation, despite the taste of blood in her mouth. Her hands shook. What had happened? What had almost happened?

She'd never expected Tom to hit her while she had the Taser in hand.

*You idiot. You hesitated.* All her sessions with Adam, and when it finally mattered, she'd tried to talk her attacker down instead. Everything had happened so quickly.

"Maybe," she whispered.

He'd... thrown Black Tom off her into a wall? Her would-be assaulter staggered to his feet, blood dripping from his nose. The stranger turned and drove a fist into Black Tom's gut, and the bastard slammed back into the tin, making a strangled sound.

Then a tanned hand wrapped around his throat and her rescuer pinned Black Tom to the tin, whispering something in his ear as he lifted him *off the ground.*

She caught a glint of silver in the stranger's hand, and Eden somehow crawled to her feet and grabbed his wrist.

"*No,*" she said.

Tension locked through his wrist. All she could see was her rescuer's black hat, dragged low over his brow. "He doesn't deserve mercy. Men like this don't go after women just once. This *puta madre* knew what he was doing."

"I wasn't talking about mercy." She might have once, but she was a little older now and the world a little starker. "If you kill him, they'll set the warg dogs on you."

She knew how it ran in towns like these. Black Tom had been sitting with friends when she'd entered the bar.

The stranger froze, his head tilting to the side, almost as if he was listening to her.

Dark stubble marred his jaw, and his skin was olive enough to hint at some indigenous heritage—or perhaps Latino. Maybe a mix.

"Please don't kill him," she said, swallowing down the lump in her throat and trying to rein in her racing pulse. Every part of her was trembling. *Adrenaline. Its just adrenaline.* Eden tried to force a joke, partly for herself. "You just saved my life and I'd prefer it if the local scum didn't lynch you for it. A dead hero's not much use to anybody."

"I'm not a hero."

"You're *my* hero," she pointed out.

Another faint twitch of the muscle in his jaw. She caught a glimpse of his mouth and that soft lower lip.

"Remember those words," he said softly. Then he pulled the blade back and drove it in lower. Right between Black Tom's legs.

Black Tom screamed and crumpled to the ground, blood pouring out of him. Eden gaped. There wasn't enough blood for him to have hit the femoral artery, but....

He just....

"You just stabbed him in the dick," she blurted.

"Justice," said the stranger, sounding satisfied. "I daresay he'll never try that trick again."

A part of her relished the bastard's pain, but the rest of her instincts were pressing her to see to the wound. Black Tom deserved it—the stranger was right, it probably wouldn't have been Black Tom's first attempt to harm a woman—but she was a healer. Eden pressed a hand over her lips, capturing her strangled groan. Her fingers twitched as if her body wanted to spring into action and stem the blood flow. Instinct. Habit. Difficult things to fight. Black Tom cupped his groin, his face white and blood welling between his fingers as he screamed.

"Leave him be," the stranger said, wiping his knife clean on Tom's shirt. He sheathed it. "If he lives, then he lives. Come."

Dogs were baying nearby and a man called out for them to "shut up" in a guttural accent. Something smashed, as if it had been thrown.

A hand locked around her wrist.

"Wait!" Eden grabbed her bag, and then almost tripped into the stranger's hard body as he yanked her back. "Thank you—"

"Don't thank me just yet." He stepped past her, pushing her behind him as he faced some threat in the mouth of the alley.

"Eden?"

She couldn't see a thing, but the tension in her shoulders suddenly dissolved.

"CJ!" she cried, shoving past, and throwing herself into the young man's arms.

She only had a moment of relief. Dogs were baying like they could smell a fox in the henhouse and wanted to get at him.

CJ. They could smell CJ.

"What happened? Are you all right?" CJ drew back and cupped her shoulders. "I heard you scream."

"I found a guide," she blurted, "but it turns out we're better off without him." She gestured toward Black Tom as she swiftly explained. "And then this guy came out of nowhere and saved me."

"Saved you?" CJ's nostrils flared as he looked over her shoulder. "Eden," he said, in a warning tone she'd never heard from him before.

"He's fine," she stressed, grabbing his tense forearm. "He hasn't made a move toward me. And we'd better get out of here. Those dogs don't like you."

"It's not just me," CJ said, still staring behind her.

A chill of premonition trailed icy fingertips down her spine.

Everything had happened so quickly. She'd been jacked on adrenaline and then focused on Black Tom. She'd never really had a chance to *look* at the stranger too hard. But he'd lifted a huge man off his feet and pinned him against the wall. He'd thrown Tom off her as if the bastard was a lightweight. A little knot twisted inside her as suspicion reared its head.

Eden spun back toward her rescuer.

Dark eyes met hers from beneath the rim of his black Stetson. The stranger's lips curved up in a lopsided manner, as if half his mouth was smiling deprecatingly.

It was the first time she'd seen him front-on.

"Told you to remember those words," Johnny Colton said, tipping his hat back so she could see his face fully.

Almost as if the action was a dare.

A shock of recognition punched through her, as if she'd been Tasered herself. She'd recognize those eyes anywhere. They were imprinted in her nightmares, and she'd pictured them again and again as she punched the bag Adam had set up for her.

He was older now. Leaner through the cheeks, and a little hungrier looking. The last time she'd seen him there'd been a hint of—innocence, perhaps, if one could use that word to describe Johnny Colton—but whatever light had remained in his eyes was quashed. Gone.

There was only darkness now.

"You," Eden choked out, her throat thick with shock.

"Me." Colton stared at her through narrowed eyes. "I know why I'm out here on the edge of the godforsaken Wastelands. But what the fuck are you doing in a place like this, angel?"

"It's been a long time, Eden," Colton rasped.

The words broke the spell. Eden slammed her palms against his chest, shoving him back, hitting him, hammering at his hard frame with her fists. Rage tore from her lips in a gasp, and her eyes turned hot and wet. "You son of a bitch!" All she could see was her brother chained in that hut. Colton shoving her through the door, locking her inside.

And Adam pleading, begging for him to let her out.

*"Please, Colton. Please. Don't make me do this,"* her brother had begged.

*"It's not my choice. Just give Cane what he wants and she's free."*

At first she hadn't understood. She'd been so frightened, dragged from her bed by this dark-haired ghost, a man who'd stolen a kiss from her the week before and flirted with her. At first she'd thought him an ally—

he'd been riding a bounty with her brother for a week—and so she'd gone with him in order to help Adam. He'd promised softly no harm would come to her if she just *played her part.*

*"I promise you'll be safe,"* he'd told her.

And she'd believed him.

Instead, he'd locked her in that hut with her newly warg-cursed brother, and used her to push Adam into betraying Luc Wade to the same fate.

"*Mierda!*" He staggered back a step.

Eden screamed her rage into his face, raking at his jaw. There were hands on her wrists, a hard body jerking her away from Colton. And then her face was pressed against CJ's chest as he rubbed a hand through her hair.

"Eden," CJ gasped. "Eden, he's a warg."

"I know he is!" A sob tore loose. Eden shook all over, fighting to control herself. She'd never felt like this before; if she'd had a weapon in her hand, she half thought she might have used it.

And that was not her.

Sucking in a sharp breath, she pushed away from CJ and got her shit together as she faced Colton. The last thing she'd ever let this man do was turn her into something she wasn't.

She could handle this.

Claw marks raked Colton's cheek. His shirt hung awry. She barely recognized herself.

"What the hell are you doing here?" she demanded. Probably up to no good, if she knew him. "Why did you rescue me? Were you following me?" Too many questions raced through her. "What kind of sick game are you playing?"

"I had no idea you were even in town. And I was trying to stay fucking lost," Colton growled. "Until *you* stumbled into my bar and turned everything upside down—"

"*Your* bar?"

"I've spent enough fucking coin in there. I might as well own it."

Eden glared.

Colton's eyes narrowed right back.

"Where'd you get the money from?" she asked hotly.

A shrug. "Here and there."

"Sounds like you're up to Bartholomew Cane's old tricks." She almost thought he flinched as she stepped forward, pushing him again. "I swear, if you're hurting people...."

He captured her wrists and snarled, "Cane's dead. And I'm free. I don't have to play his games anymore. I'm a bounty hunter, curse you. And there's good coin to be made hunting things no one else wants to hunt in the Rim and the Divide—"

"You hunt in the Divide?" CJ broke in.

"Yeah—"

"*No*," Eden snapped, turning to glare at her young comrade. No way in hell was she about to trust Colton again. "He's the last person we can trust."

Colton let her go with a rough laugh. "Don't worry, angel. The feeling is mutual. You're the last person I'd ever get tangled up with again." He stepped back and tugged the lip of his hat down over his eyes. "Didn't mean to upset you. But you shouldn't go walking around out here with strangers. The Rim's not a place for those who have any goodness in their hearts."

"You should know!"

"Wait. What's going on? You two... know each other?" CJ asked hesitantly.

"We have a history," Colton murmured.

Eden's eyes bugged out of her head again. *A history?* He made it sound as though the pair of them—

"Eden was the first girl who ever kissed me."

"That was before I knew what an asshole you were!" She seethed as she turned to CJ. "This is the dick who had a hand in turning my brother into a warg."

"I didn't turn him."

"No, but you were Cane's little lapdog. He'd never have gotten his hands on Adam, if you hadn't helped him."

CJ's eyes widened. "*You're* Johnny Colton?"

"And you would be Adam's young protégé. You were helping him hunt me down two years ago. Spent months on my trail before I lost you down south."

CJ's hand went to his gun.

Eden slammed a hand out, warning CJ to back off. He didn't know what he faced. Johnny Colton was a dangerous man, and she didn't need to look at the hard bulk of muscle in his chest, and the ammunition on his belt to know nothing had changed in that respect.

"Don't you dare hurt him," she snapped, shooting daggers at Colton. Dogs yelped nearby.

Colton froze, glancing down slowly to where her palm was braced between them, a bare inch from his black shirt. "Pretty sure I'm not the one reaching for my gun."

She wasn't touching him, but she felt like she was. A tingle shivered over her hand. A heated breathless feeling that stole through her as Colton slowly looked back up. Memories danced between them—hateful memories—and she saw the ghost of it echo in his eyes, before it vanished. A tiny hint of regret she must have imagined.

*What the hell?*

"I saved your brother's life two years ago, Eden. Adam and I are square. I understand why you're holding a grudge, but I'm a different man now. I'm sorry for the part I played in... in everything."

Of all the things she'd ever expected to hear from him, an apology wasn't one of them. "Leopards don't change their spots."

The baying of the dogs grew worse.

"Eden," CJ warned. "We need to get moving."

She couldn't look away from those heated brown eyes as Colton practically dared her to say something. His lips curled in a slow, lopsided smile. "Believe what you want of me, angel. But the kid's right. You should leave."

A dog howled nearby. CJ's nostrils flared as he grabbed her arm, and stepped in front of her. And then a chorus of bays went up, coming closer.

"CJ—"

"They're loose," CJ said sharply, pivoting on his heel to look down the alleyway for a means to escape. "Shit." Nothing. "Edie, if you run, they won't chase you. They're after me."

CJ drew his pistol and Eden grabbed his wrist. If he made a run for it and the dogs followed, everyone in town would know what he was.

"Keep her behind you," Colton snapped, turning to face the mouth of the alley.

Was he insane? They'd rip him to shreds as easily as they would CJ.

Did she care?

Two enormous brindled warg dogs slid around the corner, practically frothing at the mouth. Their eyes locked on Colton, and then the lead one threw its muzzle back and gave a hollow, echoing howl, almost one of delight.

Another one joined them, and then they launched themselves toward Colton.

"*Down*," Colton said in a low, flat voice that made Eden shiver, as if it cut through her. He held out a hand and slowly lowered it.

The dogs slunk to the ground, their howls dying off. CJ's wrist twisted in her grasp, and he went down on one knee in the dirt, and then blinked.

"What are you doing?" Eden asked.

"I don't know," CJ blurted, and she saw his foot shift, as if to power himself to his feet again. But he didn't. Instead he looked at Colton helplessly.

The trio of dogs crawled on their bellies toward Colton's feet, whining and licking at his boots. Eden had never seen anything like it.

Colton turned those blazing eyes upon her, then his gaze shifted to CJ. "Not you. You can get up."

"What did you do to him?" Eden gasped, as CJ staggered to his feet.

Colton mockingly gestured them around him. "I'd recommend you step lively, angel. If more of them arrive, I don't know if I can hold them."

The dogs whined and groveled as the three of them edged past.

"*Stay*," Colton commanded, meeting each warg dog's eyes as he backed away. The shiver of his voice went through her as if he'd stroked her inside her skin.

Then they were safely in the middle of Main Street. CJ opened his mouth, but Colton shook his head and gestured across the street to another alley. "Move."

The sound of baying grew louder. More dogs. Gritting her teeth at the fact that Colton was the one commanding them, she started running.

A hand caught her arm as she reached a junction, and Colton shoved her down another dirt-packed road. "This way."

Pounding along the streets, she didn't argue as he guided them as far away from the warg dogs as he could. Finally they pulled up in the shadow of a shanty, and Eden bent over, panting for breath as she rested her hands on her thighs.

"What the fuck did you do to me?" CJ demanded. "To those dogs?"

Colton shot him a narrow-eyed glance. But he turned his attention to her. "Go home, Eden. The Rim's no place for a woman like you—"

"You don't get to make my decisions for me," she snapped, stepping right up into his space and clenching her fists at her sides. "Adam might have forgiven you for the part you played in ruining him, but I won't ever forget it."

His eyes narrowed. "So be it."

Colton took a step back, tipping his head toward CJ. "You should keep a closer eye on Miss McClain. Take her home before she gets herself killed."

And then he turned and walked away, his long strides eating up the ground, the sound of dogs baying in the distance.

"*Easier said than done*," she thought she heard CJ mutter.

"What?" Eden demanded, feeling CJ's eyes upon her as she threw her clothes into her pack and searched the room for anything she might have left behind.

CJ leaned against the doorframe, his arms crossed over his chest. "This is a bad idea, Edie. It sounded good at the start, but the closer we get to the Divide...."

"Bad situations make for the best possible solution. If we don't get to Cortez City, then we don't get a cure for the plague."

"You don't think I know that? If we don't get a cure, then Lily dies." His voice choked off a little. "I will do anything—*anything*—to make sure she survives. But crossing the Divide by ourselves is a death wish."

"You're a warg and you were trained by my brother. So was I. We'll watch each other's backs."

"We don't even know what we're walking into," he exploded, flinging an arm out. Today's moment in the alley had bothered him; he'd been surly ever since Colton made him kneel. "Dealing with the Confederacy is a virtual gold mine. They have medicines, tech and equipment we

Wastelanders can only dream of. And this town is full of people who'd cut their own mother's throats for a bag of gold pieces. But they're not rushing to cross the Great Divide to get to the spoils. That makes me think they know something we don't."

Eden yanked her bag closed and pulled the buckles tight, pressing her lips firmly together. He was right. It was a bad idea and she knew it, but what other option did they have? If she let herself stop moving for a second, she could still feel Black Tom's hands on her belt. Still feel the weight of him pressing her down. Eden choked the thoughts down, swallowing them whole. No time for that.

She'd learned her lesson. Being able to defend herself didn't mean much if she hesitated. She was going to shoot first from now on.

"I've been through every shithole bar in this town. The only man who volunteered to help had other plans in mind. And from where I'm standing, no guide is better than one who wants to slit our throats, rape me, or steal everything he thinks we own. We're running out of time. If you've got a better idea, then spit it out."

Silence.

Worse. A lingering silence.

"There is *one* man who knows the Divide. He said so hims—"

"*No.*" Eden felt a flush of heat run through her. "Are you insane? Johnny Colton played a part in destroying my life—"

"And then two years ago he saved your brother's life. Adam admitted as much himself. Said something about a debt being repaid between them," CJ replied. "And I'm not entirely certain what I walked into today, but he saved you from that bastard, Eden. And when you tore into him, he simply took it. He didn't even bother to defend himself."

A tremor went through her. She sank onto the edge of the bed. "You don't know what you're asking of me." Heat seared her eyes. "They *used me* to force my brother to betray his best friend. *Colton* used me. He promised I wouldn't be hurt, he made me think we were riding to rescue Adam, and then he used me to blackmail Adam into betraying Luc to the same fate. Do you know how many years I've watched my brother try to put the pieces of his life back together? Adam used to keep a silver bullet in his pocket, just in case he ever lost control." She was shaking. Violently. "Because of *me*."

The world vanished in a haze of tears.

A dark shadow swallowed up what was left of her vision, and as water lashed down her cheeks, she found CJ on his knees in front of her.

"Hey," he murmured, resting his hands on her forearms. "None of this happened because of you. Adam was already inflicted with the warg curse before they even got to you. You were merely an innocent pawn meant to help them get a hold of Luc. Adam's never blamed you."

"I know," she said fiercely, scrubbing the wet from her eyes.

Adam didn't have to blame her.

He'd spent years hating himself for betraying his best friend to the monsters. Years trying to put his life back together. Drinking too much, all his emotions locked down tight, but sometimes she saw the look in her brother's eyes when the moon rose and the local chorus of wargsong lit the air.

And it had scared her, because she knew he had that bullet in his pocket.

Just in case.

"If we were in other circumstances," CJ murmured, rubbing her hand, "I'd never ask you to do this."

Eden lifted her eyes to his.

"But here's the thing: Colton owes you a debt and he knows it. I know nothing can take away the pain of what happened, but why not use him back? I *felt* him do something to those warg dogs. I don't know what it was, but he cowed them somehow. Forced them to show him their bellies—and these dogs were bred to rip people like me apart. He's not just a warg trying to leash his inner beast, Edie, he controls it. He's a bounty hunter. And he knows the Divide." A hint of something dark flashed through CJ's blue eyes. "I've been in your surgery enough times to know if you cut through the emotion of the situation and start considering your options in a logical manner, sometimes the answer you need is not the one you want."

He was throwing her own words back in her face?

"I think Colton can get us safely across the Divide," he said, pressing on determinedly. "In fact, I think he's the only chance we have of crossing it. And if you say no, Eden, then this ends right here. Because as much as I care for Lily I know she'd never forgive me for leading you into danger. So, if your final word on this is no, then we turn around now and head back to Haven. Luc said there are other options to save her."

Other options? Turn Lily into a warg and give her an amulet? "She'll *lose* her father."

CJ's expression shuttered. "She doesn't have to."

And another flush of hot-cold swept through Eden. Because there was another warg who could hand his amulet over to Lily, if they couldn't stop the plague.

This time, she caught *his* wrist when he moved to withdraw it. "*No.*"

CJ looked up from beneath dark lashes and for a moment, it wasn't a man she was looking at, but a boy. "She loves her father. Luc's everything to her. And if I can't save her...."

"No." CJ's words finally reached her where nothing else would. Eden stood, and swallowed down the thick press of conflict in her throat. This wasn't just about Lily. Her townspeople were dying too.

They needed a cure.

To get the cure they needed to cross the Rim.

To do so, they needed a guide.

It was as simple as that.

"Stay here," she said, wiping her face dry and fixing her hair, putting herself back together as best she knew how. "You're right. Johnny Colton owes me one. And that bastard better be prepared to pay."

# five

He smelled her before he saw her.

*Mierda.*

Johnny looked up as Eden swung herself into his booth, a shock of stillness running through him. She looked cold and prepped for battle, her hair knotted back into a no-nonsense braid.

He hadn't expected to see her again.

He might not have made his peace with that thought—a strange sense of unfulfillment twisted inside him still—but he'd been certain of it. Eden McClain was a chapter of his life he needed to close.

Instead, she slammed back into it with narrowed eyes, her fingers tense as she gripped the table. The black tank she was wearing contrasted sharply with her golden skin... but he was *not* going to think about her skin, tanned or otherwise.

That way dragons lay.

"What the fuck do you want?" Johnny growled out, still off-balance. Facing her twisted him into little knots he'd long thought he conquered. *Guilt.* "I thought you were leaving?"

He was the last person she'd be interested in spending time with. Which meant she wasn't here out of the goodness of her heart.

An itch of premonition trailed cold fingers down his spine.

"Mind your language. And you're right," Eden said. "The Divide's a dangerous place for CJ and me."

She reached across the table, snagged the small shot glass he'd filled with liquor, and tipped it to her lips, her mouth resting exactly where his had been.

The muscles in her throat worked and when she slammed the glass on the table, her lips were wet and slick with whiskey. Tempting. A droplet of sweat slid down between her breasts, and—

She'd said something.

Johnny blinked back into the here and now, finding her knowing gaze locked upon him. "Eyes up here," she said in a scathing manner. "I kissed you once, before all this mess begun. It's *never* happening again, so get that look out of your eyes."

He wasn't usually this slow to react. "What were you saying about going home?"

"I said you're right. It's a bad idea for CJ and me to cross the Divide. We don't know the lay of the land or the monsters that lurk within. Then there's the Confederacy and their walled cities. They're not very keen on strangers breaking into their territory."

"So you're going home?"

"I didn't say that."

Here it was. The catch. And his brain had finally started working again. "Go home, Eden."

"If I go home without a cure for the plague, then the people I love will die. Hell, there's no telling whether I'll die myself. I've been careful but we don't know how virulent this thing is. And if you think I haven't considered the risk, then you don't know me very well, Colton."

He didn't know her at all. But he recognized the look of a woman about to try and sell him something.

Johnny took the shot glass from her and poured himself a drink, tasting her lips on the rim of the glass as he sipped it. *Fuck*. Instinctively he looked toward the exits, but Eden slammed a hand over his as if she knew he was about to bolt.

"We need a guide. One who knows the Divide. One who won't slit our throats in our sleep."

"No."

"You didn't even hear me out."

"I don't need to. I know what you want." Shoving his chair back with a squeal, he reached for his hat and tossed a few coins on the table to cover his bill. It was one thing to help her brother escape, but there was something about Eden that had him running scared.

*"You promised me."*

It haunted his dreams at night. Her name was only one on a long, long list. He'd thought himself free of Cane after he killed the bastard, but seeing her again brought the truth to the surface.

How could he ever be free?

Eden didn't move, simply licked the whiskey from her finger. "Then why don't you tell me what *you* want?"

Johnny slammed to a halt as she slowly looked up at him. He didn't dare breathe. Didn't dare look away. "What *I* want?"

The devil in front of him merely smiled.

Oh, that did it.

He rested his knuckles on the table and leaned toward her. "What I want," he said, in a soft menacing tone, "is to see the dust of your bike heading back west and to know our paths are never going to cross ever again. I want to forget you, Eden."

"Do you think you can?" Those dark lashes fluttered and the hot, direct gaze she shot him almost disemboweled him. "Because I can't forget. No matter how hard I try."

His breath caught as the past rose between them.

A young, innocent girl.

His uncle's vicious demands.

And Eden McClain screaming and writhing in his arms as he tried to lock down all the choking feelings inside him, as he did his uncle's bidding and forced her inside the hut where her brother was chained.

Eden rose to her feet and glared back at him, face-to-face. Fearless. "If you don't help me, Colton, then I will *never* forgive you for what you did to me."

He could breathe again, but it didn't help remove the weight on his shoulders. This was a bad idea. A terrible idea. "What makes you think I want your forgiveness?"

"CJ has a theory you won't hurt me," she said slowly, as she watched him tense. "He thinks you owe me a debt."

"You're betting an awful lot on a kid's presumption."

"Maybe. Why did you save Adam? He told me everything that happened between the two of you in Rust City." Eden's lashes obscured her dangerous green eyes. "You risked your own life to rescue him."

*Fuck.* Colton reached for the bottle and swallowed fiercely. He needed time to think. "McClain and I were locked in warg cages. We needed each other to escape. It had shit-all to do with owing him a debt. I was trying to get out of there myself."

"You're lying."

He slammed the bottle down. "Why do you even want to cross the Divide? No sane person would attempt it. Even the fucking reivers do their best to avoid it."

"Because I'm desperate! My niece has the salt plague. She's got around twelve days before it takes her life. You might remember the girl. You kidnapped her for Bartholomew Cane a few years ago to use as bait to draw Luc into Cane's trap. It's Luc's daughter. The one that sang your praises when Luc and Riley rescued her, and told everyone who'd listen how you'd *promised her* she wouldn't be hurt. At least that was one promise you seemed to be able to keep."

Lily Wade. *Shit.* All he could see was a little girl with blonde hair and big, scared eyes. He'd never been able to stop Cane when the psychopath set upon a course of action, but sometimes he'd been able to soften the blow and protect the ones Cane meant to crush.

Sometimes.

"If I can't find a cure to save her then Luc intends to infect her with the warg curse," Eden continued in a hard voice. "That kid out there—the one that presumes too much—just told me if they have to infect Lily, then he'll give her his amulet to stop her from turning into a monster. And so her father doesn't have to."

A virtual fucking death sentence for the boy. He wouldn't be able to stop himself from turning without it, and then he'd be the monster in the night every human sought to kill. The boy wouldn't be able to stop himself from craving the death of everyone he loved, and somebody would put a bullet in his head before he made it two steps. A muscle jumped in Johnny's jaw. "Kid's a hero."

"That makes one of you."

"It does."

"Fine. You won't help me? Then let's play it your way. All I have to do is tell the men in this bar exactly what they have in their midst," Eden continued in a low voice. "The whole town's full of bounty hunters who are used to hunting wargs. How far do you think you'd get if I stand up and start shouting you're a warg?"

*Puta madre*— He sat back down with thump, and leaned closer to her. "That's a dangerous threat to make, angel. Considering who you're traveling with."

"CJ's no longer in town. He's waiting for me on the outskirts, and he knows what to do if he starts hearing gunshots."

"Well, you have thought of everything. Except this...." Johnny captured her wrist with lightning efficiency and hauled her forward, until their faces almost touched. "If he's not here, then what's to save you from me? Think

I can shut you up before you get a chance to even draw breath?" He let himself smirk. "Because I do."

"This."

Something nudged against his upper thigh beneath the table. A little electric whine began to hum.

The Taser.

It was a hairsbreadth from his balls.

He met those fierce green eyes.

Eden *dared* him to do it.

His balls felt like they hitched right into his gut, as if to try and protect themselves.

"You won't hurt me," she said with soft assurance. "That's the other thing that stands out from the night you dragged me from my bed. You went to great lengths to make sure I wasn't scared."

Oh, so the little witch thought she knew him? Thought she could control him?

Time to turn the tables on her.

"I was a little younger." *And you were an angel, taunting me with thoughts of everything I knew I'd never have.* He flashed back to the night their lives took a dangerous turn, when Eden McClain sat up in bed, clad in a thin linen nightshirt, and for the first time in his life a young Johnny Colton knew what it was to feel longing for something he couldn't quite explain. "Maybe I'm not that man anymore."

"Maybe." She leaned closer, her breath stirring against his lips. "But maybe you want to be."

"You're going to get him killed. You're going to get yourself killed."

"He's dead either way. But there's a chance we might make it if we had you."

He thought about it. He *actually* thought about it.

Eden reached across the table and captured his hand. "*Please.*"

The word cut through him like a fileting knife. But it was the action that disemboweled him. For the first time in years, Johnny felt a woman's touch stroke across the smooth webbing between his forefinger and thumb, almost as if she intended to comfort him.

And worse, it was this woman.

"Blackmail *and* a shitty attempt at seduction? You trying to pull out the big guns?"

"Please," she repeated.

*Fuck.*

He had this horrible breathless feeling inside him. *Don't get involved.* That was his modus operandi. He'd been there, tried to step into the light after he finally broke Cane's hold on him, and what had happened?

He'd ended up sold to fucking slavers and sent into an endless cage match.

Lesson learned.

There was no place in this world for a man like him. Nobody wanted a monster in their midst and it didn't matter how much he tried, there would never be any sense of redemption to find.

But....

Green eyes haunted him, the *please* whispering in his veins. In his chest. Johnny withdrew his hand, though the ghostly caress lingered on his skin. He could watch her walk out of here. He could. But how was he ever going to forget her? Would he always wonder if he could have saved her when she met her inevitable fate?

A rash of images seared his brain.

Shadow cats gnawing on bleached bones.

Blood sprayed across the desert sands.

Eden's lifeless eyes staring endlessly at nothing as the predators finished what they'd started.

*No.* A spear of ice went right through him. She was determined to do this. She wouldn't take no for an answer.

Which meant he didn't have any fucking option.

His breath eased out of him with a shudder. Eden had called his bluff. The only thing left to do was try and salvage some of this. "I don't give a shit about redemption, but I will take you across the Divide on one condition...."

Relief burst over her expression like a sun rising and that was when he knew he was in serious trouble.

"What?" Eden breathed.

Johnny kicked his chair back again. "I'm in charge of this expedition. You do what I say, when I say, and you don't argue or I swear to God I'll hog-tie you and go sit in a fucking cave somewhere with you until this is all over."

She opened her mouth, but he held up a finger and waggled it in her face. "Ah, ah, ah."

Eden pressed her lips together mutinously.

"That's better," Johnny said, and smiled at her as he drank down the last inch of whiskey in the bottle, even as he knew he was making the worst damned mistake of his life.

"Are you sure we need him?" Eden seethed, as they pulled their motorbikes to a halt at the edge of the Rim. Dust choked the air, but she knew both CJ and Colton heard her.

CJ shot her a faint smile. He'd been considerably more relaxed ever since Colton joined the party that morning. Maybe she'd be better off kicking them both off the edge of the Rim and continuing on by herself.

Maybe she was just pissed because the last man she'd ever wanted to see again was barking orders like a Confederacy general.

"Darlin'," Colton drawled, "Everyone needs me in their life. Especially the ladies."

Eden's eyes narrowed to slits.

"And you're the one who tried to blackmail me into doing this. I'm not here out of the goodness of my heart, so if you want me gone, then just say the word."

Somehow, the cage of her teeth caught the answer that sprang to mind.

"Just in case you need a little crash course on this entire situation: *You* chased me down. *You* demanded I guide you. I'm doing exactly what you asked me to do. I don't get what the problem is," Colton said, then lifted his water skin to his lips, his face tilted toward the dying light of the sun as he drank. His throat worked and Eden looked furiously away as a splash of water trailed down his lips and chin.

*This.* This was the problem.

She wasn't impervious to him.

She'd seen his gaze drop to her breasts in the bar. She knew exactly what had been going through his mind at the time. Every now and then a spark of heat flared in his whiskey-brown eyes when they met hers, and while she ought have been disgusted, she couldn't help feeling the past flash between them.

The first time she'd ever laid eyes upon Johnny Colton had been the day he and his uncle rode into her small town when she was eighteen. She'd been running errands in town for Adam when she'd burst around the corner of the general store and seen a young man bent over the horse trough, splashing water over his face. Tall, lean, dressed completely in black, he'd straightened when he'd heard her suck in a sharp breath, leaving water tracking rivulets down his throat and the open collar of his shirt.

It had been an unguarded moment.

Wide eyes. A handsome stranger barely a handful of years older than her.

And then Johnny Colton had given her the shyest smile she'd ever seen on a man, and Eden's heart had started beating a little faster.

"*Hello, angel,*" he'd said to her.

Eden hauled herself out of the memories. She'd been attracted to him the second she saw him. She'd let him use their washhouse and then stolen a kiss behind it. And it seemed—despite everything that had happened—that attraction hadn't completely died away.

*Just admit it. You're not pissed at him because he's doing what you asked. You're pissed because you can't take your eyes off him.*

"No problem," she managed to say between her teeth.

Colton smirked.

Ugh.

Turning around, he surveyed the small town nestled right on the edge of the cliffs of the Divide. "Welcome to Rimside. Location: Buttfuck Nowhere. Population: Scum of the earth. Don't drink the water. You might get syphilis."

"Cholera," she muttered. "You're thinking of cholera."

"Don't ruin my monologue."

"And stop swearing. You don't have to cuss all the time."

"I like swearing, thanks, Grandma. There are some situations where a simple *gosh darn* just isn't going to cut it." He gestured toward Rimside. "This place is a shithole filled with reiver scum. Unfortunately, it's also the only place within a reasonable distance that has access down into the Divide, without us having to pass through any of the Dead Zones around here."

Just the thought of the radioactive Dead Zones sent a shiver down her spine. When the meteor that caused the Darkening hit all those years ago, it had sent the world into an unnatural impact winter, and wildfires scorched the lands. Nuclear reactors had melted down, poisoning the area around them to this day, and everyone in the Wastelands knew to avoid them.

"Night's falling. How soon can we get down?" CJ asked.

"We stay in Rimside tonight—"

"Surely we can at least go down?" she blurted, glancing toward the sky. Evening slid across the blue expanse, a hint of shadow crawling across the horizon, like someone was drawing a blanket over the world. "We're tight on time."

"The last thing we want to do is camp the night at the base of Rimside. The bast... *very bad men* here like to entertain themselves with a specific custom that attracts all manner of critters in the Divide."

"Such as?"

"Criminals find themselves walking the plank, so to speak. Each night you'll find every predator in the Divide at the base, looking for remains. It's an easy meal for scavengers."

"Aren't *all* reivers criminals?"

Colton sighed and closed his eyes as if to ask, *why me?* "Yes. Kind of. Reiver gangs roam the countryside, but Rimside is ruled by a fellow named Clark. Millicent Clark—"

Eden snorted with amusement. "What kind of fearsome na—"

"It's the kind of name nobody is going to make fun of," he growled, "especially within hearing of Rimside. Or that somebody might just find out for themselves what waits at the bottom of the cliffs. Clark allows anyone in, but he insists upon one rule: No trouble. You'll find reivers from several different gangs in here. You're allowed to knife a man in the streets as long as you clean up the body. You can steal from other reivers. Break a few bones. But if you break any of the furniture in any of the bars, or molest any of the locals, you're going to meet Clark. He looks after his own."

"So what you're saying is watch our backs, because anyone might take a swing at us, but be careful if you swing back."

"I'll get us some rooms," he said, "and you can get some sleep while I make sure we have supplies for the trip across."

"We have—"

"Trust me. You won't have what I need. Any more questions?"

He looked at her pointedly.

Eden made a sign like she was zipping her lips.

"I wish." Colton swung off his bike and walked it toward the small settlement at the top of the escarpment, dragging a handful of coins from his pocket as the people there opened the gates.

Eden followed, struggling with the weight of her brother's old Yamaha. Colton paid to have the bikes stored, with a warning he'd be back for them in a week or so, and then helped grab one of her bags. He swung it over his shoulder with his own, barely breaking a stride.

"You don't have to—"

"I know."

The idea of him carrying her bag was personally offensive. She didn't want help. Especially not from him.

"My mother raised me to have better manners than letting a lady carry her things. Don't force me to sully her memory," he warned, as if reading her mind.

"What did she say about kidnapping?" she snapped.

Colton shot her a narrowed look, and this time it was his turn to press his lips thinly together.

Point one to her.

The smell hit her as they made their way into the main street, and she found the source immediately. A man pissed against the interior of the wooden palisade wall, swaying slightly. He turned bleary eyes upon them as the guards patted CJ down and then took a double take when he saw her.

"You're with me," Colton said, grabbing her hand and dragging her against the side that was unencumbered with bags.

Eden slammed against him, recoiling immediately. "Like hell I am—"

"Hog-tied," he said. "Cave. You and me." Then he draped an arm around her waist and let his hand rest familiarly on her hip.

"If that hand moves any lower," she hissed, "I will not be responsible for the outcome."

A thumb stroked against her hip as if to dare her. Colton's smile was pure evil. "You might as well get comfortable with me. You're my woman while we're in Rimside. Which means tonight we're sharing a room."

"When hell freezes over."

Colton's smile vanished and his hand slid from her side. "Look around you, angel. This isn't Haven or Absolution, or any of the settlements you know. This is Rimside. And like it or not, when they look at you all they're going to see is fresh meat. Unless you want every reiver in the place trying to stick his hands where they don't belong—or worse—then you can tolerate my touch. The only way to get down to the Divide is by passing through this shithole, so play your part, I'll play mine, and by the time the sun rises, you can pretend I haven't washed in a year again."

"If I need a protector, then CJ can play the part."

Colton's gaze slid toward her friend. "No offense, kid, but are you even shaving yet?"

A growl echoed in CJ's throat, but he gave her a long-suffering look. "Edie, you know I'd do anything for you, but... you're like my older sister. There's ten years between us. I don't know if I could play the part of your protector."

"And while I'm sure your friend can gut anything that moves, CJ looks young and pretty enough that he's probably going to have to watch his back too," Colton added. "Reivers aren't always that fussy."

In a horrible way, it made sense.

"Cole," CJ burst out. "Only my friends call me CJ."

Colton nodded slowly, as if to concede he wasn't a friend.

The light was fading, leaving longer shadows. A fire burned ahead of them in a rusted metal barrel. Several unwashed men in leather vests and dirty shirts warmed their hands around it. A woman strode past with the sides of her head shaved and a bright orange Mohawk standing to attention. Not all reivers were men. And the women were often the worst of the worst, as they had a point to prove.

"Wahoo!" screamed a reiver in the distance, shooting his gun into the air.

Another laughed, and a pair of drunks staggered out of what looked like a nearby makeshift bar. One of them turned to tug at the buttons on his jeans, and she looked away swiftly before she copped an eyeful of something she didn't want to see.

Eden felt Black Tom's hands on her jeans again, a sick sensation curling in her stomach.

"Fine," she said tersely. "I'm your woman. Just keep your hands to yourself unless you want to lose them."

A hand squeezed the back of her neck, the gesture both protective and confronting. "Nobody's going to touch you," Colton murmured.

"Don't make promises you can't keep." She brushed his hand off her.

"Oh, I can keep this one." His voice roughened. "Because if anyone dares to lay a hand on you, I will gut them. This way. The Saucy Wench's this way."

Eden settled her gear neatly in the corner of the room Colton had hired for the night, and then turned to stare at the narrow bed tucked against the wall. Barely enough room for Colton, let alone her. "You're on the floor."

Colton eased the door shut with a click, his large stride carrying him into the center of the room, where he dumped his bedroll. "I figured."

His presence seemed to absorb all the oxygen in the room, which was small enough to begin with. They'd be stepping all over each other. Trapped together. Breathing the same claustrophobic air.

Eden shivered. She and CJ had snatched a mouthful of food while Colton made arrangements for their descent in the morning, and purchased what looked like enough ammunition to mount a campaign on Cortez City single-handedly. The food had been terrible, and she'd felt the greasy stain of every reiver's eyes upon her. It had almost been a relief when Colton returned, because suddenly nobody was looking at her like she was a delicious morsel. He just had that air about him that said, *screw with me or mine, and you're a dead man.*

But being alone with him....

Sharing a room....

He set the lantern on the table and circled the room, running his fingertips over the walls.

"What are you doing?"

Colton paused, then leaned closer to where his fingers rested beneath a faded old framed poster that hung there, and examined something. Muttering under his breath, he took the frame down and hung his hat there, covering the pinhole.

*Oh.*

"I thought you said this was the safest place in town," she said.

"It is. Emphasis on the saf-*est*." Scraping a hand through his close-cropped black hair, he gave her a weary look. "Do you want me to fetch some water so you can wash?"

She would kill for some water and soap. The last two days had been hot and sweaty, and dust coated her skin like a glove. Everywhere. But there had to be a catch. "If you offer to scrub my back...."

Colton arched a brow. "My mother did teach me some manners."

The polite way he said it took her aback.

"Truce, Eden." He sighed. "One night of truce, okay? I'm tired and this is probably going to be the last chance I get to sleep for the next four days. Trust me. You want me as alert as I can be down there."

*Eden.* The word sat heavy in the air. So too did his request. She wasn't usually this bitchy.

"Truce," she whispered.

Colton nodded slowly, his dark eyes never leaving her face, and then he turned toward the door. "I'll fetch the water."

The second the door shut, she turned and stared blindly around the room. What was she doing? Embarking on a dangerous trek with her most hated enemy?

*Do you hate him?*

*Or do you hate what he had a hand in doing to you?*

She sank onto the bed, finally picturing the face of her true enemy.

Growing up in the Wastelands, she knew monsters. But there were monsters—wargs, revenants, shadow cats—and then there were *monsters*. Bartholomew Cane haunted her memories like a ghost, and for someone who'd been dead for three years, his image was easy to recall.

*A match flared in the darkness, and hot, dangerous eyes lingered on her in a way that made a young Eden's skin creep. Cane's rugged features held the taint of cruelty, his heavy mouth sloping down as he lit his cigar, and shook the match out slowly.*

*"You got what you wanted," a younger, not-as-world-weary Johnny Colton said, stepping between her and Cane. "McClain's going to give you Luc Wade. Now let me take the girl home. It's done."*

Ugh.

Eden dragged her hands over her face, trying to banish Cane from her mind. By the time Colton had returned with a bowl of water that even looked clean, she'd almost succeeded.

"Thank you."

A half smile twitched at his lips.

"What?"

"You're welcome," he said. "I'll go next door and make sure Cole knows how to barricade his room."

"You really know how to settle a girl's mind."

Colton's smile faded. "I don't want your mind settled. I want you wary, angel. But you should be safe tonight. Take the time to wash."

He headed for the door.

"Knock," she suggested. "And don't open the door until I grant you permission."

"Yeah, I got it." Dark eyes scoured her briefly, reminding her she was intending to get naked.

Eden's breath caught in her throat.

"I'll give you a couple of minutes," he muttered, and then slipped out through the door.

Her gaze slid to the bowl. There was barely two inches of water in it, but oh.... She burst into a flurry of movement, fetching the small bar of soap Riley had packed for her and the thin washcloth. Voices murmured next door, the walls paper-thin. Stripping out of her clothes, she knotted her hair loosely on the top of her head and set the bowl on the floor so she could stand in it and not waste a drop. Next door, the door slammed firmly, Colton's boots ringing on the timber floors.

The slick glide of soap over her skin felt like heaven.

A thin band of light stretched under the door and she could make out the large shadow standing guard, right in the middle. Water dripped into the bowl and the shadow shifted. Eden paused, the flannel draped over her right breast. A single panel of timber separated them. It felt intimate in a way she hadn't expected, and she could hear Colton shifting, hear the soft rasp of his breath.

Knew he was listening to water drip down her naked skin and splash in the bowl.

Damn it. Heat flared deep in her abdomen. Despite everything, her body hadn't quite gotten the message Johnny Colton couldn't be trusted.

*You don't have to trust him for what you want to do to him....*

*He's an attractive man,* she told herself, knowing denying the facts wouldn't make them untrue.

*Really fucking attractive*, whispered the devil on her shoulder, the one that knew no man had seen her naked in years. Eden's naughty side didn't mind swearing at all, and certain situations *did* call for cusswords. All that olive skin, stained golden by the sun. His slightly lopsided smile, which held hints of pure wickedness. Large hands, roughened with calluses. The way his jeans molded to an ass even Eden couldn't resist glancing at from time to time.

*Damn it.* She had a mental image of when she'd dropped her flask a couple of hours ago and bent to pick it up. Colton had been standing right next to her, and when she'd glanced up, her head on a level with his belt, he'd had this look on his face that stole her breath—

This wasn't happening.

And worst of all, she had one place left to wash.

Nipples pebbling—and not from the chill of the room—she dragged the flannel between her legs quickly, but it was as if everything was betraying her. A spike of sensation shot through her as the soft material rasped over her clit, and she knew if her fingers stroked there, she'd be growing wet.

"You done yet?" Colton growled.

"No!" Eden wrenched the flannel away guiltily. What was she doing? She nearly tripped out of the wide bowl, spattering soap across the floor. "Don't come in!"

"*Mierda.*" He continued muttering curses under his breath in what she assumed was Spanish. "I wasn't planning to, but you suddenly went silent."

*I was thinking about how well your jeans fit....*

Taking the full jug, she stepped back in the bowl and hastily poured it down her body. The water was lukewarm now, but it washed away all of the suds and dirt, and hopefully some of her sins.

She set a new speed record for drying herself and wriggled into fresh panties and an old shirt of Adam's that she wore to bed. The second she dragged her shorts up her legs she cleared her throat. "I'm done."

No sound from him, only that shadow beneath the door.

The handle slowly turned, as though he was giving her plenty of warning. Eden cleaned up the water on the floor, like it was the only thing that mattered in the world. There was a wet ache lingering between her thighs. Her cheeks burned and she bent over, shaking out her hair so she could hide her face.

The door clicked shut.

Eden dragged a hand through her curls, her fingers snarling in the tangles. It didn't matter how many times she brushed it, her hair seemed to revert to its natural chaotic state within minutes. Colton stared at her, his hand still resting on the doorknob, and his nostrils flaring as if he could smell her soap.

Hopefully all he could smell was the soap.

"Feel better?" he murmured.

"Thank you." She picked up the bowl and set it outside in the hall as Colton opened the door for her.

"Like I said earlier," he murmured, his gaze dropping lower than her chin when she ducked back inside. "We don't have to be enemies, or at each other's throats all the time."

Eden crossed her arms over her chest as she realized the shirt clung to her breasts, and her nipples were still firm. "Just don't make the mistake of thinking we're friends."

"I wouldn't be that presumptuous. Are you going to get in bed so I can blow this candle out?"

Fine. She slipped into bed.

"Good night, angel." Colton leaned down over the table, the reflection of the flame dancing in his dark eyes as he blew the candle out, plunging the pair of them into darkness.

Eden dragged the blankets up to her chin and stared in the direction of the ceiling. The afterimage of his face was burned into her retinas, his skin a warm golden glow on the back of her eyelids, and the slightest of smiles curving his lips. How was she supposed to get any rest tonight? How was she supposed to sleep with him in the same room?

"If you touch me, I will kill you," she said. "I have my Taser under my pillow."

"Noted." Fabric shifted. Something that sounded suspiciously like a shirt hit the floor. "But you shouldn't tell a guy where your weapon is... for future reference."

"And you might be bigger than me, but I'll have you know I can wield a scalpel like a maestro. I know all the right places to strike to render you half a man."

The zip on his jeans made a rasping noise.

Eden swallowed. Hard. "You had better not be getting naked."

The sound of his jeans hitting the floor echoed loudly.

"Would I do that?"

"*Colton.*"

He sighed. "I wouldn't do that. I would never deliberately try to make you feel uncomfortable."

She fell silent.

It was hard to trust him. She'd spent so many years painting him as the devil in her mind, but his statement forced her to reevaluate. It sounded sincere. And while he'd laid hands on her since they hit Rimside, he'd kept his touch respectful.

Blankets rustled and her eyes began to focus in the near-dark, making out a large black blur sinking into his bedroll. Colton sighed as he hauled his blankets over him, and the faint light from under the door glinted off sleek muscle.

Eden resumed her silent vigil of the ceiling, her heart starting to pulse a little swifter.

"Besides," he murmured into the quiet room. "I don't touch women who don't ask for it. I only touch them when they beg me to do so."

Eden lay so still she was barely breathing. She turned her head. "That would be a cold day in hell."

Somehow she knew Colton was smiling.

"So you keep saying. Go to sleep, Eden. You're safe. I promise. And tomorrow's going to be a big day for both of us."

# seven

Eden stood on the mesh platform as the reivers in Rimside slowly lowered them into the enormous canyon in a rickety elevator cage that looked like it had been repurposed from an old mine shaft. CJ pressed against the walls, his eyes closed and his breathing shallow as they were slowly winched down. Sweat darkened his temples and he refused to talk to her as they descended, merely shaking his head and focusing on his breathing.

Afraid of heights. Huh. *I'd have never guessed.*

Not that she could entirely blame him. It wasn't as though she was looking down at the expanse that dropped away beneath the mesh. Nope. Far better to keep her gaze fixed on the horizon and pretend they weren't a mile over nothing.

She'd gotten her first true glimpse of the Divide this morning, while Colton paid the bribes. The massive escarpment sliced through the land as though two enormous hands had wrenched the earth apart when the meteor hit over seventy years ago. Sheer cliffs dropped into the enormous canyon and she could see the ripple of undulating tors sticking up here and there within it. If she squinted she could just make out the other edge, miles away.

And that was where they were going.

But first, they had to cross the treacherous Divide. Nobody lived down there. Nothing human anyway. Few people even ventured within it, unless they were desperate. Fewer still made it across.

For the first time, she was grateful CJ had talked her into bringing Johnny Colton.

"Are you ready?" Colton murmured, and Eden realized he was watching her face and no doubt reading all her nerves.

He'd been dressed when she woke that morning, but his dark hair had stuck up in patches, and his eyes had been sleepy. Morning Colton was a sight to behold. He'd also kept to his word last night and hadn't made a move toward her.

She locked down her expression, brushing a loose curl behind her ear. "More than ready. How long is it going to take to cross this canyon?"

"Two or three days. If we're lucky. And maybe another once we're out. Depends on how well this crossing goes."

*Three or four days.* Plus the two she'd already been traveling for. She could hear the clock ticking down in her head.

Six days to get to Cortez City, at the most. She'd been banking on five. Then she had to locate the facility Chin had warned her about, and somehow extract enough of the plague cure and a vaccine to protect the rest of her people, before heading back.

They wouldn't make it in time.

The world blurred in front of her, and her lungs squeezed. She couldn't breathe.

"Kneel," Colton said sharply, his hand curling around the back of her neck. The heat of his touch broke through the icy chains that bound her heart as Eden went to her knees.

Colton squatted beside her. "It's okay. Just breathe."

"I'm fine."

"I know."

"I'm just... having a moment."

His thumb traced the line of muscle that curved beneath the base of her skull. Tension pulled there and Eden bowed her head as he squeezed gently. Oh, God. That felt incredibly good. She gave into the sensation, trying to still her racing heart.

"We'll cross the Great Divide, angel."

"I know. I will *not* fail," Eden said, lifting her head to stare out over the divide as the reivers above cranked them slowly down the cliff. She couldn't afford to. The shivery cold feeling running through her proved stark counterpoint to her words. "Whatever it takes."

"I believe you." Colton's voice sounded like a rough-edged purr, his knee close enough for her to rest her hand on.

If she wanted to.

Eden looked up beneath the brim of his black Stetson.

His expression tightened, but not before she'd seen something else in his eyes. Something she hadn't expected to see. She couldn't quite decipher the expression, but the softness of it, the emotion....

"You'd kick Satan in the teeth if you had to," he muttered. "You're going to drag me across this hellforsaken wasteland, then kick down the doors of the Confederacy and fuck up those arrogant smirks who sent this devastation west. You're going to bring that cure back to your people. I know you are."

"Language," she chided. The iron band around her lungs finally faded.

"Pardon." He sounded slightly amused.

Eden bowed her head, his hand softening on her nape as one thumb stroked the smooth skin there. Suddenly it wasn't a shiver of cold chilling her spine, but a lashing of pure heat.

"You've got this," Colton told her.

"I've got this."

Because failure wasn't an option.

She was Eden McClain, and she'd fought through blood and hell to bring babies into this world when they'd never had a chance, and to pull men back from death's door through pure willpower alone. She'd been born into a world that kicked the feet out from beneath those who faltered, and if she weakened now, then she might as well give up on all hope.

Eden pushed to her feet, taking in a slow, determined breath. "How long is it going to take to get down?"

"Two hours. Maybe. Then we've got another nine until nightfall." Colton brushed his jeans off, straightening to his full height beside her, but he was staring down at her strangely.

"What?"

"Nothing," Colton said, grabbing the rope beside CJ and staring down as if didn't have a care in the world.

The second they made camp and ate a quick meal of canned beans and salted beef, Eden crashed.

Johnny heard her breathing soften as the firelight flickered over her face and tangle of chestnut curls. He'd pushed them hard that day, trying to put some distance between them and the base of Rimside, where the predators would be lurking, and she'd started flagging a couple of hours before sunset.

Not that she was going to let him know that.

Stubborn bloody woman. He'd seen her examining the back of her heel when she poured sand out of her boots. Blisters, no doubt. But she hadn't complained once, and she'd insisted on carrying her own pack all day.

It helped, since he needed his hands free just in case anything came at them, but he couldn't help shaking his head. He'd have to keep an eye on her. He appreciated the lack of bitching, but he didn't want her dropping of heatstroke or dehydration because she didn't want to mention it.

*Whatever it takes*, she'd said earlier, and he knew Eden McClain was going to keep to that oath, come hell or high water.

Sometimes, when he looked at her, he got this rush of blood through his veins, as if her determination spurred him to new heights. He'd been drinking his life away in a rat hole, while she was battling to save lives. Made a man pause and rethink his situation.

"I'll take the watch," he said, nodding toward the kid. "Get some sleep. We break camp at dawn."

Night. A bloated moon rose in the sky above, barely days away from showing its entire face to the world.

The perfect time for monsters to come out to play.

Finding a good location to keep an eye on the camp, he eased onto a log, bringing out his hunting knife and a small branch to keep his hands busy.

Within twenty minutes, pebbles skittered down the rock face of the boulder Johnny rested his back against. He tilted his head, but he'd heard Cole starting in his direction minutes ago. Wasn't as if the young man could sneak up on him.

"Something on your mind, kid? You should get some sleep while you can."

The young warg squatted beside him, staring out into the night. "Kind of too wired to sleep," Cole admitted, scraping a hand over the back of his skull. "I tried."

"It's your fight or flight response going haywire," he murmured, shooting a glance toward the mound where Eden slept. "Over time you'll be able to control it better. Wargs don't cope well with putting themselves in danger or unknown circumstances. Too much increased adrenaline."

And they were already pumped full of hormones as it was. A little bit extra tended to tip the scales in the wrong direction. He'd have to keep an eye on Cole and make sure he was keeping his aggression under control.

The wind whispered through the narrow canyon, bringing with it a hint of long-distant warg song. Cole's scent sharpened and his nostrils flared. Johnny tilted his head, his muscles tensing, but there was no scent on the breeze and there'd been no fresh warg tracks today. He forced himself to relax, unclenching each muscle one at a time.

In the darkness of the night the kid's heart raced.

Johnny clasped his hand around the young man's shoulder and squeezed. "There's nothing out there. Breathe in and out. Let it go. Or you'll wear yourself out before you even need that extra hit of juice."

Cole's chest expanded. "Your scent just changed."

"Yeah." *I'll bet it did.*

"You smell exactly like you did yesterday in that alley."

"Do I?" He really didn't want to be having this conversation, but he'd expected it.

"How did you do it?" Cole asked.

"How'd I do what?"

Cole hesitated. "You made those dogs cringe before you, but I felt it too. I was on my knees before I could even think about it."

*Hell.*

"Okay, I'm going to have to go back a few steps if you're to understand any of this. You got it?"

Cole nodded.

"As far as I know, wargs were created pre-Darkening by the government of the time. They were trying to create some sort of elite super-soldier unit in their military. I don't know all the details, but when the meteor hit all hell broke loose, including some of their test subjects."

"Someone created this nightmare?" Cole blurted. "Deliberately?"

"Ground troops who could survive practically anything, heal from most injuries, and were faster, stronger, and owned better senses? Hell, yeah. Of course they created it. I believe the idea was to manufacture a top-secret military unit that could wipe out anything."

"Didn't they consider the ramifications?"

"Some humans like to mess with Mother Nature. Think they can control it. Or maybe they didn't care? Maybe they thought the technology was there, and if they didn't create it, then some other country or faction might get a head start on them."

"I would like to punch those people in the face," the boy muttered.

"You don't like being a warg?"

The kid looked at him like he had two heads. "No, I don't like hearing my mom's heart racing and knowing there's a small part of me that sits up and takes notice and thinks, *prey*. I don't like being looked at by all my former friends as if they're just waiting for me to lose my shit and rip them to pieces. Not too keen on turning furry, at all." His fist clenched around the amulet around his throat. "I spend every day praying this never leaves my throat. It's the only thing that keeps me safe. That keeps my friends and family safe from *me*."

Johnny tugged his shirt open, revealing a similar wolf's head talisman. "My grandfather made them. He was of the Lakota people." Reaching behind his neck, he started to lift it off. "It's a talisman to ward away evil spirits. These were created for my aunts and uncles, and passed down through my family. Reminds me of Grandfather sometimes."

But that was all it did.

"What *are you doing?*" Cole squeaked, rising to a crouch.

Johnny dropped the talisman into his palm, meeting the kid's eyes. Then he gently placed it on the ground beside him.

The kid's breath caught, and he reached for the hilt of his knife, his heartbeat accelerating.

Johnny drew his knees up in front of him, resting one hand laxly on the right one. "I'm not going to go furry. You can relax."

Cole seemed frozen in place. "You can't.... I just...."

"I don't need it," he said. "I never have. Sit and let me finish, and then you might understand."

Cole sank into a cross-legged seat, but tension remained in his body. He released a slow breath, his eyes darting to the talisman. "How?"

"I'm not the same strain of warg as you," Johnny replied. "But you could learn to control your inner beast, just as I can."

"What do you mean, the same strain? And control it? Nobody can control it!"

"Yeah, they can."

"But—"

"Just listen. I don't know the exact science behind how wargs were created," he admitted, turning his knife over and over in his hands. "But they were trying to create a soldier who wouldn't flinch in the face of danger, a pumped-up adrenaline-junkie who relished killing. You can probably guess how this goes wrong. I think the first trials failed, and the second wasn't much better, and in the end five different types of wargs were created until they finally got to a stage where their wargs weren't so volatile. You've got your alpha strain, your beta strain, gamma, delta, and omega.

"Project: Gamma was the first hybrid created. Problem was they were utterly batshit crazy. Your general run-of-the-mill psychopath warg who needs to be put down. You can't reach them, you can't teach them to control themselves, and they just want to fuck or fight. You see them out in the Wastelands sometimes—the direct descendants of the original gamma hybrids. Stink like rotten flesh from the kills they drag back to their nests, and they're generally filthy and dangerous. The second you smell that scent you know you've got to kill them. Best solution is to put a few silver bullets in them and move on.

"Wasn't exactly what the military wanted, so the scientists moved on to Project: Delta. Phase two. Not as batshit insane as the gamma variant, but still uncontrollable. Very, very occasionally you come across a delta warg out there who can fight the urge to destroy everything around it, but chances are they'll go rogue at least once in their life. I've only ever come across two. One was a killer. One was an old rogue who just wanted to be left alone, and I'm pretty sure he'd done some bad shit at some stage in his life.

"Which brings us to the alpha and beta strains. They're variants of the third hybrid created. Your alphas were bred and engineered to be leaders of their military units, once they'd finally crafted a warg hybrid that wouldn't simply murder everything it came across. Alphas have a slightly different base code, and when they're fusing—which is what I did to you and those dogs in that alley—they give off some kind of chemical scent that makes other wargs want to obey. My father called it pheromones, said it's all got to do with hormones or something. That scent says obey or die, and depending on the strain you're infected with, you'll most likely obey.

"Especially if you've got the beta strain. Similar to alpha, but they're designed to be soldiers. Militia. There's a subordinate streak in them that makes them naturally crave to be in the pack, just not at the head of it."

"And your omega strain?" Cole looked fascinated.

Johnny stabbed his knife in the dirt, his hand clenching around the hilt so tightly the timber ingrained itself in his palm. *Easy.* "Project: Omega was the last warg hybrid they managed to create. Don't get me wrong. Your alphas and betas might be more in control than the others, but most of them go warg these days. I imagine it might have been different back when they were created and had the training to resist it. Omegas, however, are the most stable of all wargs, and they give off calming pheromones.

Rarely fight, rarely turn warg. If you've got an out-of-control alpha or even a delta, an omega's about the only thing that *might* be able to rein them in."

Except for the one time in his life when it had mattered.

Bitterness churned within him. His mother had always been the aggressive one, but his father.... Hell, his father should have known better than to think anything he could have done would have talked Bartholomew Cane down.

The second Cane rode onto their small homestead, Johnny's father had been a dead man, and his mother had panicked as her past finally caught up to her.

"*Hide,*" she'd rasped at Johnny, shoving him toward the small game trail that led into the wilderness behind their cabin. "*Whatever you see or hear, don't come back. Don't let my brother see you.*"

And his father—the father who'd rarely lifted a hand against anyone—had grimly walked out to meet the lone figure on horseback. It was the last time he'd ever seen him.

The sound of a gun firing echoed through his head, and Johnny flinched.

"What's wrong?" Cole asked, as the breeze swirled past them.

"Bad memories."

He could almost feel the lingering stroke of Cole's gaze on his face. "You knew someone who was an omega?"

"My father." *And I really don't want to talk about it.*

The warg itched under his skin as if it sensed his anger. Left to brew, it would use that rage to tear its way out of him if he allowed it. Not even he was immune and the lunar tide pulled at him.

*Feel the wind on your skin and remember who you are*, his father's voice whispered in his memories. *Feel the dirt beneath your feet and use it to rein the monster in.*

Johnny breathed out slowly, letting it all wash out of him. The hate. The rage. The desire to hit something.

It wouldn't bring his father back or change the past.

The kid got the message. "So how do you know which strain of warg you are?"

"Depends who scratched you up." Johnny held his hands up, forcing the shift to stir through him. His fingers ached and began to elongate, sharp claws springing from the tips. The whisper of the night-lure became a little stronger in his veins. Every sense heightened just a fraction, until he could hear the rush of blood through Eden's veins.

"Holy shit," Cole blurted. "You can partial shift."

"Yeah. I don't know how the pre-Darkening government created us, but it's like an infection. One bite, one scratch, and you're going to start getting hairy at night. But each infection is specific to the strain of warg who scratched you. Who infected you?"

"Luc Wade."

Johnny shot him a startled look. "And you're riding to get a cure for his daughter?"

Despite the dark, he could scent the sudden flush of emotion coming off the kid. Without thinking, he reached out and rested his hand on Cole's shoulder, feeling that heavy pit of lassitude sweep through him. The calmness flooded his veins the same way adrenaline did, and Cole's shoulders softened the second he smelled it.

Pheromones.

An omega's touch.

A pity it hadn't saved his father's life.

"Lily's a friend. And I've come to terms with what happened. I have this now." Cole wrapped a hand around the pewter amulet around his neck. "Doesn't make it any easier knowing Wade cut my future short, but with this... I can live a semblance of a life. He gave this to me himself, as reparation."

Johnny eyed the amulet cynically. *If only you knew the truth....*

But he sighed and gave in. No point fucking with the kid's belief system when they were in the middle of the Divide. "I knew an alpha once—his name was Bartholomew Cane. Since he was the one who infected both Adam McClain and Luc Wade, you'll carry the alpha strain."

"Which means I should be able to control other wargs." Cole sounded out the thought, his words not quite a question. "But the second you commanded me, I went down on one knee like those fucking dogs."

"Even an alpha can bend. You're young and untrained, and you've been around two wargs since you were in your teens presumably. It's the pack hierarchy mentality. When Wade tells you to do something, I'll bet you do it. Don't even think about it mostly."

Cole stared out into the night as if he was re-running his interactions with Wade through his mind. *"Son of a bitch."*

"Don't beat yourself up. It happens when you get a warg young, and I doubt Wade's doing it consciously. He doesn't know shit about being a warg. It's most likely instinct on both your behalf, and as you get older you'll find it easier to defy him."

"Could you do that to Wade?"

He gave a faint, bitter smile. "Considering Wade managed to lock me in a cabin a few years ago and flick a match... Unlikely. It doesn't work on all alphas and depends strongly on the hierarchy. Once they're adults it's virtually impossible to make an alpha yield, especially if they're strong-willed." His smile died. "Unless you break them. Torture. Sleep deprivation. Starvation. That kind of shit." His voice roughened. "You break them down, force them to kneel to your will when you're flooding them with scent. Rinse and repeat. Do it often enough and you can twist even the most hard-core alpha to your will in a way he'll never be able to break. If you get them young, then it works even better. They can't deny you. Can't say no. You can fight it, but you're fighting your own instincts and it hurts like fuck."

A slight rustle stirred. Eden. Rolling over in her blankets, as she gave a soft sigh.

Johnny eased out his breath—and the shame that had suddenly filled him. *Fuck.* Why was he even saying this? His heart was suddenly racing, the moon beginning to whisper through his veins like a drug. He vanished the claws the second he realized he was getting emotional, staring at his all-too-human hands.

And he realized he'd given far too much away.

Cole slowly stirred the dirt beneath his heels. "You smell different to McClain and Wade. Now I know what I'm looking for I can pick up the difference. It makes me feel weird. I feel like I should trust you, and I don't know why."

"It's the omega in me, thanks to my father. My mother was an alpha. She and my father decided to infect me at the same time. She didn't want me to have to fight the rage she always struggled with, but alphas heal better than omegas, so he wanted me to have her strain too. Thought blending the two strains might help me keep my wits, and it seems to have worked."

"Double whammy."

"Something like that."

"So you're an alpha-omega?"

"Yeah. Only one I've ever met, to be honest."

"How do you know so much about this?" Cole asked. "I've never come across anyone who knows anything more than how to kill a warg."

"My father's people kept records." Pushing to his feet, Johnny crossed to the small pit where the last of the night's coals had died down. "He told me about the different strains and a couple of years ago I spent a month in the ruins of Black River Testing Facility, and managed to find some of their sealed records. They were one of the military centers that experimented on wargs."

"Do you think there's a cure?"

Wishful thinking. He kicked dirt over the coals, turning into the breeze. "Doubtful. We don't have the technology or the—"

The faintest hint of scent wafted past him.

Johnny froze.

He slammed a hand out, beckoning the kid into silence. Every hair on the back of his neck felt like it rose.

"What is it?" Cole breathed, slowly shifting to his feet.

Johnny's nostrils flared. The scent was gone. But it had been there. Musk and iron, and something faintly cat-like. If the wind hadn't shifted in that precise moment, he doubted he'd have even sensed it.

He'd smelled that scent before.

*Mierda.* Something was downwind, and it was stalking them. Worse. He knew what it was.

Tension unfurled within him. Where the fuck was his shotgun? His hand settled slowly over the gun at his belt, and his gaze shifted to the knife he'd left buried in the dirt by the log he'd been sitting on. Cole followed his glance and tugged the knife free, tensing in reaction.

Part omega or not, right now he could feel the kick of his heart and knew his scent would be sharpening.

"Don't move suddenly," Johnny said, in a conversational voice that sounded distant to his ears. Eden was still wrapped up in her blankets as snug as a bug, but he caught the glint of moonlight on her eyes. Awake and listening to them, and probably had been for a while. "Eden, can you get up?"

"What is it?" she breathed.

"Something's out there and it's stalking us." His heartbeat jacked through his ribs, and he tried to hear over its sudden drumming pulse. Except for that brief drift of scent he might not have known. There was no sound. No more scent. Nothing except the fine prickling of the hairs along his forearms and the *knowing* they weren't alone anymore.

"A warg?"

*No.* "Worse. A shadow cat."

His mother's people had called them *sombra que acecha la noche*.

And if they had any luck it would only be one.

"What do you mean shadow cats?" Eden whispered harshly, kicking her blankets aside. "You said they'd be the least of our concerns down here."

"Don't. Move. Quickly," Colton said, holding his hands out, almost as if to warm them in a nonexistent flame from the quenched coals. His head tilted slowly. Listening maybe. "We want it to think we're not aware of it."

"*It?*"

"Hopefully it. A single shadow cat will go out of its way to avoid a warg, and vice versa. Cole and I have been marking the trails all day, so it will know what we are. Usually that's enough to warn them away." Moving slowly, Colton retrieved her shotgun from her bag and shoved it at her. He reached for his knife and CJ jerkily handed it over. "They're solitary creatures except for mating season, and we're a month too late for that. But if this is an adult female with cubs and we're in her territory, she might be bold enough to attack."

*Shit.* Where were her boots? Eden spotted them and dragged them on, moving with slow, cautious movements, even as her heartbeat ran ragged.

"She might back off if she thinks we're a threat to her cubs," CJ muttered, pumping two rounds into the chambers of his shotgun.

"Unfortunately not." Colton knelt low beside a boulder, peering over the top of it as he scanned the near dark. The moon was sinking toward the horizon and visibility had dropped. Eden could barely see him; he blended into the nightscape like a shadow himself. "The females are the dangerous ones. They've got poisonous spurs, and they do most of the hunting. They'll kill to protect their territory and if her cubs are almost fully grown then they'll be with her. We want this to be a male, as they tend to be less violent."

"That's a turnaround from humans," CJ said.

"You ever broken into a woman's house when she's got kids in there?" Colton murmured distractedly.

"Neither of us has been in the kidnapping game." Eden couldn't help herself. "So I guess that's a no."

"*Puta madre.*" Colton held up his hand, gesturing for silence. "Fucking motherfucking fuck. I can see a couple of shapes out there. They're not full-grown, but they're almost adult-sized by the look of them, which makes them just as dangerous." He turned in a slow circle. "I must have caught the scent of one of them. What I don't see is mama. She's the better hunter and she'll be downwind."

This was an appropriate time for swearing. Eden swallowed her nerves. "What do we do?"

"You keep your back to the rocks," he told her. "They'll try and pounce on you from behind and crush your neck or suffocate you. Do you know how to use that thing?"

She swiftly loaded the shotgun like a pro. "Do you think Adam didn't teach me how to shoot?"

"Only as a last resort," he warned. "Stay out of it if you can. You're more likely to hit CJ or me, than anything else. A combat situation's miles away from popping cans on the range, especially when your target can move faster than you can see in the dark. Use it to defend yourself if we go down."

She didn't argue. Her face was still bruised from Black Tom's sudden blow. No matter how much Adam had tried to prepare her for this sort of situation, she was rapidly learning how far out of her depth she was.

And if they went down, she was dead.

"How many are out there?" CJ's voice pitched high.

"I've got three on my radar and a mysteriously missing adult female, but I daresay she'll be out there. They don't call them shadow cats for no reason."

*Yeah.* Eden swallowed. So named because you never saw them coming. The genetically manipulated creatures had camouflage down to a fine art.

She pressed her back against the boulder and blinked, trying to adjust her vision to the pale moonlight.

Colton gave a burst of quick orders to CJ, the pair of them standing guard in front of her. With the rock at her back, the shadow cats could only come at them in a frontal assault—which was probably why Colton had picked this spot to camp.

"What are they waiting for?" CJ demanded.

"They're still young," Colton murmured, staring out into the night. "Learning to hunt. I don't think they expected us to sense them coming."

Something landed on her head. A bug or... no, gravel. It rained down over her shoulders, and she rubbed it out of her hair. *What the...?* Eden's heart stopped dead in her chest as she heard the faintest shift of sound above her.

*Oh, shit.*

"Colton," she whispered loudly.

He jerked a hand at her. "Shh. I'm trying to listen."

"I think I just found the mother," she blurted. "It's on top of the boulder."

His shoulders stiffened and he slowly turned around, just as Eden tilted her head back. Her heart started kicking again, and a shiver of breathlessness went through her. Directly above her, a patch of pure darkness separated itself from the velvety night skies, and then a high-pitched yowl erupted.

"Shit!"

The shadow cat launched itself off the top of the boulder, aiming directly for Colton. He jerked his shotgun up and fired, the sound echoing through the night. Eden was blinded momentarily by the sudden light of the muzzle flash, a scream escaping her and the shot echoing through the night.

*Jesus.* She blinked away the afterimage, catching a glimpse of CJ darting in with his knife, trying to get the creature off Colton. The world around her jerked like a vignette of slides running through a projector. Colton was flat on his back on the ground, as if the mama cat had slammed into him. CJ smashed into the cat, as Colton flipped to his feet.

A high-pitched scream pierced her eardrums, and then Colton was cursing as the shadow swiped its claws at CJ.

It was moving so bloody fast.

And worse, the night itself seemed to be rippling with darkness.

"The kids are joining the party!" she yelled, as CJ grunted and staggered back beneath the mother's sudden assault. "Colton!?"

Trying to dance in low to hamstring the mama cat.

Behind him a shadow loomed.

Adrenaline pumped through her veins. Eden jerked the shotgun up and narrowly avoided pulling the trigger as one of the creatures launched from the boulder above her across the clearing. Colton had been right. Shooting a stationery target when you weren't in a fight for your life was a vastly different beast to trying to aim when your heart was fit to pound out of your chest.

And she might not have time to reload.

But....

It materialized out of the darkness as the glow from the embers in the fireplace lit it. She caught a glimpse of thin fur that seemed to ripple through a dozen different shades of black and gray, as if its fur absorbed the light. *Don't miss.* Her heart rabbited in her chest, and Eden focused down the line of the barrel as it launched itself at Colton's unprotected back.

She pulled the trigger.

The butt of the shotgun kicked against her shoulder like a mule, and the creature jerked and slammed into Colton's back, screaming in pain.

Easier now to breathe. Eden reloaded as Colton rolled to his hands and knees, her movements mechanical, even though a fist of nausea bloomed in her throat. The cat she'd shot twitched on the ground, but didn't move, a gaping hole in its ribs.

"You all right?" she yelled.

"Fine. Thanks," Colton snapped, and darted forward to drive his knife into one of the cubs. "Stay out of this."

"Trying to!" If she had the chance. Eden turned, jerking the shotgun around to cover both sides.

CJ went down with a scream beneath a pair of shadow cats. All she could see was a writhing mass of darkness. Stepping forward, Eden pumped both rounds into the chambers, but she couldn't gauge what was CJ and what was the predator.

"CJ!" she screamed.

A shadowy limb lifted and moonlight flashed off the curve of his knife. He plunged it into the mass atop him, and a high-pitched squeal of pain erupted.

The other cub leaped off him, landing lightly atop the boulder ten feet away from her and Eden turned on it. *Don't shoot unless necessary.* She hesitated.

But Colton didn't.

He pulled the trigger of his own shotgun, and the shadow jerked and tumbled out of view.

*Hell.* Gasping for breath, she lowered the shotgun. Had she been too late? Was he moving, or was that just her imagination? "*CJ?*"

CJ lifted his head as if to examine his abdomen, then collapsed back on the ground, breathing hard. "Son of a bitch."

"Got your back covered," Colton snapped, the back of his legs bumping into her as he fired in rapid succession into the darkness. Reloaded. Fired again. "Check him out if you can, angel."

Another feline scream. And something deeper; a low rumbling of pure fury lifted all the hairs on her arms. Eden had been about to kneel at CJ's side, but her gaze stalked the darkness, and she swallowed as she straightened. No time.

"That's two of her cubs down. Mama's not dead yet. You loaded?" Colton barked. "We've got mama and one cub left, and she's pissed."

She steadied her shotgun. "Ready."

Eden settled her back against his, searching the darkness for anything that moved. "CJ, are you okay?"

The young warg rolled onto his side, clutching his abdomen. "It was trying to rip my throat open, but my gun was in the way, so its claws barely glanced me." He sounded breathless as he staggered to his feet and looked at his hand. "Sorry. I lost the gun. It was faster than I expected."

Colton tossed him a shotgun and CJ snatched it out of the air.

"We need to drive that bitch off," Colton said. "You two stay here and guard each other's backs. I've got this."

Then he was gone, vanishing into the night like a wraith.

"Damn it! Colton!"

No sign of him. *Shit.* CJ's body trembled against hers. Eden swallowed. Without Colton they'd be sitting ducks out here.

How were they supposed to drive off a pissed-off shadow cat and her one remaining cub? Eden's mind raced. She was Wastelander born and bred, so she knew the rules.

To protect yourself against shadow cats you needed light.

Fire.

They didn't like the smell of gasoline either.

"Stay here," she told CJ.

Eden rested the shotgun on her knees and started rifling through Colton's pack for his flask. The handful of coals in the small pit smoldered pitifully. The second she doused them with his whiskey they spat and sizzled. Flames roared up. Eden kicked the rest of the kindling they'd gathered earlier onto the fire.

Eyes gleamed out there in the darkness. A grunt sounded. And another feline yowl.

"Colton?" she yelled.

*Please let him be alive.*

She had no idea what they'd do if he wasn't.

Silence settled through the night like a heavy mantle. Slowly the flames started to die down, but there was nothing moving out there. No response from Colton either.

*Shit.* The son of a bitch had a lot to make up to her, but at the same time.... She didn't want his life to end here. Nemesis or not, his death would still weigh on her conscience, and she didn't want him to be... hurt. Eden swallowed. The weight of the gun was starting to ache through her arms, and she raked the shadows for any sign of him, her ears pricking.

"Hear anything?" she murmured to CJ, who was moving between the corpses and making sure both shadow cats on the ground were definitely dead.

He looked up.

Shadows moved at the corner of her vision. Eden jerked her shotgun toward them, her finger whispering over the trigger—

"Just me," Colton called, materializing out of the night with his hands in the air. Silver warg-shine flashed across his pupils as if the lure of blood and violence brought the monster within him to the surface. She kept the gun on him a second longer—just in case—but she'd seen Adam in a worse state over the years.

Colton paused and slowly lowered his hands with a questioning twitch of his brow.

Definitely still human. A warg couldn't pull off that amount of arrogance.

Eden released the breath she'd been holding, and lowered the shotgun. "You're alive."

For a second there....

She was surprised how much the thought bothered her.

"Don't sound so disappointed."

"I'm not." Her hands shook suddenly. "Did you kill them?"

"They fled. I managed to sink my knife into mama cat, and the cub bolted." Colton's chest heaved, blood dripping from the end of his knife. He'd lost his hat in the scuffle, and dirt marred his cheek.

"Will they be back?"

"Hopefully not. But I don't want to risk it." Raking his hand through his close-cropped black hair, Colton took in the campsite. Striding toward his bag, he started stuffing his belongings back inside it. "Get moving, guys. Until the sun starts to rise, we're vulnerable. Shadow cats aren't the worst things out there, and there's enough blood here to rouse a warg from a few miles away."

"Are you okay?" Eden asked CJ, noticing the blood on his hand in the firelight.

"Fine," CJ muttered, but he didn't look at her and his voice sounded rougher than usual as he cleaned his blade on shadow cat fur.

The unusual behavior made her frown. CJ sounded like he'd swallowed acid. "Any more bleeding? Light-headedness?"

His nostrils flared and silver flashed through his pupils as he looked up, revealing how close to the edge he was. "Don't touch me."

Eden held her hands up.

With his amulet he could keep the warg trapped within him, but she didn't like how on edge he seemed.

"It's the battle rush," Colton muttered, kneeling on her bedroll and tugging the leather straps through the loops. "Give him a few minutes to get his head clear."

"And you?"

Colton pushed to his feet, tossing her bedroll toward her. "It's nothing I can't handle. We've got to get moving. Killing half their pack is enough to drive them to retreat for the moment, but they'll start following us again soon. The mother's injured, but I daresay she's brewing some serious revenge theories. They're vindictive creatures. If we can make it out of their territory, then we might be safe. They won't leave their usual haunts. Too many other predators out there, and she took a beating tonight. Might make her wary."

"That's not necessarily reassuring." She attached her bedroll to her backpack and slung the straps over her shoulders.

"It's not meant to be."

Hours trickled by. Eden staggered forward, putting one foot after the other. She could vaguely remember falling asleep when they first set up camp, but now her body ached as if she'd only managed to snatch twenty minutes or so before the shadow cats attacked.

And the second the sun started to rise, a thick oppressive heat began to make everything sticky.

*Going to be a scorcher by the feel of it.* Eden paused at the top of the trail and tipped her water canteen to her lips. Ahead of her Colton looked like a dark blur on the landscape as he roved ahead, scouting the terrain. He'd found his hat somewhere, and his loose-hipped stride caught her eye, though she didn't know why.

Eden's eyes narrowed as he paused at the bottom of the switchback. Colton rested a hand on his thigh, bending over for a moment as if to catch his breath. Maybe she wasn't the only one feeling the lack of sleep—and he'd had none.

Something felt off.

"Edie," CJ muttered, his limp long since faded as the warg within him healed his injuries. She'd checked them out back at the camp, but despite a few faint scratches across his hip and one narrow claw mark, CJ was fine.

"Yeah?" It was so goddamn hot out here.

"I can smell blood. Thought it was shadow cat for a while, but now I'm starting to feel better I realized it's not."

Eden's heart leapt. If it had been him, CJ would have admitted to it. Which left....

Her head turned, tracking Colton. He rested a hand against a rock and tilted his water skin to his lips. The stark outline of him stood out against the rising red-gold of the sun, but she wasn't focusing on Colton's hard body.

Eden's brows drew together. She'd known something was wrong. Sweat tracked marks down the dirt on his face. The side of his shirt was damp, but she hadn't noticed he was bleeding, thanks to the color of it and the darkness of the night.

"Son of a bitch," she snapped, as Colton's knees wobbled. "Fetch some wood. We need a fire, and I need boiling water. Now."

Ahead of her, Colton went down on one knee, splashing water from his canteen as he tried to catch it.

# nine

---

"Jesus Christ, let me look at it."

Blood wet Eden's fingers, leaving them tacky as she knelt at his side. Not fresh, or at least, not all of it was—but Colton's shirt was still damp enough to concern her. He had to have lost at least a pint.

"I'll heal." Colton tipped the whiskey flask up, the muscles in his throat working as Eden fussed over him. He lowered it, peering inside the mouth of the flask. "Did you drink some of my whiskey? This was full this morning, and now there's barely half left."

*I threw it on the fire.*

"Why the hell didn't you tell me you were still bleeding?" she muttered under her breath, starting to undo his shirt.

"Because we had to keep moving," Colton snapped. He looked away as he lowered the bottle. "And it's not as though I thought you'd care."

Eden recoiled sharply. He couldn't have cut her deeper if he'd tried.

All her life she'd been a healer, drawn to helping people.

She'd never turned anyone away, because that wasn't who she was.

But his claim wasn't as far-fetched as it sounded.

When had she begun to turn into this person?

Eden clearly startled him by taking the whiskey flask off him and wiping the rim of it with her sleeve.

"Hey, I need that. It's good for my...." His protest died off when she tipped it to her own lips and swallowed heartily. "But you can share if you like. Just didn't think you'd be the type."

Fire burned down her throat and Eden let it wash away the hate. If she wasn't careful, she'd tie herself in knots with it. It was already forging her into someone she didn't know—and didn't like.

"Type?" she rasped, lowering the bottle. "Why? You don't think I like a good drink?"

He bared his teeth in a pained smile. "You seem more the type who's all work and no play...."

It wasn't the first time a man had told her that. Eden's eyes narrowed. Nothing wrong with having a sense of duty. She could have a good time.

"You look like you want to say something bad," he said, grimacing. "Permission to swear at me, Miss McClain."

"Strip." She ignored his suggestion.

Colton shot her a somewhat dirty look as he tugged the hem of his shirt up, revealing the chiseled perfection of his abs. "You want to get me down to bare skin, angel, all you've got to do is say the word. But I don't need to take my shirt off."

Normally those were fighting words—especially coming from this man—but Eden's breath caught as she saw the damage. Claw marks raked across his abdomen, slashing down to his hip. The top of them was dangerously close to his sternum. She'd seen enough of Adam's wounds in the past to know this should have healed by now but the edges were grayed, the raw flesh a paler pink than she'd have expected. Tiny threads of darker gray highlighted the faint capillaries under his olive skin, as if the poison from the wound worked its way slowly through him. Sepsis, perhaps. Or something else?

"Jesus," she whispered, touching the puffy flesh lightly. Heat burned beneath her fingers, and suddenly she was moving, reaching for the medical kit she carried everywhere she went. "Hold still."

If he were human, she'd have to clean that flesh out, perhaps even surgically remove some of it. She'd have given him as much antibiotics as she dared—before she ran through her entire supply when the plague hit—and she'd have put him on a drip and spent the next couple of days monitoring him.

But he wasn't human, and she didn't have access to her surgery.

And the last thing they had was time.

"I'll live," he told her gruffly, clearly reading her expression. "Won't be the worst wound I've ever taken. Just bandage it up."

"I know we were joking about it earlier, but shirt off." Her eyes met his. "And that is not a suggestion."

"I'm fine."

"Careful," CJ warned. "She'll wrestle you into submission if you're not careful and sit on you to get what she wants. She only looks like she's small and sweet-tempered, but she's like a trapped wolverine when she wants to play doctor."

"*Mierda*." Colton tipped the bottle of whiskey to his lips again, and took another healthy swallow. Then he reached over his shoulder and hauled his shirt over his head, wincing a little as muscle flexed in his abdomen, pulling at his wound. "And I don't think I ever thought she was sweet-tempered."

"*She* is right here," Eden growled, glaring at her comrade over Colton's shoulder. A folded piece of paper slid out of his pocket. Eden frowned and went to grab it, but Colton beat her to it.

"That's private," he muttered.

Behind him, CJ sucked in a sharp breath. Colton shot him a narrow-eyed look she couldn't quite decipher, but the claw marks swiftly had her full attention.

Eden cleaned the ragged edges of the wound with a gauze pad soaked in the liquor, as Colton leaned back against the rock he was sitting on. She bit her lip when he hissed. "Normally I wouldn't bother stitching something like this—not with a warg anyway—but I don't like the look of it."

"Heat my knife," he told her, tugging it out of the sheath at his hip and flipping it so he could hand her the hilt. "Burn the poison out and I'll heal. It will just be a little slower than I'd like."

Eden turned toward the small fire CJ had made. It wouldn't have been her first choice. But Colton was right. Whatever had coated the shadow cat's claws, it was working its way through the wound. No point stitching it, and all of her herbal washes would cleanse the wound, but little else.

Which left fire.

Eden slowly heated the blade in the flames. "Are you ready?"

Colton tugged his belt through the rasp of his jeans and folded it. He set it between his teeth, his fist flexing around the neck of the flask. "Rea-rry."

Eden rested her hand on his shoulder and looked at CJ wordlessly. This would hurt and it didn't matter how conflicted she felt about Colton, she hated having to do this to him.

To anyone.

"Do it quickwy," Colton rasped, as CJ pinned his shoulders.

Skin seared as she held the blade to his mottled flesh. She'd been expecting him to at least scream but all that left his mouth was a rasped groan, and he turned his head to the side, panting through it. The stink of burning flesh made her swallow.

"Next one," she whispered, turning the flat of the blade and pressing it swiftly against the other claw mark. There were three in all, and a faint scratch where the fourth must have glanced his skin. Only two of them were deep and angry, but she swiftly cauterized the third shallow cut, just in case.

The second she was done, Colton collapsed forward into her arms, pressing his forehead against her shoulder and shuddering. The belt fell from his mouth, along with a strand of saliva, and a swift course of groaned Spanish words she couldn't decipher. Eden couldn't help rubbing her hand through his close-cropped hair, though she knew there was nothing she could truly do to comfort him.

And—

The curve of his spine flexed as he bent his neck. Scars marked his back. Hundreds of them. Eden sucked in a sharp breath, her eyes flying to CJ's.

She recognized burn marks when she saw them.

Small round burns like the end of a cigarette—or cigar, most likely, from the size of them. Some were pressed over others, deep thickened welts that looked like they'd merely built upon the base layers of scarring.

Holding the knife safely away from him, Eden stroked her free hand up his spine, cupping the back of his neck, her mind still shocked.

This was why he hadn't wanted to take his shirt off. He'd made sure the light was quenched the other night too, before he undressed.

His words from last night about how to break a warg flashed through her head: *Torture. Sleep deprivation. Starvation. That kind of shit.*

There was nothing else she could call scars like these, except signs of long-ago torture. And they had either happened to him young, before he was infected with the warg curse, or the torture had been so extreme even his super-healing hadn't been able to heal it all.

"Who did this to you?" she whispered.

"*Hijo de puta.*" Colton shuddered and clung to her arm. "Fuck." He slowly managed to lift his head, his chest still heaving. "Are we done here?"

"Colton," she blurted, grabbing his forearm.

He froze, his dark eyes dropping to her touch. Eden's first instinct was to withdraw her hand, but she tilted her chin stubbornly and let her thumb stroke, just once, over the smooth skin on the inside of his wrist.

Their eyes met.

"Don't go soft on me, angel," he said quietly. "I've lived a bad life, remember?"

Right now she couldn't think of everything he'd done to her. All she could feel was horror. "*Who?*"

He searched her gaze, as if he realized she wasn't going to leave this alone.

"You think you were Bartholomew Cane's first victim?" Each word was crisp and cool, Colton locking down his emotions hard. He reached for his shirt and tugged it back over his head. A taunting smile twisted his lips as he pushed himself to his feet. "Sorry, angel. But you spent one night with him. I spent years."

And then he stalked away into the sweltering morning, leaving her on her knees with his knife in her hand, her entire world turned upside down.

It changed everything.

Eden could barely focus on anything else all day, as Colton pushed them hard. They had to move, he said, ignoring her attempts to question him about Cane when his burns healed well enough for her to bandage them.

Which meant she had to form her own conclusions.

Thinking about Bartholomew Cane made her skin crawl. As much as Eden didn't want to admit it, she'd never thought of Colton as a monster. He'd obeyed Cane's will, but when he'd finally locked her inside the hut where her brother was undergoing his first metamorphosis, he'd been almost apologetic, and there'd been a broken-down look in his dark eyes, as if he knew she'd never forgive him.

Left to his own devices she didn't think Colton had it in him to be cruel or violent. He just wasn't the type to seek it out.

Cane had been a different kettle of fish entirely. Even now the hairs along the back of her neck rose, and the man had been dead several years, killed by Colton's own hand apparently.

Not once had she ever wondered what it would have been like to work for Cane.

She hadn't understood why Colton even obeyed the psychopath.

Hadn't given it a thought.

Just assumed he'd been there for the hell of it.

*Do it often enough and you can twist even the most hard-core alpha to your will in a way he'll never be able to break....*

Everything inside her went cold.

What if Colton hadn't been Cane's accomplice by choice?

What if Cane had used torture to break Colton at a young age, and he'd been forced to obey him? She'd heard enough of his conversation with CJ last night to understand how it might have been done.

Which meant all her preconceived notions about Colton were wrong.

Feeling breathless, Eden forced herself to mechanically chew the meal CJ had cooked when they finally stopped for the night, but the two wargs' quiet words went right over her head as she tried to replay every interaction she'd ever had with Johnny Colton.

*Sunlight drenched the street as Eden bustled out of the general store, lugging the basket of groceries she'd purchased. She was waving goodbye to Mr. Miller, all smiles and good humor, when she turned the corner and almost slammed into a young man washing his face in the water trough.*

*He had his head tilted back, and water tracked rivulets down the side of his face and his throat. A black Stetson hung on a nail on the wall, and he'd tugged his black shirt open at the collar to run his wet hand across the back of his neck.*

*Young, perhaps a couple of years older than she. All tanned skin and white flashing teeth. She'd caught him in a vulnerable, careless moment, but her tongue cleaved to the roof of her mouth, and Eden had the feeling she'd been punched in the chest.*

*Man, those jeans were tight. And he was the most attractive guy she'd ever met—which, granted, wasn't a great deal of men.*

*"I know we're in the middle of nowhere," she somehow managed to say, feeling tongue-tied and breathless, "but surely you can find yourself an actual bath."*

*Dark eyes locked on hers.*

*He froze.*

*So did she.*

*But there was a skitter of butterflies fluttering raucously in her stomach, and Eden tucked a strand of hair behind her ears self-consciously. Holy. Shit. Why had she said that?*

*"Hi," she said.*

*The stranger tugged his shirt together and started buttoning it back up. "Hello, angel."*

*"If you wanted an actual bath," she said, tilting her head toward the boarding house her father had run when he was alive, "I might be able to help you out."*

*The stranger stiffened.*

*"Eden," she said, sticking her hand out for him to shake. "Eden McClain. And my brother owns the boarding house now, so I'm fairly certain I could help accommodate you. There's a washhouse out back, and we don't have any lodgers at the moment, so you'd be welcome to use it, Mr...?"*

*"Colton. Johnny Colton," he breathed, staring at her hand as if it were dangerous. "Are you sure that's a good idea? You don't even know me."*

*"I don't know most of the people who stay with us." She rolled her eyes and dropped her hand. "Are you planning to hurt me?"*

*"No."*

*"Good," she'd told him, glancing coquettishly at him over her shoulder as she turned toward the boarding house. "Because if you were, I would have to warn you my brother taught me how to shoot and throw a knife, and he was pretty thorough about where to knee a man if he thought to get too friendly... if you know what I mean?"*

*The faintest of smiles softened Johnny's mouth and he stared at her as if he couldn't look away. He took one hesitant step after her. "Should I be worried about running into your brother too? Because if* you're half as dangerous as you say you are, then I might not want to meet him."

He was definitely flirting with her now. Wasn't he?

"You have no idea." Speaking of, Adam was somewhere in town. Eden glanced toward the main street, and then slipped into the shadows beside Johnny before anyone could tattle on her. "He's six years older than me, but you'd think he was my father. Plus he's a bounty hunter. Hunts wargs out there in the Wastelands. He's a total badass."

And if Adam caught a glimpse of her speaking to a handsome young stranger, he'd be right over here, getting all up in her business.

There was possibly a reason she'd never seen a man this gorgeous before.

"A bounty hunter?" Johnny murmured, and paused a step.

"Don't worry," she said, crossing the narrow alley behind the general store and heading for the boarding house. "He won't like you, but it wouldn't be personal. Adam thinks every guy has ulterior motives."

"They probably do."

"And what are your motives, Mr. Colton?"

Johnny scrubbed a hand over the back of his neck, glancing behind him as if keeping an eye out for overprotective brothers. The bit about bounty hunters had clearly thrown him. "My motives include getting clean and keeping my hands to myself." He paused. "I probably shouldn't be doing this."

"Relax," she teased. "You're a paying customer."

Johnny arched a brow. "Paying, am I?"

"Water's scarce. So it will cost you half a silver."

A shy smile twisted his mouth. "You're a right regular hustler...."

Eden dragged her knees up to her chest. The image was as clear as a bell. Every moment of that day she met him had etched itself in her brain, like a scar. If you grabbed a boiling pot, you'd remember the flinch of pain, no matter how many years passed, and this was exactly the same. Simply seeing Colton again bought that pain to the surface.

But now she had a chance to reconsider events, she couldn't help remembering Colton's skittishness that day, as if he'd never had a chance to flirt either. There'd been a reluctance about him as he followed her, as if he simply couldn't help himself.

He'd also been nervous, his gaze constantly roving the horizon. She'd always thought it had been Adam he'd been looking for, especially after she stole a kiss.

But what if it hadn't been?

What if he'd known exactly what sort of evil overshadowed him, and he'd been trying to protect her from it, even as he simply couldn't resist?

Eden brushed crumbs off her fingertips, shooting Colton and CJ a guilty glance. Firelight danced over their faces. CJ's face was rapt as Colton murmured something to him, turning the wolf's head talisman that kept the warg at bay over in his hands.

Speaking of the kiss....

She could almost feel it on her lips still. A swiftly stolen moment when she'd opened the door to the washroom and found Colton shaving with deft, mechanical movements, his skin bare except for the white towel around his waist.

The sight of him had stolen her thoughts. She'd stammered her apologies. He'd used the screen to dress swiftly, heat darkening his cheeks, as Eden scrambled to collect the towels—and her wits.

*"I should go," he said, as they both escaped that cursed washhouse.*

*Still reeling from her first encounter with lust, Eden grabbed his arm, reluctant to see this dream vanish. When he shot her a startled look, she wasn't able to help herself.*

*Lifting on her toes, she pressed her mouth to his, aware of the tension in his lean body.*

*He didn't move. Didn't kiss her back for such a long moment, she was about to lower her feet firmly to the ground, when he finally broke. Hands came up, capturing her face. A soft sound of pure aching need erupted from his throat, his chest, his toes—as if the sheer hunger to be touched came from so deep within his soul, it almost vibrated through him. And then he was shoving her back against the wall to the washhouse, his mouth capturing hers, and his body imprinting itself against every inch of her body.*

*It stole her breath.*

*Her wits.*

*Left her aching and vulnerable, despite the relative inexperience she couldn't fail to recognize in both of them. A clumsy, sloppy kiss, full of need and unspoken desire, and a burgeoning hunger on her behalf.*

*"What have we here?" a voice called, cutting through the haze of desire like a knife.*

*Johnny shoved away from her as if he'd been burnt.*

*"You should go." Johnny's soft smile turned hard all of a sudden, and he gave her a little push behind him as a stranger appeared out of nowhere, his malevolent shadow separating from the*

*ones he hovered within on the veranda, and the ever-present glow of his cigar burning like hot little embers.*

"Oh, no need to run along, young lady," the stranger called, sounding exactly like someone's jovial uncle. He winked as he breathed out a wreath of smoke. "I'm sure Johnny's manners will get better."

"She has things to do," Johnny replied flatly. "And her brother's around. Her bounty hunter brother."

"A bounty hunter brother, huh?"

The sight of the sudden intensity of the stranger's eyes haunted her until this day.

Bartholomew Cane.

*I drew him right into Adam's life.*

Eden shuddered, bowing her head to rest on her knees. *Stop it. It's not your fault. You had no way of knowing what Cane would do to Adam.*

Easier to say than to believe.

But now there was another aspect of the puzzle to uncover, one she'd never thought about before.

Knowing what she knew now, had Colton been trying to protect her from the real monster? She'd almost forgotten how he'd shoved her behind him, putting his body between them as if to protect her.

*I didn't want to remember it.*

And why had he kissed her back in the first place?

It was the one piece of the puzzle she'd never been able to fit into place. Because *she'd* started it. She'd gone after *him*, so despite the guilt and hate twisting her into knots after everything that happened, she could never believe he'd just done it to toy with her, or to use her.

"Are you all right?" CJ asked, breaking through the ever-looping repeat of her thoughts.

"Fine," Eden managed to mutter.

But the questions wouldn't go away.

And whether Colton refused to discuss it or not, she needed to know the answers—if she had any chance of sorting through the confused jumble of emotions in her chest.

He'd spent most of his life being hunted, one way or another, so he knew when a predator was stalking him.

Even if it was the prettiest damned predator he'd ever seen.

Johnny's eyes narrowed as Eden circled the fire and knelt at his side, bringing her medical kit with her. He'd seen her haul it out of her pack earlier. He was pretty sure she'd packed more in the goddamned kit than she had in the way of clothes. The only personal item he'd seen was a hairbrush she tugged out constantly, as she retamed her curly hair, again and again throughout the day. Prepared for any emergency, except humidity.

"How are you feeling?" she asked.

Tension slid through him. There'd been a certain look in her eyes ever since she saw his scars, and it made him panic. "The same way I did an hour ago when you asked."

"I want to check your wounds," she said, tapping on the hem of his shirt. "Off."

"You've checked them twice. They're getting better." *End of story.*

He didn't know why her sudden attention unnerved him so much.

Or why he both craved and feared it.

"I want to check them again," she said, without a single trace of heat in her voice.

"Leave it alone, Eden. Pretending to give a damn doesn't become you." He rolled to one knee, about to get the hell out of there. Nothing had changed. Nothing. He couldn't trust this new form of truce between them. "*Mierda.*"

A hand punched him in the shoulder lightly. "Language."

"You speak Spanish?"

"I don't need to speak Spanish to know you just swore. And I do care." Her voice softened. "I do."

Johnny reached for the flask in his bag. "Yeah, well, what are you going to do about it?"

Sharp eyes watched every move he made. He could see the judgment in them. Then sudden soft dawning, as if she'd had a realization about him.

"What?" he all but snarled.

"You get your flask out whenever I push you," she murmured, resting her hands on her thighs.

*He did?* "Maybe you're driving me to drink?"

"Maybe you're using it as a crutch, every time I get close enough to stir your emotions."

"I'm not emotional." He was a goddamned omega warg.

*And half alpha.*

"Oh no, you're fine," she mocked. "You're not helping me because you feel guilty. You don't owe me a debt. You're just crossing the Divide—which might get you killed by the way—for the heck of it."

*Smart-ass.* He tipped the flask to his lips and swallowed. Not much left but damned if he'd give her the satisfaction of resisting. As if what she'd said bothered him. "I seem to recall blackmail."

"I seem to recall some dick luring me out of my bed with promises I shouldn't have trusted before he threw me in a hut with a transitioning warg. But I'm also starting to wonder if my recollections of certain events aren't clouded by my own emotions about everything that happened between us."

Johnny froze. "I knew Adam wouldn't hurt you. He loved you. I knew he'd give in to Cane's demands."

*And I didn't have a choice.*

If he'd fought Cane over it, then the consequences would have been bad.

For her.

He'd spent years trying to deny Cane by then, feeling the kickback of pain as Cane broke him to his will. Years of torture. Years of losing the fight, bit by bit, until sometimes it was easier in the end if he *didn't* fight.

The second Cane saw him kissing Eden McClain, Johnny knew the bastard would try to destroy her—if only to ensure nothing ever came between Johnny's "loyalty" to him. In some sick and twisted part of his mind, Cane had thought of Johnny as his ally. His nephew. His possession.

*"You ever run like your mother did, and I swear I'll burn your world down around you. I'll find you, no matter where you hide. I'll repay you for every ounce of your treachery. You belong to me, boy. You understand?"*

His only option at the time had been to yield to Cane's will. Bring Eden along, throw her in the hut, use her to get what Cane wanted from Adam.

If he'd hesitated....

If he'd stood against Cane....

Then Cane would have killed her. Slowly. Painfully. And he'd have made Johnny watch, after he'd broken him again.

*When did you stop fighting? When did it become easier to give in, just a little? When did you become numb, even as a part of you died, over and over again?* He wished he didn't know.

The lesser of two evils. How many years had he spent making a choice between the lesser of two evils, so he wouldn't rouse the devil in Cane?

"Tell me about Cane," Eden whispered.

"*No.*"

He didn't want to think about Cane ever again. *I killed him. I finally killed him.* But he still felt the ghost of Cane hanging over him, every damned time he woke up.

*I am what he made me.*

It made him feel sick, even now. Especially now. He tried to move again, but Eden leaned forward, her weight resting on his thigh. "Don't," she said.

A chill ran down his spine.

"He hurt you, didn't he?"

"What part of *no* don't you understand?"

Grabbing her by the hips, Johnny threatened to tip her onto her ass in the dirt. Eden grabbed a fistful of his shirt, and glared at him as if to say; *I go. You go.*

Somehow she was almost on his lap. She straddled his thighs, using her weight to keep him there, but his gut churned with too much emotion to let himself enjoy the experience.

"I thought I'd be the last person you'd ever want to roll around on the ground with."

"You are."

"Do you want to check my wound or not?" Johnny snapped. "Because if you do, then fine. Check it. But I'm not talking about Cane. Not now. Not ever. Your choice."

Eden's lips pressed together. "I'll check your wound."

As she climbed off him to fetch her kit, he almost thought he heard her mutter, "*But don't think I'm going to give up.*"

⟶　⟵

Colton slumped on the bedroll with his hat over his face, the blankets drawn up under his chin. His chest rose and fell in steady movements, and he began to snore softly. Eden watched him from across the fireplace, still not quite certain how to take the day's revelations.

Colton had wanted to take first watch, but she'd taken one look at him and put her hands on her hips.

"*You'll be no good to anyone if you keel over from blood loss and lack of sleep.*" He'd started to protest so she'd held her hand up. "*Five hours. Give me five hours of sleep, and I'll let you out of bed. Otherwise, I'll simply get CJ to take you down and I will tie you to your goddamned bedroll. We'll both keep watch.*"

She wasn't going to think about his reply about beds and just who'd be tying whom down, but at least he'd finally complied.

And started snoring almost immediately.

Stubborn bloody men.

Eden glanced to where CJ was keeping watch, and kept sewing the hem on his shirt. It was the least she could do, and she needed to keep her hands busy.

Four days down.

Halfway across the Divide.

One warg injured; two dead shadow cats.

*Guess I can call that a win,* she thought with a sigh as she tied off her last neat stitch. Adam had taught her how to sew when she was a kid, and she needed to keep her hands busy, or else that internal clock would start ticking loudly again.

*Hopefully Lily's okay.*

*Argh. Don't think about it. There's nothing you can do for her—except keep pressing on.*

Finishing CJ's shirt, she set it aside and glanced to where Colton's sat folded beside him.

Sewing the rips in his shirt felt a little too personal, but she didn't know how else to thank him. Plus there was the queasy feeling inside her whenever she thought of how bitchy she'd been toward him.

*Guy nearly passed out because he didn't think you'd care if he were bleeding or not.*

Then there were those bloody scars.

And the violent churn of emotion in him when she brought up Cane. She recognized fear when she saw it, which only added to the mystery.

The least she could do was mend his bloody shirt.

Moving quietly, so as not to wake him, she grabbed his shirt and tugged it into her lap. The blood had dried and it would need a wash at some point, but *waste not, want not* was the personal motto of anyone born in the Wastelands.

Something crinkled in his pocket.

The folded piece of paper that had fallen out earlier.

She hadn't been too curious then, and his injuries had swiftly distracted her, but Eden slowly slipped the piece of paper out and looked at it.

*Thou shalt not read someone else's private communications.*

Eden always obeyed the rules. Hell, most of the time she *made* the rules.

But....

Maybe it was private—maybe it was information she needed to know about. His reaction when she'd seen it had been just weird enough to make her want to look.

*Don't you dare.*

She squeezed her eyes shut, fighting against her curiosity. She needed to know the truth about Cane. She needed to know why Colton's betrayal had hurt her so badly. She'd spent years avoiding relationships, because she couldn't trust a guy. Years trying to control every aspect of her life, so it couldn't blow up in her face.

She was screwed up, and she knew it, and if she could just work out the knotted mystery of Colton's *why*, then she might be able to move on.

*One glimpse to see what it is, then you put it back.*

Easing the paper open—it was a folded letter by the look of it—she caught a small photo that fell out of the center. *What the hell...?* The shock of recognition she felt when she saw the image cut all the way through her.

Because it was *her*.

A photo of her, taken many years ago when a photographer came through her parents' town. The only photo she'd ever had taken.

And suddenly Eden knew she wasn't going to put the letter back.

She couldn't even fathom where Colton might have gotten it. The last time she'd seen this photo it had been in Adam's— *Adam*. Of course. It had been in Adam's wallet in his riding bag, which Colton had stolen when they parted ways after the escape from Rust City. She could vaguely recall Adam muttering something about "the bastard" stealing it, when he'd finally ridden north with Mia at his side.

But why did he still have it?

And why was it tucked in his pocket, right over his chest?

A weird little feeling went through her. Eden sank onto a log near the fire, swiftly unfolding the letter.

*Dear Adam...* it began.

Her eyes swiftly scanned the words of greeting. One of many she'd written to him during his year of exile following the revelation he was a warg.

Which was, once again, courtesy of Johnny Colton.

If he hadn't shot Adam in the chest, she wouldn't have had to remove Adam's amulet and force him to go warg in order to save his life. Her brother wouldn't have been forced out of the town he built and—

—And he'd have never met Mia.

Eden frowned, her hands crinkling on the paper as she got to the end of the page.

*...I write to you today to let you know I'm getting married. I always dreamed you'd walk me down the aisle, but now I have to concede I shall do this alone.*

She flipped over the page, knowing what was coming. She'd been tired and frustrated and lonely, and she'd written this letter in the heat of the moment and sent it along with CJ to track her brother down after three months of not hearing from him.

*Ha. Had you fooled, didn't I? Let's be honest; there are no men in the Wastelands who are interested in me, and vice versa. But I wanted you to think what it would have been like if I was getting married, and you missed it.*

*Missed it because you were being stubborn.*

*Missed it because you're hundreds of miles away from me right now.*

*Missed it because you're dead in a ditch and I don't even know.*

*Please don't be dead.*

*I miss you so much. I wish you'd come home. Your place is here, and I'm keeping your room ready for you in the hopes that one day I'll turn around, and your shadow will fill the door....*

It rambled on, but Eden slowly lowered the letter, her heart skipping a beat. She knew every line of it by heart anyway.

What did this mean?

Johnny Colton had been keeping the letter she wrote to her brother in his pocket, and from the frayed edges it had seen heavy use.

And she didn't have a damned clue why.

# ten

His chest itched like a bitch.

Johnny sat up slowly, prying his bandages away from the claw marks. The skin beneath was slick and whole, the bandages matted with rusted flecks of blood. He could still feel the pull of the wound deep inside, however, lingering with malignant fingers. That sensation would be gone by tonight, but it made him feel slightly vulnerable.

A couple of inches to the left... hell, not even that, maybe an inch and a half, or a twist of the angle of the strike, and he wouldn't be here.

Wargs were difficult to kill. Not impossible. And that bitch had been packing some serious vindictive urges over the loss of her kits.

*Lucky. You were lucky.*

*No, you were careless.* And the reason for that was wearing a white tank that revealed tanned arms, and a tight pair of jeans. He could feel that flash of desperation again as the shadow cat launched itself off the boulder, and he'd known Eden wasn't safe. Something had come over him. Something he hadn't really felt before. Something that lingered like a snarl of rage in the back of his mind.

Rage? Or another emotion? He poked at the feeling, but there were no answers there.

"Good morning," Eden said, eyeing him with what could only be described as a dangerously female look.

It asked questions, that look. It kept secrets. And it promised a world of trouble, though he wasn't quite certain how to interpret what type of trouble.

When it came to Eden McClain, it could be anything.

"Morning," he muttered, looking about for his bloody shirt. "You were supposed to wake me."

"We made do."

The shirt was folded neatly nearby, and his stomach suddenly dropped to zero gravity as he remembered the letter he had in the pocket. Her letter. The one she'd been curious about yesterday. Not that she knew her own hand had written it.

Stupid. There was no reason for him to have it still. He should have burned it long ago, but—

But.

Johnny stretched and hauled his shirt toward him, relief slamming through him when his fingers crushed the stiff paper in its pocket. He turned the move into something natural, as though he'd only been reaching for his shirt.

Eden returned to her task of frying breakfast—the smell of which had woken him. The way she leaned over the fire gave him a healthy view of her cleavage. "How are you feeling?"

"Alive. That's what counts, isn't it? How's the boy?"

She glanced toward the other set of blankets. "Dead asleep. I think you wore him out yesterday. Do you want breakfast?"

"Why? Is it poisoned?" He tossed back the blankets with a snort.

Only to feel a set of eyes glaring at him. "No. It's not poisoned. I just thought you'd like breakfast. And I wouldn't do that."

"You'd be tempted."

Eden stared into her fry pan as if it held all of the mysteries of the universe. "I'm a healer. You were hurt"—her voice dropped—"defending me. I'm trying to make amends."

This was weird. She'd been weird last night too. "Who are you, and what have you done with Eden McClain? Because I'm pretty sure the real version has been busting my balls for the past couple of days. Call me suspicious, but I'm not certain I trust this polite bullshit."

At all.

Eden tilted her closed eyes to the sky as if silently praying for strength, before she leveled a force-one glare on him. "I won't pretend I wanted you with us on this mission, but CJ was right. We wouldn't have made it this far without you. We both would have died, if not for you."

"What are you trying to say?"

"I'm sorry," she ground out.

"For what?"

"For busting your balls," she grumbled, looking like she'd rather be doing anything other than apologizing. "If I hadn't been such a bitch, you wouldn't have been hiding your wound."

This was territory he hadn't quite expected to stumble into. Johnny scratched at the stubble on his jaw. "It's not as though I would have told you I was injured anyway. It was just a—"

"If you say 'scratch,'" she growled, "I swear I shall commit an act of violence."

"Right." *Fuck.* What was he supposed to do?

People didn't apologize to him.

Especially not her, when he'd never be able to repay the debt he owed her.

"Stop looking at me like that," Johnny muttered, as she clearly searched for the right words to say. He shouldn't have said anything about Cane yesterday, but she'd caught him at a weak moment. The second she laid eyes on his back, she'd changed.

Eden's lashes hid her troubled green eyes. "I never.... I didn't realize you weren't with him of your own volition. I just thought—"

"Yeah, I get it." *We are not delving back into that again.* "How about we pretend last night didn't happen?"

"If we pretend last night didn't happen," she pointed out, "then I'm back to acting like a bitch."

"You weren't a bitch." This was the most awkward conversation of his life. He scraped a palm over the back of his neck. "I've done some pretty terrible things to the people you love. You have good cause to hate me. I *shot* your brother a couple of years ago."

Did it matter if he hadn't wanted to do any of them? Cane had merely ground Johnny's will beneath his heel like one of his fucking cigars.

His pulse flickered a beat at just the thought.

"Don't remind me. I'm focusing on the part where Adam survived. And on the part where *he* was going to shoot you, but you were quicker."

Johnny stared at her tense profile. "I'm sorry," he said roughly. *I didn't want to do any of it.* "I know you probably don't want to hear it, but I am sorry, Eden. I never wanted to... hurt you."

*Ever.*

She glanced his way. "Thank you." Soft words. "I think I do need to hear that."

Silence.

A thick, awkward silence that was full of Cane, even if the questions in her eyes remained silent, as if she knew he'd refuse to talk about it.

Eden scraped chopped onion into the pan. "I've been thinking we should probably call a truce. While we're traveling together, anyway."

"Truce?"

"You know," she deadpanned. "I don't spit in your breakfast, and you don't call me 'angel.'"

"Can't say I can promise that."

Eden shot him a heated glare.

He held his hands up in surrender. "But... I can probably try." Some part of the devil must have been in him, because he smiled. "Don't pretend to be friends, Eden. I can see you're struggling with this. Don't pull a muscle."

"How about not-quite-enemies then?"

"I prefer nemeses," he replied, every sarcastic volley easing the tension within him. This he could handle.

"Sounds bloody."

"You did hold a red-hot knife to my skin yesterday."

"Contrary to popular opinion, I didn't actually enjoy it," she muttered. "Speaking of..."

"All healed over."

"Even so"—she arched a pointed brow at him—"I'd like to have a look at it after breakfast. This is not a request."

Johnny stood, suddenly desperate for a piss. Something told him arguing would be futile. She had that look about her. "You just want to get me out of my shirt again, angel."

A faint curse caught his ear as he strode off into the bushes. "I'll give you *angel*."

"What was that?"

"Nothing," Eden muttered. "But I'm definitely spitting in your breakfast."

Despite himself, he smiled.

Johnny staggered into the sagebrush, hauling his shirt over his head and trying to surreptitiously rearrange his morning wood. "Give me a chance to wash my face and wake up."

Or more to the point, to take care of business.

He washed up at the creek, the splash of water on his face sloughing off the last remnants of sleep. Behind him, he could hear Eden dishing up breakfast.

It was no surprise to realize having her here, being around her, bothered him. It was like resurrecting ghosts he'd long thought buried, and last night hadn't helped.

*"You won't ever escape me, boy,"* said Bartholomew Cane in his head. *"Even if I die, I'll haunt you until the day you finally kick this mortal coil."*

His mother's screams overtook him, thrusting him straight back into that horrific moment when Cane locked his mother inside their house—and lit it on fire.

The *only* reason his mother was allowed to live was because Johnny begged for her life. *"I'll do anything...."*

And he had done anything.

He'd killed people on Cane's whim, granting them swifter deaths than they'd have ever earned from Cane, and he'd called it mercy, even as something inside him shriveled up and died. He'd borne the brunt of years of abuse that would forever show on his skin despite the fact wargs healed from almost anything, when the man who called himself his uncle turned to those darker moods that afflicted him.

And when Cane decided he wanted to make more wargs, Johnny had gone out and found candidates for him. No matter what it cost.

He squeezed his eyes shut.

The one person he'd never wanted to make a warg was Adam McClain, but when he'd tried to divert his uncle, it had all gone pear-shaped.

Cane could scent out weakness like he was part bloodhound.

It wasn't hard to understand why his mind was dredging up the past. Eden McClain brought with her a whole package of unfinished business, and his feelings about her were complicated. It would be easy to push her into the little box in his mind that he relegated his past to, but she kept pushing her way back *out*. He owed her a debt he could never repay and that was all this was, but at the same time, she also represented a whole shit-ton of confusion for him.

Want. Need. Yearning.

He'd read the letters she'd written to her brother dozens of times, when he was alone on the Rim riding a job. They called to him, luring him into a world of warmth and family and belonging he hadn't felt since he was fourteen and Cane destroyed his family. They whispered to his dreams at night, tempting him with visions of her. He'd created an image in his mind, an idol of Eden McClain that was sweet and loving, and everything a secret part of him longed for.

The reality had smashed that image to pieces.

Eden *was* sweet. She was loving. Just not for him. No, for him she was stubborn, infuriating, hardheaded, frustrating, and brave, running headlong into danger regardless of the risk to herself. She drove him fucking crazy. She constantly argued with him. She knew *everything*, even when she was wrong.

And he wanted her.

Nemesis or not. Wary ally or not.

Wanted her beneath him, wanted *inside* of her.... His cock roused at the thought and Johnny swore under his breath. He couldn't get those breasts out of his mind. He could picture his hands on them, his mouth. He wanted to fuck his way into her in a way he'd never felt before.

This was *supposed* to be about repaying a debt.

And right on cue, Eden called out, "I *will* eat all your bacon if you don't come up here and get it pretty damned soon. The only thing that's stopping me is the thought you're an invalid, and as a doctor I should be getting some decent food into you."

*Sweet Eden McClain, my ass.* Johnny growled, but he instantly felt better. He could trust *this* version of her. He could banter with her all day, as long as shit didn't get personal. "I'm not a goddamned invalid. And if you eat my breakfast, you're going to be doing all the dishes for the next few days."

"How are you going to make me?" She was transferring food to his plate, her back to him as he strode back to camp. All that hair was tangled down her back as if she'd run her hands through it. Seeing it out was rare enough he actually stopped in his tracks and blinked.

"I'm bigger than you," he pointed out, though he still felt like she'd kicked him in the gut.

The sun picked out golden strands in her honey-brown hair. He had this sudden, impulsive desire to run *his* hands through it.

*Fuck.*

"I fight dirty," she shot back, casting him a glance over her shoulder, dark lashes half obscuring those almond-shaped eyes. "Just to warn you."

*You sure do.* "I remember."

He grabbed the plate she'd made him, glaring back at her as he shoved a mouthful of the hash she'd cooked into his mouth.

The taste of it exploded there like a punch. Johnny stiffened, chewing slowly. *Jesus.* He eyed the plate more carefully. Had it all been a carefully concocted lie? The truce. The joking about poisoning him....

"What's wrong?" Eden bristled, setting her hands on her hips, and he realized she hadn't deliberately burned breakfast. Not with that look on her face, like she almost dared him to say something about it....

"Nothing." *You're a terrible cook.* He ruthlessly shoved another mouthful of food in, forcing himself to chew. He needed the calories. And he was a Wastelander, born and bred. You didn't waste good food in the Wastelands.

Though the term "good food" might be somewhat of a misnomer. What had she done to it? There'd been salted bacon in his pack that had cost him a small fortune, though the end result was what one could term charred. Johnny swallowed. Maybe he should have told her to eat it, and taken his chances on an empty stomach.

Eden's eyes gave new meaning to the word "dangerous."

Maybe not. "We're running behind your schedule." He cast a swift glance at the sun as he ruthlessly shoveled the rest of breakfast into his mouth, chewing mechanically. "It's nearly seven."

"You needed to sleep," Eden said, though a flash of frustration crossed her brow. "So does CJ. He's starting to look a bit worn around the edges."

"And we've slept." He scraped the plate, crossing to where the boy curled up in the nest of blankets. "Time to get moving again."

Tomorrow he wouldn't be sleeping in.

No. *He* was making breakfast.

"Where'd you learn to cook?" Eden murmured, resting her head on her hand as she watched Colton stir the cornmeal for cornbread that night. Out in the dusk, birds chittered as they fluttered about in curiosity. It was early to set up camp, but Colton had taken one look at this spot and pronounced it defensible.

He wasn't budging, no matter how much she wanted to get another hour or two behind them. And CJ had backed him, collapsing with a groan on the ground, and a plea for mercy. Today had been a hard, merciless push.

Tomorrow they'd be climbing the escarpment, and end up in Confederacy territory. Butterflies whirled in her stomach at the thought. She could give CJ and Colton an earlier night.

"My mother taught me," he muttered, almost too quiet to hear. There was calmness about him in this moment, as though the action was almost meditative. Colton grabbed the fry pan and gave it a swirl, sending chopped bacon and onion sizzling around the pan. As he set the pan back on the rack, he glanced her way. "Where'd you learn to cook?"

And... there it was.

Eden scowled. "Don't think I didn't see your expression this morning when you were eating breakfast."

A faint smile danced over his lips. "You're officially banned from desecrating my fry pan ever again."

Of all the nerve. She sucked in a breath... and deflated. "Okay, fine. I just wanted to help. I know I'm terrible in the kitchen. Adam used to do most of the cooking when we lived together. My talents run in other directions."

Adam had mostly taken over when it became clear Eden had other things on her mind.

"You can help by not helping. How can you be so bad at it?"

"I was training to be a healer when I was a teen," she admitted. "And I get distracted. Cooking always seemed to be something necessary to sustain life, but not... not intellectually stimulating like my textbooks were. I mean, I like the finished product but I never have the time to go through the process."

"Sustain life? Yeah, that pretty much covers it."

She watched him stirring the mix in the pan. "You like cooking."

Odd to think of Colton in any way as domesticated.

He shrugged. "In my family, home revolved around food. My mother was always in the kitchen. It helped calm her and she'd had a rough childhood. I think she wanted to make our house as homely as she could."

"What happened to her?"

Dark eyes flashed to hers, then looked away. "Why do you think something happened to her?"

"Because you speak in past tense when you mention her, and your voice gets a little soft."

"Eden—"

"It was Cane, wasn't it?"

The muscles in his cheeks tensed as he poked the items in the pan with an intense focus. "Yes."

"You don't like to talk about him."

"Would you?" Moving stiffly, he reached for the flask in his pack. "Why so damned curious?"

"Because I think I was wrong about you, and now I want to know the truth."

Colton tipped the flask to his lips, then winced and held it out, shaking it up and down. A drop of liquid hit the ground but nothing else, and Eden squirmed away, remembering when she'd thrown it on the fire. "Bloody. Fucking. Hell. I'm out."

And clearly trying to change the subject. "Language."

He flashed her an intense look. "This situation—"

"Doesn't require it."

"You're probably right, because I've got no intentions of discussing Cane or my mother. Now... I'm pretty sure I saw a flask in your bag when you were bandaging me up."

"You would be correct."

He stared at her.

She smiled sweetly. "What makes you think I'd give it to you? That flask is for medicinal purposes only."

"I think my claw marks are playing up."

"Nobody likes the Boy Who Cried Wolf."

"How about the Wolf Who Would Like A...n F'ing Drink?"

She stared at him.

"Because I did not swear?" he suggested.

She fetched the small flask of medicinal whiskey she had in her medical bag. "Use sparingly. It's all I have."

Colton uncapped the flask and took a decent swallow. "Now I know you want me to bare my heart and soul. Are you trying to get me drunk, Eden McClain?"

"Yes," she deadpanned. "I have ulterior motives and want to get you drunk in the middle of the Great Divide. Sounds like an excellent way to die."

He laughed. "I never knew you were so uptight."

"I am *not.*"

"Doesn't like swearing. Doesn't approve of drinking too much. Please tell me you're not a virgin."

"I have—occasionally—said a rude word. I just don't think they have to be part of every sentence you utter. I drink with my friends. And no, I'm not a virgin." *Though I might as well be.* "Stop looking at me like you think I'm a prude."

Colton slowly unscrewed the cap, offering her the flask as if he dared her. "All work, no play. No wonder you're tense."

"Are you serious?" She sat up straight. "The reason I'm tense is because I'm on a tight timeline, while you don't seem to give a damn."

"Can't travel at night," he pointed out. "You could join me."

"I don't even like you. Why would I drink with you?"

He shrugged. "Didn't think so...."

*Screw him.* Eden captured his hand and brought the flask closer to her lips. She tipped it up and drank, watching him all the while, her hand covering his.

Their eyes met.

And suddenly she realized how it might look.

Eden froze, lowering the flask. A slow heated smile spread over his mouth, as if he could read her mind.

"Don't worry, *mi corazon*," he said, with a faint, half-mocking lilt to his voice. "I'm not getting ideas. You're the last woman I'd ever touch. Your brother would skin me alive."

A little flutter went through her at the words as she hastily swallowed the burning mouthful of whiskey. "You're the last man I'd ever *allow* to touch me."

But that was a blatant lie, as evidenced by the rasp of her nipples against her bra, and the sudden wet heat in her panties. Eden spilled some of the whiskey down her hand as she hastily screwed the cap back on.

His smile was pure evil. "Do you know the best thing about being a warg?"

"There *is* something good about it?" Her heart skipped a beat.

Colton leaned closer, as if breathing in her scent. "You can tell when someone's lying to you."

"You're dreaming if you think I'd ever lay hands on you. That's *not* a lie. Truce or not."

Even so... She licked the whiskey off her fingers and paused the second she realized his gaze had turned hot and he was watching her, like a hunter scenting prey.

A long breathless moment.

The seconds ticked out, as Eden considered her feelings. There was a part of her—a very small part—that liked having him watch her like that. Knowing he wouldn't touch her without permission.

Knowing he wanted to.

It made her feel powerful.

It made her pussy clench.

Eden unfroze and slowly finished licking her fingers, taunting him the entire time with her eyes. *Ask me how uptight I am now....*

Colton sucked in a sharp breath. "Hate sex," he growled. "You. Me. And one night in which to get all this out of our systems."

"*Hate sex?*"

"Let's not pretend you're ever going to forgive me. But every time you look at me, your eyes are saying one thing, and your mouth another. You don't like me, but there's a part of you that wants to be under me."

"Who said I'd be *under* you?" she shot back, leaning close enough to breathe in his exhale.

Colton's lips curved in a slow smile. "I said. Because I can guarantee if you give me a single hint the answer is yes, you won't be the one doing the fucking."

Holy. Shit. Her heart was racing almost too fast to hear anything else. In this context, that word was exactly the right one to use.

"That itch you can't scratch," he whispered. "I know you feel it."

Eden smiled sweetly at him and waggled her fingers. "That's why I have these. Let's just say… I can scratch my own itch."

Heat gilded the dark depths of his irises. His nostrils flared. "Tell me… is it as good as the real thing? Because my hand does the job too, sweetheart, but there's something to be said for the feel of someone else's hands skating over your skin, and their teeth sinking into your shoulder. Something to be said for soft lips between your legs, and a fist wrapped in your hair, and—"

Eden sucked in a sharp gasp. She could almost feel his touch on her skin, his words painting a picture she could feel. "I'm not that desperate."

"Or is it just the fact it's me that makes you itch that pisses you off?" Colton's fingertips ghosted over her chin. "Because I'm fairly fucking certain you're wet right now."

Colton's thumb dug into the muscle on the inside of her leg. He went to one knee in front of her, his thumb sliding up, stroking her inner thigh. "Are you wet, Eden? Are you thinking about it?"

"I—"

"I can hear you," CJ suddenly called out, from where he was on watch.

Eden jumped. *Jesus.* What was she even thinking? Hate sex? With Johnny Colton? *Bad idea. Bad.*

Shame her body wasn't getting that memo.

Colton scrubbed his large hand over his mouth. "Good," he called back. "That means nothing else should sneak up on you."

The moment was broken. Eden sucked in a sharp, shuddering breath and pushed to her feet, taking the flask with her. Good God, she'd actually been thinking about it. Worse. She'd been craving it.

*He's right. You're tense. That's why this makes sense. It's just an itch to scratch, just a little bit of pressure to relieve....*

"Eden?" His voice came out low and hard, as if he could feel her pulling away.

"Never going to happen."

"Think about it," Colton told her, then pushed to his feet, dusting his knees off. His dark eyes looked like molten chocolate. "Or stop torturing me."

# eleven

Eden blew out a deep breath as Colton fetched a larger log and dumped it on the fire.

Damn him.

She was hot and wet and flushed again.

And that fucking itch was back.

"I swear to God you drive me crazy," she muttered.

His lips quirked as he kicked the log into place on the coals. "Likewise. Are you doing the dishes, or am I?"

"You cooked." *It was only fair.*

"Darlin', I plan on cooking all the meals out of self-preservation, if nothing else. Doesn't mean you have to wash up all the time."

"Careful. I'm going to remember that." Eden pushed to her feet, searching for the fry pan so she could fill it with water and set it on the coals to soften the remains of dinner.

Anything to get away from Colton for a moment.

"You finished with your plate?" Colton called out to CJ, who'd drawn the first watch.

Eden turned her back on him, her cheeks hot. She'd been too long without a man. That was the problem. Grabbing the pan, she used the spatula to scrape out the crust on the bottom of it. Nope. Definitely needed to soak.

"CJ?" Colton's voice sounded strange.

Two seconds later, a hand rested on her shoulder. Eden looked up sharply, but Colton wasn't looking down at her. Instead he peered into the shadows of the night.

A familiar nervousness flooded through her. "Shadow cats?"

Again?

Her heart skipped a beat.

Colton knelt at her side. "Not sure. But there's got to be a reason he's not answering."

Boots scuffled over granite somewhere out there in the dark. Colton's head snapped in that direction, tension radiating through his body, and then he cut her a quick look, slashing a hand as if to say, *stay there.*

Clutching at his knife, he vanished into the shadows of the night.

Armed with a fry pan and a spatula, Eden squatted by the bedroll, not daring to move. *Damn him.* What the hell was out there? What had he heard?

And where was her gun?

She saw the barrel of the shotgun near her pack and edged toward it, cocking her head to listen as she put the pan aside. The breeze whispered through her clothes, and she thought she caught a faint grunt.

"Why, what do we have here?" drawled a voice.

An enormous man leaped up on a boulder, his body lit by firelight. He wore a gray tank with the sleeves cut off, and muscle flexed in his arms.

Eden snatched the double barreled shotgun and rolled onto her back on the bedroll, pumping two rounds into the chamber and holding it steady on him. "Don't move."

Shadows shifted in the corner of her vision. An Asian woman melded out of the darkness, holding a spear. Her clothes were dark gray; a long tunic that left her arms bare, held together with black leather straps.

And then another woman to the right of her, who looked like she wrestled men for a living.

Eden was surrounded.

"Colton!" she yelled.

No response. Just a muffled grunt and then a hooting sound, out there in the night.

Another voice lifted, hooting back.

A flash of silver went through the stranger's eyes, and Eden's lungs seized up. Wargs. She was surrounded by wargs. She almost pulled the trigger in her fright.

"Stay back."

"You've only got two rounds in that chamber, sweetheart." The man grinned at her, pacing back and forth, almost as if he was taunting her. "And there's three of us."

"There's silver in the bullets, so whoever I hit first is going down." Eden deliberately swung the shotgun toward him. "And I don't think I like your tone, so it might be you."

"Put the gun down," said the muscly woman. "You won't be hurt."

"Forgive me if I'm not very trusting." Eden stared along the barrel, and swallowed. Her gaze dropped to the stranger's chest. No amulet. Full night was still an hour away, the moon not quite fully in the sky yet, but.... Letting go of the shotgun was probably not a great idea. "Why the hell haven't you gone warg?"

The man glanced toward the dark-skinned woman.

"Why the hell haven't your friends gone warg?" the woman returned.

"Because they're not monsters."

"Maybe we're not either?"

"Put the gun down, before I take it off you," the man said, his voice dark and low.

The second she lost that gun Eden was vulnerable. "I think not."

"Then we're at an impasse." His weight shifted forward, onto the balls of his feet.

"No, now we're at an impasse," came Colton's voice as he melded out of the shadows. Another man leaned stiffly against him, with Colton's arm locked tightly around his head, tilting it to the side. Colton held the tip of his knife to the flickering beat of the stranger's jugular. "I'm assuming this is one of yours."

The stranger's eyes narrowed, and his glance slid sideways.

"If you're looking for the others, three of them aren't coming," Colton muttered. "They had a sudden pressing appointment with the sandman."

"Are they dead?"

"No."

A faint smile graced the stranger's face. "You're good."

"Thanks."

"But we're better," said another voice, and suddenly there was CJ, forced to his knees as another pair of men materialized out of the night. One of them pressed his shotgun directly to CJ's temples.

"Drop the knife," said the stranger. "Or we'll kill the boy."

Colton's eyes narrowed. "If I drop the knife, what's to say you won't kill the boy anyway?"

"Pinkie promise," said the stranger with a smile. "If you're a good little warg, nobody needs to get hurt."

"Just do it, Colton," she cried, the shotgun getting heavy in her hands. Eden crawled to her knees, holding the shotgun up in surrender. *See?* She swallowed. "Let CJ go."

"Eden," Colton warned. "They're wargs."

"Noticed that, thanks."

It didn't change her decision. If there'd been any sign of hairy rage erupting out of any of them she'd have never let go, but they were human. Potentially open to negotiating. And they could have killed any of the three of them, but they hadn't.

"Eden," Colton warned.

Eden set the shotgun down, and slowly pushed to her feet, hands in the air.

"Kick it toward me."

"No. I'm human and you're not. You know you can get to me before I can lift the gun. I did what you wanted as a show of respect." She locked eyes on the man holding the shotgun to CJ's head. "Now you lower your weapons. You said we wouldn't get hurt."

"I'm the one giving the orders here. This your woman?" said the stranger, leering at Colton.

"Yes."

Eden's heart skipped a beat as the stranger captured her chin and tilted her face toward him.

"She's pretty," he mused.

"Rath," said the muscly woman, and it sounded like a warning.

Colton shifted.

"Just playing, Bobbi."

Nobody was watching her. Nobody expected her to cause trouble. Eden's hand slid to her belt—and her emergency precaution.

"You keep your fucking hands off her," Colton growled, and the knife in his hand drew blood.

"Maybe I'll have some fun with her." The enormous stranger grabbed her and wrenched her back against his chest. His hand rested a little too comfortably on her waist.

"Hey!" She wriggled, but his grip was merciless. "You promised."

"What's your name, sugar tits?"

"Eden." There it was again. Eden seethed. "You don't happen to know a guy called Black Tom, do you?"

"Can't say I do. Why? Friend of yours?"

Eden uncapped the syringe behind her back with her fingers, and swallowed. "Not exactly."

"What's your man's name?"

"Johnny Colton."

She could feel his breath stirring her hair, and her eyes met Colton's. Unlike everyone else, he'd noticed the syringe in her hand.

"You want to have some fun with me?" Rath murmured, but she knew he was watching Colton. His enormous arm locked over her chest, and the hand on her waist began to shift, moving up.

"Not really."

"Pity. Now we have both your friends, Colton," Rath said, sliding his hand up and down the side of her ribs, his fingers brushing against the under curve of her breast. "But I think since I've got the prettier one, you might start paying attention. Put the knife down. I won't ask again. If you hurt Lincoln, you're a dead man."

"You fucking touch her like that again, and I'll kill you," Colton growled.

"I put my gun down," she said, "because you swore you wouldn't hurt us. You just broke your promise."

"Gun in the air, Rodriguez," Rath called.

Instantly the man holding the shotgun to CJ's head lifted it, aiming toward the sky. He kept a hand wrapped in CJ's collar, to keep him on his knees.

"Now you, Colton," Rath said. "Let Lincoln go."

The second the knife shifted, the warg Colton had been holding hostage jammed an elbow back into Colton's ribs. Lincoln lashed out as Colton jerked the knife away, and slammed a fist into Colton's thigh.

*Shit.*

Mayhem erupted. Rath grabbed her by the throat, just as Eden stabbed the syringe in his side and pumped its contents into him.

Rath roared, his grip slackening just enough for her to get away. She staggered forward, but Bobbi tackled her. Eden slammed to the ground, her ears ringing, as a fight broke out.

A knee drove into the back of her thigh and Eden found her face smushed into the dirt, her right hand yanked up behind her back. The syringe fell from nerveless fingers.

"What did you do to Rath?" Bobbi demanded.

"What the hell is going on here?" snarled a woman's voice.

A trio of women melted out of the shadows, but it was the one standing on the rock, her fingers laxly gripping a spear who'd spoken. Her head was shaved, and her skin gleamed like polished ochre in the evening shadows. Gold handprints adorned her brown skin, glimmering in the faint dying light of the tangerine sun. Within moments, Eden suspected the light would fade and the gold handprints would vanish with it.

All the men stepped back, except for Rath, whose heels were still drumming on the ground as he twisted and screamed.

"Second." One of them bowed. "Strangers in our territory. Two of them are wargs—"

"I have a nose," said the woman, leaping off the rock and crossing to Colton. She wore a leather halter top that bared her midriff and a pair of cerulean blue trousers that vanished into her combat boots. "What did you do to Rath?"

Colton arched a brow. "Nothing."

Bobbi hauled Eden to her knees.

"That was all me," Eden said, suddenly the center of attention as Rath's mouth began foaming. "I just shot your friend up with a concoction of colloidal silver. If he doesn't get medical attention shortly, then he's going to have a hell of a night."

Wargs hated silver. It burned their skin, and her injection would be doing the same—on the inside.

"If he dies, then so do you," said the woman, striding toward her.

"He's not going to die." Eden held her hands up. "He just might feel like he is for an hour or two. There's not enough silver in the mix to kill him."

"Fix him," the woman snarled.

"I can't. His body will process it eventually. But in the meantime, maybe he'll learn some better manners."

The newcomer's dark eyes locked on her. A thin gold line curved under both her eyes. "Better manners? He didn't touch you, did he?"

"His hands got a little loose, Nnedi," Bobbi grumbled. "I warned him."

"Next time he does something like that, Bobbi, you have my permission to take him down." The newcomer—clearly a leader of some sort—lifted her boot and pressed her weight down on the middle of Rath's chest. He wheezed, froth foaming from his mouth. "I was going to help you get back to the caves, Rath, but now I think you're on your own. You know my rules."

She pushed away, and the man rolled onto his side, reaching helplessly for her. "Please...."

"I am Nnedi," the woman tilted her head. "Second of Shadow Rock pack. And the three of you are under my protection. Come. We will take you back to Shadow Rock until the alpha can decide what to do with you."

Eden only wished that didn't sound quite like Nnedi intended to lock them up and throw away the key.

Colton remained on his knees, his hands cupped behind his head and blood dripping from his nose. Around him sprawled the slumped bodies of three wargs.

"You look like trouble," Nnedi said, kneeling in font of him to assess him. "I hope you're not going to be trouble." She jerked her head to the men holding him down. "Let him stand. Take their weapons, but give them room to move. We will not harm you if you do not retaliate. Am I clear?"

Eden exchanged a look with Colton. What was going on?

But she trusted Nnedi. The woman's manner was brusque, and she clearly held a lot of respect here, for nobody would meet her eyes.

"Understood," Colton said, as he was helped to his feet.

A sudden crash made them all turn sharply.

CJ hit the ground, not bothering to put his hands out.

"CJ!" Nothing could stop her from running to his side. "What did you do to him?"

The man beside him looked shocked. "Nothing. I didn't touch him, I swear. He just collapsed."

"CJ," she demanded. His skin felt feverishly hot beneath her hand. "CJ?"

Nnedi knelt at her side, sniffing delicately. "He's been poisoned."

Eden gasped. "Poisoned?"

Nnedi hauled up his shirt, displaying the angry red scratch on his side. "Shadow cat poison."

"But it's just a scratch. I checked it out, it barely even broke the skin. He was fine. Colton was the one who'd been cut up." But CJ had been the first to collapse on the ground when they made camp.

And the welt was angry and red now.

She should have been paying more attention.

Nnedi sank back onto her heels. "Come. The sooner we get home, the sooner he can be treated. He too is going to have a very long night."

"What do you think they intend to do with us?" Eden whispered as she followed him through the winding canyons the Shadow Rock pack led them to.

Johnny's nostrils flared. "Don't know. They're all wargs though."

Which meant nothing good.

Usually.

He glanced back at the makeshift stretcher some of the wargs had rigged up. Cole was on it, his hand slumping off the edge as they carried him. Eden saw the direction his gaze traveled in and dropped back to check on her charge. She pressed a gentle hand to Cole's forehead, frowning with concern.

*Mierda.*

One tiny scratch and the kid had gone from laughing and shrugging off the shadow cat attack, to passing out. It hadn't even been a full wound. Merely a scratch. Eden looked guilty, but fuck that, because he hadn't noticed the kid getting sicker either.

"The boy will be fine," Nnedi said, falling in beside him. "We have healers who can see to him, and they are used to dealing with shadow cat poison. He's lucky we came along when we did."

Johnny didn't fully understand Nnedi's position in the hierarchy of this pack, but she seemed to hold enough power to make even the most grizzled warg back down. They'd wanted to tie his hands behind him, knowing who the dangerous one was, but she'd countermanded the proposition.

*"They are under my protection,"* she'd spat instead, *"which means they are my guests. And we will treat them as such."*

Then she'd given him a look that clearly said, *don't fuck with my trust.*

"So how does this work?" he muttered, examining the narrow canyons that soared above them. Torchlight played over the rose gold of the sandstone, and striations of color lay exposed in the bedrock, revealing years and years of different types of rock layered upon each other. "A group of wargs living together here in the Divide? I'd have expected that to get messy."

Nnedi strode at his side with a loose-hipped grace. "Not at all. We are not like those scavengers that prowl the plains. We are pack. We are stronger together, and weak links are removed to keep the pack safe."

Weak links meaning... wargs who had an issue with their inner beast, he guessed. "How long have you been down here?"

"Since the Darkening, in one way or another. And yourself? What brings you down here to the Divide? It's a place few strangers dare enter, so we're not entirely used to having company. You'll have to forgive my wargs their manners. Life is dangerous."

How much to reveal? "We're heading for Cortez City. Want to do a little trading there."

"A dangerous supposition, for the chances of paying the price of your lives is more likely than that of receiving any gains. The Confederacy rarely deals with outsiders." She snorted. "They don't like any outside views corrupting their sheep-like populace. Too hard to keep feeding them lies. And they don't like wargs."

"Sounds like you've had some experience with them."

"Some," she admitted, and her dark eyes shifted toward him. "What are you hoping to trade for?"

His shoulders stiffened. Nnedi was far from stupid, and she had to scent the doubt swimming off him. He forced himself to breathe slowly, his racing heartbeat slowing to a crawl as he brought his omega side to the fore. Calmness slid through his veins like a drop of oil landing on a pool of water. It could spread across the surface of him, enveloping him in its shielding embrace, but deep inside the furnace burned.

"Medication," he admitted, watching her eyelids soften as she subconsciously breathed in his pheromones.

"There's a virulent disease afflicting the humans in the Wastelands. Eden seems to think the Confederacy have antibiotics that might treat it, perhaps even a vaccine."

"The Confederacy don't give anything away for free."

*True.* "Her people have mining rights the Confederacy wants to get their hands on. She's authorized to grant those rights in exchange for the medication she needs."

He glanced back toward Eden, just to check on her. Having her so far away made the monster within him flex, shrugging off its shroud of calmness. If something happened he'd never get to her in time....

"She is your woman?" Nnedi followed his gaze.

"Yeah." He didn't know how these wargs lived, but he'd seen enough of the Wastelands to know how events usually played out. "She's mine. If anyone touches her, I'll kill them."

A faint flicker of a smile curled over her lips. "I wasn't asking for her sake—I'd have their heads if they touched her without permission." Dark eyes raked him from head to toe. "But there are a lot of single women in the pack, and *you* might need her at your side to keep your jeans intact."

He... wasn't certain how to take that.

"All that smooth, olive skin, and pretty eyes?" Nnedi smirked. "You're going to be like an oasis in the desert and some of my girls are thirsty. They're going to be disappointed you're taken."

Heat crawled up his throat. *Jesus.* Was this what Eden had to put up with all the time?

"Are you actually blushing? Oh, you are just too cute. Hey, Amara!" she called. "Pretty boy here is blushing. We've got a live one."

"Ignore her," said a man at his side. "She's just pissing in your bedroll. Nobody's going to touch you either."

Nnedi laughed, a full-throated sound. "José, you take all the fun out of life. You could have let me make him sweat a bit longer."

"As long as your men keep their hands off Eden, we won't have a problem." He could handle himself. It was Eden he was worried about.

"They won't touch her." Nnedi sounded assured. "I'll have their heads if they do."

"And when the moon rises?" The warg within him was always content to doze the days away, as if sunlight weakened its hold on him, but night always brought the monsters out to play.

He could control it.

Mostly.

But an entire pack of wargs? Maybe they should have taken their chances and made a run for it, but he would never have been able to get both the kid and Eden out of there safely, and the chances of her leaving Cole behind? Slim to none.

"When the moon rises," Nnedi said coolly, "nothing shall change." She glanced at the amulet he wore around his throat. "We of Shadow Rock control the shift—not the other way around."

"You do? How?" It was something his parents had been able to do, and Cane had beaten it into him when he finally got his hands on him. But Johnny had never met another warg out there who was in control. Not even Cane. He'd been so desperate to get his hands on the amulet's Johnny's grandfather had made, as if that could stave off his madness.

"Do you know how wargs were created?"

"Pre-Darkening, in a lab. Yeah. I know a bit. Just don't know how."

"Wargs were created with nanotechnology and used to form a special branch of the pre-D government's military that was supposed to be the best of the best. The perfect soldier."

"Nanotechnology?" he breathed. There was the missing link in the stories his father had told him, and the records he'd found at Black River.

"Tiny microscopic particles that can warp the DNA of a regular human and manipulate the genome. I don't understand how it all works, though I daresay the Confederacy has better records than we do.

"Our legends state the subjects who volunteered to become these super-soldiers weren't used to the nature of the beast. They were violent and emotional, overwhelmed by their increased levels of testosterone and lower levels of cortisone and serotonin. But some were able to handle it.

"Shadow Rock is formed of the descendants of those who survived the Darkening. When the comet hit, it ruptured the walls of one of the compounds where a certain military group was being held. The government was considering whether to terminate the project—and the Alpha-Beta group—when they managed to break free of the facility."

"Black River," he murmured.

"You've heard of it?"

He'd been there. Seen the fallout and the prison cells where more than just wargs had been experimented upon. "Not a nice place, if you ask me."

"I've never been," Nnedi said, "but I suspect you're correct. My grandmother was one of the test subjects. With the skies turning black from the impact cloud, she and the rest of the alphas found shelter. There was a division among the group, and what was left—thirty-seven men and women—formed Shadow Rock. We've been together ever since.

"Of those that split from the pack, they wandered through the Wastelands and went it alone. Some forgot their conditioning; some didn't care to remember it. And some were simply broken from what they'd been through during their time in the laboratory. They gave in to the beast and ravaged the Wastelands, killing with abandon and rage. Of their victims, those that survived began to change. It took years before we realized a simple scratch could pass the nanotech on and corrupt the host. The newly formed wargs were not like us. They'd never been taught to control themselves, and when the shift came over them, they gave in to their darker halves.

"But we are Shadow Rock. We remember our ancestors, and we remember our pact. We are trained to control ourselves from birth. We are not monsters. We are elite. This is why we do not fear the moon. What about you?" Nnedi asked. "I expected you to turn when we had you surrounded."

"Is that why we're still alive? Because we didn't?"

"Yes."

"It didn't seem like a sensible option." If he'd let the monster within him out, he might have killed half of them or more. But there was a fair chance he'd also turn on Eden if she panicked. "I refuse to lose control."

"It's the only reason you're alive. It's curious to find another skinwalker out here, let alone two. The boy could be excused if he turned this once—his injuries make him weak, but you.... The alpha will be very curious about you."

His head turned toward her sharply. "Skinwalker?"

"Warg who walks in a human skin."

"What if one of your pack loses control?"

"If we cannot control it, then we are silenced. Forever. We dare not let the rage eat at the heart of the pack. It is a grave sacrifice, but we all understand."

His thoughts raced. Once upon a time, he'd lived with his mother and father in a small homestead, high in the mountains. They'd all been wargs, and his father had taught him the Way early in life. It was all he knew, until the day Cane knocked on their door, revealing another warg—albeit one who followed a different path.

Since then he'd seen the mindless monsters that roamed the Wastelands, hunting for prey and fighting each other for spoils.

But he'd never come across others like *him*, except for Luc Wade and Adam McClain, who'd managed to trap the warg within them with the amulets.

He hadn't realized how much he hungered for it. The company. The acceptance. People who wouldn't look at him as if he was a monster.

He'd tried to be human once before, and look how that turned out.

The bastards sold him to slavers.

But maybe, just maybe, there could be a place for him among other wargs.

Johnny's gaze raked the canyon ahead. The sand beneath their feet was compressed with dozens of trails. And a faint shape on a ledge far above him resolved into a warg in a pair of khaki pants and vest. Another on the other side of the canyon. They were nearing the heart of the pack's territory, if he wasn't mistaken.

And for the first time since Cane rode into his life, Johnny actually felt breathless with possibility.

Eden swallowed her wonder as they strode through the canyons. Each curved wall soared high above them, until it felt as though the light was only a mirage. She couldn't see the source of it, or where it was coming from, just the aftereffects. It kissed its way down sandstone rock, highlighting the gold shimmer of the paint on the walls. Handprints and finger-drawn suns gave way to a sleek pack of running wolves. Someone had blown clouds of charcoal around the wolves so it seemed as though they were sprinting into pure darkness.

Beauty.

Beauty the likes of which she'd never seen.

And a story.

As they ducked beneath an overhang, plunging into darker caverns, the charcoal on the walls overtook almost all of the sandstone. Shimmers of gold paint rippled here and there, as their torches grew closer.

"It's the Darkening," she whispered, reaching out to trace her fingertips an inch above the paint.

A warm body shadowed her own. Colton. "Yes. The people here remember the years that followed the meteor impact. It's a warning to be passed down from elder to child." He pressed ahead, lifting the torch Nnedi had given him higher. Figures began to emerge from the darkness. Men with spears, wearing the headdress of a wolf. "Nnedi said they're all descended from the original warg soldiers who were created by the pre-D government. They escaped the laboratories when the meteor hit, and made their own way in the Darkening."

Writing etched its way across the next wall, but it wasn't a language she knew.

"Fear not the dark, fear not the light," he translated, bending lower to track the writing. "Fear dark without light. And light without dark. One consumes, one burns. And both must be mastered to…. I can't make out this bit."

"Wargs," she whispered. "They're speaking of wargs."

Colton looked up, light falling across his face. "Yes."

A hint of wonder lit his face, and Eden paused, transfixed by how it made him seem so much younger.

She understood his wonder. Adam would love to see this place. Ever since he'd been transformed, he'd hated his other half, but what she wouldn't give for him to see how he could live with it without conflict.

Children laughed somewhere ahead of them as they entered the caves Nnedi led them to, and all her nervousness fled.

"The main cavern is this way," Nnedi called.

Curious faces began to peep out at them as they worked their way through the cave system. The roof opened up, soaring high into the darkness. She couldn't see where it ended, but there were no stars glittering there, so she guessed the roof was made of rock.

Dozens of people lingered in the main cavern. Several of the women wore brilliant blue outfits similar to Nnedi's, and most of them carried weapons of some description.

Colton moved through the crowd, and pale hands reached out to brush against him. Women's heads turned all across the main cavern, some of them standing to see him better. He looked a little unnerved by the attention, as if he was so used to living a life in the shadows that he'd never been looked at so openly.

"I think you're popular," Eden whispered. "It's those pretty eyes."

"It's the fact I'm not related to half of them," he muttered back, slipping his hand into hers and squeezing. "I told Nnedi about us."

*Us?* She met his gaze sharply.

"It's okay, angel," Colton muttered, staring at her intently. "No need to hide our relationship here. Nnedi knows you're my woman."

And he squeezed her hand.

Back to the whole "you're my woman" thing. She sighed. Ever since Nnedi arrived, she'd felt the threat level evaporate, but she wasn't certain she wanted to sleep alone. Not with CJ going to the infirmary, and dozens of wargs everywhere.

Plus, they needed to plan.

As lovely as the caves were, time was running out.

"What are we going to do?" she breathed in his ear, looking up as though examining the painted mural on the wall. "We can't stay here."

"We're not going anywhere tonight." He slung his arm around her waist, his hand resting laxly on the small of her back. Just a man hugging his woman. "We have to wait for this pack leader."

"Colton," she warned. He didn't understand. She'd already wasted too much time. Lily would be starting to suffer from the salt plague by now, and they hadn't even reached the other side of the Great Divide.

"I've counted sixty-three wargs," he whispered, brushing a curl behind her ear with his fingertips. "And that's so far. We can't run, angel. We don't know how many of them are out there, but from the sentries I saw posted, there's enough. They know the lay of the land, and Cole's not well. Be patient. We'll speak to the alpha as soon as he arrives and hopefully we'll be on our way come morning."

*What if we're not? What if—?*

Colton's fingers shivered over her cheek, alighting on her lips. Eden focused on him in surprise.

"I know you hate giving up control," he whispered, "but you have to trust me."

Eden bit her lip.

"Let's get a lay of the land," he murmured. "We need to know where the infirmary is, and how to get out of here. Don't get separated. We might have to leave at any time."

Sounded good to her.

At the end of the cavern, a pair of men waited for them, wearing dove-gray clothes. One of them had a shock of white hair, his eyebrows and lashes the exact same shade.

"Victor," Nnedi said, leaping up onto the dais in a single bound. "Where's Arik?"

"The alpha is hunting," said the albino, bowing his head. "You have found intruders?"

"Guests," Nnedi corrected.

"We will prepare quarters for them, and offer our healers for your friend." He bowed politely in their direction. "My name is Victor, and I am the seneschal of Shadow Rock."

"What about CJ?" Eden asked, watching the stretcher head across the cavern. Without her.

"My healers will see to him," Nnedi assured her.

Colton stepped forward. "Do you know when—"

"Later," said the albino sharply, and then he graced them with a softer smile. "The alpha shall have answers for you, and you can visit your friend after you're refreshed. Until then, friend, relax and enjoy the company of the pack. You are free to wander our caves, but I should warn you: these are dangerous lands, and we have people on watch outside. It would not be wise to leave the caves, in case you are mistaken for intruders. Bobbi shall accompany you throughout the caves, to ensure no harm comes to you within them."

"We'll keep that in mind." Colton managed a smile as he grabbed her hand.

Their eyes met.

*Trapped,* she told him silently.

*For now,* he returned, with a faint arch of his brow.

# twelve

Johnny paced the small room they'd been shown to, keeping his back to Eden as she washed. A pile of furs rested in the corner—a bed he presumed—and a washbasin and jugs of water had been set out for the pair of them. A loose curtain hung over the door, woven with exquisite skill. It reminded him a little of some of his mother's craft. Through it he could just make out the shape of the warg who waited out there for "their protection."

"Are these quarters?" Eden murmured. "Or a cell?"

She'd picked up on the same thing he had.

"This place smells like wolf," he muttered, rubbing the back of his neck. "And I don't know if I like the sound of this 'alpha.'" As far as he was concerned, the excitement he'd felt earlier was sloughing off as their position became clear.

Nnedi had pulled the wool over his eyes with her talk of guests and being protected. A smile, a joke, a story about the origin of wargs, and suddenly he'd been at ease. She was good.

Water dripped behind him. Johnny squeezed his eyes shut as his cock roused. He'd been on his very best behavior ever since they were shown to the room. The second Eden saw the water her eyes lit up, but with their guard, he couldn't exactly wait in the hall. And she'd had blood and dirt on her skin. He'd seen her excitement fade when she realized he couldn't leave, and hence she couldn't make full use of the amenities.

Until he very pointedly turned around and said, "Soap's in my bag."

Every moment alone with Eden was becoming torture.

Especially now she'd begun to trust him. It made his chest ache a little, for she'd have never allowed him to remain in here with her two days ago.

Which meant he couldn't do a damned thing to destroy that fragile olive branch.

He wanted her trust, curse it. He wanted more than that, if he was being honest, because there was a heat between them he ached to explore. Today's flirtation had gotten out of hand, and it only stirred his hope.

Eden wanted him. He hadn't missed the look in her eye, the way she squirmed when he told her exactly what he wanted to do to her.

Eden Fucking McClain ruined him with but a single sultry glance. He couldn't help feeling like there was a mountain of unfinished business between them.

And if he couldn't ease the tension, then something inside him was going to erupt.

"You done yet?" he muttered, scenting her soap.

Fabric shifted behind him. "Nearly."

He shifted the hard ache behind his jeans.

"Safe," she murmured, and he could make out the sounds of cotton being dragged over skin.

Johnny turned around slowly.

The first thing he noticed was her bare legs. Eden dragged the hem of her clean tank down, black to match her no-nonsense panties. Catching him looking at her legs, she arched a brow and reached for her jeans.

"You might want to make use of the water too," she said, screwing her nose up. "You've got blood on your shirt."

*Later.*

He had to rein himself back in. They had an escape to plan, and Eden was proving the worst kind of distraction, right when he needed his wits about him.

Glancing toward the door, and the muscular woman standing on guard outside, he stepped closer to Eden. She paused as he caged her against the wall with his arms. "Fancy a kiss? It's been a long day."

Instant suspicion.

Johnny pressed a finger to her mouth before she could say something that might ruin his plan. Eden stilled, the press of her lips softening beneath his touch. He mouthed, *kiss me*, and her gaze lowered to his mouth as he leaned closer.

Blood rushed right to another area of his body as he breathed in her exhalation. Taking her hand he slid it up his side, knowing the woman outside the door would hear their breathing deepen and the rustle of fabric. Johnny turned his face at the last moment, brushing his cheek along hers. Eden shivered as he nuzzled her hairline.

"Need to get a look around," he whispered, right in her ear.

Eden nodded. She turned her head to his, their faces so close their lips were almost touching. A tilt of the head toward the door said, *what about her?*

He drew back, encouraging her hand to keep exploring. Their eyes met and he pressed his fingertips between her breasts. Moving his lips silently, he mouthed, *Cole.*

Eden's gaze grew thoughtful, and she made a complicated gesture he thought meant, *I'll go check on CJ and take her with me?*

He tapped his chest. *They'll be watching me.*

As far as they were concerned, Eden wasn't the threat. If he drew their eyes, then she might get a good look at this place.

It was dangerous, sending her out there alone.

But he suspected she'd be safe, especially since Nnedi's scent had held no trace of a lie when she promised nobody would touch Eden.

*You need to look around,* he told her with a flick of his hand and fingers.

*Got it.*

She leaned up suddenly and kissed his cheek, her mouth making a loud smacking noise. Johnny stilled, breathing in the scent of her soap.

"I want to check on CJ," she said out loud.

He played along. "Not alone."

"I'll take Bobbi."

"Watch your back," he murmured. "I'll have a quick wash, then head back to the main cavern and see what I can discover. I want to know more about this alpha."

And his *pack*.

Because, while Johnny could protect her from the wargs running wild in the night, he wasn't certain if he could take on what seemed like an organized pack.

Especially if they had no intention of letting him and the others leave.

"I will," she said softly, slipping through the door.

Urgency pressed upon her as Eden made her way to the healing room.

They didn't have time for this.

But there wasn't much either of them could do right now. She was so frustrated she could have screamed.

"Here's the infirmary," Bobbi said, gesturing to a small door. A lot of the carved doors bore only curtains, so it was surprising to see sturdy timber.

"Thank you." The infirmary wasn't too far from their room, and she'd managed to map out the landscape as she went. Not much to go by, but a start.

Easing open the door, she slipped inside. A candle burned in the corner, and a form melded out of the shadows. Nnedi. The other woman looked up when she entered.

"Couldn't stay away." Nnedi shook her head. "He'll be fine."

"Would you stay away, if this was one of yours?" Eden asked, slinking onto the bed beside CJ.

They'd stripped him of his shirt, and a yellow stain marked his skin where the single scratch bloomed against the swollen flesh. She still couldn't believe such a tiny mark had felled him.

"No." Nnedi snorted.

"You're a healer?" Eden asked, looking at the pestle and mortar the other woman was working.

"My mother was a healer," Nnedi replied. "I'm a warrior, but she taught me what she knew, and I'm the one they turn to when we need field dressings or combat medicine. Wargs don't get sick, in general, but there are a few humans among the pack—those who don't want to be infected, or those who are too young—so we have a few healers here. I volunteered, however."

CJ twisted on the bed, wracked by fever dreams.

Eden soothed his sweaty dark hair off his forehead. "He should be getting better."

Wargs could heal from almost anything.

Nnedi ground something into a paste. "It's the poison in the shadow cat's claws. It kills a human instantly, but it takes longer to kill a warg. Most of the time we can push through it, but occasionally it's too strong. I need to draw it out."

"But Colton was hurt too." And his claw marks faded, once she'd bandaged them. "His injuries were deeper than CJ's, and yet they seem to have healed by now. Completely."

"This," Nnedi said, pointing to the reddened flesh around CJ's claw marks, "is from a female. The male's spurs are laced with enough poison to wound and irritate, but the female's poison is lethal. It's so they can protect their cubs. Your man must have been slashed by a male."

"How long will it take for him to heal?"

Nnedi shrugged. "A couple of days. I need to draw the poison, and give him a chance for the wolf within to heal him."

*Days?* Eden looked up in dismay. "But...."

Nnedi seemed to read her mind. "You cannot force him from his bed any earlier, or you might kill him. Even now, it might be too late. He needs time and rest."

They didn't have time. But she couldn't allow CJ to suffer. Eden sat on the edge of the bed, and tucked CJ's hand in hers. What were they going to do? "How far is it to the other side of the Divide?"

"The Confederacy side? An hour. Then half a day to the top."

The timing was growing tight.

Eden swallowed the lump in her throat and squeezed CJ's hand. She needed him with her. When she'd set out on this quest, he'd been her voice of reason, her shadow. Without him....

She'd be alone with Colton.

And judging from the tension between them today, that would be disastrous.

"What's the rush?" Nnedi asked.

Eden took a deep breath. "Have you ever heard of the salt plague?"

Nnedi looked up from her pestle. "No."

"It's a bacterial infection that was genetically engineered by the Confederacy, according to one of their defectors. One of their generals was testing it on human subjects when another general found out. The project was shut down, I think, but... it somehow found its way to the Wastelands. According to the defector, there might be a cure in Cortez City.

"Nnedi," she pleaded, grabbing the other woman's wrist. "We can't stay here. If we do, then my family and friends will die and there's no hope for the rest of my settlement. We're not a threat to your pack. I promise we won't breathe a word of you to anyone. But we have to get moving. I *need* to find that cure."

Nnedi's lips thinned. "That is not an answer I can give you."

A knock sounded at the door, and a stranger poked their head inside. "Nnedi? Arik's back."

"Arik?" Eden asked.

"He's the one you need to convince to let you go," Nnedi said.

But she didn't sound hopeful.

Eden found herself back in the main cavern, though now it had come alive. Packed with people, torches ringed the walls, and everyone seemed in a celebratory mood. Laughter echoed ahead of them loudly as Nnedi wove her way through the crowd. It parted around the tall warrior, and Eden scurried along in her wake, looking for Colton.

There was a natural stone dais at one end of the room, and that was where Nnedi led her. A pair of enormous men embraced on top of it, and Eden recognized Lincoln, whom Colton had put a knife to the throat of. She didn't know the other man, but when he drew back, clapping a hand on Lincoln's shoulder, she blinked.

Had to be Arik.

He towered over the others, his long chestnut-colored hair in a knot on top of his head, and a thick beard trimmed neatly across his jawline. A large tooth hung on a leather thong around his neck, and she was pretty sure it was from a shadow cat. The guy was ripped, with the kind of heavy, bulky muscle that had to come from hard manual labor.

His chest was also bare and oiled, with a gold handprint pressed over his left breast—a tattoo, she suspected, as it looked like someone had crushed pure gold and inked it into his skin. The only thing he wore was jeans; even his feet were bare.

Someone gave her a nudge from behind. Colton materialized out of the crowd, his body heat warm as he brushed against her.

"You want to be alone with him?" He tipped his head toward the man on the dais.

"*No.* Doesn't mean I'm not aware the guy is hot. I'm not blind and contrary to popular opinion, I'm not a prude."

His eyes grew sleepy-lidded, the dark of his pupils burning. He turned back to the front, his lips pressed tightly together.

*What was that?* She nudged him back, but Colton ignored her, and all she could think about was the heat of his eyes when he'd turned around and seen her in just her tank and panties.

A little shiver ran through her at the memory. *Oh, shit.* She was in trouble, she knew it. Keeping her hormones under control had been easier before she and Colton signed a truce.

Now?

It was becoming ridiculously easy to be around him. They'd somehow started leaning on each other, making plans, joking....

Even as that tension between them threatened to boil over every damned time he looked at her with those smoldering eyes.

*Hate sex.*

The problem was, she was pretty sure that wasn't the right way to describe the way she felt about him.

Eden didn't quite glance his way, though she couldn't help being aware of the heat that existed in the air between them. She could remember that long-ago day he'd kissed her. The hunger. The fierce need.

The betrayal.

*Ouch.*

Getting involved with Colton again was the last thing she should be thinking of, but a part of her couldn't resist being aware of him.

A part of her heard the words "hate sex" and thought that was an excellent idea. Which was madness. Or was it?

*Be honest. A) Johnny Colton's an extremely fine example of a man. B) There's unfinished business between you. You've always known that. C) He might not be as guilty of hurting you, as you've always believed.*

*D) How can you ever move on, if you don't confront everything that lingers between you?*

Easy to think.... She wasn't the one who refused to discuss the past.

"Arik," Nnedi called, leaping up onto the dais and striding toward the enormous newcomer.

Dark eyes flickered toward them, and the man turned, capturing Nnedi's hand and drawing her against him, his forehead bowing to rest against hers. He had to lean down to do so.

"They're together," Colton muttered. "I'd keep my eyes off him, if I were you. Nnedi would bury you alive, and then I'd have to step in—"

"You're so gallant."

Arik's eyes flickered their way as Nnedi murmured to him, one hand on his enormous chest.

"Welcome to Shadow Rock," Arik said, gesturing them closer. He sank onto a chair, legs spread wide, and his forearm resting on his thigh. "My second tells me you're on your way to Cortez City."

Here was her opening. Eden swiftly explained about their mission, giving it her all. "We're running out of time," she pleaded. "We have to leave as soon as possible."

The Alpha's face remained impassive. "You won't see the inside of Cortez City. Its walls are thick and the Confederacy doesn't like outsiders getting in."

"Then we just have to figure out a way over their walls," Eden shot back, growing a little vexed. "Or under them. Or around them. I can't go back to watch the people I love die without at least *trying*. I know a man inside. He might agree to meet with me, if I can just figure out a way to—"

"You have a contact?"

"Miles Wentworth."

Stillness radiated through him, and if she hadn't known any better she would have suspected he knew the name.

A flicker of something dangerous roamed through Arik's hazel eyes. There were flecks of gold mixed among the brown, as if a painter had flicked gold paint from his brush onto his canvas.

"I understand your desire," Arik finally said, leaning back in his chair. "It doesn't negate the truth; you can't get inside Cortez. It's impenetrable."

*Nothing's impenetrable.* But there was no point arguing with him. He'd made up his mind. "We shall see. In the morning I'll check on CJ. If he's feeling a little better, we intend to head on."

"And if he's not well?" Nnedi asked.

Eden knew what CJ would tell her to do. She'd seen Nnedi tending him and knew he was in safe hands. "If he's not better, then we will have to go on without him—if you would agree to tend him?"

Colton stirred at her side, and Eden looked up into his eyes. *Please.* She couldn't do this without him, and despite the change in circumstances, the plan had to remain the same.

He nodded faintly, and relief flooded through her. Eden pressed her hand to his back, a silent *thanks*.

"I will tend the boy," Nnedi said, her hard face softening.

Arik turned his head toward her, his brows drawing together. "He is an untested warg," he murmured, censure in his voice.

"I will vouch for him," Nnedi said. "When he is better, CJ can be tested."

Arik pushed to his feet, and Eden felt the tension in the room shift.

They'd all been making plans around this man, a potentially volatile alpha, and she could see he didn't like it.

"You are strangers in our territory," Arik said, "and one of you drew blood."

"Arik," Nnedi said under her breath.

He moved forward, and Eden took a step back as he loomed above them on the dais.

"My second has granted you guest rights for the night. Tomorrow you intend to leave. But first"—Arik held up his hand to still the murmur of the watching crowd—"there is a reparation to see to."

The crowd grew a little closer, and Eden shook her head. "Reparation?" she demanded. "What sort of reparation? Your men attacked *us*."

A hand came to rest in the middle of her back.

Just a light warning.

"Is this how you treat guests?" Colton murmured. "We've obeyed your rules, and given over our weapons in good faith."

Lincoln began stripping off his vest with a faint smile. "You misunderstand, friend." He touched his throat, where Colton's blade had kissed it. "You owe me a debt, Colton. You drew the blood of the pack, now you must pay the price. Maybe I'll take that pretty little piece at your side as repayment."

Colton stiffened.

"What's going on?" Eden whispered, horrified she already knew the answer.

"Blood for blood. If your man wants to keep you," Arik called, "then he needs to fight for you."

A chorus of howls went up.

Some of the men in the galleries beat their chests, and others stomped their feet. Eden took a step back, unable to stop herself from counting. A full pack. She and Colton had no chance of escaping. Suddenly the alpha didn't look so pretty. *Dick.*

"Munin," Nnedi bellowed. "To me."

Almost instantly, Eden found herself surrounded by over a dozen of the women in azure blue. Most of them had spears. Some had guns, and others wore knives in the sheaths at their hip. All of them bore a black raven tattoo on their upper arms. The same raven Nnedi wore, though hers was gold.

Colton spun around, his gaze seeking hers, but the tension in his shoulders softened when he saw what Eden had.

All of the women held their spears out.

Toward the alpha and his men.

"Munin rejects our alpha's claim," Nnedi stated. "No woman can be taken by force. It is not our alpha's right to grant this woman to another without her permission."

Arik's lips thinned, and the howling died off. "Nnedi—"

"I will guard this woman with my life to prevent such a thing," Nnedi said, her voice softening dangerously.

The enormous warg swore under his breath, and then strode along the natural platform toward them. "My apologies. Poor choice of words on my behalf. But he will fight to prove himself worthy."

"I granted them guest rights."

"With respect, Second," Arik snapped, "you had no right to grant guest rights without my approval. These people are strangers and two of them are wargs. Our prime purpose is always to protect the pack."

Eden didn't dare breathe. Without the Munin, she and Colton wouldn't survive. But Nnedi was challenging her pack's alpha, and there were only fourteen of the Munin here, and at least fifty... maybe sixty men.

"With respect, Alpha," Nnedi called, putting her hands on her hips. "You're being a dick."

Silence.

Absolute stunned silence filled the canyon.

"Would I dare bring enemies into the heart of my pack?" Nnedi snarled, stepping forward through the ranks of her Munin. "Do you doubt my intelligence? Or do you suspect my loyalty? Either way, you show doubt in my abilities as second of this pack."

Nnedi reached behind her neck and began untying the leather thong there, the wolf's claw on the end of it dipping between her breasts as she drew the necklace free. Holding it out, she dropped the claw in the dirt.

The woman beside Eden sucked in a sharp breath, but otherwise the Munin remained silent.

Despite the packed galleries, Eden could have heard a pin drop.

The alpha's gaze locked on the claw, then slowly lifted.

Nnedi stared back, and Eden was kind of glad she wasn't on the receiving end of a look like that.

"It is not you I doubt. But this warg has not passed the tests, and the moon is rising," he said gruffly.

"This warg faced a dozen of our warriors with a knife at his woman's throat, and he didn't lose control," Nnedi replied. "I consider that my test."

"Nnedi." Arik's face tightened. "There are children here. He must prove he is in control of himself, without a doubt. I am not asking anything that any warg here has not proven. We all face the fire. We all hold the flame. Or else we burn. I will not change the rules, not for anybody."

A murmur of agreement sprung up in the gallery.

What did it mean? Eden took a step closer to Colton, reaching for his sleeve.

Nnedi's lips thinned. "The woman is human."

"Fine." The alpha looked seriously pissed as his attention returned to Colton. "Your woman has guest right. She will be safe, regardless of the outcome of this fight. But you are an untried warg walking into my home, without having proven your mettle. You have drawn the blood of one of mine. You will fight and you will show us you are not one of the monsters. Or you will die."

"So all I have to do is prove I can hold this form?" Johnny said, remembering what Nnedi had told him in the canyon.

"And survive," Nnedi replied, gesturing the circle of women around them closer. "Prepare him."

Survival might be the more difficult task. He'd caught a glimpse of his opponent, and while Johnny knew he was good, he hadn't been able to test the mettle of the other wargs here yet. Lincoln was an unknown, and he didn't like the unknown. He'd had a gun the last time he took Lincoln down, which made the odds uneven. This time it would be body against body. No weapons.

"What sort of man challenges someone who's been recently wounded?" Eden snarled. Strands of her curly brown hair had managed to escape from her ponytail, and despite the fact she was only human, she stepped right up into Nnedi's face, her hands on her hips.

"A warg who cannot heal himself is weak," Nnedi replied flatly. "A warg who cannot control himself is weak. A warg who cannot fight to protect himself is—"

"Yeah, yeah, we get it," Eden replied.

"It doesn't matter whether he is healed or not," Nnedi muttered, her lips pressing thinly together as she shot Arik a hard look. "The alpha has decreed your man shall fight for his right to survive, and so it shall be."

Tension existed there, if Johnny wasn't mistaken. Could he use that to help them get free of this place? "Is this going to cause problems between you and your alpha?"

"He is my chosen," Nnedi said, with a shrug. "Eight years ago we stood before the pack and pledged ourselves to each other, and he placed the claw at my throat to show our bond. However, he has displeased me. I shall not put the claw back on until he apologizes and proves he is a man I can give myself to."

Oh, shit. Not just the leader and his second, but a man and wife.

"I'm sorry," Johnny murmured. "We didn't mean to—"

"Arik makes his own choices." Nnedi sounded completely assured. "You did not force his hand. And as he likes to say—it is up to each of us to prove ourselves worthy. So let him prove himself to me."

Someone started tugging his shirt buttons undone. Another woman began on his belt.

"Whoa." He grabbed her hand.

"You can keep the jeans on," Nnedi said, "but a belt gives your opponent leverage."

He slowly released the belt. Good point. Heat still flushed through his cheeks though, as they stripped his shirt off him. Eden gave him a faintly amused look, her gaze lingering on his bare chest.

*Focus*, he told himself sharply.

Johnny took in the circle of wargs and the way several of them were dipping their hands into a clay bowl and pressing powdered handprints to Lincoln's chest. Drums sounded as wargs packed the cliff shelves and gallery, looking down at the sandy floor as they hooted.

It wasn't the first time he'd been forced to fight for entertainment reasons, but as Johnny glanced toward the alpha, he saw something reflected in the man's dark eyes. This wasn't just for laughs.

"What happens if I kill him?" he asked.

Eden paled.

"I would advise not killing him. Lincoln is Arik's younger brother."

"So all I need to do is force him to submit or cry mercy?"

"It is a fight until you cannot keep fighting anymore," Nnedi replied steadily, using a pestle to grind something to dust in her clay mortar. "This ends when one of you is no longer able to get up."

"And what about Colton? Is Lincoln going to pull his blows?" Eden demanded. "Or is he going to try and kill him?"

Nnedi's expression said it all.

"This is bullshit," Eden exploded, her vehemence startling him. "You said we were guests. Is this how you treat your guests?"

"It is not my call to make," Nnedi responded sharply.

"Hey." He grabbed Eden's arm and dragged her in close, mimicking a man comforting his sweetheart. His voice dropped as his thumb stroked her upper arm. "It's okay. I'm not going to let anything happen to you, and Nnedi will protect you if this goes south."

Conflict waged war in her green eyes. "Jesus Christ, Colton. How about you focus on yourself?"

She was worried? For *him*?

No. Couldn't be. She needed a guide and with Cole down and out for the count, he was it.

"This isn't my first time fighting like this. I'm good at what I do, Eden."

"Good. Because I'm going to be pissed if I have your death on my conscience."

That was more like it. "Can't have that."

"Boots off," Nnedi instructed, examining the white powder in her bowl.

Johnny stared over her shoulder toward his adversary. Several of the pack gathered around Lincoln, painting a thin line of black down the center of his face.

Something stirred in Johnny's blood, as if the war music called to him. He could feel Eden's hands on his body, as she knelt and tugged his boots off.

"The amulet too," Nnedi instructed.

Eden hesitated as she straightened, and he read the train of thought in her eyes. It was the one thing that kept her brother Adam from turning, despite the pull of the moon. She hadn't seen him take it off in front of Cole.

Johnny lifted the amulet over his head, handing it to her. "Keep it safe for me, angel. It was my grandfather's. I don't need it—I never have—but it holds sentimental value for me."

The handful of women with Nnedi began rubbing oil all over him. He knew it would help him avoid Lincoln's grip, but he couldn't help noticing Eden's eyes on him. One of the women's hands slid low across his abdomen and Eden's gaze followed it. It was hard not to think about what it would feel like if that were Eden's hand, skating low enough to brush the top of his jeans.

He caught the woman's hand before it skimmed any lower and his body started focusing on Eden beneath him, rather than on the task ahead.

The woman giggled.

A hand slapped his back. Nnedi walked in slow circles around him and slammed her powdered hand against his skin to leave a print. Another of the Munin pressed one to his stomach. The giggler.

"Enjoying yourself?" Eden muttered.

"Are *you*?" He quirked a brow, and heat painted a pretty red across her cheeks.

"Don't get hurt. *Please*."

He stared into her eyes, as the entire cavern vanished around them, trying to work out what she was trying to say. "Whatever happens here, it's not your fault."

Her thumb brushed against the inside of his wrist as she lowered her eyes, trying to say something and failing. "I forgive you," she finally whispered.

"*What?*" he demanded, the pit of his stomach freefalling.

Eden slowly looked up from beneath those thick, dark lashes. "I don't know the truth of everything that happened between us. You won't tell me. But.... I forgive you. I forgive you for your part of what happened to me. To Adam. I know you never truly wanted to hurt me."

Every inch of him ran cold with shock, his heart suddenly thundering along in time to the beat of the drums. A distant howling filled his ears—the other wargs screaming for him to enter the ring. But he was trapped in this moment, his entire world wrenched out from beneath his feet with three little words.

He had the feeling he'd never be able to right himself again. Of all the times to tell him this.... It cascaded through him, like someone setting a spark to the fuse of a thousand suppressed emotions.

He didn't deserve forgiveness. Especially not from her.

But those words filled him, forcing the darkness that lingered deep within his soul to flee into the recesses of his empty heart, where they could no longer touch him.

He hadn't realized how much he'd craved forgiveness.

Johnny's eyes narrowed on her, as Nnedi gestured the women away from him.

"Go," Nnedi said. "And fight with honor."

Hands pushed him. Pulled him.

All he could see was Eden.

It was stupid.

Reckless.

He didn't even know where the urge came from. But as the wargs began howling for him to enter the makeshift ring, he slid his hand behind Eden's neck and dragged her against him.

Eden's hands slammed against his chest as Johnny captured her mouth. The surprised exhale of her breath filled his lungs as he explored her lips. No time for finesse. Only hunger. Tongue lashing teasingly across her lower lip, and her hips grinding against his. Eden's palms skated up the back of his neck, her body softening as she kissed him back.

He'd dreamed of this moment a thousand times. She didn't know what she gave him with her forgiveness, and her need. Intangible necessities he still couldn't quite touch, more a dream than a reality still, but growing heavier and more real with every lash of her tongue.

Three... four seconds at most. By the time he stepped back, he was wearing a faint smile and her eyes were so wide, he could see dozens of the torches in the cavern reflected in them. It made her eyes look like a night sky. It made him feel like he could steal half the light of the world just by kissing her again.

"In case I never get another chance," he murmured, as she put her fingertips to her lips.

Then he stepped through the opening in the circle of wargs and headed for his destiny. The drums beat faster as he strode through the narrow tunnel of hooting wargs. Some clapped his back, others shoved their faces in his, screaming at him. Thumping their chests.

He ignored them all.

The only thing that mattered was survival.

# thirteen

The main cave echoed with shouts and the deep throat ululations Eden had heard earlier. But the tone had changed. It had been a song of welcome earlier, whereas now it reminded her of violence, of power, of the sheer, unblinking exhilaration of a people preparing themselves for war.

Nnedi climbed the natural dais, gesturing for her follow. Eden clambered up the stone, just as the others circled the pit below. Its floor coated with sand, it bore faint ruddy stains that made her throat catch. Clearly not the first time blood had been spilled here.

Colton flexed his shoulders, muscle gleaming beneath the coating of oil they'd rubbed all over him. They'd pressed white powdered hands all over his back and shoulders, a stark contrast to the red ochre handprints that stained Lincoln.

Lincoln had an inch or two on him, and broader shoulders, but Colton had him beat when it came to pure, hard slab of muscle. Every inch of him was rock, from his shoulders to his eight-pack, whereas there was a softer layer of muscle on Lincoln.

Arik lifted a gourd-shaped pot to his brother's lips, and Lincoln grabbed it with both hands, red liquid dripping down the sides of his mouth as he drank.

He lowered it, and Arik turned toward Johnny.

"Drink," the alpha said, his eyes glittering as he lifted the hollowed-out gourd to Johnny's lips.

"What is it?" Colton demanded, his nose wrinkling.

"Kaga," Arik replied. "We call it Fire in the Blood. All our warriors must drink it before they face their testing. Master the fire, and you master yourself."

"It's an enervative," Nnedi called. "It will stimulate your system and make it harder to control your darkness. Lust, rage, violence.... Everything is magnified."

Eden swallowed. *Don't do it....*

But he merely nodded and drained the rest of the gourd.

Wargs screamed in satisfaction as he lowered it, as if he'd done something they approved of.

"Can your man fight?" Nnedi murmured at her side.

*He has to.* Eden's breath came short and sharp. Her lips still tingled from where he'd kissed her, but she couldn't focus on that.

*He kissed me.*

*Shit.*

"He can fight." Adam had told her of the arenas of Rust City, where both he and Colton had been forced to fight for their lives for the enjoyment of the slavers who ran the town. She'd refused to listen to the story once she knew Colton was involved, but she'd heard enough hints of what Adam went through to know Colton had to be good if he'd survived that.

"Challenge has been made," Arik called, holding his hands up for silence. "Shadow Rock belongs to the mighty." *Hoo-ra*, bellowed the wargs. "It belongs to those who control the darkness." *Hoo-ra*. "And now, if our guest wishes to keep his head he must prove he is mighty enough—controlled enough—to have a claim on it."

Eden's fingers dug into her palm. Colton rolled his shoulders and windmilled his arms, looking calm and at ease as Lincoln preened with his arms wide as he turned in slow circles.

She'd brought Colton into this.

The past no longer mattered. His debt to her was gone.

If he died, she'd never forgive herself.

"Come on," she whispered to herself. "Kick his ass."

Colton's gaze lifted to hers as if he'd heard her, the faint edge of a smile haunting his lips, and then he and Lincoln began circling each other.

"Fight!" shouted a fierce, bearded warg with hair the color of fire.

Lincoln charged forward, the movement sharp and sudden. Eden's fists curled into hard knots as she bounced forward on the balls of her toes. The crowd pressed closer to see, and she could barely make out what was happening over their heads.

A loud "ooh" echoed through the cavern and the sound of fist hitting flesh echoed. Blood spattered across the crowd.

"Damn it." She couldn't see. Shoving past the man next to her—*Jesus, it was the alpha*—Eden scrambled up onto the lip of a rock, where she could finally make out the action.

Lincoln wiped his mouth, his hand coming away bloody as Colton merely held his fingers out and gestured at the bigger warg. *Come at me*, said those taunting fingers, and relief flooded through her. Not Colton's blood.

Not yet.

"Get 'im, Linc!" someone screamed.

Colton's knees flexed, and then he met Lincoln's charge, driving forward and slamming a shoulder into the younger man's midriff. Lincoln flew up over his shoulder, his eyes widening.

"*Hoo-ra!*" came the echoing cry through the canyon as Lincoln slammed into the dirt.

A shiver of relief flooded through her.

Too soon, perhaps. Lincoln flipped up onto his feet, and this time his eyes were wary.

They slammed together, again and again, grappling, their feet straining in the sand, flexing to get a better grip. Colton moved like a lithe snake, changing grip, forcing Lincoln to halt his attacks and concentrate on defensive moves.

Something was happening to both of them. The veins in Colton's throat throbbed, and Lincoln's eyes held the silver sheen that betrayed a warg.

"He's turning," Eden whispered, swallowing hard.

"It's the kaga," Nnedi muttered. "It's difficult enough to hold the transformation back when sober, let alone with kaga in your blood."

Eden paced along the shelf, trying to see better, butterflies darting in her stomach. "*Hold it.* Come on, you can do it."

Lincoln threw his head back and roared, his teeth elongating. He lashed out with his hand and claws gleamed on the end of his fingers. Slash marks appeared across Colton's chest.

Slamming against each other again, they fought and twisted for position. Colton went down with a twist as Lincoln kicked his knee from the side. A punishing punch followed it, and his head snapped to the side.

Eden's stomach knotted up. *Get up. Come on, get up.*

But Lincoln wasn't having any of that.

Their freedom hinged on the outcome of this fight.

Colton's life lay on the line.

Eden felt sick.

Colton hooked his foot behind Lincoln's and using a whip-swift snap of his legs, took Lincoln down. Then they were on the ground, shifting, grabbing, using every inch of their bodies to gain the upper hand.

A fist punched into Colton's ribs, but he'd trapped Lincoln's arm behind him. With a jerk of his hips, Lincoln managed to get free, but not for long. Colton took him down, swinging behind him and locking his forearm around Lincoln's throat, trapping his head there with his other hand.

*Yes!* She didn't dare breathe.

Lincoln's face went red as he kicked at the sands. He dug his claws into Colton's arm, but Colton merely ground his teeth together and flexed his arm tighter, his legs locked around the other man's waist.

Eden swallowed hard, as Lincoln's bare feet kicked once more. Twice. And then he went still, his body slumping onto Colton's embrace, and his fingers falling open as his hand hit the sands.

Silence fell around the cavern, the drummers drawing to an abrupt halt.

Someone sucked in a sharp hiss of breath.

Colton dumped Lincoln's unconscious body on the sand, then stood, blood gleaming on his heaving chest and his skin slick with sweat and oil. He stared up at Arik, tilting his chin just a little arrogantly. "Call it. Or I'll kill him."

The alpha's lashes fluttered as he surveyed the scene. With a sharp nod, he turned and gestured to the man who'd started the fight.

It was over.

Relief sank through her, like lead through her veins.

For a second....

Eden's eyes met Colton's across the arena, her chest rising and falling. Sweat and oil gleamed over his skin, and the heat in his eyes practically incinerated her. She could taste him again on her lips, as though the phantom kiss consumed her.

"*Hoo, hoo, hoo,*" the wargs started chanting, slamming their left fists against the right side of their chests.

Someone held a water skin up to Colton's mouth, forcing him to drink it—or drown.

Eden rubbed her arms, feeling jittery. She didn't know what was wrong with her. It hadn't been her down in that ring, but the sight of it... of the graceful moves, the threat of danger, Colton's oil-slicked body, all of it ratcheted a tension inside her she hadn't known she was holding.

He looked good.

Like some brutal warrior, marred by sweat and blood, and damn her hormones, but she couldn't help feeling something stark flare in response.

*It's just the adrenaline*, she told herself. Adrenaline and stress made one hell of a potent combination.

Lowering the water skin, Colton met her gaze, and the intense gleam in the liquid dark of his pupils made her swallow.

They could have been alone in the cavern.

And from the look in his eyes, he knew exactly how she was feeling right now.

Arik stepped off the dais and landed in the ring in a squat. He straightened, his smile thin as he surveyed his brother's unconscious form.

"You have won your right to be one of us," he called, slapping a hand on the thick muscle of Colton's shoulder. "Now we celebrate."

The pair of them clasped hands, Colton's white teeth flashing in a smile. Someone bought more kaga forth. Wargs spilled around Colton, swallowing him up as they all sought to touch him.

"You've got to be kidding me," Eden said, rubbing the gooseflesh on her arms. "Now they're all friends."

"Men," Nnedi snorted. "There will be many sore heads come morning."

"I think I need a drink myself," she muttered, pushing past Nnedi as the sounds of celebration began to spiral through the cavern.

Eden moved through the dancers, trying to ignore the press of bodies against hers as she tried to get some air.

She'd had a generous mouthful of kaga before realizing it didn't just affect wargs. Her heart was racing in time to the drums, and her head felt like it was ready to explode. Her fingers curled around the pewter amulet he'd given her for safekeeping.

CJ's injury. Lily's illness. Time ticking down like a bomb about to go off in her face. Johnny Colton slamming back into her life. Finding her own goddamned letters in his pocket.

Seeing the momentary glint of vulnerability in his eyes when she touched the scars on his back before he looked away.

The feel of his mouth on hers.

All of it formed a volatile mix, fusing into a pressure cooker inside her, until Eden thought she was going to scream.

She needed to get out of here.

Before she did something stupid.

Something she could never take back.

The drumbeat throbbed through her veins until her heart was racing as she pushed through the crowd. Or maybe it wasn't the drum at all, but the pulse between her thighs.

She caught a glimpse of Colton tracking her, moving like a shark in her wake. All tanned, oiled skin, those handprints standing out starkly, as if to show her where to put her own. Hungry dark eyes.

Eden stared back, and once again she could feel her lips tingling. Colton's lashes shadowed his eyes as he started pushing through the crowd toward her.

*Hell.* She ducked into the passage that led to their room, finally free of the cloying heat of bodies. A glimpse back showed wargs flinging their heads back and stomping the ground in time to the music. Nnedi had pushed Arik back into the shadows of the cavern, where they were having a heated argument, and someone threw an entire jug of water over the crowd from the lip of the dais.

And there....

Colton himself, finally slipping free of the mass of heaving bodies. He stood out against the torchlight behind him, a dark shadow carved from pure stone. Eden rubbed her mouth, her nipples hardening as she turned and darted down the passage, shooting glances over her shoulder to see if he was following.

He came for her, as if drawn by the look in her eyes.

Maybe he could sense it—or maybe that same echoing throb rang through his body, and he needed the release too.

Eden couldn't breathe. Need fisted like a tight knot inside her. Her skin ached, as if she could almost *feel* his hands upon her.

And then she was.

A hand locked around her wrist, spinning her around. Her back hit the smooth slope of the wall, and suddenly Colton was in her space, barely touching her, just looking. "Where are you going, angel? The party's back there."

An inch separated them. It wasn't enough. "Here's your amulet." She shoved it toward him. "I think... I need some air."

"Put it on me," he breathed, bowing his head toward her, and letting her wrist go.

Eden froze. Lifting the chain, she draped it over his head, letting the snarling wolf's head fall into place in the center of his chest.

All she could breathe was the heated scent of the oil on his body. Her hand fluttered between them as if to fend him off, but she wasn't sure if that was what she truly intended. Hands had swiped through the palm prints on his chest, and white paint dragged across his abdomen.

"Are you sure that's what you need right now?" he whispered, resting one palm flat against the wall on the side of her head.

Eden glanced up from beneath her lashes and as he leaned closer, her fingertips brushed against the hard flex of his abdominals. Every inch of her skin seemed to ache, as if it was begging for his touch.

She turned her face to the side, trying to escape the intensity, but there was no avoiding the truth.

She didn't want him to go.

"Eden?" he murmured, fingertips resting against her chin. "What's going on in that head of yours?"

She took a deep breath. Another. What was she doing?

*Scratching that itch....*

Courage seemed to fire through her, and she grabbed a fistful of his hair, jerking his face to hers. "You were right. We need to get this out of our systems. I can't think when you're here. I can't focus. I can't ignore this bloody itch."

He drew back, dark eyes searching her gaze so hungrily, she suddenly wondered exactly what he was looking for.

And whether he'd found it.

"Say no," Colton demanded, one hand clenched on the wall beside her with white knuckles. "Because I am this fucking close to misreading the look in your eyes, Eden."

One last chance to avert this head-on collision.

Eden's gaze slid down over him like a hot caress, and suddenly she didn't want to avoid a thing.

Her throat felt raw. "You're not misreading anything. Fuck. Me. *Please.*"

# fourteen



*You're not misreading anything....*

"Hate sex," Eden breathed.

Johnny's entire body stilled. "Hate sex?"

He had the sudden, angry feeling this wasn't what he wanted at all. *Not like this.* But then her hand was on his chest, splaying directly over one of the handprints there, and the look in her eyes.... Jesus. How could a man resist her?

"You. Me. And everything that burns between us."

He was losing the battle. They could discuss their situation later. Right now, he just wanted his hands on her. It fired through his brain, and then suddenly it wasn't enough to just touch her.

Johnny grabbed the back of Eden's scalp, dragging her into his arms as he lowered his head.

Their mouths met, Eden's body wilting against his as a moan echoed in her throat.

It wasn't the sort of kiss he'd given her before; a taste, a tease, something a little more chaste than this....

This was pure, unrelenting mouth fucking. Days of frustration. Years of guilt and twisted memories running him ragged. He stabbed his tongue past her lips, forcing her to open for him, and feeling the lush stroke of her own tongue as she yielded. Kissing Eden was better than all his feverish imaginings had led him to believe. There was doubt in her eyes when she looked at him, but all of it evaporated the second he laid hands on her. She kissed as if she wanted to steal his breath—his *soul*—as if she couldn't survive another moment without the feel of his mouth on hers.

The drumbeat in the cavern echoed through his veins, and the kaga felt like someone had lit his blood on fire. Johnny pushed into her, his aching cock pressing against the hollow between her thighs. Not enough. Never enough. He wanted inside her now.

Somehow he broke the kiss, panting as he leaned against her. The kaga made it hard, but he wasn't about to mistake a single thing here. "Last chance to say no, Eden."

Hands slid down his chest. "Don't stop."

Permission to unleash every last ounce of hunger he felt upon her. All his dreams were coming fucking true.

And suddenly he couldn't hold himself back anymore.

She kissed him as though someone had lit the fuse and fire sparked along it, about to hit the powder keg. Hands tearing at the buttons on his jeans, her teeth sinking into his lower lip.

Johnny captured her hips and lifted her as Eden wrapped her legs around him. Then he was striding blindly toward their room, her greedy hands raking up his back, the bite of her nails digging into his scars.

He hissed as he shoved through the curtain that was all that shielded them from the outside world. Wrenching it closed, he managed to set her back to the wall, and then he was thrusting against her, his tongue invading her mouth with urgent need.

He grabbed the hem of her tank and hauled it up, revealing the soft skin of her abdomen beneath his hands. *Fuck.* His cock felt like a battering ram. Eden broke the kiss just long enough to drag the tank over her head, and then she was tossing it aside, both hands capturing his face between them, as her lips met his again.

Years of desire bloomed within him.

This woman. Damn him for a fool, but this woman got under his skin in a way no one ever had.

She'd been young and innocent as a girl, heart-stoppingly lovely.

In every letter she'd written her brother, there'd been an aching loneliness and love that shone through. He'd craved some part of that affection on those long, lonely nights out there in the Wastelands alone, when he couldn't resist opening one of them and pretending they'd been written for him.

His dreams of her had been relentless, an odd mix of guilt and desire.

But Eden McClain in the flesh was like a bomb going off in his hands. Under his touch, she ignited like wildfire, hands sliding up his chest, then dancing low, teasing along his belt buckle.

He grabbed her hand and curled it around his erection, drawing back to gasp a breath. This close, he could see the glazed shock of lust in her eyes, and she squeezed him, biting her lip.

Not once did she look away.

"Bed," she breathed.

Johnny kissed her throat, biting just hard enough to earn a gasp. Hauling her away from the wall, he staggered toward the pile of furs on the floor.

"I don't have condoms." Getting his hands on one was difficult, as production was strictly controlled by the Confederacy and they cost too much on the black market.

And it had been a long time since he'd needed one.

Three or so years, right before a village in the badlands sold him out to slavers and made him realize he couldn't trust anyone.

Eden's hands clasped at the back of his neck. "I had my injection a couple of months ago. I'm safe for another month at least. And I'm clean."

Johnny sank to his knees, his hands cupping her ass. The second he hit the furs he pushed forward, spilling her onto her back. "So am I."

Just one more benefit of being a warg.

"Are you sure about this?" he gasped, a single moment of hesitation rocking him as he knelt over her. "Because you're not going to be able to pretend this didn't happen in the morning...."

Eden grabbed the amulet around his neck and hauled him down. "Shut up and kiss me."

Sounded good to him.

Johnny captured her mouth again.

Her heated hands slid up his chest and over his shoulders, nails raking down his oiled skin. Johnny worked his way down her throat, trailing his tongue along her pulse.

Eden's bra was black cotton, and he delved beneath her with one hand as she arched her spine. Then it was off, and he dragged it aside, capturing her nipple with his heated mouth.

"Oh, God!"

Laving attention across her breasts, he somehow managed to get the straps off her arms without breaking his kiss. "You have the best fucking tits," he breathed, suckling hard. "You don't know how much I've wanted to get my mouth on them."

"Jesus, Colton." Fingers dug into his hair as she lifted her head off the fur. "I want you. *Now*."

Before she could reach for his jeans, he reared up onto his knees. "I'd like to oblige, darlin', but I've been dreaming of what I'm going to do to you for days."

He undid her belt, even as she ran her pale hands up to cup her tits. *Fuck*. He bent as he jerked her jeans open, kissing the smooth skin of her abdomen. The wet, musky scent of her cunt drew him to her, and he dragged her panties aside and nuzzled into her pussy, barely able to get a taste. He needed her jeans all the way off.

"Oh, God," she moaned, her fingers curling in his hair.

Tugging her jeans down her long legs, Johnny threw them aside, and then hooked both thumbs under the hem of her panties. Half tempted to rip them off, he dragged them slowly out from under her bottom, revealing the thatch of brown hair between her thighs.

"Are you wet for me, angel?"

He couldn't resist any longer.

Wrenching them down her thighs, he buried his face in that hair, breathing her in. The second he got her panties free, her thighs parted and Johnny tongued her wet slit, getting his first full taste of her. Eden cried out, her spine arching and her thighs clamping around his head. Forcing them wide, he settled in to feast, smelling the soap she'd used earlier.

Hate fuck or not, he didn't intend to rush a damned minute of this.

Eden McClain had haunted him for years.

He wanted to imprint every second of this encounter in his brain, until he couldn't remember their hateful past, only this. New memories to replace the old, an encounter forged out of the forgiveness he desperately needed from her.

Tilting his head, he suckled hard on her clit, alternating that with the slow, heated lap of his tongue. Every gasp that came from her lips felt like victory, and he teased her as the pressure built within her, tracing slow, lazy circles, flicking his tongue lightly against her when her fingers dug into his scalp and her body silently begged him to lick hard.

"Colton," she breathed as he thrust his tongue between her slick folds. A soft scream broke over her lips, and she arched in response, her thighs clamping around his head.

Nothing had ever tasted better than the slick wetness of her desire. Nothing had ever sounded as good as her soft cries of ecstasy as she came.

*I could spend all day eating Eden McClain out.*

But her fist was in his hair, dragging him insistently up.

And as much as he wanted to prolong this, he also knew he was getting dangerously close to the edge himself. Jerking the buttons of his jeans open, he kissed her throat again, shoving her hips wide.

"Ready?"

"Yes!"

He thrust into her wet heat, his jeans still half-on.

Eden cried out, flinging her head back as her spine arched.

Johnny buried his face in her throat, fucking her with short, ferocious thrusts. Her body sheathed him like a glove, molten with heat. A good thing he'd worked her over, for he could sense the warg within him climbing to the surface. It wanted to fuck. Hard and fast, and brutal. The last thing he wanted to do was hurt her, so he ground his teeth together, fighting back against the rush of blood through his veins.

It was as if she felt him trying to rein himself back. "Harder," she breathed, nipping at his lip and digging her heels into the back of his thighs. "I want to feel it tomorrow. I don't mind the bruises."

So be it.

She'd called it hate sex—he'd even been the one to jokingly suggest it—but there was nothing of hate in this. Only pure, rapturous pleasure. The chance to worship her body with his, to take what he so desperately wanted from her.

Pinning her wrists to the fur, he gathered them in one hand and slid the other down to drag her knee up between them. The angle made her cry out.

"That's it, angel." Burying his face against her throat, he bit his lower lip as the pressure in his balls began to mount. "Come, *mi alma*."

Her body clenched.

"*Eres una mujer hermosa y obstinada*," he whispered hotly, in her ear. "*Eres hermosa. Eres mío. Mi dulce sabor del cielo....*"

"Sweet Jesus," she breathed. "What are you saying?"

He gasped against her throat. She liked that. Every inch of her clenched around him until he was seeing stars.

"Scream for me," he panted, arching his hips to ride over that spongy little spot deep inside her. "Scream my name, darlin'."

*Can't hold on much longer....*

*Fuck.* He gritted his teeth together, his thrusts slowing. Eden's spine arched, her breasts meeting his chest as he pinned her wrists down and told her how fucking much he loved this in Spanish.

"Oh, God," she breathed. "Oh... my... *God*. Colton!"

The word burst out of her in a rush as her body gave a spasm around his. Johnny captured her scream with a kiss, feeling his own orgasm hit him like a lightning bolt. Pinning her beneath him, his spare hand fisted in her hair, he bucked into her as heat swept up the back of his spine and he came.

Thousands of nights alone.

Thousands of blood-soaked days beneath a blistering sun.

And for one perfect moment, it was all worth it for this one glimpse of heaven. Johnny collapsed atop her, sweat slicking both of their skin as he gasped for breath. Boneless. Empty.

At peace, for the first time in years.

And whether she hated him or not, for that one moment her hand clasped the back of his neck as she dragged him into her embrace, and Johnny Colton finally knew what it felt like to not be so alone.

# fifteen

Morning came. Johnny could feel it tingling in his veins, even deep beneath the rock, as if the warg subsided within him like a contented cat.

Or maybe that was just the aftereffect of finally getting rid of some of this sexual tension between them.

Movement shifted, a soft body wriggling against his as the sheets lifted. He'd taken her again last night before they both collapsed in a sweaty mess and he'd curled around her. Eden had fallen asleep before she could move, and he'd buried his face in the back of her neck and pretended this was real.

But with morning came all those thoughts he was refusing to think of, and the fact this had *actually* happened between them last night.

He could feel stiffness stealing though her warm body as she slid away from him like a thief in the night. So that was the way it was going to be. Couldn't say he was surprised.

Pretend to be asleep and let her sidle out of here as if nothing had ever happened? Or take a chance?

Johnny cracked open one eye.

Eden shrugged from the bed of furs, the curve of her spine a shallow canyon in the topography of her back. Her hips flared wide and he caught a glimpse of the undercurve of her breast as she reached for her tank and panties.

*Damn.*

He was hard and aching in a second, remembering the feel of her beneath him, the taste of her pussy on his tongue. Johnny shifted, his cock aching as memory teased him.

Eden tugged her panties up her long slim legs, bending over just enough to taunt him, before the scrap of black cotton hid the white globes of her ass and her wet pussy from view.

Johnny lunged across the pile of furs and snagged an arm around her waist. "Where do you think you're going?"

Eden gasped, then shivered as he kissed the slope where her shoulder met her neck. "It's morning."

"So it is," he murmured, brushing another kiss just behind her ear.

Her spine arched as her head fell back to allow him better access. The thick tangle of her curly hair fell over him, smelling of the soap she used. Eden didn't push away, but tension lingered in her spine, even as the rest of her began to surrender.

Inch by softening inch.

A sucked-in breath....

The hardening of her nipples.

"It was one night, Colton." Her voice roughened, though he could scent her brewing desire. "I scratched your itch. You scratched mine. Let's not pretend it was anything else."

*Morning after regrets.* Wasn't that a punch to the throat? One he should have seen coming....

"If you think my itch is scratched, then you have another think coming." Johnny kissed his way across her shoulder. He could almost feel her slipping through his arms, like a dream that scattered upon waking. A part of him wanted to grab hold with both hands and never let her go.

"I want to fuck you again," he whispered.

Funny how she didn't protest the use of that particular word in this instant, as if it somehow distanced them.

"*Quiero hacerte el amor,*" he murmured, kissing the flickering beat of her pulse, suckling there. His right hand slid lower, cupping the weight of her breast. "*Quiero ahogarme en ti y nunca dejar ir.*"

Eden gasped as he nuzzled in against her neck, his erection pressing hotly into her bottom. "Colton!"

"Say my name," he breathed, sliding his roughened palm down the smooth slope of her waist and over the curve of her bottom. "I want to hear it on your lips."

"Johnny."

He urged her forward onto her hands and knees, his palm teasing the edge of her panties. Trailing his tongue down her spine, he felt her rock back into him, and then his questing fingers were delving beneath the edge of her panties and sliding down between the smooth curves of her ass.

Reaching for her wetness....

She was still slick with his cum from last night, and he had two fingers inside her before either of them realized it.

Johnny dragged the cotton aside, liking the way it made this feel a hundred times naughtier. Then his fingers found the soft pad of her clit and Eden shivered as he began to stroke her.

He dragged her panties down to her knees, revealing the heated flush of her pussy. Another taste. Too hard to get exactly where he wanted here.

He bit her ass, delving deep with his fingers and stroking her.

Nudging her thighs apart, he tugged her panties off her lower leg and then forced her hips wide. Eden's fists curled in the sheets as he nudged against her with the tip of his cock. Slipping in an inch, withdrawing. Another inch. Teasing her with slow, shallow thrusts until she was begging him for more.

Hissing out a breath, he drove himself slowly within her, feeling her body yield to him until he was seated deep inside her. Resting there.

"Fuck me," she whispered, reaching back to squeeze his hand.

That word again.

The muscles in his spine tensed at the sound of it on her lips. He loved that word—had dreamed of her saying that exact combination to him—but the second he heard it from her lips, he knew she kept saying it so this couldn't turn into something else.

"*Please*."

*Not like this.*

Spilling her onto her back, Johnny resettled between her thighs, grinding his cock against her clit. Resting on his forearms, he smiled as he met her dazed eyes. "Maybe."

She gripped his upper arms, rubbing up against him as he mercilessly ground against her. Johnny pulled back every time he felt that quiver run through her, and frustration danced through her eyes.

"Damn it. Are you trying to torture me?"

*Yes.* "If you want to get off," he whispered, "then you know the rules."

Her gaze sharpened.

"My name, Eden. I want to hear it on your tongue. Tell me how much you want me."

She turned her head away with a moan. "I *hate* you so much right now."

He took the hit, flinching a little. She didn't mean it. Not that way. But it echoed in his ears, a full body slam, and he finally had to admit to himself how much he cared about her response.

"Fine." Johnny withdrew, lifting up onto his forearms and knees, and Eden's eyes went wide as she realized he meant to roll off her.

"No!" She locked arms and legs around him, dragging him back against her. "I want you inside me so badly. Please, Johnny." Her voice softened. "Please."

Desperate to earn some sort of reaction from her, he captured her mouth slowly. Eden yielded, her body opening like a flower as he pressed inside her with a slow thrust.

He made love to her mouth, his hips moving against hers with slow, rocking thrusts. Sliding his fingers between hers, he pinned her hands to the furs, rubbing over her clit, grinding the base of his cock there until he could feel her body clamping around his.

She came with a soft sob, sinking her teeth into his shoulder. Pleading with him. *More. More.* But he wasn't going to break, not this time.

Johnny let himself feel every inch of her, imprinting her on his skin, his memories. He knew this would end—there was no future for them, not with the weight of the past between them and her brother looming like a stark, imposing figure in the background.

But, just this once, he let himself make love to her.

It would be very, very easy to want to stay here, in her arms, forever.

A hand locked over his shoulder and then Eden pushed him. "Over," she whispered.

"Still wanting to be on top, angel?" Arching his hips, he gave a taunting thrust, searching for her G-spot. "Maybe I'll let you, if...."

"If?" Eden tried not to react, but he could see her eyes losing their focus as her attention turned inward.

Another slow thrust. He felt her shiver, her body locking around him like a glove again.

"Say my name," he encouraged again, brushing his lips against her ear. "Tell me how much you love the feel of me inside you."

Her eyes narrowed.

He smiled and kissed the tip of her nose, then slowed his pace to something glacial, barely moving. *Say it, or I'll make this go so slow you'll be begging me....*

Eden bit her lip, arching against him, trying to push him faster.

He slid his hand up her hip, rocking into her with devilish slowness. Eden McClain might be as stubborn as a rock, but he was about to teach her just how patient he could be. He brought her hand to his mouth, kissing her fingertips, suckling one inside his wet mouth, and staring into her eyes.

Her lips parted. "You are an evil man," she breathed.

"I like being on top." He gave her another nudge, a tiny little rock of his hips. "I guess it depends how much you want to ride me, *mi alma.*"

Eden kissed his cheek. "I love the feel of you inside me, Johnny." She licked his ear, sucking the lobe into her mouth until the ache of it went right through him. "What do you want me to say? That I can't resist you? Even though I probably should? That last night was the best sex of my life? Well, then I'll say it. I can't resist you. I tried, but I wanted you too damned much."

Good enough. He felt breathless. Grabbing her by the hips, he rolled them both.

Straddling him, she sank down, taking his full length. Johnny's lip curled. Fuck, that felt good.

"Ride me, angel. Show me what you've got."

It was meant to be a game—he recognized that immediately.

She wanted to repay the torture, to drive him as crazy as he'd been making her, but what she didn't realize was that she'd already done that. Being with her, knowing this was most likely all he'd ever have of her was torture enough. If he'd wanted to punish himself, he couldn't have come up with a better means than tasting Eden, just once, before she walked out of his life.

He shoved himself upright, hugging her close so his mouth could find her tits as she rode him. Eden moaned, her hips canting against his.

He told her how much he wanted her, the Spanish tripping from his lips with ease the more he used it. It had been forever since he'd spoken the language, and it brought with it a feeling of belonging, a reminder of all he'd lost. A home. A family. Love, even if it was familial. He could hide here in the words, knowing she didn't understand him. Knowing he could reveal himself, splay his heart wide open, and she'd never, ever know.

They came together, his arms still around her and a kiss on his lips.

It was the best fucking moment of his life.

Eden wilted over his chest as he collapsed back, breaths shuddering as her pussy tightened around him in hot, tight pulses of aftershock.

Johnny slid a caressing hand up her spine, scraping her hair out of the way. He stroked it gently, enjoying the feel of it. Eden lived and breathed control, but her hair had a mind of its own. He buried his face in it, breathing in her soap, loving the fact they were still joined.  Closing his eyes in pleasure as her fingertips grazed the stubble on his cheek, as she unconsciously petted him.

He wanted to press her hand to his cheek and pretend this moment would last forever.

Slowly she lifted her head, lashes fluttering over dazed eyes. "I think I have a new appreciation for hate sex."

Like a dash of ice water to the face, the dream was broken.

Johnny froze.

"Mmm." That wasn't what had just happened, and they both knew it. "Speak for yourself."

She looked at him sharply.

Johnny sighed, pulling out of her and spilling her to the side. *Eden McClain, you sure know how to ruin a moment.* He rolled to the edge of the bed and hunted for his jeans, the sweat chilling on his skin as his heart rate began to return from the stratosphere.

Behind him, he could hear her sitting up.

He dragged his jeans on, feeling vulnerable. Buttoning them up, he turned to face her.

Eden looked like she'd been fucked every which way. Her hair hung in knotted tangles, her lips swollen and her eyes wide. She'd dragged the blankets up around her breasts as if his words had threatened her.

"What do you mean by that?" she whispered.

His heart skipped a beat. Facing down a ravaging pack of shadow cats was nothing compared to baring his heart.

Johnny knelt on the bed, pressing three fingers beneath her chin and lifting her face so she couldn't look away. "You've been haunting my dreams ever since I met you. What happened here last night.... It had nothing to do with hate, angel. Call it that if it makes this easier, but you should know, what I feel for you is nowhere near hate. Not at all."

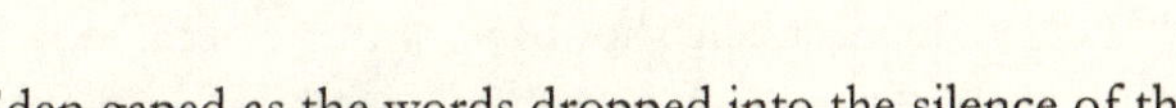

Eden gaped as the words dropped into the silence of the room like a bomb detonating. "*What?*"

Morning Colton was a sight for sore eyes. All mussed hair, dark eyes crinkled with relaxation and seductive good humor. Fucking into her so slowly this morning, that perhaps fucking wasn't the right term for it at all. His thumb stroked her jaw, and she had the horrible certainty she was about to lean into his touch.

"You heard me," he whispered.

And oh, shit, but she was somehow doing *this* with Johnny Colton.

Eden slid toward the edge of the bed, needing clothes. Something to shield herself. Anything. "I heard you," she admitted, "but...."

Her mind went blank.

*Where the hell was her tank?*

She snatched it off the floor, swinging it over her head and managing to get it on beneath the protective shield of the blanket. Her heart pounded like last night's drums, but her mind was an angry buzzing of *oh, shit.*

She needed a moment to recover—because she'd *never* expected this.

*Didn't you?*

*I mean, the guy's carrying around your letters. It's not because he needs kindling.*

"I heard you," she repeated, the second she had her tank on. Suddenly she could think again, even if her inner alarm bells were still blaring *abort*. "I just think now's not a really great time—"

"Let's be honest," he shot back, with a cynical look in his dark eyes. "Never's going to be a really great time for this conversation judging by the look on your face."

Never sounded like an excellent idea.

"Good point. So how about we skip it? We should get dressed," she said, wincing a little as she dragged her jeans up her bruised thighs. No pretending it hadn't happened; she was dripping with his cum and needed to wash. "We need to get going."

Start packing for the trip.

Pretend this never happened.

"Chicken shit," he said, his face shuttering as she managed to do her fly up, and reached for her boots.

"Colton—"

"It's fine," he snapped, raking a frustrated hand through his hair. "Probably not the best time to start this. I get it. Itch scratched and all. Guess I'm good for something. Good enough to fuck. Good enough to get you where you need to be."

Anger fired in her chest. Damn it, she had no right to feel guilty. "You're not the only one who's spent all those years feeling haunted by what happened. You said you were sorry and you didn't want to hurt me, but it doesn't change the damned fact you did." Her voice roughened. "I might be willing to forgive you, but I don't even know what He-Who-Shall-Not-Be-Named did to you. Or why you fell in line with him."

How could she let herself accept what had happened between them last night wasn't just stress and attraction?

Because if she did....

*You just slept with the guy who nearly destroyed your brother.*

Eden flinched.

"Yeah, right. You want me to bare my soul? Consider it bared," Colton snapped. He jerked the curtain open and held it for her. "Arik said there are natural springs along the corridor if you want to wash up. First turn on your left. Go and wash my fucking scent off your skin. It will make it easier to forget what happened."

Eden stared at the hard line of his jaw.

Was that hurt she heard echoing in his voice?

Couldn't be. This was Johnny Colton.

But he sounded pissed enough that—

"You're coming with me?" she asked in a small voice.

Silence.

Her heart started pounding a little faster. She couldn't do this without him, even if the thought of continuing on with him alone suddenly felt like she was walking into a minefield blindfolded.

"Someone has to keep you from getting killed." His lips thinned. "And I made a promise. Contrary to popular opinion, I don't break my word once I give it."

She grabbed her pack, and then paused in the doorway, uncertain why she didn't feel more relieved at the thought.

*Because he made it clear this isn't the end of it....*

But it had to be.

How could there be anything more between them?

Adam loomed like a silent force over her shoulder; he'd never allow it. And as much as she wanted to say she could ever trust Colton with her heart, Eden didn't know if that was possible. Forgiveness was one thing, but actively handing him her heart on a platter?

She'd locked it away after Colton betrayed her, and never, ever let herself give it again.

Except....

It would be very easy to turn Johnny Colton into an addiction she never wanted to quit.

Far too easy to start falling for that dangerous smile, and the way he whispered words she didn't know in her ear as he thrust into her.

Because while she might have no clue what he'd been saying, the look in his eyes and the tone of his words told a complete story.

And when she'd been in his arms, for a second she'd forgotten everything that lay between them.

Forgotten all the reasons she shouldn't be doing this....

"I don't know what you want from me, but if it's anything more than what happened here last night, then I don't think I can give it to you," she whispered and didn't know who she meant those words for. "I need to keep my head, keep my focus—"

"Didn't know I was messing with your head." He crossed his arms over his broad chest, and she tried to keep her gaze from dropping to the muscled flex of his pectorals.

"You're not."

"Then what's the problem? I'm not getting to you, Eden. There's nothing between us except mutual attraction. Last night didn't mean a damned thing. But here's what I can't understand—if it was just a fuck, then there's no reason we can't continue fucking, is there?"

"You know I don't like that language—"

He took a step closer, trapping her in the doorway with the curtain draped over one arm. "What do you want me to call it? You're the one dictating the terms and telling me what this is—and isn't. So tell me.... What would you prefer to call what happened here last night?"

His eyes dared her.

Eden took a step through the curtain, nearly tripping over her feet.

"It's not—We shouldn't complicate things," she blurted. "Last night happened. Nothing we can do about that. But if we continue on together, then there need to be rules. Once we cross into Confederacy territory, it's going to get dangerous." Her words firmed as she found safety in clear, rational statements. "One of us will need to be on watch at night. No more sleeping together. No kissing. No touching—"

"Understood." Colton's dark eyes remained cool and untouchable. "Can't afford to forget ourselves, can we?"

She ignored that. "Right."

He looked disappointed somehow, as he pushed away from her.

"Fine. Go check on Cole so we can get going. We'll discuss this later. Both of us have sore heads this morning. It's probably not the time to go into this."

Then he let the curtain fall shut in her face, his dark form moving behind it.

Eden's body ached in places that hadn't felt a man's touch in years.

An overprotective brother and a narrowing pool of potential hookups meant her bed had seen limited action. It had never really bothered her—she had far too much work to do, and she'd given up on finding good sex after a few lackluster encounters—but the bruises on her skin and the tenderness between her thighs this morning were a taunt.

Because suddenly she knew what good sex was all about.

Johnny Colton fucked as though he wanted to consume her. In the heat of the moment, she'd given in to the tension between them, and now she could never forget it.

And look where that had landed her....

What the hell did he want from her? Now she had some distance from him, she'd thought it would have been easier to work her way through the muddle in her head, but she was a mess of contradictory thoughts and feelings.

*What do you want me to call it?*

*I don't bloody well know!*

Nnedi looked up as Eden burst into the infirmary. Eden skidded to a halt and realized she hadn't even knocked. Hadn't even been keeping an eye on her surroundings at all.

Colton could do that to her.

"Morning," she said, somewhat warily.

One of Nnedi's eyebrows arched and the woman smiled faintly. "You look... refreshed."

*Oh, Jesus.* She knew. Eden had scrubbed every inch of Johnny Colton off her body in the heated pools, but she could feel his hands on her skin still. Worse. The argument between them was burned into her mind. "What the hell was in that kaga?"

Nnedi threw her head back and laughed. "It's an enervative. A rush of blood. Helps a warg's stamina."

"So I noticed." She felt like she had the hangover from hell. Sighting a jug of water on the stand beside CJ's bed, she poured herself a glass.

"Good night?" Nnedi's eyes sparkled.

Eden drained the glass. *Understatement.* "The kind of night I'm not going to forget in a hurry, and let's just leave it at that."

"Guess you finally bagged your man."

Eden looked up sharply.

"You didn't wear his scent on your skin when you arrived," Nnedi said, clearly interpreting the look on her face. "It was clear you two hadn't been sharing a bed for a while. It's why some of the males around here were testing his claim."

Eden eased onto the edge of CJ's bed, smoothing a hand over his forehead to test his temperature. "We kind of haven't shared a bed before."

"Argument?" Nnedi asked gruffly as if thinking of her own most likely cold bed.

"No. It's... a long story. We're not together."

"Looked like you were together last night." Nnedi snorted. "Smells like you're together this morning."

"It's complicated." This morning only made matters worse. What had he been whispering in her ear in Spanish? Because the look in his eyes wasn't just *let's have fun. Let's fuck, Eden.* No, there'd been a glint of possession there she hadn't quite known how to interpret.

*Say my name....*

She closed her eyes. Forced herself to think. "We're not in a position to be examining the precise implications of this. We need to get to Cortez City, Nnedi. Any chances your alpha is going to let us go this morning?"

Nnedi started picking up discarded bandages. "He's not *my* alpha." Her voice lowered. "Not anymore. And he's curious about Colton. Lincoln's good in the ring, so I daresay Arik's wondering just how good your man is."

"He's not a threat," she pointed out. "We're leaving."

Without CJ. Eden brushed her hand over his forehead. His lashes stirred, but he didn't wake.

Eden took CJ's wrist and felt for his pulse. Nice and steady. She reached for his forehead again, but it was hard to tell whether his temperature was high or whether that was simply the nature of the beast within him. The full moon was only days away, and that always set wargs on edge.

A thick mud poultice covered his wound.

Eden's throat felt thick with guilt. "I didn't even notice," she said quietly. "It was barely a scratch. Colton's wounds were far worse."

"He'll heal," Nnedi promised.

That wasn't the point.

Rage flared, hot and potent. Maybe she was tired, but she had the sudden urge to break something. "I'm a healer. I should have noticed CJ had a fever. I should have realized Colton was bleeding the other day. I've been so distracted of late. Everywhere I look someone wants a damned piece of me."

The plague, the council, lack of sleep, and then Lily....

And worse.... "I should have suspected there was something wrong when Miles Wentworth missed two meetings. He'd been sitting near that mine for six months, trying to work out a trade agreement with us, and all of a sudden he just vanishes? Gives in? I thought he was showing me how pissed off he was."

That bastard knew what was coming for them, and he hadn't even bothered to warn them. Damn it. She'd had dinner with him and he'd made his interest in her quite clear. She'd even entertained the thought of obliging him—wasn't like her other options had been overwhelming at that point, and while something about his smile set her on edge, he'd also been charming enough. The urge had just never been strong enough.

Despite the fact Riley had pointed out—loudly—it had been a long, long time without a man to warm her bed.

*Until last night....*

Nope. She shied away from those thoughts immediately.

"You're only human, Eden. You can't foresee a plague. And Wentworth's Confederacy. They don't consider anyone outside their walls to be worth a damn thing."

"He could have warned me." If there was anything she hated more than feeling powerless, it was betrayal.

"Maybe he was hoping the plague would wipe out your settlement and then he'd have exactly what he wanted without having to give you a damned thing—or wait for your decision."

Eden's heart beat a little swifter. It was an outrageous thought. She couldn't even conceive of.... No. Wentworth had met her people, walked among them and shaken their hands, smiling his stark white smile with his perfect teeth.

*But,* said a dark little whisper in her heart.

*"I have quotas to meet,"* Wentworth had said to her in their final meeting, his lips pulling back off his teeth in a sign of frustration for just one second. *"I'm sorry, Miss McClain, but I have a little bit of pressure on me back home to close this deal, or start looking elsewhere. The settlement of Haven has access to another mine. Granted, it's miles to the north and would need more work to make the conditions safe, but I* have *to give my father something."*

"You okay?" Nnedi asked.

"I need to get to Cortez City as soon as possible," she said, her ears still ringing a bit from the shock Nnedi's words had caused. She needed to know the truth—had Miles Wentworth known the plague was about to hit?

Or... had he been involved in spreading it?

It was a manufactured biological weapon, after all, one supposed to be locked away in a sterile lab....

These things didn't just escape.

She felt cold all the way through. "Do you think you could look after CJ for me? At least until he's better? I hate leaving him behind, but surely he'll understand when the fever breaks."

After all, whatever it takes....

CJ knew that. He'd tell her to keep going, to try and save Lily.

"He'll be safe here. I'll see to his care. I promise I'll—" Nnedi's head turned toward the door.

Someone knocked.

"Come in," Eden called, before realizing this wasn't her infirmary.

A huge form lingered in the doorway, his tawny hair bound back in a topknot. Eden's breath washed out of her as she laid eyes on the hulking alpha of Shadow Rock, and Nnedi stiffened.

"A word, my second?" Arik asked, hovering beneath the lintel as if didn't dare enter the room.

"I'm not your second," Nnedi replied tightly. "I told you that last night. If you can't trust me to lead in your absence, then there is no point in me wearing your claw."

Just what Eden needed—to be caught up in a marriage dispute. She glanced toward the door. "I'll just...."

"I'd like to speak to you too."

*You... do?*

"This plague," Arik said to her, "how virulent is it?"

"I don't know, but I suspect it will prove highly contagious. Henry Chin said it was manufactured by the Confederacy as a bio-weapon, so I daresay it's meant to wipe out thousands."

Underneath his tan, he paled slightly. "And you think you can find a cure in Cortez City."

"Yes."

"You'll never get inside the city." Arik took a hesitant step through the door, earning a scowl from Nnedi.

"So you said."

"The walls are too high and all the gates heavily guarded. They have barcode scanners to make sure you belong to the Confederacy, and if you don't have a barcode tattoo they won't let you through. They don't like outsiders coming in. Don't want to risk one of them getting loose and telling their little sheep about the truth of the world outside their walls."

"We have to try," she protested.

"I know. Which is why Lincoln and I are going with you."

A second warg filled the doorway, scowling at her with his arms crossed over his chest. He still had a black eye, but no other sign that Colton had knocked him out.

"Wait, what?" Eden gaped.

"You can't leave the pack," Nnedi said abruptly. "Who will lead? Who will—"

"My second will lead," Arik replied, turning that intense focus upon his wife. "I can get Eden and her man inside Cortez. There's a way in and out, though nobody else knows of it, and it won't be fun.

"Shadow Rock is not wholly comprised of wargs," he murmured, returning his attention to Eden. "There are people here who choose not to accept the gift, and the children are vulnerable until they are turned. If I don't help you, then this plague might touch us, even here."

Nnedi caught his arm. "You can't go back!"

*Back?*

Arik's head bowed, and he breathed in his wife's scent, shifting on his feet. "I'm the only one who can get her inside Cortez, Nnedi. You want me to prove I trust you? You want me to prove you should be wearing this"— he dragged the necklace Nnedi had cast aside out of his pocket—"then you need to let me do this. Let me make amends. Let me protect our pack. Let me prove you have my heart, my trust, my everything."

Holding out Nnedi's hand, he put the necklace on her pale palm and closed her brown fingers over it.

"If you are captured—"

"Then I'll face nothing more than what Eden's man will face," he murmured.

The pair of them stared at each other.

"What Colton will face...?" Eden repeated, her eyes narrowing. "What will Colton face if we enter Cortez?"

Gold-bronze eyes turned on her. "The Confederacy leashes their wargs, Eden. If they get their hands on him, they'll lock him away in one of their military prisons and never let him out. Or they'll kill him."

# sixteen

Everything was packed, and he'd resupplied with Shadow Rock's generosity. Johnny looked around the small room he'd shared with Eden. Not a sign of them remained behind, only their scent.

It felt weird, staring at the empty room. Everything had changed between him and Eden in the space of a single night, and yet there was no visible evidence of it. Only a thickening feeling in his throat, a pressure behind his ribs.

Eden was getting to him.

*Getting?* Asked a sarcastic part of him he tended to think of as his inner asshole. It liked to throw truth bombs in his face.

*Fine. Gotten.* Johnny rubbed his chest. *You are so fucked, Johnny-boy.*

Because it was clear she didn't feel the same way.

What the hell had he been thinking? That they could ever have something between them? That there was any sort of future between them after they'd gotten their hands on this cure?

He was half tempted to ask Arik what was in that fucking *kaga*, because he'd forgotten for a second who he was.

How many times did he have to reach out, only to have the brutal truth thrown in his face?

Years of living on Cane's leash had taught him not to yearn for anything for himself, or else Cane would destroy it. The one time he'd given into his aching loneliness, he'd brought hell down upon Eden, and torn her life apart.

And then he'd finally managed to break Cane's hold on him for just long enough to put a bullet in the bastard's head.

In the months following Cane's death, he'd had this static sort of buzzing in his head, as he tried to put himself back together. For the first time in his life, there'd been no consequences for his actions. No reason not to make his own way, and do what he damned well wanted.

He'd searched for his mother, but by then it was too late. There was no sign of her, and nothing but ashes where their homestead had been. The Coltons kept to themselves, and nobody he spoke to in the nearby towns even knew who he was talking about.

He'd found a town. Bitter River. He'd walked in out of the darkness to find the residents celebrating a local marriage. People. Laughter. Dancing. A welcome he hadn't expected to find. He'd stayed one night. Turned it into two. Then a week. Started thinking maybe he could find a place to settle, when one of the local widows rested a hand on his shoulder one night and smiled at him as she offered him a drink.

And then he realized the truth when he woke from a drugged stupor to find himself in a cage. He didn't belong anywhere. Bitter River had sold him out to fucking slavers to keep them off their own backs.

He should know better than to want more from Eden.

All he'd end up doing was get his fingers burned again.

Or worse.

*I don't know what you want from me, but if it's anything more than what happened here last night, then I don't think I can give it to you...*

*Yeah. Bullet to the chest right there.* At least she was fucking upfront about it, but he didn't understand why he couldn't simply bury the faint nudge of hope inside him.

Brisk footsteps echoed along the stone floors outside. He'd recognize that determined stride anywhere, and his chest hitched as he girded himself. It had been an hour since he'd seen Eden and he'd managed to pull himself back together, but the second he heard her coming, the warg within started scraping its claws along the inside of his skin.

Johnny hauled his pack over his shoulders, settling it into position. Grabbing Eden's pack off the floor, he'd started toward the door when she burst through the flimsy curtain, her curls tangled in a ponytail and her face flushed with color.

"I can't let you do this," she blurted, pushing a hand against his chest.

He captured her hand against his chest, a little shocked she was touching him after what she'd said earlier. "Do what?"

"I've been speaking to Arik and Lincoln about the Confederacy." Eden looked up, her dark lashes framing the intense green of her eyes. "You can't come with me to Cortez City."

*What the actual fuck?*

"Like hell I can't." Fear flooded through him. "Jesus, Eden. You're not walking in there alone. You need someone to watch your back. Someone to make sure—"

"Arik and Lincoln are coming with me," she said bluntly. "Arik's been inside Cortez before, he can get me inside again. He said he knows a man who might be able to help me access what's left of the Radisson-Meyers Syndicate laboratories. That's where the cure is."

*What?*

He knew he'd pushed her earlier, but to do this....

"No," he said sharply. "I'm not going to allow you to walk into a place like that without protection."

"I'll have protection."

"Two strange wargs who may or may not be allies?"

"Not the first time I've trusted a stranger who may or may not be an ally." She tipped her chin up stubbornly.

Johnny's eyes narrowed, his voice coming out thick and heated. "I wasn't a stranger. Our lives have been intertwined for years. Why? Is this about last night?"

*This morning?*

"No. It's got nothing to do with last night." She looked away, two spots of color blooming in her cheeks. "It's not safe for a warg to enter the city."

That took him aback. Not safe? Was she actually worried about him? What did that mean?

Was there a chance she felt more for him than she claimed?

"Pretty sure you're planning on entering with two of them at your sides."

*And I'm calling bullshit on this having nothing to do with what happened between us.*

"Arik knows the city," she replied, her voice firming. "He knows what he's walking into."

"And I don't?"

She wrapped her arms around her middle. "You've helped me more than you could possibly know. You don't owe me anything anymore. Consider your debt repaid—"

"Like fuck," Johnny snapped. She wasn't just going to pat him on the shoulder and send him on his way like a good little boy. "You don't want me there because of what happened between us? Fine. I'll keep my hands to myself. I won't push you, angel. I know you've got a lot on your mind, and you're not ready to deal with us—"

"There is no us."

He breathed out. Slowly. She was under a lot of pressure. They hadn't even come close to broaching the elephant in the room. And this was the worst possible time to deny her statement. Still.... Maybe it was finally time to fight for the one damned thing he wanted in this world? "There's something between us, Eden, whether you admit it or not, but I understand this isn't the time. I'll shelve that discussion, but you need to know it's going to be revisited. One day."

She tipped her chin up stubbornly.

"As for me accompanying you? That isn't your decision to make."

"I—"

"You can't control everything, damn it. Stripping me of the ability to make this choice? That's bullshit." He stabbed a finger in the air toward her. "And you wouldn't like it if I did it to you. Pretty sure you'd be branding it under 'male territorial bullshit' or something. Give me one damned good reason to even consider this."

"I don't want to see you get hurt! If you're captured the Confederacy will put a shock collar on you, and lock you away in one of their facilities—they call them training facilities. That's where they mold their wargs into good little soldiers, and don't pretend you don't know exactly what I'm talking about. I heard everything you said that night to CJ. They'll hurt you, and it will be my fault. I should never have asked you to come."

It all gushed forth from her lips like blood from an arterial wound, and for a second he had no idea what to do. *My fault....* They'd been skirting around the Bartholomew Cane issue for days as though it didn't exist, but he'd managed to glean enough from her to realize it affected her to this day.

She blamed herself for what happened to her brother.

She worried for the people she might not be able to save from the plague.

And now she was looking at him as though she didn't want to add him to the list of people she hadn't been able to save.

"Well, you didn't exactly *ask* me to come. I seem to recall blackmail *and* a shitty attempt at seduction," he joked, the words completely bypassing his brain and leaping from his mouth before he could catch them.

The second they hovered in the air, he had this sensation, like the ground dropped out from beneath his feet. *Uh-oh.*

Eden reared back, her eyes shocked and wide, and Johnny saw utter devastation flash through her eyes, as if he'd just confirmed every fear she had. He had no fucking idea what to do, how to help, how to....

*Touch her, you idiot.*

Johnny grabbed her by the shoulders, squeezing gently. "Eden." His voice roughened. "Breathe."

"I am breathing." She dug the heels of her palms into her eyes as if to hide from whatever she'd seen when he'd said it.

Tremors wracked her. Not massive, Eden-shattering tremors, but a shiver that shook through her from head to toe, as if her lungs were pulsing, trying to suck in air, but she was too afraid to let herself, just in case a sob escaped.

"I didn't mean it like that," he murmured, easing her into his arms. Every inch of her was tight and restrained, and she wrapped her arms around herself as if she didn't want to wrap them around him.

*Because you're an utter dick....*

"It just came out. I wasn't thinking." The creeping lassitude of his omega half began to assert itself, but for the first time in years it wasn't helping him.

Or her.

"You know what this life is like, angel. I could have died a hundred times in the past. I've come damned close to it at times. If something happens to me, it's because I put my own feet on this path. You're not responsible for me."

*Not yet, anyway.*

*Maybe never.*

But her fear softened the argument they'd had earlier because she wouldn't be so bloody upset if she didn't give a damn, would she?

That cursed nugget of hope stirred in his chest.

Johnny stroked her hair. It was the thing he adored most. And as he stroked, he felt her begin to soften in his arms, her face pressed firmly into his chest.

More than anything that had happened between them last night, this felt like they both took a dangerous step forward into... whatever the hell was building between them.

"Want to tell me what's bothering you? What flashed through your mind when I said that?"

"Is it so inconceivable I might actually *not* want to see you end up in a Confederacy prison?" A little bit of snap came back into her voice.

*That's the spirit.*

Eden McClain with her eyes blazing and her hands on her hips was a force to be reckoned with.

He didn't like it when the determination in her eyes was replaced with something sad.

"You're worried about me," he repeated, just to make sure he'd gotten the facts right. "You don't want me to come because you're worried the Confederacy will get their hands on me?"

"They break wargs. Arik's been there. He said they shock them, again and again. Use drugs to confuse them. Beat them down. Torture."

"Yeah," his voice thickened. "I know what they do. You want to know the truth? It scares the fuck out of me. Because I've been there. I've broken before. I know... I know what could happen." His gaze focused on her face, thumbs tracing the array of freckles that splayed lightly across her cheeks, as he gave her a little piece of the Cane puzzle. "You know what scares me more? The idea of you walking into that trap without me. Of not being able to protect you. Not knowing what's happening to you. Maybe never seeing you again.... I can't do that."

Eden looked up, misery written across her face. "I spent nearly ten years wearing guilt over Adam on my shoulders. I don't want.... If anything happened to you, and it was my fault.... You're right. I blackmailed you into coming."

"Trust me, darlin'." He stroked his fingers down the back of her neck. "You couldn't have forced me if you'd tried. I came because I couldn't stay away—"

"Because *I* insisted."

"Because I couldn't let you cross the Great Divide by yourself, no matter how much I tried to talk myself into it. You're not the only one who knows what guilt feels like. I owed it to you to try and make amends." He felt a shiver run through her as he turned his hand, so his thumb rasped against the soft skin just behind her ear. "I'm a fully grown adult, Eden. I made a choice to escort you and whatever happens, that's on me. Stop trying to take on the weight of the world. I get it. I know why you're doing it. I—"

"You *don't* get it. Adam had a silver bullet in his pocket. He kept it with him all the time, just in case...."

Johnny's fingertips stilled on her skin, hearing the distress in her voice. "Did he use it?"

"What?" She looked up. "*No.*"

"Maybe your brother wasn't carrying it 'just in case.' Maybe it was something he could put his hand around, as a reminder, when times were grim and the warg was threatening to push its way out of his skin. Maybe it helped him breathe a little easier, knowing it was there. And Bart Cane turned Adam into a warg before he even sent me to fetch you that night. All he wanted from you was leverage to force Adam to lure Luc Wade into the same trap. You never had anything to do with what happened to your brother, Eden. It was a done deal by that stage. Say it."

"I...."

"Never had anything to do with Adam being forcibly turned into a warg."

"I never... had anything to do with Adam being turned," she mumbled.

It would have to do.

"And if something bad happens to me, it's not your fault."

She looked up mutinously.

Johnny pressed a finger to her lips. "It won't be your fault. Say it."

"It won't be my fault—"

He kissed her, stealing the words from her lips. No tongue this time, just a gentle exploration. Eden's hand softened on his chest, her lips tilting to his, and a soft moan coming from her—

"No." Eden broke away, resting her forehead against his chest.

"Sorry. I just broke one of your rules, but you broke one first. You touched me."

"You are not distracting me like this."

He couldn't help smiling, just a little. *Oh, angel.* This morning he'd wondered if there'd been anything more between them than sex on her behalf. Her confession seemed to unknot some of the tension within him.

*It's not just me.*

"I don't need to distract you. The decision's made. I'm coming with you."

Eden breathed out a shaky laugh. "Three alpha wargs in a high-pressure situation? I just know this is going to go well."

"Depends on who's in charge."

"Me," she said, drawing away from him. "I'm in charge. And if anyone argues they can go home."

"Got it."

"And the rules stay the same," she blurted. "No kissing. No... Nothing else."

He stared at her for a long time. She'd kissed him back. He could afford to give her a little bit of space.

"Your rules. Which mean, if you ever want to break them, I'm down for that. Your choice."

Eden swallowed. "Okay."

She turned to leave, but he grabbed her waist before she could take a step.

"All I want in return is to know one thing.... When you agreed to have hate sex with me, was that really how you felt?"

Eden bit her lip. Hesitated. Finally gave in. "I don't hate you."

"Not even a little bit?" He leaned closer.

She shook her head. Whispered, "Not at all. I was angry with you. Or not at you. Just angry. I don't know. And you've been pushing my buttons for days. I don't know what's going on in my head. With you."

*Yeah, I get it.*

Seemed to be the sum total of his feelings at the moment too.

"Good." He tilted her chin up. "It was angry, messy, exploding volcanoes of emotion sex, but it wasn't hate sex. And your buttons need to be pushed every now and then."

Eden gripped both of his wrists, her eyes lifting to his. "That's why you were shitty this morning, isn't it?"

"I wasn't shitty."

She arched a brow.

His breath exploded out of him. "Fine. I was a little pissed. Best night of my life, and you practically slapped me on the ass and said, *thanks for the good times, but no thanks.*"

"Did you want me to say something else?" she asked slowly and lifted her gaze to his.

Johnny stopped breathing. It was one thing to be pissed with the way she'd used his body to scratch an itch, another to actually be the one to put his heart on the line.

But he was tired of playing the lone wolf.

"Yes," he said simply.

Her mouth parted, her eyes widening.

"Later, Eden," he murmured. "You and I have a lot to discuss, but I think we need to get our heads in the game. We're going to cross into confederacy territory today and go get your plague cure. You and I. Whatever it takes, Eden."

Eden looked like she was trying to read between the lines, but she finally nodded. "Whatever it takes."

# seventeen

No kissing. No touching. No sex.

The perfect set of rules to keep things strictly business between them as they made their way out of the Great Divide.

Why then, did Eden feel like the ground had just dropped out from under her feet?

She could no longer pretend Colton wasn't interested in her. They'd gone from mortal enemies to reluctant allies, to... something else... in the space of a week.

It was defining that "something else" that left her thoughts scrambling and made her feel breathless. Because she panicked every damned time she thought about it.

Even if he didn't push her, as he'd promised. No, she was the one pushing herself, going over everything that had happened in Shadow Rock, as if to try and make sense of it all. Colton's manners remained perfectly polite.

Just distant.

And if she was being honest with herself, she didn't like the space between them.

She kind of missed the way he'd point things out in the distance, and tell her where they were. Or capture a lizard scuttling through the rocks to show her, opening her eyes to a new world she'd never truly noticed. For all the not talking they'd done in the first couple of days, she was starting to realize he'd always been at her side as if some strange force drew them together even when she'd been holding him at a distance.

He was patient as he helped her up the escarpment. Didn't offer her a hand—as per her no touching rule, he'd pointed out with a grin—but he stayed with her every step of the cursed journey, calling a water stop every time her body started flagging. The mess he left her mind in was a great distraction for the climb, except she was no closer to solving the problem by the time they'd reached the top.

*Maybe you need to stop thinking about this like a mathematical equation that has a solution,* said a snide little voice inside her head. *You like him. You're attracted to him. And it scares the hell out of you.*

"Nearly there," Johnny muttered, as she paused near the top of the escarpment.

"You keep saying that," she panted, bending over to rest her hands on her thighs. "And every time we climb the next cliff, there's another one behind it."

"Here, let me take your pack," he said, reaching for the straps.

"No. It's okay." Eden shot up ramrod straight, clinging to the straps. "I can do this."

"Fine, Miss Independence." He backed away, hands in the air, a frustrated look on his face. "Don't say I didn't offer."

She stared after him as he bounded up the next slope, leaving her behind. The tight line of his shoulders spoke volumes.

Eden sighed.

So far, nobody had killed each other, though they'd come close this morning when Arik and Johnny had a fricking death-staring match over who would go first up the escarpment.

Apparently alpha wargs had a natural hierarchy, worked out through pheromones, swagger, eye contact, and probably a hundred other little things she didn't even notice.

Apparently, Arik and Johnny hadn't yet managed to work out who was at the top of the food chain.

"Awkward," Lincoln said, bringing up the rear. "What's going on between you two?"

Despite the fact he'd forced Johnny into a death match, Lincoln was swiftly becoming the easygoing member of the group. Arik was his older brother, hence Arik was above him on the invisible chain of command; Johnny had kicked his ass in the ring, hence Johnny was above him.

He found it all highly amusing.

She was merely getting a headache from all the testosterone.

"Nothing," she grumbled, staggering after Johnny.

"Oh yeah, looks like a whole lot of nothing," he said. "Kind of like Arik and Nnedi this morning. That was a lot of nothing too."

Arik had given his wife a hard kiss on the mouth before they left, and while she hadn't pushed him away, Nnedi also hadn't been wearing his claw.

"That's completely different," Eden snapped. "Your brother and Nnedi are married."

*Johnny and I are....*

*Still to be determined.*

"Currently that definition's a little rocky," Lincoln replied, with a shrug. "My people have simple rules. If you take a man's claw, then you accept his suit. If you discard his claw, then you're a free woman. Hence why Arik has a bug up his ass today."

"You mean, he isn't normally this surly and dictatorial?"

"Ehh." Lincoln held his hand out flat, then wiggled it this way and that. "Okay, you've got me there. He's being his usual bossy self. But he's a little snappier than usual. Arik used to have a sense of humor, before...."

"Before?"

Lincoln winced. "Not really my place to say. Before the Confederacy got their hands on him. Let's just leave it at that."

She looked at him sharply.

He'd challenged Johnny to a death match. She was finding it really hard to hate him, however, because now they'd fought it was as though there'd never been an issue between them, in Lincoln's eyes.

*They're not human,* she told herself. *Their culture and rules were completely alien to her.*

"It doesn't help that you're an unattached female, who Colton's clearly trying to lay claim to. Arik's not interested, but he's being forced to yield to Colton on small matters, so it doesn't look like he's a threat. He's not used to yielding on anything."

"Really?" she drawled, a bite of acid in her voice. "This has all got to do with some Neanderthal-style chest-beating?"

Lincoln shot her a long look, then grinned. "I think I know why Nnedi likes you." The smile died. "It's not that simple. We've spent years trying to still the rage, and choke down the warg when it rises within us. There are rules we obey, as pack, which makes everything easier. Important rules. One warg is the Alpha. Every warg beneath him slots into a certain hierarchy. You either obey the ones above you, or you fight for the right to take their place. If you're interested in a female, then you lay claim. If she accepts you, then you mate. If she doesn't, then you walk away and you don't look back. This is the way of pack, so the madness and rage doesn't tear us apart. It's not just a set of rules we made for the fun of it, but a way of life, Eden. We're not human. We never will be. And we can't afford to give into our emotions."

He shot her a long slow look. "Colton and Arik are so equal, it's hard for me to see who fits where. And you're the one saying you're in charge, but you're not a warg. Arik's trying. Give him that. He's pigheaded and domineering, but he knows he messed up. He's trying to right wrongs. He's trying to yield to you and Colton, even as all his instincts are screaming at him to take over this little expedition. It's not as easy as you think it is. The full moon's out tonight too, which makes everything just that little bit harder. And not just for Arik."

She glanced ahead, to where Colton strode up the switchback.

"His woman just rejected his help," Lincoln added, a little quieter. "We can all sense it, and it's igniting the tension. Maybe if you don't want him, then you should tell him. Make it clear to him there is nothing between you and never will be."

The words gave her a queasy feeling deep inside.

"I said... no kissing," she muttered. "Or anything else."

"Ah," he breathed. "You told him you had no feelings for him, and there was nothing between you, and he should move on?"

"I said...." Her voice trailed off.

*I said... I didn't know.*

*And he said we'd talk.*

Ahead of them, Colton paused at the top, looking back at them. For a second their eyes met, and her stupid heart started beating a little faster. Then his gaze shifted to Lincoln, his lips thinned, and he turned away from them, vanishing over the lip of the horizon.

"I know this isn't my place to say this," Lincoln said softly, "but you should be clear about your intentions. He has hope, Eden. Hope that something might be forming between the two of you. I can see it every time he looks at you as if you're his whole world."

"He looks at me like I'm his world?" she blurted.

"We have a saying in Shadow Rock," he said. "*'When you know she's the one, not even the moon can tear your eyes from her.'* So yes. He looks at you like you're the moon in the sky, and that is saying something, for a warg."

"It's complicated."

"Do you want him or not?"

He didn't understand. "There's so much about us you don't know."

"Do you *want* him or not?" Lincoln repeated.

"I don't want to be hurt," she snapped.

"None of us want to be hurt. It's a risk, to be sure. But what's your other option? Bury your heart until you can pretend it doesn't exist? What's waiting for you back home? Apart from the people you want to save?"

She nearly missed her next step.

Because the answer was clear.

Not a damned thing.

Reaching the top of the escarpment left them standing in a foreign world. A forest of bleached white timbers stretched out before them for miles, looking like the crucified remains of twisted skeletons. The wood was rotting and nothing grew there. Ghost forests, Arik told them, before warning them to keep an eye out for mutos.

Eden's calves ached from the mountain of switchbacks they'd just climbed, but she resolutely set her pack and sucked in a deep breath. She could do this.

They weren't quite in a Dead Zone, where the radiation poisoned the ground, but close enough to come into contact with those poor souls whose bodies had been warped and twisted, the mutations handed down genetically from when the nuclear reactors burned down during the Darkening. The Confederacy enforcers hunted mutos down when they saw them and put them out of their misery, but there were enough of them around to make passing through the forest dangerous, according to Arik.

Wasn't much to eat here, after all, apart from unwary travelers.

"Lincoln and I will scout ahead," Arik shot over his shoulder, as the pair of wargs slipped into the trees.

"You do that," Johnny muttered.

And suddenly she realized she was alone with him, with Lincoln's earlier words echoing in her ears.

Johnny hauled out his battered flask. He'd managed to refill it in Shadow Rock. "You need a rest?" he asked, in a gruff voice.

She could read the tension in him now as if Lincoln's words opened her eyes to an entirely new world. Johnny didn't look at her. Just tipped the flask to his lips.

"I'm okay," she said quietly, dumping her pack off her back and reaching for her water flask. Sweat wet her back where the pack had rested, and she suddenly felt so weightless she suspected she could almost float away.

A part of her wished she could just float away.

"What were you and Lincoln talking about?" he asked, as she drank.

She almost spilt water all over herself. "What?"

He repacked his flask as if it suddenly held all his attention. "He seemed to have a lot to say."

"He was just... explaining a few things about warg life."

Dark eyes flickered up.

"About Arik trying to rein in his dominant side, and you and Arik being on a par on the hierarchy, and how that's causing problems here."

Johnny scowled. "It's not going to be a problem. Arik knows the terrain, so he can lead. It makes sense."

She eyed him. "And you're okay with that?"

He shot her a frustrated look. "It's only going to be a few days. Then life goes back to normal. No more Arik. No more Confederacy. No more—"

*You.*

He didn't say it.

"What do you plan to do once this is all over?" She screwed the lid back on her flask.

"Plan?"

"When we get our cure?"

Eden watched him search for the answer, her heart clenching a little when she saw he didn't have one. It was the first time she'd thought of where she'd found him, and what he'd been doing at the time. Bounty hunting. Buried in a bar. Alone.

"I don't know," he said finally. "Thought I could linger in Shadow Rock for a bit, but I can't see myself settling in under Arik. Continue hunting monsters, I guess."

She felt breathless. "Does it make you happy?"

*No.* She saw it in his eyes. Saw the weight of debt and guilt.

"It's the only thing I'm good at," he replied, as he stood and slung his arms back through the straps of his pack. "And it's not like I have a variety of options."

"That's not true. I've seen you with CJ. He said you've been helping him sort through some of his emotions about his transformation, and how to deal with keeping his inner warg under check. You're good with him." The second she said the words, she realized it was true. Johnny had a teacher's soul.

All along she'd been thinking of him as the dangerous man who helped tear her life apart, but was that merely a response to what he'd become under Bartholomew Cane?

Who would he have been if Cane hadn't swept into his life?

She barely knew what Cane had done to him, but she could guess enough.

Her lungs unlocked, and Eden released the breath she'd been holding, as her mind put those crucial puzzle pieces together. Johnny wasn't a killer, not at heart. No, he was ridiculously patient, a man with a surprisingly nurturing side he hadn't been able to put to use.

A lone wolf hungering for a pack.

"There could be a place for you at Haven," she said slowly. "Luc Wade made a home for himself there with Riley, and Adam's begun repairing a house from the damage the reivers did to it a few years ago. A couple of humans live there, but it's rapidly becoming a home for those wargs who can keep their humanity."

"You think there's a place for me at Haven?" Incredulousness underscored his expression. "You think your brother would ever let me live beside him?"

"Yes, I think he would. Adam said he'd forgiven you for what happened after Rust City. And.... Maybe you could help him deal with his warg side? He's always rejected it. Always hated it."

But what if there was a chance Johnny could help Adam come to complete terms with who he now was?

Maybe it would never heal all the damage, but what if it could soften her brother's scars?

"That was before he realizes I'm sleeping—"

"With his sister?"

Johnny shut his mouth, but Eden pushed on, feeling a little breathless now. It could work. "Losing a loved one to the monsters is the one thing every Wastelander fears. There aren't enough of the amulets to go around to save everyone who gets scratched up. But what if you could teach them to control it? What if you could use your omega side to stop wargs from giving into the monster within? You could be the one person who could bring my community back together. They wouldn't have to fear your kind anymore. Humans could live side-by-side with those afflicted with the warg nanotech."

A healer, just like her.

"You want me to teach your brother—and others—how to control and accept themselves?"

"Yes!" she cried. "You can't tell me you were happy roaming the Rim by yourself. I saw the way you looked at the Shadow Rock pack. You want what they could give you. A home. A sense of belonging. And I know a part of you needs to atone for the past." Moving slowly, she rested her hand on his arm. "You could have all of that at Haven."

A breathless laugh escaped him. "Eden—"

"*Please*. Please consider it."

"Fine. Let's play this game of pretend. What happens if I return with you to Haven, angel?"

She blinked. "What do you mean?"

"You've skipped over one crucial element. You. Me. Your life is in Absolution, not Haven. How do *we* work in this little dream you have going? Are we over? Do you pat me on the back and send me on my way, grateful you managed to rescue me from a life of nothingness? Do you give in every now and then, when that itch is back? Am I the dirty little secret your brother doesn't need to know about? Or...."

She swallowed. "Or?"

"You tell me what the alternative is," he challenged.

Eden looked away, staring blindly through the bleached bones of the ghost forest. She hadn't had a chance to think about the future. "Everything's been happening so quickly...."

Johnny pushed away from her. "Yeah, I thought so." He gave her a faintly self-mocking smile. "It's a nice thought, Eden. Thank you for offering me a place to live. But I've been many things in my life, all of them forced upon me by another, and you know what? I'm done. I'm done feeling shame and hating myself. I'm done pretending to be something I'm not. If there's one thing I refuse to be it's your dirty little secret. It's not good enough. So if that's all you have to offer me, then I'll see you to Cortez City, and I'll see you home, but I won't be staying in Haven. I won't be someone you can use for sex whenever you get the urge. Because that would break whatever's left of me, and I refuse to let you do that."

"That wasn't what I meant—"

But he was walking away, his shoulders broad in the wretched sunlight. Eden scrambled after him.

"Wait! Don't just walk away!" she called. "Talk to me. Please. I know you're afraid—"

Johnny's head turned, the broad rim of his black hat shielding his face. "I'm afraid? Right back at you, darlin'. You want to talk about the future? Well, you just let me know when you've made your damned mind up."

Then he vanished between the forlorn carcasses of the trees.

There was a horrible taste in her mouth. She knew it well. She'd been stewing herself in it for years.

*Good enough to fuck,* came those damning words again.

She wanted Johnny to have a chance to find a place for himself, to be happy, but was she prepared to let him in enough to do that at his side?

Instinct said *no*.

The part of her that said *ouch, hot plate*, also said, *ouch, broken heart*.

He'd hurt her once before.

She'd always thought herself remarkably well adapted, considering what she'd been through. She'd fashioned a safe life for herself. A routine, a job, a home, a brother, a family, people she loved. Everyone in Absolution came to her for advice. She had a surrogate niece and nephew. She had everything she ever needed. Maybe her home felt a little empty at night, but she was useful. Maybe her heart tugged every time she cuddled baby Tommy and reminded herself she was getting on in years now, but it wasn't her fault there were no men who lit a fire within her. She'd told herself for years it sucked that her love life was as barren as the Wastelands around her, but at least the rest of her life was perfect.

But was that the truth?

Or had she merely walled her heart away so she'd never get hurt again? Plenty of men had asked her on dates in the past. She couldn't entirely blame Adam for her lack of a love life. He'd been gone two years, and she'd still been as celibate as a nun.

No men? *Ha.*

There was a man standing here right now—one who destroyed the careful fabric of her world and made her question everything—demanding to know where he fit in *her* life.

Johnny Colton struck a flame within her that was so overwhelming it threatened to sweep her away.

And it was *because* he threatened her guarded heart, because of the sheer intensity of the passion between them, that she'd refused to paint herself within the picture she'd offered him.

"Fuck," she whispered, because that word was somehow completely apropos.

Everything *had* happened quickly.

That didn't mean what she felt for him wasn't real. She'd been battling for days, trying to fix a label to what he meant to her. Trying to somehow fit him into the order of her life, in a nice, safe fashion.

*You're attracted to him, but that's okay because maybe he wasn't the monster you thought he was.*

*You had sex with him, but that's okay because you're under a shit-ton of stress.*

She'd made excuses for everything that had happened between them, so she didn't have to examine the root cause of why she couldn't deny this man.

*You have feelings for him.*

*It would be very, very easy to fall in love with him.*

She had a sudden brief flash of a future, this time with herself woven through the tapestry.

*Lazy mornings in his arms in bed. Soft kisses. The smell of sizzling bacon when she woke because he'd banned her from the kitchen, and taken over those duties himself. Arms slipping around her waist from behind, and kisses nuzzling her neck, as he pulled her from her work and reminded her she'd been at it all day. Someone to talk to about her daily frustrations. Someone to listen to. A baby on her shoulder, one with black, black hair and beautiful olive skin. And a smile on his face when he returned from his own work during the day; the smile of a man at peace with himself.*

It wasn't just a future created for Johnny, to fill the hollows in his heart, but one for her too.

It was, if she let herself believe it, a possible future that brightened all the cold moments of her own life, and filled the void she'd barely even realized was there.

And it frightened her so much a shiver of cold ran through her.

Not because she knew he'd break her heart—but because she was afraid to give him the chance to try.

# eighteen

Cortez City loomed out of the grasslands like an iron behemoth, the wall that stretched between it and its fellow city-states running like a ruler across the land. Built to keep out the wargs, the reivers, and probably the Wastelanders, it was solid concrete that stretched twenty feet high.

A dam shimmered beneath the sun to the north of the city. The wall enclosed Cortez. Eden squatted at Johnny's side and handed Arik's binoculars back to him. They'd settled into a wary sort of truce again, and she hadn't been able to say a damned word with Arik and Lincoln at his side.

"You're right. There's no way in."

"Not through the front gates, anyway," Arik muttered.

"Okay, Captain Man-bun," she muttered. "How do we get in?"

Arik crouched low as he crossed the ground to where they'd left their packs. "Same way I got out. Follow me."

Scrambling north toward the dam, he kept the pace up. Eden's breath came in harsh pants, and she noticed Johnny followed on her heels, almost as if was prepared to catch her if she fell. Eden didn't know if her fitness sucked or if she was simply worn out after most of the week on foot, but by the time they got within range of the dam, she was struggling to put one foot after the other.

"Water break," Johnny called, forcing the two wargs ahead of her to stop.

"I know what you're doing. You don't have to stop for my sake," she said, though she bent over and rested both palms on her upper thighs. "I can do this."

Johnny helped her ease the pack off her shoulders. He'd packed them, and she'd noticed hers was suspiciously lighter this morning. "I don't doubt you can. But the three of us aren't human, Eden, and you shouldn't be trying to keep up with us."

*Eden.* She almost missed the "angel."

But it was her own damn fault.

"I hate being weak."

"It's not weak," he pointed out. "It's playing to your strengths. I'm sure when we get to the lab, you're going to be thinking circles around me. I'll just be there to lift heavy things and shoot people."

She couldn't help laughing, and it cut through the tension between them. Shattered it. "You're a little handier than that."

Johnny's mouth softened as if he could sense the olive branch she was extending.

"I also give great oral," he said, waggling his eyebrows up and down, and Eden lost it.

"True."

He offered her his water flask, and she tipped it to her lips and drank thirstily. Climbing the escarpment had knocked the wind out of her sails. Everything ached, from her calves to the tips of her ears. Mostly her calves.

All the tension from the morning had vanished. She didn't have the energy to fight with him.

And truth be told, he'd promised to shelve any future discussions, and simply reverted to his flirtatious, devil-may-care self.

She could pretend too.

"So I know the no-touching law is fully in place, but.... I could help ease some of your aches and pains."

"What do you have in mind?" she asked warily.

Hands softened on her shoulders, and Johnny rubbed the spot just above her shoulder blades. Eden groaned as he worked tense muscles. "I think I'm going to melt if you keep doing that."

"Maybe I should save these magic hands for later?" he teased.

"If you just hit on me, I should warn you I don't have the strength to even reciprocate in the near future." All that sleek, sexy muscle would be wasted on her tonight.

Possibly tomorrow too.

"Besides," she muttered, "that's against the rules."

"I'm already breaking one."

"I'm pretty sure you're planning on breaking more than one."

"Only a rub-down, Eden." He leaned closer, his voice softening. "I'm not interested in *just* sex. Maybe it's my turn to say, if you want more then you have to give more."

There were a thousand complications in that sentence. She looked at him helplessly.

Could she trust him?

"Don't overthink it," he said, no doubt reading her like a book.

"You have met me."

"Yes." He grinned. "Kind of think I'm getting to know you intimately by now."

She blushed. And that was weird too, because she felt a little bit like a girl with a crush.

What was happening to her?

"Can I ask you a question?" she blurted.

"Yeah."

"It contains a bit of a confession too," she admitted, as his hands kept rubbing her neck, thumbs sliding along the sore muscles there.

"Now I'm curious."

"You know that letter that fell out of your pocket the night you were injured?"

"Yeah," he said, his voice roughening.

"I stole it when you were asleep and looked at it."

Eden glanced behind her as Johnny's hands came to a complete rest on her shoulders.

His face remained neutral.

"It was my letter," she whispered. "One I wrote to Adam, years ago. I know you took off with his bag when you slipped away after Rust City, but I guess... I guess I'm curious as to why you kept my letters."

A sudden chill swept over her, as the heat of his hands dropped away. Now he was reaching for his flask.

"Johnny?"

He took a mouthful of water, the muscles in his throat working. With a sigh, he lowered the flask, scrubbing a hand up the back of his neck. "What do you want me to say? I didn't realize they were in the bag until it was too late. I meant to burn them. I tried once or twice, but somehow I couldn't do it. I never forgot you. And sometimes it gets lonely out there on the Rim." Dark eyes flashed to hers. "Sometimes I used to read them, and pretend we hadn't met the way we did."

Her heart broke a little for him.

A smile curled over his mouth. "Mind you, I remembered you as this sweet, young girl who loved her brother, and hated my ass. I could picture you through your letters. Loving. Generous. Frustrated with a brother who wouldn't come home. Reminding him of everything he had waiting for him. I had this whole image of you in my head. My angel. Then you threatened to Taser my balls, and I kind of realized the Eden McClain I thought I knew was nothing like the real thing."

"Ha, ha." Her heart thrilled a little. "You had a thing for me."

"Darlin', I've had a thing for you since the moment I met you," he pointed out dryly, tipping the flask to his lips again. The smile vanished from his face. "Just never expected you'd ever look at me the way you did that night in Shadow Rock. Or kiss me back."

Butterflies took flight in her stomach.

"And I know it scares you, so I guess... What you do with that information is up to you."

Arik loped back down toward them. "How are you feeling?" he asked, in the carefully mild tone of a man who wanted to get the hell out of here. "Not a good place to stop, sorry. Got an hour to the tunnel, Eden. Can you do it?"

Right now, she felt like she could float away, those damned butterflies were fluttering so hard.

Walking though?

Maybe.

She took a deep breath and held her arms out so Johnny could slip the pack onto her back. "I've got this."

"We're getting close to patrolled territory now. Keep an eye on the sky for drones," Arik said, mostly to Johnny and Lincoln. "They sound like a swarm of bees, have heat-seeking abilities, and miniature rocket launchers attached to them. Heat-seeking range is generally two hundred feet, so we can't afford to be surprised. They're all run by AI back in Cortez—"

"A-what?" Johnny asked.

"Artificial Intelligence," Arik replied. "It's all computer controlled, but they're designed to alert enforcement should they go down, or spot anything. If that alert gets sent, we'll be knee-deep in drones and enforcement will send a squad out to check. It's the last thing we want."

Eden stumbled forward, her thighs groaning.

And of course they were going up a small slope.

"You were a Confederacy prisoner?" she asked Arik, to take her mind off things as they trooped along a narrow track that looked like something goats would use.

He hauled his pack higher. "Yes."

Lincoln caught her eye and shook his head as if to say, *don't go there.*

But Arik surprised her. "They captured Nnedi when we were eighteen. The alpha at the time refused to go after them, so I headed for Cortez. My family practically raised her, so I couldn't just move on the way everyone else expected. Knew I couldn't sneak into the city, so I walked up to the gates. They took me down, and I woke up in Camp Ragnarök. Head shaved, barcode on my wrist, chained and naked. Took me three months to find her. The women have their own barracks."

"Took you another three years to get out," Lincoln muttered.

No wonder Arik pissed dominance and bled arrogance, as Johnny had muttered to her at lunch.

"But we did get out," Arik replied. "I got her back; that's all that matters."

"I'm surprised she didn't want to come along," Eden said.

Arik's shoulders stiffened.

"That's why he brought me," Lincoln replied. "If he took himself out of the equation, I'm the next warg who can rule the pack, which means if we're both not there...."

"Nnedi had to stay behind," Johnny muttered. "Bet that went down well. Nothing like being told you should stay behind so you don't get hurt."

She looked at him.

Johnny arched a brow.

Despite their conversation, she still felt uneasy at the thought of what she was leading him into.

"There's the dam," Arik said, crouching as he paused on the top of a hill next to some sagebrush. He pointed to the base of the wall. "We go in through there. There are all sorts of service tunnels and water drainage pipes. It's not going to be fun, but you can do it if you're strong enough. And the enforcers patrol the top of the dam, but they're not really keeping an eye on the drains."

"Lead the way, Cap," she said, before her aching body could talk her out of it.

They were so close to Cortez City and her cure, that she could almost feel it in her hands.

*Tick tock.*

"You ever get the feeling this is too easy?" Eden muttered, as she landed in a tunnel.

Johnny had dropped her through the grate. Water splashed around her ankles. Or at least she hoped it was water.

Johnny landed beside her, water skating up her jeans. Above them, light bled through the grate, but the tunnels were black.

"Wait for it," Arik warned. "The best bit's ahead."

Light bloomed as Johnny lit a torch. Its flame hissed in the near dark, but at least she could see.

"Excellent," she muttered. "A billion steps?"

"Not... quite."

They sloshed through the tunnels, with Arik in the lead. Eden's feet began to numb. She'd never been in water this cold. Most of the time in the Wastelands, water was warm.

A trickle of light began to take the edge off the darkness, along with the rushing sound of water. It sounded like... a waterfall.

And Arik headed straight for it.

"We don't have to jump off anything, do we?"

"Nope."

A sheet of water broke the tunnel ahead of them, and light filtered through it. Arik vanished under the spray. Then Lincoln. Eden squealed under her breath as she darted through it, getting instantly soaked.

Light broke over them as she found herself on a narrow ledge in a man-made cavern of some description. No, a hollow tower. Far above them, she could see the sky. Below them, the water vanished into nothingness.

"How good are you at climbing?" Arik called, peering up through the hollow tower. Water sloshed down its sides, as if they opened grates to change the level of the dam above them.

And wasn't that a thought? All that water, the concrete groaning against its weight....

"I used to climb the tors as a girl," she admitted, a little breathlessly. "Hunting rocs where they nest. But that was a long time ago."

And her thighs and calves were already aching.

Arik and Johnny exchanged glances.

"I can haul her up if we harness us together," Johnny replied.

Arik nodded shortly. Clearly it would have to do. He and Lincoln began tugging an assortment of ropes out of their packs.

Johnny held the harness out, allowing her to step into it. Arik had supplied the climbing equipment. Apparently it was what teens in Shadow Rock did for fun before they became adults and were expected to climb freestyle.

Johnny's tanned hands snapped the harness into place around her waist and thighs, testing the give in it. He worked the carabiners efficiently, and hooked the pair of them together with a thick, stretchy rope that had about twenty feet in it. "If you fall, I've got you."

"Who's got *you*?" she snorted, rubbing her hands together nervously.

A faint smile flickered over his mouth. She loved this particular smile of his; a droll *ha-ha* on the surface, with a shyer undertone of shared amusement. Johnny held up his hand, forcing his claws to extend. "Trust me, darlin'. I won't fall."

It was kind of gross.

In a fascinating, unusual sort of way.

Adam couldn't manage the partial shift; he'd spent years denying his nature. She'd seen Luc go claws out once or twice, but never up close. Eden sucked in a breath, staring at Johnny's suddenly monstrous hands. His fingers were covered in thick, dark fur, and his claws gleamed like obsidian.

He stiffened as he noticed her interest.

Eden reached out slowly, brushing her fingertips over the sleek fur. It thinned out where his hand met his wrist, becoming nothing more than the dark hairs on his arms. Softer than she'd expected.

"I've never seen a warg up close," she admitted.

Silver streaks flared out around his pupils like a corona in the dark field of space. "Trust me, you don't want to."

*I know.* But she turned his hand over, curious about the difference in anatomy.

Something so hateful, she'd spent her entire life running from it.

It was merely a set of claws.

"Let's do this," Arik muttered, staring up at the inside of the hollow tower. There was a narrow ladder embedded in the wall, but it started about fifteen feet up. Water sluiced over it.

Johnny's claws retracted, the hair absorbing back into his skin, revealing a normal hand once more.

Lincoln knelt, cupping his hands together. His brother stepped into them, and Lincoln threw him up into the air. Arik only just caught the bottom rung of the steel bars embedded into the concrete. Biceps flexing, he hauled himself up with pure arm strength, catching the next rung. Pulling himself up, arm over arm, he began the climb.

*Oh, heck.*

In Absolution, Eden managed to run several mornings a week, purely for stress relief. It had been several weeks since she'd fit one of her runs in though— thanks to her sudden busy workload—and as she stared up through the hollow core of the concrete tower, doubt began to creep through her lower abdomen.

Eden knew three things: A, it was a long way up; B, she was a human, not a warg; and C, while the strength and precision of her hands was undisputed, particularly with a scalpel, her upper arm strength had been crafted purely from lifting a spoon of cake to her mouth.

She liked cake.

"I don't know if I can make it. My arm strength isn't my best quality."

"Sure you can," Johnny replied. "You're going to go in front of me, and I can help you when your arms start getting heavy. Once we hit the ladder, you can use your legs too. You'll be fine. The one thing I don't doubt is your determination."

Eden wiped her sweaty palms on her cargo shorts. She stared up at the first rung. It was a long way away.

"Ladies first," Lincoln muttered, holding his cupped hands out for her.

"Just remember, angel. Your cure's at the top," Johnny muttered.

Right. She could do this.

"*Motherfucker*," Eden groaned quietly.

Not the first curse word that had come from her in the past few minutes. When Eden swore, he knew she was reaching the end of her endurance. Johnny climbed up behind her, his body curving around hers. "Need a break?"

Reaching around her, he grabbed the rungs and clenched.

Eden let go, her weight pressing against his chest. He breathed out, feeling the slow burn in his biceps. It had to be hurting her. Not once had she complained when they crossed the Great Divide. She'd gritted her teeth on the way up the escarpment, but didn't whine. No, when Eden was struggling, she tended to get quiet, turning that significant focus inward until her body was merely a machine pumping blood through its systems.

"I can't do this," she moaned, resting her forehead against the wall.

"Well, you're almost three-quarters of the way up, so it's closer to the top than it is to the bottom. Come on. One rung at a time."

Eden gritted her teeth and set her hands back on the bars. Water splashed over them, which didn't help, as she took another step.

"When's your birthday?" he asked her, letting her track ahead again.

She looked down. "What?"

"Figured now's as good a time as any to get to know each other." Johnny hauled himself after her, straining under the weight of the wet pack. It was made of oiled canvas, so at least everything within would be dry, but he swore it was getting heavier.

"June tenth," she called back down. "What about you?"

"The eighteenth of September."

"Are you telling me this so I can bake you a cake?"

Johnny looked up in surprise and copped a faceful of water. Swearing under his breath, he wiped it away. "Not a big fan of cake."

She laughed as she hauled herself up. "Cake in particular, or my cake?"

"Dare I eat your cake? Isn't it supposed to be my birthday? I thought they were meant to be pleasurable days," he teased. Not that anyone had ever offered to make him a cake anytime recently. He could vaguely recall his mother doing so once, but that had been years ago. Hell, the most he ever treated himself to was a swig of whiskey.

"Fine," she called back down. "I'll get Maggie to make the cake, just so you don't choke on it. I'm in charge of the present. And I'll warn you: I've got ideas."

"Sexy ideas?"

"Maybe."

Pleasure radiated through him. He'd been trying to distract her—and maybe that was all this was—but she was speaking in terms of the future as if she imagined he'd be in it.

Despite the brief salvo, she fell quiet again.

They climbed for another few minutes, and he could sense her slowing down. She paused again, resting her head on the bars and trying to take the tension off her arms.

"Nearly there," he called. It had been a long day, and the strain was starting to show in her. Stars glittered in the sky above them. They weren't as bright as those you saw in the Wastelands, probably due to the proximity of the city.

Pushing up behind her again, he looked up. "Five more rungs, Eden."

A head appeared, outlined by the velvet dark sky.

Arik.

"Need a hand?" he called, over the roar of the water.

It was drier here, near the top, with the sluice gates below them. Mist clung in the air. Johnny nudged Eden up one more rung. Her hands shook with the effort.

"Lean on me," he offered, crawling up behind her legs.

Step by step they reached the top. Arik helped haul her over the lip, where she collapsed on the ground in a panting heap. They were in another tunnel that branched off toward the city. Lincoln hauled himself over the edge behind them.

Eden groaned. "You might have to go on... without me."

He could just make out Arik pressing a finger to his lips up ahead.

"Easy now, darlin'," Johnny whispered, stroking her hair as he squatted beside her. His thighs ached too. "We're getting closer to the surface. Got to keep your voice down."

The other two wargs vanished into the darkness, and despite the fact he and Arik were getting along like two cats trapped in a burlap sack together, he was actually grateful they were there.

Gave him the grace to look after Eden, rather than worrying about what was out there in the dark.

Eden sat with her head bent, her entire body trembling, and her forehead resting on his thigh. She didn't look like she could move.

"You got any more water?" she asked. "I've got a headache."

He put his pack aside and handed over his flask. "Not long now, angel. Night's falling, which means we can get some rest."

"Where?"

"That's what Arik's seeing to."

She slumped against him after she'd drunk her fill. Johnny rubbed her shoulder. A part of him didn't like seeing her in so much pain, but he was helpless to do anything about it. Just had to keep telling himself all she needed was rest.

Footsteps sloshed in the tunnel. Johnny sighed in relief as he turned his head. "It's about damned time—"

He broke off abruptly as a shadow loomed in the mouth of the tunnel, clad in an array of high-tech body armor. A tall figure with a shaved head, and warg-silver eyes that shone in the faint moonlight. Every inch of him looked hard and well-fed, and his boots gleamed in a way no Wastelander's ever had.

*Oh, shit.*

"Who the hell are you?" demanded the stranger.

Shoving Eden behind him, Johnny reached for the knife at his belt and threw it in one smooth move toward the stranger's throat. "Stay behind me, Eden!"

The stranger flung up a defensive hand, the knife glancing off the black gauntlet on his arms. He pressed his fingertips to some sort of earpiece, and Johnny suddenly realized he couldn't let the bastard alert his friends.

Driving to his feet, he started sprinting.

Johnny slammed into the other warg, and Eden went down on her knees as the rope between them jerked. She wrenched forward, scrabbling to grab something as she was hauled across the floor after them.

"Arik!" she screamed.

The two wargs tumbled over each other, Johnny getting the upper hand and slamming the soldier's head into the concrete. A pair of claws slashed up and jammed into Johnny's side as the stranger bucked beneath him, and he went flying over the stranger's head.

Eden grabbed the rope hooked from her harness to Johnny's and jerked it up sharply just as the stranger made to leap over it. He went flying forward, thrown off balance, and Johnny managed to get to his feet, black spatters of what she suspected was blood splashed across his jeans.

They slammed together.

Over and over, wrestling and punching. In the dim moonlight, she could barely make out who was who. She saw her shotgun strapped to her pack, and scrambled over the floor toward it, jerking it free and—

Freezing.

Arik had cautioned them over and over against making any loud noise. The dam would be lightly patrolled, but all it would take would be one mistake to have the entire Confederacy raining down on them.

The rope around her waist jerked.

Eden's knees went out from under her, and she lost her grip on the shotgun. The pair of wargs rolled toward the lip of the hollow tower they'd just climbed, and Eden's eyes widened as Johnny shot her a sharp, panicked glance.

Then they vanished over the edge, his claws lashing out helplessly for grip.

And failing.

*Gone.* He was gone.

The rope snapped taut, and the sudden slam of his weight against her harness nearly bowed her in two.

"Johnny!" she screamed, yanked toward the edge.

Jamming her feet out, her boot heels locked against the inch-high lip of concrete that circled the ledge. She pitched forward, almost upright, her arms windmilling—

"Got you!" Lincoln bellowed, hauling her back against his chest.

The harness cut into her skin, and Eden screamed in pain as Johnny's weight swung like a pendulum from her waist. Then Arik's fists wrapped around the rope, easing some of the strain. The pair of them fought to haul her away from the edge.

The rope jerked.

"Kick him off you!" Arik bellowed into the emptiness, and Eden finally realized she wasn't just holding the weight of one man.

"*Son of a bitch.*" Lincoln's arms were almost crushing her ribs.

Eden threw her head back, forcing every inch of willpower into her straining thighs, as she choked back another scream. The rope jerked, and Arik almost lurched forward.

Eden grabbed his shirt. If he went, they'd all go.

A sudden cry echoed up through the tunnel, and the rope suddenly slackened.

The three of them collapsed back on the ground.

Eden grabbed the rope, hauling it hand over hand—

No weight.

Nothing.

One of them must have cut it.

"No!" She scrambled toward the edge, leaning over it, her heart squeezing in her hest. "Johnny?"

Her voice echoed through the hollow core.

Nothing moved.

Only an endless splash of water that vanished into the darkness below. Her heart jacked into her throat, her eyes darting—

And then a hand locked around one of the rungs of the embedded ladder, water spraying off a dark shoulder.

"*Please, please, please, please, please,*" she prayed, as the figure hauled himself up out of the shadows until she could finally see his face.

Johnny.

It was Johnny.

Eden collapsed onto the ground, panting for breath. Safe. He was safe. Tears of relief burst out of her, and a hand squeezed her shoulder as Arik stopped beside her, and peered down.

"Is he dead?" he called softly.

Johnny ground his teeth together and kept climbing. Slowly. "Put my knife in him," he growled out. "Hopefully the fall did the rest."

The second he made it to the top, Arik hauled him up to safety. Eden wasted no time. She threw her arms around him, wincing at the sharp ache as the harness's straps cut into bruised flesh.

"Oh, my God," she breathed. "Are you okay?"

There'd been blood on his jeans. And it washed in thin rivulets of watery gray down his face. Eden pulled back, hauling his shirt up and examining the claw marks there. "I need more light!"

"I'm fine," he murmured, capturing her hands.

"You're bleeding—"

"Just a scratch." Johnny gave her a faint, tired smile as if to remind her of the last argument they'd had about "scratches".

"That had better be a joke."

"It is. Nothing a night's sleep won't heal."

Capturing her face, he pressed a faint kiss to her lips. Eden grabbed his wrists, and kissed him back, her heart still pulsing like she'd run a race.

She'd spent days pushing him away and telling herself nothing could come of this.

She'd almost lost him—this time for real.

And suddenly she realized none of it mattered.

Not Adam. Not the threat to her heart. Not even the past.

She broke the kiss, trying to catch her breath. "Don't *ever* do that again."

"Fall off the top of a high building?"

"No! Put yourself in danger. Get hurt. You almost—" She couldn't say it.

"It's okay," Johnny said roughly, his eyes dark and wondrous as if he saw exactly what she couldn't put into words. "I get it, Eden."

She hugged him tightly, resting her head against his chest and just listening to his heart beat, as he wrapped his arms around her.

"You scare the hell out of me," she whispered.

Because he'd been right.

There was something growing between them, and it had the ability to rip her heart clean out of her chest if something went wrong.

Johnny stroked her hair. "Right back at you, angel."

Eden slowly looked up.

"We'd better get moving," Arik called softly, hauling his pack over his shoulders. "Best-case scenario—the bastard's dead, and his superiors don't notice him missing until morning. Worst-case scenario? Well, I'm not sticking around to find out."

"Ready?" Arik whispered. "We're directly under a suburban area. It's just a quick climb, and then we should be able to haul ourselves out through one of the stormwater grates."

Johnny helped Eden to her feet. "Nearly there," he promised. "Then you can get dry and crawl into your bedroll."

She'd begun flagging badly, and though she wasn't limping, he'd seen the marks on her skin where the harness nearly jerked her over the edge with him.

They staggered through the dark, Arik leading the way. No time for the torch now.

Pausing beneath a stormwater grate, he watched Arik vanish through it. Then Lincoln. Johnny lifted Eden, and Lincoln reached down and hauled her through the opening.

Leaping up, he caught the edge of the grate and hauled himself out into the fresh air. A moon hung swollen in the sky, casting soft light down over the city below them.

Arik crouched in a squat, lifting his water canteen to his lips. "Welcome to Cortez City."

Before them stretched a landscape the likes neither of them had ever seen before.

# nineteen

"Here we are," Arik whispered. "We made it."

Eden stared about herself in wonder. Lights glittered as though someone had put the stars themselves on earth. She couldn't escape the size of the city.

She'd been pushing herself all week, focusing on getting to Cortez. A tiny part of her hadn't believed they'd make it.

But they were here.

Buildings pressed together, all glittering steel and panes of glass that stretched so high into the sky Eden could barely see the top of them. Wide roads spanned below them, strangely empty. The roads were wide enough to drive a herd of a thousand cattle along them, and they were perfectly straight. In fact, everything was laid out into neat grids, and every building was square or rectangular. Thousands of little windows loomed in the side of each building, like a spider's eyes.

She couldn't escape the impression she was being watched. Maybe that was the point; Henry Chin had spoken of yearning for freedom, after all, and despite its glory, its technology, there was a creepy feeling of eyes boring into her back, no matter which way she turned.

But the thing that surprised her the most was how clean everything was.

Everything bore the stamp of the Confederacy; a half sun in the center of a circle, its rays radiating outward like a new sun rising from the ashes of a former empire. All the roads seemed to point toward the center of the city, where a massive building towered over everything else, comprised of a tiara of five towers built adjoining one another, with the one in the center spearing toward the heavens.

"That building looks like it's giving the middle finger," Johnny mused. "Do you think they realize they're saying 'fuck you' to the rest of the city?"

"Pretty sure," Arik muttered. "That's where the general will be, along with all his boot kissers."

She was staring at a world she could never in her wildest dreams have imagined. The sheer scope of the technology astounded her. Enormous square screens were mounted to the walls, flashing in bright colors in the night. They looked like a bigger version of her datapad, and images of people flickered over them. A scene of thousands of people in an enormous square appeared, waving dark green paper ribbons as a parade of cars drove along the narrow space in the center. A man in a crisp white uniform waved at the crowd with a dignified expression. White and green. The Confederacy colors.

"That's a general," Arik muttered. "Don't know which one, since it's been a while since I was here, but they rule the Confederacy with an iron fist. Each general rules a territory, and virtually owns his own city. Seven generals; seven territories. There was a coup about forty years ago, and ever since the military overthrew the leaders of the time they've been in control."

"There are so many people," Eden breathed, watching the screen.

"Yeah." Arik scrubbed a hand over his face. "They like to play their clips over and over. The military controls what people see, which means they can dictate what sort of information gets out. Expect to see a lot of parades and crowds cheering. But nothing real. You won't see the grimy underside, or the people who disappear just because they broke some imagined law."

All the people on the screen looked so clean. Their clothes were sleek, and everywhere she looked the men were clean-shaven, and the women wore their slicked-back hair in neat buns or braids. Military-style clothing seemed to be in fashion, with most people wearing varying shades of gray, black, or Confederacy green.

She felt very small, and dirty, and ragged. Every inch of her clothes had been repaired multiple times over the years, and her boots were scuffed, the soles thin. Dirt edged beneath her nails. It was something she'd never thought about until she walked into this place.

They'd never be able to blend in here.

"Cortez City's just a military outpost," Arik murmured. "This is nothing compared to the enormous city-states further in the interior. The Confederacy considers Cortez to be out in the sticks."

"What would they think of us?" Eden whispered, staring from one end of the city to the other. Despite her aches and pains, the sight was enough to distract her.

"Most people don't know much about the Wastelands to the west," Arik replied. "Like I said, information gets filtered. All they hear about are the monsters and the reivers. Nobody goes outside the walls. If you do, then they say you might get contaminated. Who knows what's out there? Radiation. Disease. Wargs and revenants. Ghost forests filled with mutos. Better to stay within the walls, where the military can protect you." He sounded disgusted. "They used to show a program in the warg camps about how *lucky* we were to be taken in. They've given us so much, so we should give back. It was our duty to play cannon fodder, because we were serving a bigger cause. Worse, some of the wargs believed it."

Thunder rumbled overhead, thick boiling clouds rolling in across the Wastelands. All three wargs looked up.

"Time to find some shelter," Arik muttered. "That storm's probably going to help. If the enforcers have wargs out on patrol, then they won't smell us if the rain washes away the scent. This way. We'll bunker down somewhere, then plan our next move on Radisson-Meyers."

Bunkering down somewhere consisted of housebreaking. They'd discussed simply tying a family up and leaving them in the cellar, but Eden didn't approve—at all—so she'd insisted on them finding a place that was empty.

The house was four times as large as her home in Absolution, and looked like it had been vacant for a while, though the rooms were sparsely furnished. Sleek furniture, and polished concrete floors. There was little ornamentation though, and a certain efficient coldness to the interior. Despite all the accessories, she much preferred her home.

"Right now we stick out like sore thumbs," Arik said as they gathered in the kitchen, around what was left of the dinner he'd hauled out of the icebox.

Lincoln picked through it, rolling a pea dubiously across the plate. He'd tried to eat the pale gray square on the corner of the plate, then gagged and spat it back out again. "Not meat," came his assessment.

"Shower, clean up, and I'll see if I can steal some Confederacy clothes from somewhere," Arik continued. Holding up his hands, he roughly measured her shoulders.

"Do you need one of us to come with you?" Johnny asked.

Arik shook his head. "I know how to act and what to say. You'll only give me away if someone spots us."

"Arik." Lincoln took a step toward him.

"You too," Arik said firmly.

The two brothers eyeballed each other, and Lincoln finally looked away. "I don't like it."

"Noted," Arik replied.

She could understand Lincoln's reticence. He'd lost his brother once, and now she was starting to warm up to the pair of them, she could see the way they watched out for each other. There was love there; the kind she felt whenever Adam was home. Sometimes it was smothering, but without it—

She'd be alone.

The way Johnny was.

Her eyes widened, just a touch, as she realized what his life was like. He'd mentioned a mother. But no one else. And he'd been alone in that bar when she found him, sinking into liquor as if there was nothing else to do.

But the second they set out through the Divide, Johnny slipped into the crew as if he belonged there. Worse. As if a part of him hungered for company.

She suddenly felt like she'd unlocked the key to part of Johnny's secrets.

"Eden can get some rest," Johnny said.

She'd been struggling to keep her eyes open, so didn't argue. Her feet tingled, as if they'd simply done too much today. "You might have to carry me to the bedroom."

"Can do."

"I'll sound out my contact, Derek Mayhew. Shadow Rock uses him to get our hands on black market goods, so he'll be aware we're coming. Nnedi would have managed to get in contact with him. I'll see if Mayhew can get us some intel on the Radisson-Meyers laboratories, and see what we're dealing with here," Arik said.

Eden rested her head down on her arms. She was so tired. As much as she wanted to get out there and get started, she simply didn't think she'd be able to even stand. Just a moment to rest her eyes....

Strong arms tucked under her, and she swayed awake to find herself in Johnny's arms. The room was dark, and there was no sign of Lincoln or Arik.

"I fell asleep?" she murmured.

"You've earned it," Johnny replied, tucking her head against his shoulder as he strode toward one of the bedrooms.

She'd insisted upon sleeping in what looked like the spare bedroom, a little discomfited by the idea of sleeping in someone else's bed.

Sinking onto the bed, she groaned. It was *so* soft. "You want to stay with me?"

"Do you want me to?"

She didn't even have the strength to think her way through the minefield. "Of course I do."

The bed dipped as Johnny joined her. "Want me to rub your back?"

"Is that a trick question?"

It took both of them to get her clothes off. Her fingers simply didn't want to work properly, and her deltoids and shoulders screamed with every movement.

"Do you know the worst thing?" she muttered. "We have to go back down that bloody ladder."

"Roll onto your stomach, and think of nicer things."

"Like your hands on my skin?"

He started with her feet. Eden groaned as she slumped facedown on the bed. "That feels.... Oh, God."

"Better than sex?" he teased.

"Maybe."

Depending on the situation. Right now, it was a definite yes. Sex seemed too energetic. Too much work. Maybe when she got some sleep, it might hold more interest.

He moved slowly up her calves, his touch easing the strain from her muscles. It was a pity she never got to enjoy it.

Within a minute, her eyes had flickered shut, and she tumbled into sleep.

Johnny jerked awake, his heart in his throat and Cane's cigar burning holes in his back. A shadow moved over the top of him, and he reacted without thought, slamming his assailant onto the bed beneath him, and locking an arm around their throat as they cried out—

A woman.

The scent of her soap flooded through him.

Eden.

*Mierda.* A chill ran all the way through him as he let her go. "Angel?" he managed to croak, heart beating a million miles an hour.

She flopped onto her side, a slim hand curling around her throat.

He wanted to touch her. Wanted to hold her. But his hands were shaking so badly he could barely prop himself up on his knuckles, and he was terrified if he did touch her, he might forget where he was again.

"I'm okay," she panted, her eyes forming little black holes in the night as she looked up at him in a manner that seemed to see straight through him. "Are you all right?"

Johnny nodded. "Best not to touch me when I'm dreaming."

"That wasn't a dream," she said slowly, pushing her way upright. "That was a nightmare."

He had to get up. Had to start moving. There was a metallic taste in his mouth and a strange ringing in his ears. He forced himself to feel the carpet beneath his feet as he slid from the bed, to think of nothing beyond the sensation of it. Cracking the window open, he settled onto the seat nestled there, the cool breeze skittering over his face and washing away the sins of the past.

The wind traced cold fingers over his damp chest and hair. Sweat. It slicked down his spine and dampened the edge of his briefs.

"Want to talk about it?" Eden asked softly, watching him from the bed, her bent knees tenting the sheets.

*No.* His throat felt full of angry wasps. "I'm so sorry. I didn't— I thought you were someone else."

Eden watched him over the top of his knees, and he sensed the moment she opened her mouth to ask—and then didn't.

Because he was the one who'd slammed the doors shut in her face each and every time she brought it up.

He cleared his throat. "Want to join me?"

She kept her expression neutral as she slid from the bed, but there was a certain knowing sort of sympathy in her eyes he shied away from. He reached out a hand instead and dragged her into his lap. Eden's weight and warmth broke the chill, and he rested his chin on her shoulder, closing his eyes for a brief second as he tried to compose himself.

"Bad dreams?"

*Always.*

Outside the city lights gleamed like a thousand stars. Not quite dawn, by the look of it. Johnny's arms tightened around her. "Yeah."

"Tell me about him," she whispered. "Not for my sake, Johnny, but for yours. You can't keep this all locked up inside you. It's not healthy."

He wanted to lock it all up forever and throw away the key, but clearly, his mind wasn't having any of that.

"I don't...."

She stroked his hand patiently.

"I can't...."

The memories stole his breath, and with them his thoughts. He wanted to try and explain somehow but didn't know where to start.

"When did you first meet him?"

*There.* There was a starting point. "When I was fourteen," he managed to say. "He was my mother's brother. I never knew about him. Never even heard his name, but she was always looking over her shoulder for something. And one day that something finally rode into our lives...."

It started to spill from him in a gush as if someone had opened the spillway on the dam outside Cortez City. Pouring through the sluice gates of his soul, as he tried not to let the memories drown him.

His father walking out to meet the stranger. His mother shoving him toward the trails behind his house.

*"Whatever you see or hear, don't come back."*

But he had, hadn't he?

That single pistol shot ricocheted through his memories again, and somewhere in the sagebrush, a young boy slammed to a halt, his heart leaping into his throat.

*Don't look back.*

But he looked.

And he saw his mother screaming and fighting as Cane hauled her toward the cabin with contemptuous ease.

Smelled the smoke spiraling into the air as Cane stood there with his cigar and watched flames lick up the side of the cabin.

Heard her screams. Heard her banging on the locked door.

And despite her words, her training, the never-ending litany of what he was supposed to do if someone ever came upon them, a young Johnny's feet turned back toward the cabin.

*"You want to save her life, boy?"* Cane had demanded, squatting in the dirt, as if to make himself appear unthreatening as Johnny approached, his gaze sidling toward his father's fallen shotgun.

Anything.

*"Then hold out your arm. You make a single fucking noise and she burns."*

The first hiss of the cigar on his skin.

The scream he somehow trapped within him.

It felt like hours.

Probably only lasted seconds.

He'd stared defiantly into Cane's eyes, letting his uncle see the hate, the rage, and the desire to kill him with his bare hands.

But Cane's eyes lit up in gloating ecstasy as if Johnny had done something that pleased him immensely. And he'd turned and shot the lock off the door to the cabin, before hauling him to his feet.

*If you come with me, then she lives.*

A thousand threats over the years.

*If you run, I'll hunt her down and scalp her myself, and tell her why. I'll tell her you betrayed her.*

*If you scream, then I'll turn my horse around and track her down. You know I will.*

A thousand trapped screams.

The burning stink of his skin.

Again.

And again.

And again.

"It amused him to try and break me," he whispered, staring sightlessly out over the city. "And he knew it would cut my mother up on the inside to know he had me. I can only guess from the scars on her skin that he did the same thing to her before she somehow escaped him. He used to ramble about it all the time. About her betrayal. About my father. They deserved to die. They'd stabbed him in the back by running off together, and punishing me was his favorite way to get back at them."

Eden shifted in his arms, trying to read his face. She looked sick. "I'm so sorry. I never knew."

"He'd break me down, fuse me with his scent, and then force me to do something," he admitted, in a rough voice. "Little things to start with. Things you can't refuse. *Fetch me a cup*. You don't know what it's like to consider the danger of giving in. Is it worth fighting him? For a cup? You give in once, and it stops hurting. It's one step off a small cliff. Then the next request comes. And the next. Before you know it, you're conditioned to do what he wants you to do. It gets harder to refuse him and it hurts more when you do. The worst thing is, Eden, toward the end he didn't even need to burn me or torture me. If I fought his will, I'd feel the pain. It was like my own system was trained to give it the feedback he desired—"

Eden turned in his lap, somehow managing to straddle him. She wrapped her arms around his neck, her breasts in his face, but for the first time, he didn't feel a single lick of desire in him. "It's okay."

He ground his face against her shoulder and sucked in a huge breath of air.

It was beyond hope to believe she'd touch him at this moment. Beyond anything he'd ever expected. He felt dirty all over, but Eden's hands stroked up his spine, her scent stealing through his chest like a blazing warmth whenever a surge of panic went through him. He'd have accused her of having some omega inside her if he didn't know better.

This was forgiveness.

This was compassion and empathy, and all the things he'd never dared believe he'd ever have.

This was everything he'd read in her letters and pretended not to dream about, not to give a shit about. Not to hunger for.

She damned near broke him harder than Cane had ever managed because Eden made him vulnerable in a way Cane couldn't.

He couldn't fight the way she made him feel.

Or how much he needed her to hold him.

"I should never have touched you that day we met," he whispered, knowing he'd never apologized enough. "I knew he'd be nearby. I knew he'd hurt you if he laid eyes on you. But I couldn't resist going with you." The words broke a part of him he hadn't known he was holding back. "It had been so long since someone had touched me. So long since someone had smiled at me. I needed it so badly, I couldn't help myself. You were an angel, and though I knew better, I couldn't walk away from you."

"Sshhh." She captured his face in her hands. "It's not your fault. Cane was a monster who destroyed both our lives. There's nothing you could have done to stop him. He tortured you until he managed to overpower your will. He tried to break you, but he didn't succeed. He couldn't destroy the core of who you were, no matter how hard he tried."

He kissed her palm.

"It's not your fault." Her voice gained strength. "None of it was ever your fault."

"I should have fought harder—"

"No." Eden glared at him, like some mighty avenging warrior. "I get it. I do." She gave a breathless laugh. "Of all people, I truly understand. But none of this was your fault."

"None of it was my fault," he rasped.

It might take him a decade of saying it to believe it, but this was a start.

The warm cup of her hand stroked down his cheek. "There's a courage and warmth inside you he couldn't destroy. Now I know you I can see who you are inside, Johnny. I want... When we're finished here, I want you to come home with me. To Absolution. Haven. I don't know where. Just as long as you're with me."

She bowed her forehead against his, as his heart sped up. "You were right. There is an *us*. There's something there between us I want to explore. I don't know how this is going to work. It scares me. But I want to try—"

Johnny captured the words on her lips.

His hands slid up her sides, shirring the fabric of her tank, as he explored her mouth gently. Eden kissed him back, her hands locking around the back of his neck. He almost couldn't believe she was in his lap. Saying the things he'd wanted her to say. Agreeing to this crazy proposition that had somehow fallen from his lips—

"Bed," she rasped, drawing back from him with glazed eyes.

"Are you sure? What about your rules?"

"Fuck the rules," she said, and kissed him again.

Johnny lurched to his feet with her in his arms, staggering blindly toward the place he'd feared only minutes ago. He'd been trying to be good ever since that night in Shadow Rock. Having an audience wasn't exactly his idea of a good time, and Eden had been so exhausted last night she'd crashed and burned like the meteor that plunged the world into an impact winter nearly seventy years ago.

"Let me make love to you," she whispered, as he laid her reverently down upon the sheets as if she knew he'd already promised her his heart and soul that morning in Shadow Rock. As if she knew he'd made love to her when she'd been trying to keep this strictly physical between them.

"As you wish," he breathed, as she pressed him down onto the bed, and swung her leg over his thighs, straddling him.

Eden captured his mouth again and this time he felt the difference in the kiss, as their palms locked together, their fingers threading through each other.

And whatever tension had been lingering in his spine, vanished as she made him forget everything but this.

Dawn arrived, bringing with it a new sense of peace.

But not, unfortunately, a new body.

"This is where we're meeting your contact?" Eden asked, walking stiffly into the bar behind Arik. She felt like she was eighty.

He'd managed to set up a meeting with this Mayhew, whom he said was an information broker and hacker.

She couldn't come to terms with what that actually meant, though she supposed in a world where every piece of information was available on the Confederacy-controlled Fednet, it might be a lucrative proposition.

Johnny hovered on her heels, looking well out of his depth. She understood how he felt. Arik had led them through a maze of dark alleys and twisty streets. The section of town they were in wasn't like the structured and sterile streets she'd first seen.

Even Cortez City had a dark side, it seemed.

"He said nine o'clock, sharp." Arik scanned the darkened interior of the bar.

It wasn't what she'd expected to see. The walls were concrete—like the rest of the city—and cigarette smoke hazed the air. Despite the fact it was midmorning, there were over a dozen patrons in here. A table with painted numbers on it stood in the center of the room, and a man threw a pair of dice across it. Another pair of women lingered in a dark corner, their heads close together as they sipped from elegant glassware. Everywhere she looked, people held hushed conversations. This wasn't so much a bar as a place to meet.

"There he is." Arik nodded toward the corner.

A man stood by one of the tables, the faint flicker of a cigarette gleaming as he watched the game in front of him with rapt attention. He wore a black, nondescript tunic, similar to what Arik had dug up for Johnny and his brother, the material clinging to his chest. It seemed most of the people of the Confederacy wore the same sort of thing, as if being one of many was the fashion, and individuality could be dangerous.

She couldn't see the stranger's face. Somehow he'd positioned himself beneath a hanging light, and it was so bright it obliterated the details, merely forming a halo over his blond hair.

Derek Mayhew rolled a pair of dice over the back of his fingers. Sleek, she would have said. Dangerous. He examined them, pausing on her. "Arik." A faint smile toyed over his lips. "It's been a long time."

The pair of them clasped hands.

"Was hoping it would be longer," Arik admitted. "Didn't plan on ever coming back. Did you get the information I requested?"

"Please." Mayhew looked amused. "Now I'm insulted."

Arik swiftly introduced the pair of them. Lincoln remained outside, surreptitiously standing guard.

"What information?" she asked.

Mayhew gestured toward a steel door. "I have a rule, Miss McClain. Don't ever discuss your affairs in public. You never know who's listening in."

He snagged a glass and a bottle of brandy off the bar and led them to a small concrete room down a flight of stairs that looked suspiciously like a bunker. The second the door was shut, he gestured for her to sit at the small metal table in the center of the room. "The room's been swept."

She glanced at the floor.

"Of bugs, Miss McClain," Mayhew said sarcastically. "I mean we can speak freely without fear of someone listening in."

"Oh."

"Got what you need," Mayhew said, tugging a datapad from inside his tunic. His fingers darted over the keys. "Radisson-Meyers project. Bligh had it behind a firewall, but I got through an hour ago."

The screen flashed with information.

"Project: Chimera," he said, with a smug smile, reading through his notes. "A super plague."

"I don't understand," Eden said. "Why would you help us?"

Arik leaned back against his chair, looking stoically bored, even as his eyes scanned the room. "Derek owes me a favor. He was trying to find a way to get into Camp Ragnarök to steal some military secrets a few years ago, and I was looking to get out. I gave him what he wanted, and he gave me what I wanted. We can trust him. He doesn't like the Confederacy any more than we do."

"You *are* Confederacy," she pointed out.

Mayhew smiled as he uncapped the bottle of brandy and filled his glass. "Yes, I am. Needless to say I'm doing my damnedest to overthrow the current system. Arik tells me you have information that might assist in taking down some big shots." His smile became somewhat frightening. "I want that information. Tell me what's happening out there in the Wastelands. Tell me about your plague."

Political bullshit. She sighed, and told him what she knew.

"Now your turn," she replied. "What have you got on Project: Chimera? Particularly about its cure?"

"I did a little research today," Mayhew admitted, turning his brandy glass around in slow circles on the table. "Last year, Lieutenant Bligh swept General Radisson from power. There was a court martial, mention of illegal experiments, a lot of smoke and mirrors. But they managed to keep it all off the las-screens and out of public view. According to the official memo, General Radisson resigned thanks to a terminal diagnosis he'd just received.

"But… from the information I just found on Bligh's private server, Radisson's scientists manufactured a disease by tweaking the genetic structure of several different bacteria. They call it the Chimera Plague."

She stared at him. "Why? Why would they do that?"

Mayhew's mouth thinned unpleasantly. "It's never been used, but it was developed to counter a threat from the Northern Hegemony states. They were hit harder than we were by the revenant plague, and resources in the north are grim, especially with their winters. We've clashed with them in the past over resources. A group of their agitators unleashed anthrax upon some of our military officials a decade ago in response to a trade deal that soured, and so we dedicated a great deal of resources to finding something that could return the favor, before the Hegemony sued for peace. The project was officially sidelined, but it turns out Radisson's cousin, Nigel Wentworth, was in charge of the laboratory and he didn't get that memo—"

"Nigel Wentworth?" she asked sharply. "Any relation of Miles Wentworth?"

Mayhew's eyes looked somewhat dreamy as he leaned forward. "They're brothers. Nigel's the eldest, the scion of the Wentworth family. His baby sister, Addison, is ranked highly in the military. Miles, as the middle child, has a lot of pressure on him to succeed. Nigel's a genius, and Addison's ruthless. Miles, unfortunately, hasn't managed to achieve very much, no matter what he's turned his hand to. His father managed to get him a starring role on the

Confederacy's mining expansion project, and gave him one last chance to prove himself. You might have heard of it."

No wonder Miles had been so desperate to bring the settlements to the table.

"He needed the Copperplate deal," she whispered. And desperate men could do desperate things.

There was a horrible certainty swirling through her.

"Miles knew the plague was coming. He had a plague map of all the places hit. His team was vaccinated *before* they arrived to officially meet us. Until then he'd been sending couriers, and we spoke over the radio several times. His initial offer was rejected."

"I wonder," Mayhew teased her, "how our dear Miles predicted a plague?"

The breath went out of her. "He knew because he unleashed it. We'd denied his first offer, and were negotiating the second. He kept pushing us to make a decision, but Bart wanted more."

She had no proof, no evidence, but the dull pit in her gut told her the truth.

Who else had access to the plague?

Who else was desperate enough to risk it?

"And Miles had a deadline to keep," Mayhew said. "He needed the mine, signed, sealed, and delivered, and so he must have decided to get rid of the competition. Confederacy miners would be vaccinated. The plague would wipe out most of the settlements, so there'd be no need to strike a bargain. He could simply swoop in and take it, and there'd be nobody to protest. It's not as though the Confederacy has much contact with the Wastelands, so the chances of anyone discovering Wentworth deliberately slaughtered thousands was obscure. He could feed the committee whatever information he wanted."

Eden breathed into her cupped palms. "How could he do this?" Anger burned like a hot coal within her. "He knew he'd wipe out thousands of people."

"He's a Wentworth, Miss McClain." Mayhew gave a cynical smile. "They don't tend to think of the cost, as long as they gain." Eyeing her hotly, he pushed the brandy across the table toward her. "Here. Looks like you could use a mouthful. It's one of the finest brandys the Confederacy has to offer...."

Far too early to be drinking, but Eden set it to her lips and swallowed heartily. That bastard. No, that absolute, miserable wretch. If she got her hands on Miles Wentworth, he was going to regret it.

Fire burning down her throat, she pushed the brandy glass back, half full. Mayhew nodded to her, then lifted the glass as if in cheers. "He's a weasel, no doubt."

"And a cure?" Johnny asked, reaching out to stroke her neck. "What about a cure?"

"They have a hydrogel solution of nanoparticles that targets the actual bad bacterium and breaks down its cell walls within twenty-four hours, without attacking the healthy bacteria in the body. It's the only thing the bacteria aren't resistant to. It's also designed to recalibrate the electrolyte imbalance in a patient safely. One injection will deliver a sustained release of nanoparticles over the following three weeks to protect against resistance. You get the full course without forgetting to take it, with zero side effects."

"Where's the cure now?"

"That's the problem," Mayhew replied bluntly. "As I said, Nigel was working the laboratory under orders from General Radisson. They were caught testing the disease on live specimens. Radisson went down for it behind closed doors, and his understudy, Lieutenant Bligh, stepped into his shoes. The Radisson-Meyers laboratories were closed on Bligh's orders, and the contents of the laboratory transferred to the military labs at Camp Ragnarök, where Bligh could keep a closer eye on it. Nigel Wentworth was transferred across to continue his project, despite the fact Bligh hates the Wentworths."

Her face drained of heat. "He didn't go down for his crimes?"

"He was under orders from Radisson," Mayhew replied. "He got a slap on the wrist, but the man truly is a genius, and he'd served Bligh's purpose; he helped put Bligh in command with everything he knew about the experiments. I believe his testimony destroyed Radisson's legal defense during his court martial. I'll bet every credit I own they cut a deal."

"Nigel sold Radisson out to save his own skin," Johnny murmured.

"Yes."

"So Bligh has the plague, the scientist who created it, and now, the cure." Mayhew tipped his brandy to his lips. "He's not as dangerous as Radisson—he can be reasoned with if you present him with an argument that appeals to him—and he despises the Wentworths, which is a point in his favor, but he's not in charge for no reason, Miss McClain. Bligh won't want this information to get out to the general public, not after the Radisson fiasco. So he's going to want to bury any leads on this plague."

"Plus we can't get anywhere near Camp Ragnarök," Arik growled. "There's an entire squadron of wargs there, and it's locked up tighter than your granny's drawers."

Eden felt like she couldn't quite catch a breath. "Then how do we...?"

Johnny squeezed the back of her neck. "We know where the cure is now, we just have to get to it. That's step one covered, angel."

"I highly recommend not breaking into a military camp," Mayhew said, sipping his brandy.

"You did it," Johnny replied, his voice roughening. "You got in, and Arik and Nnedi got out. How'd you do it?"

Mayhew bared his teeth. "With great difficulty. I had to hack the security system and take out the electrical grid—without dropping the electric fence around the warg barracks. I had a team of highly trained professionals to watch my back, and we set off a distraction further afield to take the focus off what we were doing."

Johnny pushed to his feet, leaning on the table. "Then do it again."

Mayhew merely smiled, crooking his little finger as he threw back the last inch of brandy in his glass. "Whyever would I do that? I wanted information about what Wentworth was up to. Now I have it, and I just have to find proof so I can bring Miles and Nigel Wentworth down. I feel for you, truly I do, but you're asking me to risk my life, and I can tell from the look of you that you don't own enough credit to tempt me. It's not personal, but I rather like breathing. I don't take risks unless there's a substantial gain on the table. I'm not a gambler, Mr. Colton. Unless I'm guaranteed to win."

He stood up, setting his glass down. "Good to see you again, Arik. Best of luck with your endeavor. I suggest you forget about your plague though. Stay here, far away from its clutches, as I plan to."

# twenty-one

Two hours later, Johnny sunk onto the bed.

"Damn it!" Eden curled her hands into fists, her knuckles splaying white. "I've come all this goddamned way to find a cure I can't get my hands on. We've got one day before we *need* to start the return journey. How are we supposed to manage that in one day?"

"Hey." Johnny caught her hands and dragged her onto his lap. This wasn't like her. "Remind me of the part where you said you'd give up? I distinctly recall hearing you state you would do *whatever it takes* to get your hands on that cure. You blackmailed me into guiding you. You crossed the fucking Divide, darlin'. You looked death in the eye and put a bullet in its skull, and managed to work out how to break into a territory that's heavily guarded. You are not going to hold up a white flag now."

"I can't steal it," she retorted, putting both hands against his chest in her agitation. "I can't seduce it out of them with a smile and a please. And I can't pay for it."

"Then how are you going to get our hands on it?"

"I don't know!" She pushed him away from her, eyes darting wildly. "I don't have the answers! I haven't from the start. All I've been doing is putting one foot in front of the other, and trying to keep playing with every new hand I've been dealt." Her voice broke. "I don't know how to win this fight. I don't know how to save my people."

The sorrow in her eyes damn near broke him. Eden had always carried the weight of the world on her shoulders, and her sense of duty was impeccable. Too damned impeccable. She put everyone else's needs before hers, no matter how much it cost her.

For a woman who liked to control her world, the idea of failure was the worst thing that could happen to her. She'd never been afraid of fighting; she was afraid of letting others down.

Johnny drew her into his arms. Eden shook her head as if she felt claustrophobic in her distress, but he simply wrapped his arms around her and rested his chin on her head. "Breathe. You're stressed out and I know you're thinking of that bloody clock in your head. Take a moment, angel. I know you've got the answers. You're too fucking smart for your own good, but you're not going to get them if you panic."

"Your omega bullshit doesn't work on me," she murmured, but she wrapped her arms around his waist and surrendered.

Johnny smiled. "It's just a hug, smartass."

"Trying to stimulate my oxytocin levels, huh?"

He brushed his face against her hair, pressing a gentle kiss just above her ear, his voice dropping. "I love it when you talk intellectually to me... even if I don't understand half of what you're saying."

"Are you trying to hit on me?"

"Nope."

"You're using your sexy voice," she accused.

"I have a sexy voice?"

Eden laughed, her racing heartbeat slowing down with every second in his arms. She tilted her face to his and the laughter died, her green eyes turning serious.

Her gaze slowly dropped to his mouth.

"Want a back rub?" he murmured, his cock swelling at the heat in her gaze. He slid his hands down her sides.

"Not quite." Eden stretched up on her toes, her mouth seeking his—

And winced.

"Ouch," she said, letting her heels hit the floor.

"Still sore?"

"You have no idea," she muttered.

"Then let me." He swooped down and captured her mouth with a hard kiss. All the blood in his body rushed south when Eden returned it without a single hesitation.

Johnny caught her under the ass, hauling her up into his arms. Eden wrapped her hands around his neck, not breaking the kiss. Then her arms draped over his shoulders. *All mine.*

Eden broke free with a moan.

"We don't have time for this," she whispered.

"Can't do anything until Arik gets back from checking out Camp Ragnarök." He lowered her onto the bed, kneeling one knee between her thighs. "So we could spend the next hour pacing back and forth and worrying about something we don't have the answer for just yet. Or... we could get rid of a little bit of nervous energy. Fuck a little. Maybe a lot."

She shivered. "Language."

Johnny kissed her mouth as she lay back beneath him, most of his weight resting on one hand. The other traced the curve of her breast. "Sorry."

"You're not sorry at all."

"You're right." He was utterly unrepentant when it came to her.

Eden's hand curled up the back of his nape. "Why do I have such a hard time saying no to these proposals of yours?"

"Because you find me irresistible."

Her hand slid through his dark hair. "I used to think I had willpower."

"Then you met me."

She smiled, even as she rolled her eyes. "Then I met you."

Johnny pressed a kiss up under her jaw, his cock pressing insistently against his jeans. Eden gasped, arching beneath him, her hand clenching around a fistful of hair as he ground his erection between her legs. *There.* Right there. He felt the shiver run through her.

"So which one is it?" he whispered, tugging open the buttons on her shirt. "Are we going to fuck a little? Or a lot?"

"That depends on you," she murmured, "because you're going to be doing all the work. I can barely move."

"Not going to be a problem at all, *mi alma*," he whispered. "Lie back and let me love you."

Eden nuzzled into Johnny's arms, breathing in the scent of his skin after he'd delivered one earth-shattering orgasm after the other. She'd thought she felt boneless yesterday, but he'd worked her over pretty good before dragging her into a cuddle. She felt like she owed him an orgasm. Maybe three. Damn the man smelled good. It was one part musky heat; one part sweat and soap; and the rest an intoxicating combination that was purely Johnny himself.

"I'm not sure if your omega shit *is* affecting me," she muttered, stroking a hand over the heated flex of his bare stomach. "Every time I start to get overanxious, you send me into this relaxed state where I can suddenly think again."

"Pretty sure it's just my superior oral skills. Not my pheromones."

She punched his arm and he laughed, rolling her onto her back and coming over her. "Worked out the solution yet, darlin'?"

Eden shook her head, tension suffusing her bones. "I—"

He captured her mouth, pressing a heated kiss to it. By the time he lifted his head, she could barely breathe. Thinking was beyond her with the ghost of his kiss branding her lips.

"Yes?" he asked, that wicked half smile taunting her. "Maybe we need to keep experimenting. You clearly need a bit more oxytocin, or whatever it is."

"I'm pretty sure it's the hit of serotonin," she murmured, with a sigh. "Post orgasmic bliss."

Johnny dove under the sheets, kissing his way down her abdomen. "Let me assist then."

Eden squealed as he brushed his mouth across her ticklish flanks. "Johnny! Stop! We've wasted too much time. I can't— You can't—"

He licked his way to the seam between her legs, raining featherlight kisses across the curve of her hip, and all of her protests died a soft death. Eden moaned, her fingernails digging into his scalp as his tongue circled closer.

Closer.

She held her breath.

But the kiss she wanted didn't come.

One hand trailing lightly up and down the back of her thigh, until her skin shivered with goose bumps. Every inch of her began to tighten, like a screw. And Johnny nuzzled across the patch of curls covering her mons, his heated breath whispering over her wet skin.

Torture.

"Johnny," she breathed. Begged.

"Yes?"

He blew warm air across her sensitive skin.

"Oh, God," she moaned, her spine arching. "What are you doing to me?"

"Waiting."

"For what?" Her breath began to come in short, sharp pants. She pushed his head lower insistently, but he merely trailed his tongue down her inner thigh.

A growl hovered in her throat. Damn him.

*Damn him.*

"You know what I'm waiting for," he teased.

For her to beg.

"*Please.*" She simply didn't have it in her to wait.

"Please what?" A smoky whisper that stirred her curls.

"Kiss me, Johnny," she begged.

Johnny cupped his hands under her bottom, spreading her hips wide as he lowered his head to feast. "Oh, I'm not thinking about kissing you, darlin'." He traced his tongue just above her clit. "Nothing as civilized as that. I'm thinking about fucking this wet little pussy with my tongue. I'm thinking about making you scream. I'm thinking about forcing you to surrender every scrap of self-control you own, until we both know who owns you."

"You talk too much!" she panted.

"Do I?"

"Yes, damn—"

Johnny suckled her clit into his mouth, and every thought fled her mind as a stab of pleasure went through her. She'd been joking about him talking too much. Those heated words got her off almost as much as this, but... Jesus. That tongue. It felt like he knew her own body better than she did. Every teasing flick sent a shiver darting through her, and she could feel the wave about to break over her.

"Fuck," she gasped. "Fuck, please."

Johnny lifted his head just briefly, his dark eyes shining with pure wickedness. "Eden McClain," he chided. "Your language."

She shoved his head back between her legs, so close to the damned edge that she didn't care about manners. Or control. Or dignity. She just wanted to come.

Johnny laughed against her flesh, the sound vibrating through her. Then that delicious mouth was consuming her, devouring and licking, his tongue plunging inside her, pushing her higher and higher....

All the tension within her suddenly exploded out, and she was pretty sure she actually screamed. Eden's heels dug into the back of his shoulders. Johnny suckled hard, as if her utter devastation wasn't enough and he wanted to wring every last greedy drop of pleasure from her.

Until he finally lifted his head.

Eden collapsed on the bed, wrung out and panting, trying to make sense of her body—or what was left of it.

Stubble rasped against her hip as he crawled over her, and he wiped the slickness from his mouth with the back of his hand, his eyes twinkling. "Judging from the way you were pulling my hair I'm going to guess you liked that."

"I didn't hurt you, did I?" she breathed, wincing a little as she remembered grabbing fistfuls of his hair right before she came.

"I'm pretty sure I'll survive."

Smiling smugly, he rested his arms on either side of her head as Eden's heart raced. Her thighs parted and his hips slid into their cradle, his erection focused on only one thing.

But it was the look in his eyes that consumed her.

Eden didn't dare look away, her heart feeling like it was fragmenting in her chest. *Warning: Danger ahead*, some part of her whispered.

Because being in his arms felt like finally coming home to a place she'd longed for, but had never been able to find. There'd always been something missing in her life. Seeing Riley with Luc, and Mia with Adam, and the happiness they all shared had only exacerbated the situation. She'd thrown herself into work instead, so she was too tired to even regret how cold and empty her bed was when she crawled into it at night.

This… felt a little like what she saw between the others.

*You are falling bad….*

The first thrust took her slowly, as Johnny nuzzled her lips with the same dedication he'd given to her pussy. Kissing him was almost as delicious as having him eat her out. The man's mouth ought to be given an award.

He thrust inside her slowly, each move echoing that of his tongue. This wasn't fucking so much as a slow, intense session of lovemaking. He'd done this to her that morning at Shadow Rock, as if he wanted to make it last forever, his mouth and hips trying to tell her something he wouldn't put into words.

Eden clenched around him, trying to make him lose control. He drew back and grinned at her, and the next thrust came a little harder.

"You're beautiful," he breathed, "*Eres la luna que me consume, el sol alrededor del cual giro. Te amo mi angel.*"

"What are you saying?" she whispered, so close to the edge she could feel it crumbling beneath her feet.

"You drive me crazy."

Then she was lost in a sea of sensation, wracked by the waves of pure pleasure that rolled through her. Each thrust pushed her higher until she could barely breathe. Johnny slammed into her, a quiver running down his spine as he grunted, and finally collapsed atop her.

Tension pitted deep within her as she stroked her hands up his sweaty back. She liked this. Too much. She adored kissing him. Lying in his arms, it felt like nothing would ever be able to touch her here. She felt safe.

But for how long?

Johnny lifted his head, his breath catching and his heart pounding as if he'd run a hundred miles. "What's wrong?"

"Nothing's wrong." She lifted her mouth to kiss his lips, but he turned his face away, before looking back at her insistently.

"Eden?"

He could feel the tension curling through her, which, considering she should be suffused with post-orgasmic bliss, left his stomach knotting up.

"There's nothing wrong. You destroy me," Eden whispered, her fingers stroking his arm. "Each and every time."

"Then why are you biting your lip like that's a bad thing?" The horrible feeling was back, leaving him a little breathless, like something was squeezing his lungs.

The words *I think I love you* whispered through his mind, but he choked it down before he could betray himself.

Because he wasn't certain if she felt the same way.

A small frown furrowed between her brows. "Because I can't control my world when I'm with you. I forget what I'm supposed to be doing. You're a distraction I don't need."

"That's not a bad thing," he murmured, lifting away from her, his slackened cock wet with his cum. "You can't control everything, angel. Least of all me. This is a negotiation between us, in which we both get to meet in the middle. I have something you want; you have something I want."

"Which is...?"

*You. I want you.* Johnny curled onto his side. Damn it. He felt breathless again. Was he really going to say this? "I know this is fast—"

Eden suddenly clamped her hand over his mouth, her eyes punching wide.

"What?" he muttered, behind her palm, as she sat up like she'd been shot.

"Holy shit," she whispered. "I have something they want. They have something *I* want. That's it. That's how I get my cure."

The breath rushed out of him. *Fuck.* He'd been about to tell her how he felt, and *now* she had her epiphany? "You have incredibly bad timing."

But Eden wasn't listening.

She rolled out of bed, reaching for her clothes. Within three seconds she was tearing her jeans up her legs and trying to find her bra, wincing as her body clearly reminded her of yesterday's climb. Bruises shadowed her hips from the harness. He'd tried to be careful with her, but she was coated in blackened marks from head to toe.

"Bless your wicked mouth. I need to work out how to contact General Bligh."

# twenty-two

A plan formed as Eden headed for the bathroom. It was risky and relied on elements of pure luck, but she just might be able to pull it off if she was clever. Arik returned just as she'd had her epiphany, but she'd sent him out to track Mayhew down again, in the hopes he might be able to get a message through to the general.

But first, a shower.

Eden stripped her clothes off, turning on the water. Hot water poured out of the showerhead, gallons of it. She was used to a trickle, and this was more luxurious than she'd ever known.

Closing her eyes, she stood under the spray as long as she could. Hot water sluiced away the aches and pains of the last couple of days' exertion. Tomorrow would be worse, she suspected. Unused muscles obliterated by sudden exertion. Leaning her forehead against the wall, she lost herself in the drum of the water on her skin, thinking about all she'd learned about the bacteria and the cure. They needed a way to get into the military base, and Mayhew could do it, but how to talk him into helping them? She had something General Bligh wanted, but what about Mayhew? Without him the entire plan fell apart.

It was only when the water ran cold that Eden hauled herself upright. She must have almost fallen asleep, or into some sort of semi-trance. The traces of yesterday's headache began to ache behind her right eye. She needed more sleep.

No time for that.

She turned the shower off and started drying herself. Beads of perspiration clung to the mirror, so she wiped her fingers across it.

She was just about to flip her head upside down and towel dry her hair when something caught her eye.

A chill ran down her spine as Eden used the towel to dry the mirror instead, her heart starting to beat a little faster.

She leaned closer.

There.

The beginning of a rash blossomed on the middle of her chest. It was so faint she almost mistook it for stubble rash from Johnny's jaw, except for the fact she'd been staring at tiny red dots exactly like these for the past two weeks.

All the heat drained from her face.

Headaches. Muscular aches. Thirst. She'd put it down to a strenuous couple of days, but the truth stared her straight in the eye.

She had the plague.

Eden walked out of the bathroom, a towel wrapped around her hair and her skin pink from the shower.

Johnny glanced up from the map he was poring over with Lincoln. He was about to look back down when something about Eden's expression set off alarm bells.

"What is it?" he demanded.

"Promise me you're not going to freak out," Eden said, in the sort of voice that made his stomach drop.

Johnny considered her. *You don't say something like that unless you're fairly certain someone is going to lose their shit.*

"No promises," he growled. "Why? What's wrong?"

Swallowing hard, she began unbuttoning her shirt. "I've been a bit headachy in the past couple of days, but I assumed it had to do with everything that was going on." Her fingers fumbled on a button.

"Eden?" His voice sounded hollow. Outside of him. He had the sudden sensation the world was dropping out from under him.

He knew, before she told him.

"I'm in phase one," she whispered, holding her shirt open just enough for him to see the faint hints of rash on her chest.

Cold shivered through him.

Johnny's heart squeezed into a tight little fist in his chest, and it was all he could do to stop himself from swaying. *No. This couldn't be happening.*

Eden cleared her throat, still not quite meeting anyone's eyes. Her lashes fluttered toward Lincoln, then she glanced down again. "I'm so sorry. It's likely I was infected with the plague when I stayed at Shadow Rock. Anyone who came into close peripheral contact with me *might* have been infected, as it can be spread by airborne contamination as well as body fluids. Symptoms don't tend to show for around three to seven days after exposure. If I'd known...."

"It's all right, Eden," Lincoln said simply. "I've spent the past couple of days with you. You wouldn't have put them at risk if you'd suspected. You're not that type of person. And we'll get our cure."

He couldn't believe how calmly she was taking it.

"So what do we do?" Johnny demanded, throwing his arms wide. "Hope and pray Bligh comes through?"

"We've got time."

"How much time?" he demanded, his voice rising. "We can't wait for Bligh and hope he gets your message. We can't rely on his good conscience. He might just lock us up and throw away the key."

Or worse.

He hadn't misunderstood what Mayhew was saying about burying any sign of this plague. If Blight discovered Eden was infected....

A hand clamped down on his shoulder. Lincoln. "Settle down," the other warg said.

The fucker was *fusing* him....

Johnny saw red. He broke the warg's hold on him, and Lincoln hit back, their arms locking. Johnny slammed him into the wall, and Lincoln's breath hissed out between his teeth.

"Calm the fuck down or I'll put you down." Lincoln snarled, capturing his wrist.

Rage enveloped him, his voice growing deeper as his vocal chords started shifting. "You think you can?"

"Johnny!" A voice. Eden's voice. He felt her hand on his shoulder then, and the breath snarled out of him. Her face loomed in front of him. "Stop it! He's right. You need to calm down."

He looked down at his hands, and realized he wasn't staring at human flesh anymore.

Another slither of ice through his veins. He hauled himself up short. *Fuck*. He'd almost gone warg. Lincoln stared at him like he didn't dare move, his cheekbone swelling.

Johnny reached deep, searching for that part of him that belonged to his father. It was harder to find than he'd expected. His heart beat a hundred miles an hour, and all he could see was that damned rash.

Eden wrapped her arms around him. "It's going to be okay."

Wasn't that a punch in the face? He was the one who should have been consoling her. Eden knew exactly what the plague could do. She had to be scared.

"I'm sorry," he whispered. "I wasn't expecting that. I just...." *Lost it*. "I can't lose you, angel."

"You're not going to," she reminded him.

Calmness washed over him like a sluice of cold water as his omega half rose. His skin itched with heat as he pulled back, forcing his body to shift. Hair vanished along his arms, and his fingernails ached as they transformed.

He'd never in his life come so close to flipping that switch before. A part of him had almost thought itself immune.

*It's her*, said the darker part of himself. *She does this to you. You're too involved. Too twisted up emotionally in her.*

Having no one might have been both a blessing and a curse. He breathed out a helpless laugh. All this time, and the warg had been sitting there beneath the surface of his skin, waiting.

"Are you okay?" he asked hoarsely, drawing back and looking down into her upturned face.

Eden swallowed. "No. But now I know how my patients feel. I can't afford to fall apart right now. And I've got plenty of time."

"Bullshit." She wasn't going to live with the threat of this over her head any longer than she needed to. "I'm done sitting around waiting on the Confederacy. We have to crack the military labs tonight."

"Arik tells me you have important information for me," Mayhew said, looking bored even through an eight-inch monitor.

"I do," Eden said, swallowing hard.

"I'm not interested in playing games, Miss McClain. I told you this morning I don't take risks for no gain. So what's changed?"

She let out a slow breath and started unbuttoning her shirt. "This."

Mayhew's eyebrow arched as she worked the first three buttons open. "Intriguing, to be sure, but a strip show isn't something I can't view any day of the week, for the right price."

She opened her shirt, revealing the rash across her chest. "I didn't notice it this morning. It was only after I got out of the shower that I saw it." And since then, it had only darkened and spread. "I have the plague, Mr. Mayhew."

He froze, and then his fingers continued rolling those ever-present dice over the backs of them. "I'm sorry to hear that, Miss McClain."

"You should be," she replied bluntly. "There's a chance you were exposed to it this morning. You won't know for another three to seven days, of course, and you might be lucky. But you did share your drink with me. Wanted to show me the finer aspects of Confederacy life."

The color rapidly drained out of his face.

"It's a virulent disease, passed along through body fluids," she continued, reeling off the facts. "Blood, semen, saliva. You drank out of the glass after I did. I'd recommend you start a course of antibiotics, just to make certain, but as you know, the plague's immune to them. It might help ease the fever, a little. It might prolong it. But within two weeks there's a chance you might be dead... unless you'd care to beg General Bligh to open up his laboratory to you. Maybe he will. You know him better than I do.

"And of course, there's the risk to your loved ones, the people around you. It didn't take much to set it off within the population of Absolution."

"Did you know?" he snapped, clenching his fist around his dice.

"Of course not," she replied tightly. "Regardless of how much I want that cure, I would *never* risk the lives of innocent people."

"Fuck." He pushed away from his monitor, pressing his fist to his mouth. A muscle in his jaw ticked.

"We're going after the labs tonight," she told him. "We need your help to get us in."

Dark eyes cut toward her. Mayhew laughed humorlessly. "And in return I get a booster shot of the hydrogel. This seems to have played out very well for you, Miss McClain. You've finally given me incentive."

The strain got to her then. "It hasn't bloody well played out in my favor at all! You think I want the plague?" The clock in her head was ticking down again. She had a day or two before the fever hit. If she didn't get a handle on this cure, she'd be out of action.

Then what?

Mayhew wiped the sneer off his face, looking pale. He nodded. "Fine. I'm in. What's the plan?"

"You tell me," she replied. "You're the one who knows the military base inside and out. You're the one who can hack the schematics."

Mayhew smiled. "First step: We need a distraction."

"Sure you got your shit under control?" Arik asked, his eyes roving over the military labs below them.

Lincoln must have told him about the earlier episode.

Johnny checked all his guns, his hands moving over them with unconscious ease as he mentally prepared. "Locked and loaded."

"Just don't want to be going in there with a ticking time bomb," Arik said coolly.

"I'm fine."

"You don't look fine."

"Can we just focus on the mission?" It was the only thing keeping his heart rate normal.

Arik returned to studying the military base below them. "I get it, you know. When they took Nnedi.... They all told me to mourn her as if she was dead. Nobody could get in and out of the city-states, they said. If I tried, I'd probably die.

"But they didn't know I was a dead man anyway. I never realized how I felt about her until that moment. She was mine. My woman. And I'd let her slip through my fingers. I'd never see her again, unless I got off my goddamned ass. I could feel the warg beneath my skin, all hot rage and blinding pain. I trashed my room and when I came out of it, I thanked my lucky stars nobody had been in there. So I headed for the city, knowing if I stayed they'd have to put me down in the end. I was dead either way; at least if I tried to get her back, we might have a shot."

Johnny glanced toward him. "What's it like in there?"

"Bad."

He scrubbed at his mouth. "It's my worst fear," he admitted softly. "My uncle was a bad man. Broke my will to his when I was barely a kid." He swallowed. "Made me do a lot of things I'm not proud of. You think it can't happen to you, but I *know* it can."

Arik's face remained implacable. "They test you to see if you're truly broken. Make you do things you don't want to do. Put a bullet in a friend's skull. Break your own arm. Any hesitation, any resistance, and they take you away and throw you back in the hole. Work you over again. It's relentless. You start reacting. Obeying." His voice softened. "It took me three years, but I could feel myself bending to them. It's easy to pretend you're invulnerable when you're out here. The only thing that saved me was Nnedi. I knew she was in there. If I focused on her, then they couldn't break me. Lincoln doesn't get it—thinks nothing's strong enough to break his will down—but then he's never faced the reality of it before."

Arik glanced at the watch Mayhew had given him. "We've got five minutes."

"How's that distraction coming along?" Johnny asked.

Arik put a hand to his ear, pressing the comm device Mayhew had given him. "We all sorted?"

Static echoed through both their earpieces. "You don't rush a maestro," Mayhew shot back. "Are you in place?"

"Almost."

"Then get your asses in place."

# twenty-three

"On my signal," Derek Mayhew's voice whispered in his ear.

Johnny crouched down by the fence. It felt weird having another man's voice in his head, but he had to admit it was handy.

"Three, two, one...."

A spark flared in the distance. A couple of lights went out along the fence. In the distance a dog barked. Warg dogs. Brilliant.

"Move," Mayhew directed. "You've got a minute window before I flick the electrics back on and you need to be inside that fence."

He and Arik were going in first to clear the way. Behind him, Lincoln hovered over Eden. Both of them were dressed in Confederacy green. He didn't know where Mayhew had gotten the uniforms, but at a glance they might pass for Confederacy soldiers. Mayhew waited with them, using a datapad to take down Ragnarök's electricity.

They crouched low and ran. Arik used wire cutters to snip the lowest strand of the fence, then they were both rolling under the fence and moving to take up position. So far, so good. Adrenaline pumped through him, until the night seemed to come alive.

Johnny looked back, gesturing with his fingers for Eden, Mayhew, and Lincoln to make their move. He scanned the darkness, covering them. Nothing moved, and then they were through the fence, and the faint electric whine began again as Mayhew flicked the security systems back on.

Arik gestured toward the end. Johnny nodded, holding his shotgun low.

The laboratories were on the opposite side to the barracks, thank God. The last thing they needed was Confederacy wargs scenting them.

Johnny rubbed a hand over Eden's spine, sharing a questioning look with her. *You okay?*

She rolled her eyes. *I'm fine.*

He was pretty sure there was more to it in her head, but he merely moved on. She wouldn't appreciate him hovering. Time to hit the labs.

A warg suddenly melted out of the shadows. One second there was no one there, and the next Johnny could smell him.

It was one of those moments where both of them were downwind and hadn't expected the other.

Johnny recovered quicker, perhaps because he'd been anticipating enforcers around every corner. He leaped forward, jamming the butt of his shotgun against the soldier's head.

The bastard staggered, but didn't go down. A hand chopped toward his throat, and the gun was knocked from his hands. Johnny moved inside his next strike, delivering a punch to the warg's ribs. One, two, then a hard uppercut that snapped the warg's head back.

Johnny stepped behind him, dragging the warg back against his chest. Slamming a hand around his throat, and another over his mouth, he took him down, kicking his feet out from under him.

"Stay down," he hissed, holding the warg against his chest.

The warg struggled, his heels kicking in the gravel as Johnny stared into his eyes and fused him with scent.

"That's it," he murmured, as each kick became a little weaker. "Stop moving."

The soldier slumped in his arms.

"Nice work," Arik muttered, and there was a somewhat wild look in his eyes. Arik would be getting a lungful of those omega pheromones too.

Johnny knocked the soldier out, then flipped him over and hastily hog-tied him, ripping the warg's tunic and stuffing some of the material in his mouth. No point killing him. The blood would only draw attention, and if they needed to rely on Bligh, then a trail of dead wargs would do nobody any good.

"Any more?" Arik muttered.

"Not that I can see or hear." His heart raced.

"Let's go get our cure then."

Breaking into the lab was Eden's first experience in breaking the law.

She hadn't been there when Johnny popped the lock on an upper window of the house. But this was different. She kept jumping at shadows, expecting wargs to leap out at every corner.

The four guys moved like a well-oiled machine. Johnny and Arik rode point, with Lincoln guarding them from behind. She and Mayhew were in the middle, tasked with keeping out of the way until required.

Fine by her.

Mayhew slipped a cord into his datapad, and then slid the other end of it into some sort of plug on the keypad to the door. She didn't fully understand what he was doing, but it worked like magic. The keypad lit up, and then the door was hissing open. Mayhew collected his cord, and they were in.

"You're very good," she noted, as Johnny and Arik slipped ahead of them to clear the way.

"Child's play."

"Oh, everyone in the Confederacy can do it, can they?"

He smiled at her. "Computers always made sense to me, Miss McClain. Spent a lot of time locked up in juvenile detention, and there was a guy in there who knew code. Taught me a little. He was pure genius, and when we got out.... Well, the Confederacy likes to say all its citizens are equal, but they're really not. I wanted to feed myself and didn't want to end up back in juvie, so I had to learn how to get credit." He waggled his fingers. "I can steal everything that's not nailed down with a touch of my datapad."

"Mayhew," Arik called. "Another locked door. You're up."

The labs were all locked down for the night, with bulletproof doors at certain intervals. Mayhew cracked them, one after the other, until they were in Wing C. A sign on the wall said Infectious Diseases.

Mayhew examined the map he'd pulled up on his screen. "Gold mine." He pointed to a door. "This one."

The door gave with a hiss, leading into a sterile laboratory. Rows of fridges with glass fronts lined the walls. She could see hundreds of vials within them, labeled neatly and barcoded. And a certain sort of breathlessness went through her. A giddy *you did it*. Victory. Relief. She could save Lily. She could save Ian and all the others of Absolution who were inflicted with the salt plague. A thousand furious emotions pressing in on her from the inside out, and—

"What the hell?"

Eden slammed to a halt as a man's voice broke through the room.

It went through her, thin as a sharpened stiletto.

A cut. A slice.

Miles Wentworth.

He looked up sharply from where he'd been reading some sort of document a second man had slid in front of him. She hadn't seen either of them from the outside, tucked as they were in the corner, and as Johnny sucked in a sharp breath, she realized she wasn't the only one.

Their eyes locked together, and Eden felt trapped in a vortex where Miles's mouth dropped open in shock as recognition flared in his dark eyes, and she knew the same expression was painted across her own face.

"*You,*" she whispered, her heart starting to thunder through her veins.

He took a step back as if she'd spat the word at him. As if it carried a weight that could dissect him. His gaze tracked sideways, a furtive move that compounded his guilt.

The truth was etched on every inch of his body and face.

"You know these people?" the man at his side asked, and Eden saw in the thick dark slashing frown of his brows a similarity between them.

Miles turned and bolted for the bench in the middle of the room.

"Stop them!" Mayhew yelled. "If they hit the panic button—"

"Don't move," Johnny snarled, pointing his handgun directly at Miles. It had been provided by Mayhew, and a thin green dot bloomed right in the middle of Miles' forehead.

He skidded to a halt.

A shotgun pumped as Lincoln turned his weapon on the other man, who'd been in the process of reaching for the datapad attached to the wall.

"Miles *and* Nigel Wentworth," Mayhew mocked. "What are the odds? Here we are looking for whoever was behind a certain plague ravaging the Wastelands, and who should we find but the Wentworth's themselves. Daddy

Wentworth's going to be quite unamused when he discovers the pair of you dabbling in things you shouldn't be."

"Miss McClain," Miles managed to gape. "What the hell are you doing here?"

"What the hell am I—?" Her fury burned to the surface, turning her incandescent with fury. This man had tried to murder hundreds, possibly thousands for a fucking mine.

Eden didn't even realize she was moving toward him until he threw up his hands with a yelp. Her fist was moving independently of her and slammed right through his ineffective guard.

Miles's head snapped back as her punch landed, sending him staggering into a tray of tools. They smashed to the ground, the violent echo of their landing ringing in her ears.

"You murderous bastard!" She hit him again, driving the blow through her knuckles and not her fingers, the way Adam had taught her. "You fucking prick! You unleashed a gods damned plague on us as though we weren't even human. You thought you'd wipe out my settlement just so you didn't have to pay more to get your greedy hands on the Copperplate mine. Admit it!"

"I didn't!" Miles bleated. "I had nothing to do with it!"

Rage consumed her. She turned to find Johnny right behind her and snatched the spare pistol from his belt. Eden drove the muzzle right into Miles's forehead until it left a white ring of pressure on his skin. "Then tell me how a Confederacy-manipulated plague suddenly managed to afflict Wastelanders? Tell me how a bacteria that could only be found in this fucking lab made its way hundreds of miles west, where it started killing *my* people." Her hand shook. "Explain why your men were vaccinated against it before they even arrived!"

"I don't know! I don't know!" Tears and snot ran down his face as he cowered.

"Henry Chin told me everything!" Eden clicked the safety off, her vision narrowing down the line of the pistol as she stared into his pathetic eyes. "You deliberately infected Wastelanders, so you could move on the Copperplate mine without paying the price we wanted."

He finally broke, nodding furiously. "I'm sorry. I'm sorry. I did it! I needed the deal. You don't understand—"

For a second she actually considered pulling the trigger. The violent urge to end this man filled her like a poison.

"Don't do it, angel," Johnny said softly. "You know you'll always regret it."

*I want to. I want to so badly....*

"Miles?" Nigel croaked. "Is this true?"

She saw it in his eyes and wanted to end him. "You *don't* deserve to live," she managed to say, pushing harder with the pistol, until the scent of urine stung her nostrils. Miles slowly sunk to his knees, shaking, quivering, cowering before her like the pathetic bully he was.

"Please," he gasped. "Please don't hurt me, Miss McClain! *Please.* I'll do whatever you want. I promise."

"His death is not worth your guilt." A hand rested on the small of her back. "Easy, darlin'. Let's leave some of him behind to pay for what he's done."

Eden tore the pistol down, clapping a hand over her mouth as she gasped. She shook. Violently. She'd almost shot him. Almost murdered a man. He didn't deserve to live—not after what he'd done—but she wasn't a killer.

She refused to let Miles Wentworth twist her into something she wasn't.

Eden let Johnny take the pistol from her, and collapsed into his arms. He caressed a hand down her spine.

"Beautiful," Mayhew breathed behind them, a red light blinking as he held the datapad up. "Got it all on tape—confession and all. You're going down, Wentworth. Both of you."

Nigel's head snapped up. "I had nothing to do with this. I didn't know he'd taken some of my plague samples!"

"*Your* plague samples," Mayhew spat. "There's going to be a lot of people who start asking questions about what you've been up to, Nigel."

"Are you okay?" Johnny asked, as Nigel bleated something at Mayhew.

She looked up. Nodded. There was a hollow mess in her heart as if her anger had suddenly flamed out. All she felt was exhausted. "Yeah. Better now I hit him."

A smile bloomed over his dangerous mouth. "It was the perfect punch. Adam taught you well." His smile died. "But now it's time to get to work, angel," Johnny murmured, holding his gun on Miles. "This is your part of the action."

Arik set up by the doors, gun held ready as he stared into the darkened corridors.

"What are we looking for?" she asked Mayhew shakily. Every fridge was neatly labeled, with a strange barcode on the front.

He shrugged. "There's nothing in the database. It's like this thing doesn't exist, except in rumors of what brought down Radisson."

Lincoln grabbed Nigel by the scruff of the neck and hauled him toward the fridges. "Where's the cure for the plague?"

"I don't—"

Mayhew put a gun to Miles's temples. "Get the fucking cure, Nigel, or I'll spray your brother's brains all over the floor. If that doesn't inspire any action, then you're next. We're a little short on time."

"The nanoparticle solution's called Ener-V," Nigel bleated. "That's what you're after to cure the plague. The vaccine should be in the same fridge."

Eden scanned label after label. Despite the chill in the room, her hair was damp with sweat.

Phase two was about to kick her in the teeth.

"Here it is!" she called, finally finding the right label.

Mayhew scanned the strange code on the front of the fridge. "Give me a moment to check if these are the right vials." He looked at Nigel. "It's coming up as password protected. I could break it, but it would take a while. What's the password?"

"I can't—"

Mayhew put the gun to Nigel's head. "I actually don't need you any more, though I'd prefer to double-check."

"NKW773X," Nigel yelped.

Mayhew's fingers danced over the keypad. The datapad pinged. "Got it. This is definitely it. There's an entire section on Ener-V in the database. The vaccine's on the bottom shelf."

Eden eased open the fridge. Each syringe was preprepared, and they lay in neat racks. Hundreds of them.

"Get a refrigerated transport box," Mayhew called. "You'll need to keep them cool."

He showed her what he meant. There were small silver briefcases in the corner with a cooling pack attached, and foam inside them. Hundreds of cutouts lined the foam; the perfect size for the vials. She didn't understand half the terms he used, but when he adjusted the temperature dial on the side of the box, she could feel the foam pads begin to chill.

"Start packing them in," he instructed.

"Inject yourselves first," Johnny cut in, looking away from the door for the first time. Their eyes met. "Just in case we lose those cases."

Eden swallowed. He'd been tense ever since she told him she was infected.

Mayhew showed her the instructions on the datapad.

"How are you getting all of this?" she asked breathlessly as she prepared the small syringe and his arm.

"Magic." His smile came quick, and she quite suspected he was getting some sort of thrill from the night. "They don't even know I'm in their system."

He hissed out between his teeth as she injected him with the full contents of the vial. Then it was her turn. A little whisper of relief went through her as she swiped the alcohol swab over her upper arm. She hadn't wanted to think too much about the disease, but it'd been on the back of her mind, gnawing away like termites.

"Pinch here," she instructed.

Mayhew blanched. "You're kidding, right?" He held up his hands and backed away. "Sorry, Miss McClain, but I don't do blood."

She *almost* looked at Nigel Wentworth, but there was no way she was letting him put his hands on her.

"Here." Johnny handed his gun to Lincoln, and strode toward her. "Want me to do it?"

She nodded. Johnny pinched her skin together between thumb and forefinger, and stabbed the syringe needle deep into the muscle. Eden winced as a flood of pure cold pumped right into her arm.

He rubbed her arm and dragged her against his chest. "Thank God."

"I'm okay."

A shuddering breath tore through him. "Just let me hold you for a second. You weren't okay, and it's been driving me crazy. I'm not afraid to die, Eden, but I couldn't handle it if anything happened to you."

"Right back at you, big guy."

He drew back and looked at her, his eyes filled with emotion. Then he hauled her in close, and Eden let him hold her.

One hand slid up the back of her neck, sinking into her hair. Eden closed her eyes and took a moment to just breathe. She was starting to get dangerously addicted to these hugs. For a man who'd spent years riding by himself, he was more affectionate than she'd expected.

Or maybe just hungry for affection?

She wrapped her arms around his waist and squeezed tight. "We did it," she whispered. She had her cure. She could save Lily, and the rest of her patients. "I couldn't have done this without you."

"Never doubted you for a second, angel." Johnny stole a kiss, tension easing through his shoulders. "Got in, got the cure, now we just need to get out. Then you and I are celebrating."

Eden rested a hand against his chest. "You got something planned?"

Johnny gave her his crooked smile. "You. Me. Dinner and a little privacy."

"Can we focus?" Arik growled under his breath.

"Right." Johnny straightened, his relieved cheerfulness fading off him as if he forced himself to lock down his emotions. "Let's get the hell out of here."

He helped her pack two of the refrigerated cases. Eden wanted to take as much of the vaccine and Ener-V cure as she could. She hated not knowing what was going on back home. Who knew how many people were affected? With this, she had enough of the cure for three hundred people. It would have to do to start with.

"What do we do about these two?" Lincoln asked, gesturing toward Nigel and Miles.

The sound of Arik removing the safety on his gun echoed loudly through the room.

"No," she said sharply, pressing a hand to her temples. "It's too easy. They should suffer. I want them to suffer." She looked at Mayhew. "What are you going to do with that footage?"

He gave her a lethal smile. "I think the good citizens of the Confederacy deserve to know what's going on behind the closed doors of Ragnarök."

Complete ruin. The Wentworths would lose everything. Possibly even end up on the wrong side of General Bligh, if this erupted in his face.

"I need Bligh."

Just in case there were more than three hundred plague victims.

"Then I'll hold it over Bligh's head. I don't think he'll be very happy with the Wentworth's."

"Perfect," she said, with a brisk nod, though her gaze lingered on Nigel and the uneasy way he shifted. Instinct made her tense. His smile seemed out of place.

"What's that smell?" Johnny asked, rubbing his nose. "Smells like—"

The second he said it, her gaze shot to Nigel.

Nigel snatched at a small tap on the bench, and gas began hissing into the room. Further along the bench, another tap shimmered in the air as gas trickled silently from its nozzle. He must have slipped it on when they were distracted.

"Don't shoot!" she screamed as Nigel suddenly bolted for the panic button.

Arik hauled his pistol into the air, just as Johnny leapt for Nigel. He slammed into the scientist, but it was too late.

An alarm began blaring, and the lights suddenly cut off, plunging them into a sudden darkness. All she could see was the red glow flashing from the alarm in the corner, and the flash of shadow moving as Johnny lifted his weapon and pistol-whipped Nigel with it.

"You fucking piece of snot," he snarled, and Nigel whimpered and hit the floor.

"Oh, shit," Mayhew said, looking around frantically. "We need to get out of here."

"What about them?" she demanded, gesturing to where Miles cowered next to his brother's fallen body.

"Justice will just have to wait. Move!"

"They know we're here!" Johnny yelled, as they sprinted along the hallway. "How many are we expecting?"

"Full squad of twenty," Arik yelled back. "They won't know exactly where we are at first. They'll be waiting for commands from central, and central will be sending drones out."

"On it," Mayhew called.

The lights in the hallway had been cut, and the only illumination came from the red alarms, pulsing in and out.

"Time for that diversion, Mayhew," he called, grabbing Eden by the arm and hauling her close against his side, just in case.

She pounded down the hallway with him, but he could hear her breath rasping. While the injection was hopefully starting to work, her system was still ravaged, and she wouldn't have the strength to keep this up for long.

"With pleasure," Mayhew said, fingers racing over his datapad. "Let's confuse them."

Outside, a series of explosions rocked the air.

The ground shook, and Johnny could just make out screams and confused yelling in the distance. "Do I want to know what you just did?"

"Comms are down." Mayhew gave a sinister smile. "It seems someone's taken over their drones. They're attacking the barracks, keeping the wargs within pinned down."

"Shame." Johnny allowed himself a tight smile.

"I live for this shit."

They skidded around a corner.

"Remember the exit plan," Johnny snarled at Eden. "As soon as we're out, we're heading for the storm water tunnels. No time to waste. Mayhew's going to cover us from the inside."

She nodded, her eyes wide.

"Incoming!" Arik yelled, slamming the pair of them into the wall as gunfire suddenly barked.

"*Fuck*." He cupped his arms around Eden's head, as hell opened up around them. There was a doorway there. Just enough cover, if he and Arik pressed tight.

Mayhew found himself in the middle of the line of fire. He spun the other way, using the steel case to shield himself. Bullets punched into the case, and one hit him in the side. He went down, the case hissing pressurized gas.

"Mayhew?" Eden screamed.

"Got him." Lincoln had been last. He grabbed Mayhew by the arm and hauled him back into the corridor they'd come from, leaving a smear of blood on the tiled floors.

Mayhew groaned, cupping his side. "My datapad."

It lay on the floor in the middle of the hallway.

"*Go, go, go,*" called a tinny voice near the exit.

Heavy booted feet drummed on the floor, coming closer. At least one squad had managed to clear the barracks.

He hoped they were only human.

And that it was just one squad.

"Without that datapad," Mayhew gasped, "none of us are getting out of here alive."

Johnny poked his head out of the doorway. Over a dozen black-clad figures in full riot suits clomped toward them. One of them yelled when they saw him and pointed. Light flared as a gun retorted. *Ping. Ping. Ping.* Bullets bit into the back wall.

Pinned down. Shit.

"We've got to get moving," Arik warned.

"Count of three." He grabbed Eden by the arm. "Get the datapad."

"One... two...." Arik counted.

"The cure!" Eden held her hand out imploringly toward the shattered case.

"Down to one case," he yelled, shoving her back down the corridor they'd come from on the count of three. "We've got enough for over a hundred people. It will have to do."

Arik slid across the floor behind him, as bullet fire barked in the hallway. He had the datapad and shoved it toward Mayhew as he gained his feet.

Lincoln was tucked under Mayhew's shoulder.

"Let's get moving!" Arik remained at the back to cover them in Lincoln's place.

Down the hallway, past Infectious Diseases.

They hit a T-intersection, and Johnny paused. A set of steel bars was slowly descending from the ceiling. *Shit.* "They're locking down the facility and trying to herd us."

"This way," Mayhew gasped, limping past them, bloody fingers holding his datapad. "There's an exit at the back."

At each intersection, the steel bars were descending. Arik cursed behind them as he tried to spit enough bullets back toward the squad to keep them at bay, but conserve their ammunition.

"Stay with Lincoln," Johnny said to Eden, giving her a little push. "I'll help Arik keep them off us."

Mayhew plugged into a fuse box. "If I can get us through here, we have a clear run to that exit."

They were dangerously in the open here. Johnny saw the enforcers' red dot bloom right in the center of Arik's chest as he swung his rifle off his back.

"Get down!" he screamed, slamming into Arik.

They hit the floor, Arik sliding across the polished concrete with Johnny atop him just as gunfire turned the air above them into a hailstorm of death. Bullets slammed into the wall ahead of them, pitting the brick, and Johnny buried his face in Arik's shoulder before someone called out sharply behind him.

It stopped.

*Eden.*

Lincoln crouched behind a steel box, his hand holding Eden's head down. "The cure!" he yelled, pointing at the briefcase on the floor behind them. He'd clearly shoved her out of the way, and she'd dropped it.

No way was Johnny losing that briefcase.

Without it, Eden's people would die.

Sprinting low toward the case, Johnny heard a loud groan echo in the ceiling. A wall of bars began to descend, and red lights flashed at intervals along the ceiling. *Shit.* No wonder they weren't shooting.

"Code black," one of the enforcers yelled into his radio. "We have a code black in the Wing C. All units. I repeat, all units."

Skating to a halt, Johnny bent to grab the case and tore back toward Eden. The bars ahead of him cranked down inexorably, separating him from the others. He wasn't going to make it. He wasn't going to—

Johnny threw himself into a slide, one foot flung out before him.

At the last second he thrust the case ahead of him, and it flew beneath the bars just as they crashed into the floor. Johnny slammed against them, his knees bending with the force and his body colliding against the silver-coated steel. He jerked back with a hiss as the silver burned him.

Too late.

He was trapped on the other side.

"Johnny!" Eden screamed, throwing herself at the bars.

Behind him the enforcers advanced, lifting their rifles. Red dots glowed to life across Eden's chest.

"Down!" he yelled.

Arik wrestled her back, tossing the polished steel case to his brother. "Damn it, Eden. We've got to go."

Arik looked at him helplessly, and Johnny understood. He wasn't getting out of here. They had no time. Barely any ammunition left. And the enforcers were right behind him.

There was a tight clenching in his chest as if the cage of his ribs fought to contain his heart. His ears were ringing, and all he could see was the shock and fear on Eden's face.

He loved her.

He'd found more of himself in the past week than he'd ever dared to hope for, thanks to her.

Someone needed to make the decision.

"*Go*," he whispered, dread sliding through his veins as he crawled to his feet, putting his body between the enforcers and Eden. "Get her out of here. Get her safely home."

"No!" Eden struggled, driving her elbow into Arik's ribs, her expression frantic. "*No!*"

She got free. Hit the bars again, rattling them with her tiny fists. "Mayhew!"

"Eden, stop it," he demanded, curling his hands over hers. A shiver of nerves ran through him as he cast a look over his shoulder—their window of opportunity was narrowing, and the longer they delayed, the stronger the chances of them getting caught.

Enforcers hammered down the corridor toward him. Two of them knelt at the sides, bringing their rifles to bear on him. He could almost feel the red lasers of their sights burning right between his shoulder blades. A helpless sort of anticipation stole his breath. If they pulled those triggers, there would be nothing he could do about it.

"We've got to get these fucking bars up," Eden snarled, looking for some sort of electronic fuse box.

"Eden," he snapped.

She looked at him helplessly, and he saw his fear reflected there.

"Whatever it takes," he said desperately, reaching through the bars and stroking a hand through her hair. "That's what you promised, angel. You've got your cure, you've got—"

"Not you!" she cried, her heart bleeding through the words. "I can't lose you, *no*."

He met Arik's eyes over her shoulder and nodded grimly. "I'm not getting out of here." And they wouldn't either, if they didn't hurry. "You have this one chance, Eden. Don't waste it. Go and save Lily. Save your people. They won't kill me if I don't force their hand. The Confederacy takes wargs alive."

"Throw your weapons on the ground," called a tinny voice behind him, as if to punctuate his words. "This is over."

Not for Eden and the others.

"*Go*," he insisted.

"Johnny," she begged.

He'd been holding the words close, biding his time, hesitant to say them when he wasn't sure if she returned the sentiment, but now there was no point. "I love you," he told her hoarsely as Arik dragged her back. "You made me believe I didn't have to be alone anymore. And I'll come for you, Eden. No matter how long it takes me. No matter how much it costs me, I will survive. I promise. Now go and save your people, before it's too late."

"*Love you*," she mouthed, and he wasn't sure if she was simply repeating the words in shock, or trying to tell him she felt it too.

Arik muscled her away from the bars, and Johnny's ribs constricted. He had this horrible feeling he'd never see her again. Time seemed to slow down. The ringing in his ears enveloped him.

Then she was gone, Arik literally carrying her through the door Mayhew had just jacked open.

The shitty feeling in his chest felt somewhat akin to panic.

"Turn around slowly."

Arik would get her out, and she could complete her mission.

He had to believe that.

Slowly Johnny cupped his hands behind the back of his head, and forced all of the fear out in one nervous exhale. Enforcers surrounded him, their stunners held low as he slowly turned.

All he could do was try and survive.

If Arik could escape Camp Ragnarök, then so could he.

# twenty-four



*Whatever it takes....*

How she hated those words.

Locking down her emotions, Eden crossed to the bed, pressing a hand to Lily's temples.

"Will it work?" Luc rasped, his beard thick and black, his hands clenched between his knees as he sat beside his daughter's bed. From the smell of him and the rumpled shirt he wore, he hadn't moved from Lily's side in days.

Eden prepared the nanoparticle syringe. "It worked for me. Took a few days to shake off the fever"—and she was still a bit achy in her joints—"but my rash is clearing, and my temperature's back to normal."

Hopefully, Lily wasn't too far gone.

It took a couple of days for the nanoparticle hydrogel she'd injected to work completely. She'd barely managed to vaccinate the human pack members of Shadow Rock before the sweats started, though her sweats had been nowhere near as bad as the plague victims in Absolution.

The fever had her in its grip by then, and she could barely remember crossing the Divide in the back of a jeep driven by Lincoln and CJ. Arik had stayed in Shadow Rock to make sure his pack was safe, but he'd provided an escort of Munin for her, as a debt repaid for when Johnny slammed him to the floor before he was shot.

*Johnny.*

Thinking about him only caused her heart to constrict like she was having an angina attack. There was no time for that. She had to believe he was safe and alive, and she would have time to get him back.

*They will die if you don't get out of here now....*

How had she ever thought him violent and selfish?

Right now, she needed to focus on those who might not be safe.

It was all that was keeping her on her feet right now.

Blinking away the surge of pain, she turned to Luc. "Has she kept any water down of late?"

"Barely," he replied, his voice rough from lack of sleep. "She's been incredibly thirsty all week, but yesterday she started to get listless. Not as thirsty."

Not a good sign.

"No word from Adam?"

"I sent news north through the radio chain," Luc replied. "No reply. He might be out of range. Was expecting to spend the month there. So Riley sent a message north with her friend, Jimmy. He'll find him."

She felt restless without Adam there. She'd survived a year apart from him when he went into his self-imposed exile two years ago, but he'd always been a presence in her life. Despite the fact he drove her crazy at times, when

Adam strode into town, she felt like she could relax. Her brother might try and take over, but he could handle anything the world threw at him.

She really, really wanted a hug from him right about now.

Eden set up the drip she'd gotten from Absolution, unnerved by how hot the young girl was. The red rash that accompanied the plague was all over Lily's chest and her heartbeat was far too fast, her blood pressure low. The antibiotics Eden had given her at the start had helped, Luc had said, until the last couple of days.

Leaning on the bed, she rubbed an alcohol-soaked rag over Lily's deltoid muscle, and injected the entire solution before withdrawing the syringe. Lily shifted on the bed, making the faintest of protests, but didn't rouse.

Eden stepped back and took a deep breath. The first step down.

She'd handed over most of the solution and vaccine in Absolution when she got what she needed for Lily, but she hadn't paused to stay. Absolution had an entire medical team. Bart had gotten in her face, demanding she stay and "see to her duty" and it had been all she could do not to punch him.

She'd given everything she had of herself to save her people.

She'd risked her life, and lost the man she loved.

She owed Bart nothing.

"And now?" Luc demanded.

"Now we wait," Eden said, sinking into the stuffed armchair beside the bed. Her eyes were so heavy she could barely keep them open. "Wake me if anything changes."

It worked.

Lily's breathing eased over the next couple of days, her fever swiftly dying down. The hydrogel injection was a slow-release system that would feed her the full dose of antibiotics manufactured specifically for the chimera bacteria over a course of three weeks.

When Lily woke, it was the first time Eden let herself cry.

She spent the next week buried in the quarantine tents, or helping to vaccinate the long line of people from outside of Absolution. They lost most of the first round of victims, including Ian, who was simply too weak to recover, and Eden cried as they buried him, before she dried her eyes and got back to work.

She barely had time to eat, and sleep was snatched when she hit the end of her endurance. She didn't dream of Johnny—she was simply too exhausted—but he filled every waking moment of her days.

They wouldn't kill him. They used wargs as soldiers in the Confederacy.

Broke them to their will.

The thought made the knot twist even tighter within her, but she couldn't think of that. Johnny would survive, no matter what they did to him. He was strong, and he knew she'd come back for him.

She'd promised.

All she had to do was get through this week, and figure out how to break one warg out of a highly secured military facility in the middle of a walled city-state full of people who were gunning for her head.

Piece of cake, right?

Saving Johnny Colton seemed an impossible task.

But Eden had dealt with impossible before, and as she'd learned in Cortez City, to get what you wanted, you had to work out what your opponent wanted too....

The problem was, she no longer had just one opponent. And this time she was working alone.

Step one had been secured, thanks to Mayhew. She'd given him the letter she'd prepared for General Bligh, and he'd promised to get it to the general. A day ago, the radio room in Absolution had called her aside; General Bligh had received her terms and was interested in discussing the matter.

Miles Wentworth had been arrested, and his case was due to be processed in Cortez City in a month's time. Eden had agreed to be a witness, and Bligh was going to send a helicopter for her. Mayhew had dug up some damning evidence—somehow it was released to the general public—and the general had been smoothing affairs over by shipping out large quantities of the vaccine to the settlements.

She had time to breathe, and now it was time to turn all of her attention on rescuing Johnny.

She just needed to wrangle a herd of ornery cattle into line. Easier said than done, but she'd run through all possible scenarios in her mind, and prepared her retaliating arguments.

The council waited as Eden strode through the doors to the meeting room in Absolution; Meredith Hammerstein arguing with Ben Whitshaw at one end of the table; Maggie Carpenter nursing a mug of tea at the other end and staring at nothing with bleary eyes; Bart Carpenter, Maggie's greedy brother; Alan Cummings, rifling through documents as if he'd never seen the terms listed in them before; and Susan Hawker, who was probably going to be her staunchest opponent here.

Susan straightened with a scowl. "You're late."

Eden didn't take her seat. Instead she rested her hands over the back of the vacant chair left for her. "Sorry. Didn't realize you had anything better to do. I was too busy saving lives."

Maggie wrapped her hand around a mug of steaming chamomile tea and slid it toward Eden. "*And* we appreciate it. We all know we owe you the lives of nearly everyone in this town," she said, with a pointed look around the table. "Have you had any sleep?"

*Sleep. God.* Eden's eyes felt grainy enough she suspected half the Wastelands were embedded beneath her lids. "I'll sleep when this is all over. Have you had a chance to look at my proposal?"

Alan looked up from the page scrawled in Eden's neat handwriting. "These terms are nearly half what they were before."

"You're right." Eden feigned shock. "*And* I was lucky to get that out of General Bligh. It seems the Confederacy is done playing your games. You were going to grant them the Copperplate mining rights a month ago if they agreed to all your terms. They accepted. And then you got greedy and added gold to the list, and Miles Wentworth clearly decided killing off the locals would be a more profitable exercise. Considering I helped foil that plan and am now *trying* to salvage the deal for the sake of Absolution, I think you can grant me a little bit of leeway."

"What's this?" Bart demanded, stabbing his finger at what Eden knew would be item five.

"It's an additional term," she said, her voice settling into a steely resolve. "And it is *not* negotiable."

The Confederacy didn't count wargs as people. She needed leverage if she was going to get him out.

"You're basing this entire agreement around the life of one warg?" he protested.

The slimy little bastard was probably thinking of the money that had slipped through his fingers. He was the one who'd talked the majority of the council—bar Eden and Maggie—into adding gold to the original terms.

"Yes." She stared him down. "I am. If Bligh doesn't agree to this one term of mine, then it's off the table."

It wasn't Bligh she was trying to bluff. She would never deny her people the chance at medication and food they desperately needed, but the council didn't need to know that.

Because she didn't have any other options of saving the man she loved.

She'd seen where Johnny was no doubt being held. Sneaking into a Confederacy-controlled city was one thing. Managing to break into the military camp, find the one warg she wanted to rescue, and escape? Impossible.

She'd spent all week putting her people first—saving their lives. It had broken her heart to do so, but every time she thought of Johnny, she remembered his last words to her. *Whatever it takes.* If it had been her own life on the line, a choice between him and her, then she wouldn't have suffered a moment of doubt. But there'd been too many innocents to consider. The Confederacy wouldn't kill him. They'd try to use him. It was standard operating procedure for them, and she had to believe he was still alive.

Eden wasn't a warrior like her friend Riley. She couldn't take up a gun and shoot her way through to the man she loved. All she had was diplomacy, a deal the Confederacy might accept, and a will of pure steel.

And if Susan, Bart, or Alan thought they could sway the rest of the council against her, then she was here to prove them wrong.

"You don't have the authority to decide that," Bart exploded.

"Eden," Alan's tone sounded a little more conciliatory, "I understand your circumstances, but wargs are wargs. Thou shalt not suffer a warg to live." He glanced toward Susan. "That's the rule we've always lived by, to keep our people safe. It's a horrible rule, but we have to protect—"

"It's the way we lived in the past." *Thank you, Alan.* She didn't bother to roll her eyes at him and point out that of all people in this room, she knew the most about wargs. *But please, do explain just how dangerous they are... and use small words so my poor female brain can understand.*

Alienating him would not help her cause. Putting up with his bullshit might. But there were limits to how long she could let him prattle on.

"What the six of you don't know," Eden said, sucking in a slow breath, "is that there are options now for those afflicted with the warg nanotech. We can't cure it, but—"

"Thought you said there were limited amulets," Alan protested.

"There are. I'm not talking about the amulets. I'm talking about wargs learning how to control the beast within without one. I'm talking about how the Confederacy uses wargs as foot soldiers, and trains them to leash their inner wolf." Not that the council needed to know about the shock collars and "breaking" sessions. That wasn't a solution either. "Johnny Colton knows more about wargs than anyone else I've ever met—including Adam. He doesn't need to wear an amulet. I've never seen him turn. Not once. I've never seen him come close to it. And he offered to teach CJ how to control himself. Imagine what it would be like to live in a world where being clawed up by a warg was no longer a death sentence—or worse?"

Susan's lips thinned. She'd personally put her husband in the ground six months before Adam's status as a warg came out, and in her grief she'd been angry enough at Adam's deception that she'd voted to cast him out of Absolution.

Eden had never held that against her. Every Wastelander grew up knowing you had to put a bullet in your loved ones if they were scratched or bitten by a warg. It was considered a mercy. But Adam's revelation about the amulet that kept him human had shattered the other woman. In Susan's place, she might have been bitter too.

But she'd never have retaliated the way Susan had.

"Maybe it's too late for those we've lost," Eden said softly to her. "But what if we could save those who'll face such a future dilemma? There aren't enough amulets. Nobody knows how to create them." Though Johnny had hinted the amulets themselves might not be responsible for halting the warg, merely a placebo effect. "Our children. Our brothers and sisters. Our husbands and wives. If you help me get Johnny back, there might be a way to save future generations."

Susan stared at her fiercely, her lower lip trembling with suppressed emotion. Eden didn't know whether it was a good or bad sign.

"Why don't we stop wasting everyone's time?" Bart broke in. "Wargs are the least of our concerns. We can deal with them the same way we always have. Clearly your emotions are engaged, but this has to be a business deal, Eden. And what you've put on the table for us is a shit deal. We're giving up a damned mine for this."

*Greedy fucker.* "It's goddamned better than nothing, and it's not like we have the resources to mine it."

Alan shoved the documents away from him. "I'm with Bart. If this general is open to negotiations, then we have another shot. We can get more."

"You want us to give up the rights to Copperplate for a weaker deal, Eden," Ben said softly. "I'm sorry. But I cannot vote for this."

"My vote's with you, Eden," Maggie growled. "As you say, it's not like anyone else has managed to bring the

Confederacy back to the table. We know what happened last time we got greedy."

Meredith looked like she'd bitten into a rotten apple. "I need time to consider our options. Sorry, Eden. I'm not for or against. I'd like to take a week or so to assess."

Johnny might not have that time.

She looked sharply toward Susan, her heart sinking in her chest. *Please. Please.*

Susan stared down at the table, drumming her fingers slowly.

"Fine," Eden said, locking down all of the emotions that afflicted her. She'd been prepared for this. Eden drew the chain over her head—the one that marked her as a councilor. "Then I resign."

"*What?*" Meredith blurted.

The chain clanked as it hit the table. Ben—who'd been leaning back in his chair—straightened abruptly. A gasp came from Maggie.

Bart, however, looked rapturous. They'd always butted heads. "You've done a lot for the council," he said sanctimoniously—the prick. "Unfortunately, we will have to accept your resignation and take over the—"

"I also intend to leave Absolution," Eden said, cutting through his monologue. "You are welcome to attempt to contact General Bligh, if you can work out how to reach him. You might have to remind him who you are, and you'll also be competing against an offer from Haven, which I'm helming."

Six voices cut over the top of each other, echoing off the walls.

"You can't leave!" This from Maggie, who looked stricken. "Your place is here."

"What offer?" Bart.

"*Haven?*"

"Who's going to run the medical team?"

"No. We need you. The medical team needs you."

"Eden, please reconsider...."

"How do we contact Bligh?" Bart again.

Eden held up a hand, letting their voices wash over her, until they fell into silence. "I am done dealing with this council." A little bit of heat suffused her voice. "My brother built this town. Adam forged Absolution out of nothing, and gave a home and a place of safety to every person I see sitting around this table." She glared at Ben. "He took a bullet for you." Another glance speared Meredith. "He rescued your son when reivers took Milton prisoner. And three years ago, when you discovered what he'd been hiding, you cast him out, despite the fact he'd spent years holding the warg within him at bay." Her throat felt dry as she locked eyes with every councilor in the room. "It was Adam's choice to walk away and I knew if I fought you on it, it would be one vote to six in favor of banishment. He was gone before I woke up, and even though it gutted me, I felt I had a duty to stay and continue training up my medical team, as there was no one else to step into my role.

"I have *never* asked you for anything. Except this." The muscle in her jaw ticked. "Johnny Colton is the one item I've added to the list. One life. The life of the man I love, a man who sacrificed himself so you could have the cure that saved the lives of every damned person in this town. Some of you might not even be here if it wasn't for him." Angry tears dampened her eyes. "Once upon a time, this town believed in looking after its own. We opened our gates to those who needed it. We gave our food to strangers and watched each other's backs. I don't know where we lost our way. Maybe it was Adam's secret coming out, I don't know. But warg or not, Johnny doesn't deserve to be repaid for his sacrifice with contempt. He doesn't deserve to rot in a Confederacy prison while we go about our lives without a care in the world. So if you want to deny the deal I've discussed with Bligh—medicine for Absolution, resources to teach our healers more about medicine, food supplies, gasoline—just because you're greedy and Johnny's a goddamned warg? Then go ahead. But I won't be here to listen to your shit."

Eden took a steadying breath. "The settlement of Haven owns access to the escarpment mines to the north. They're a little further out of the way, but there's copper there too. And they're willing to ask for less. You want to know why you're getting half the original deal? Because Haven's in on it too. I think that's fair. They took in those who couldn't find a place here, and they've accepted others who don't belong anywhere else. They need food and medicine just as much as we do. I *could* negotiate a deal for both Haven and Absolution. But that choice is up to you. And my price is not negotiable. If you won't help me rescue the man I love, then screw all of you. I will save him myself, and you will get nothing."

Someone cleared their throat behind her.

Eden turned, half-blinded by rage. How much did she have to give these people? The fucking blood from her veins?

There was a large shadow in the doorway.

A tall man, wearing a black ten gallon hat.

Her heart took a sudden mad leap in her chest as she straightened away from the table. "Adam?"

Luc Wade came into the light, hands in his pockets. Eden's hopes fell. For a second she'd thought it was her brother. The one person she could trust—the one person who took all her troubles away and promised to deal with them. Luc ignored the rest of them, simply gave her a crooked smile as if he knew exactly what was going through her mind. "Sounds like Absolution's loss is Haven's gain. Want some help packing your bags?"

The rest of the council gaped at him as if he were a ghost sprung to life. Wargs weren't welcome in Absolution, and the last time Luc had been here, he'd caused an epic shit-ton of trouble.

She'd never understood what Riley saw in him before—until she fell in love with Johnny. Luc might have been one part villain, one part ruthless mischief-maker, but he adored his wife and he was a damned good father.

And he'd clearly heard enough to play along with her proposal.

"I would *love* a hand," she said.

She made it two steps toward him before chairs scraped across the floors behind her.

"Wait!" Susan called.

And relief flooded through her.

# twenty-five

The door gave an electric buzz behind him.

Johnny lifted his head, tension dripping down his spine. He pushed away from the barred windows he'd been staring through, his fingers aching as blood rushed back into starved digits. He'd lost track of time, staring at the thin sliver of blue sky he could barely see, his thoughts drifting to better times....

Of lying on a pile of furs with Eden's panting body beneath him.

Of watching relief cross her face when they finally received the cases full of hydrogel that would save her people.

Of watching a smile creep shyly across her mouth when she finally warmed up to him.

And finally, that one last time, when he'd told her he loved her as Lincoln and Arik hauled her away from him.

The trick of dissociating from his current surroundings had saved his sanity in the past. He'd needed it to survive the past couple of weeks. But now he needed to be in the moment.

A handful of guards came through the door, splaying out before him with baton-like stunners in their hands. They all wore flak vests and riot masks, with plastic shields guarding their faces. Four of them. As if he couldn't put them all down if he wanted to.

"Hands behind your head, L-234."

*L-234.* He bore the fucking barcode on his wrist, and that was all they'd called him in the interim. Johnny Colton had ceased to exist the second they brought their electric-stunners down on him in that hallway three weeks ago.

Reluctantly, he lifted his hands and clasped the back of his shaved head. One of the guards moved closer, lowering his stunner as he approached with the warg-proof cuffs they used with a heavy hand. Another guard lifted his gun and pointed it directly at Johnny. Clearly they hadn't appreciated what had happened three days ago, when his temper finally snapped.

Likewise.

His ribs had finally stopped aching. Wargs healed fast, but the enforcers treated them like animals. Any assault on their guards earned a heavy-handed retaliation, and they hadn't stopped kicking him until he lost consciousness. They didn't speak to him unless it involved ordering him around. They'd stripped his name from him, started trying to break him to their will.

It was nowhere near as bad as what Cane had done to him, but fear curdled his gut whenever he found himself alone.

Because he'd broken once. He'd bent, and he knew it.

And maybe they couldn't get to him, but maybe... maybe they could.

*I would rather die than become someone's pawn again.*

"Hands behind your back, L-234."

Perhaps it would be easier to go out this way, with a clean bullet to the chest? His lungs started to squeeze, and he couldn't get a full breath at the thought.

*Eden. Think of Eden. You can survive this. You can escape.*

*She's not the type of woman to leave you behind.*

But who'd come back for a man like him?

The cuffs snapped into place as he slowly consented, the dull burn of fear flushing through him. He'd told her how he felt about her, but everything had happened so quickly. Eden would come for him; he knew her too well to doubt that. But there'd be other people around her, trying to talk her out of it. A whole Confederacy between the pair of them.

And if her brother, Adam, had anything to say about it, Johnny would probably find himself rotting here. Adam might have forgiven him for what happened all those years ago, and there'd even been a hint of camaraderie between them when they parted ways, but they weren't friends, and if he had a single clue Johnny had put his hands on Adam's sister....

*Face it, you don't have a single friend in the world.*

The radio buzzed on one of the guards' hips. "Is the prisoner secured?"

The man lifted it. "Yes, sir."

"Make sure he's cleaned up. Give him the works. Then bring him topside."

"Sir."

Johnny's eyes narrowed as the guard lowered the radio. This was new. They spent most of their time either brutalizing him or throwing him in a cell with one of their pet alphas to see if the warg could bring him to heel.

He'd enjoyed turning every single alpha they'd tried to use against him. So far nobody had worked out how he'd managed to do it, though they'd taken blood tests and were quite excited about the slight differences in his DNA and nanoparticles.

Apparently, a lot of records had been lost during the Darkening. Black River Testing Facility, way out there in the Wastelands, had been a black site according to the records he'd flipped through when he'd been poking around out there. It was possible Project: Warg had been so far off the books that when the Confederacy formed post-Darkening, they weren't aware of it.

All their research had been on alpha and beta strain wargs they'd captured from the Wastelands to form their new lupine unit.

He was their first omega.

"This way," the one in charge said, and the guard behind him prodded him forward.

And Johnny was just curious enough to obey.

The shower cells were stark and empty. Just a row of showerheads, with drains set in the concrete floors. Uncuffing him only long enough to strip him down, they gestured him under the shower.

"No trouble," the guard in charge snapped. "We've got orders to bring you before General Bligh, preferably in one piece. I'm going to be pissed if you force me to break the general's orders."

Someone shoved him under the shower and turned the cold water on. Another tried to scrub the dirt and blood from his skin, but Johnny curled his lip and snarled, snatching the soap himself.

No fucking way.

He cleaned himself as best he could, and toweled dry when commanded. They wouldn't let him handle the razor himself, using one guard to pin his head in place, two on each of his arms, and another to shave him.

Something was definitely going on.

"No trouble," the guard in charge repeated, once he was dressed and cleaned. "Or you'll regret it."

They'd even given him shoes.

Dragging a hood over his head and cuffing him again, they led him through the main building where hundreds of wargs were locked away in barred cells. He'd been kept in solitary, and presumed he'd stay there until they deemed him subjugated. He could smell other wargs, hear them shifting in their cells as they passed, but nobody said a damned thing.

These were the Confederacy's special warg forces, comprised of soldiers and not individuals. Not anymore. He'd tried to speak to some of the alphas that tried to break him, but there was no spark in their eyes anymore. Just puppets trained to submit to the Confederacy's whims. It made his skin crawl.

The stale scent of warg pheromones stained the air, even through the hood. Then a hand in the middle of his back shoved him out of the room, into something small and dark. The swish of doors closing made him feel slightly claustrophobic as he found himself trapped on either side by the warm bodies of the enforcer guards. Suddenly the ground lurched and he staggered. Up. They were going up in one of their little metal boxes.

Another hiss of air as the doors finally opened, and there was wind on his skin, rippling his shirt against his chest. An engine roared somewhere nearby, and the black hemp of the hood grazed his face as they walked directly into a headwind.

"Where the hell are you taking me?" he yelled, breaking the first rule they'd ever taught him. *Wargs don't speak.* But he was too unnerved to obey. Maybe there was an execution ground out here somewhere, so they didn't get blood all over the floors. Or maybe they were simply going to throw him off the edge of the building?

That didn't explain why they'd shaved him or given him shoes, though.

"Silence." Another shove.

*One of these days....* He could feel his claws itching beneath his skin.

"General." The guy who'd pushed him sounded instantly respectful.

"Get that goddamned hood off him," snarled a voice thick with command. The stranger's voice dropped, though Johnny could barely hear him over the roar of that engine. "Jesus. I didn't tell you to put a hood on him! I said *clean him up*."

They dragged the hood off, leaving Johnny blinking in the sudden sunlight. His eyes hurt after being trapped so long in the dark.

Blades winked as they rotated slowly in the light, the flashes of sunlight blinding him. A black helicopter loomed on the launchpad nearby, a handful of people standing just outside the rotor circle, though he couldn't make them out. It still took his breath away, seeing something like the helicopter. These fuckers didn't know how good they had it here.

Though he suddenly realized he wouldn't trade the Wastelands for all the tech in the Confederacy.

"Johnny?"

A whisper carried to him on the wind.

His heart punched into his throat.

And there was a slim figure in denim jeans and a white shirt, her long chestnut curls bound into a tight bun as her eyes lifted to his. The second she stepped into the sunlight, it surrounded her like a haze. Or no, maybe a halo of pure golden light that surrounded her entire body.

*Eden?*

The breath punched out of him, his heart plummeting like it had leapt off a cliff without the rest of him. He was dreaming. Had to be. Johnny took a half step toward her, before the twist of the cuffs reminded him exactly where he was.

He had the unmanly feeling he was about to lose his shit. His vision blurred once again, but this time it wasn't from the piercing sunlight. She'd come. She'd actually come for him.

"Remove his cuffs," said the general.

An electronic click, and he was free, rubbing at his wrists.

He barely had time to catch his breath before Eden launched herself against his chest, sending him staggering in a circle as he wrapped his arms around her and breathed in the familiar scent of her hair wash.

Johnny captured her face between his hands as he found his feet, though he had the feeling he'd never catch his balance again. "Angel? What are you—?"

Soft lips captured his, stealing the words from his mouth. Johnny moaned, drinking in the taste of her. But it was one thing to kiss her—something he'd been dreaming of for weeks now—and another to see her right back in Confederacy hands.

*She came back. Right into enemy territory.*

*Who knew what Miles Wentworth's family would do if they heard she was back?*

Johnny broke the kiss, breathing hard. He squeezed her tight, his mind still reeling. What was she doing here? What had she done to earn his freedom? He couldn't believe she was real. "You came back?"

*For me?*

"Did you think I was just going to leave you here?" she asked, a tear sliding down her cheek. Eden suddenly shoved him in the chest. "Damn it, Colton. Who do you think I am?"

*The woman of my goddamned dreams.*

He kissed her again, a silent apology for doubting her. Of course Eden McClain would storm the Confederacy to get him out. It was his own worth he'd doubted. Every inch of him ached with shock. He still couldn't believe she was here, running his hands up and down her arms as if to confirm the truth.

"Sorry to break up the reunion," drawled a very familiar voice. "But I'd rather we get the hell out of here before some Confederacy cumstain decides the only good wargs are either dead or leashed."

Johnny jerked away from Eden, his breath ragged.

"Wade." Johnny's breath caught in his chest when he saw who else was there. Luc Wade was the last person he'd have ever expected to see. The last time they'd met, Wade's woman put a bullet in his chest, and Wade decided against finishing the job. But he was almost grinning now, as if to see Johnny undone made his fucking day. "Long time, no see."

"Colton. Not long enough."

Eden gasped, but Wade merely held up his hands. "I owed you a favor, Eden. I'm here to help spring his ass, but I don't have to like him."

Definitely easier to pretend they didn't have a whole fucked-up history. He was dangerously close to feeling like the world was shifting beneath his feet as it was. "Aw, shucks. And here I thought we'd sit down and reminisce about old times."

"Which old times? When you kidnapped my daughter and shot me in the knee?" Wade asked coolly.

"I was kind of thinking of the night you barred the doors to the house I was sleeping in, and set it on fire."

"You got out."

"Lily was safe," Johnny pointed out. "I didn't let Cane touch a hair on her head."

*Touché.* Wade's eyes narrowed as his gaze collided with Johnny's. "You and I are long overdue a certain talk. But we can shelve it until we get the hell away from this place. It makes my skin crawl."

*You have no idea.* Johnny wrapped an arm around Eden's shoulders, still shaken by the fact she'd come back for him. "Agreed."

"Besides," Wade gave him a wolfish smile, "I'm kind of anxious to get home. There's a certain reunion I'm looking forward to seeing even more than this one. You and Eden? McClain is going to just *love* that."

"As you can see, Miss McClain, the Confederacy intends to hold up its side of the deal," said the general, who'd been watching the entire affair with a faintly disapproving look on his face. "If you would sign the agreement."

A secretary in a prim suit stepped closer, opening his briefcase and presenting a set of documents. Eden signed with a flourish.

"Eden," Johnny breathed. "What did you do?"

What had she given up to get him out of there?

"Don't worry, Colton," Wade mused, looking completely unconcerned by the idea of being surrounded by people who thought him an animal only good to be caged—but then he'd never been on the receiving end of their treatment. "Eden received the original contract terms for the Copperplate mine, except she managed to split the benefits between both Haven and Absolution. You're just a bonus. I think the good general thought throwing you in instead of the gold was a win-win situation, but you should have seen the fat little piggys in Absolution squealing about it."

Johnny stared at her, speechless.

"The settlements have a new agreement," Eden confirmed, sliding her hand into his. "We're going to be assisting the Confederacy with their new mine development program. The general has even offered us a helicopter ride home. Shall we?"

He couldn't think of anything he wanted more. The sooner they got out of here, the better. He squeezed Eden's shoulder. "Let's go home."

For the first time in years, he actually had one.

And it was wherever she was.

# twenty-six

A sudden loud banging woke her up. Various members of the council had come knocking since their return, but Eden had ignored them all. This was her time. Eden lifted her head off Johnny's chest and scraped her tangled hair out of her face. "I thought I told you all to go away and leave us alone?"

"Eden, open up."

*Adam.* That was Adam. Eden grabbed the sheet to her naked breasts and shoved herself upright, her post-orgasm languor sloughing off her instantly. He was back from the settlement of New Hope, where Mia's sister and her husband had settled. Finally home.

Except she hadn't figured out how to tell him about Johnny.

"*Oh, shit,*" she breathed. A scalded sound echoed in her throat as she looked sharply at her lover. "You need to hide."

"Where? Under the bed?" he whispered. "Do you think I'll fit?"

She shot a hopeless glance toward the en suite bathroom. "In there!"

"Ashamed of me?" he asked with a nonchalant yawn. He'd spent the past week in and out of bed with her, and he'd finally stopped waking up in a sweat, though he wouldn't speak about what had happened inside the training center. Not yet.

"Of course I'm not ashamed of you!" Eden shot a look toward the door. A large shadow blurred the thin slice of light that streamed beneath it. "I'm trying not to get you *killed*."

Johnny rested back on his elbows and arched a dark brow. "He's already smelled me. And he can hear us." He stroked a hand down her spine, smiling a mischievous smile. "I guess we get to discover just how much your brother thanks me for *saving his life two years ago*."

The last few words rang out loudly, and Eden slammed a hand over his mouth, but it was too late.

Silence.

A thick, *judging* silence.

Then someone was hissing words outside. Mia, by the sound of it. Probably trying to talk Adam out of murder.

Good luck with that.

"Give me a minute," Eden called, shooting out of bed and trying to locate her clothes. And panties. *Jesus.* Where—

Johnny pointed up. The scrap of her cotton panties hung from the light fitting. Her face flaming, she leapt up and hauled them down. Johnny lounged in the sheets, looking for all the world like he had no intention of moving.

"Get dressed," she hissed.

Still smiling that lazy smile, he tossed the covers back and slung his legs over the edge of the bed.

Eden whipped a shirt over her head and tugged her jeans on. Adam might have forgiven Johnny for the part he'd played in his warg curse, but there was no way in hell her overprotective, judgmental brother would let Johnny get away with putting his hands on her.

The second she was dressed, she cracked open the door.

"Adam! You're home!"

"Oh, hell no," Adam ground out, his gaze shooting straight over her shoulder and locking on Johnny, who'd just pulled his jeans on. He stabbed a finger toward him. "You fucking bastard. You son of a bitch—"

He nearly mowed her down, but Eden hadn't grown up with an overprotective older brother for nothing.

"Hey," she yelled, slamming her palms against his chest. "It's good to see you too."

Adam slowed, his nostrils flaring as he looked down at her. "What the hell, Eden? You're *sleeping* with Johnny Colton?"

"Long story," she shot back.

"Then give me the fucking short version. Riley sent her friend Jimmy to track me down and tell me I better get my ass back here as soon as I could. Something about a plague, and Lily dying, and you all wrapped up in it." Adam scraped a hand through his short tawny hair. "We returned as soon as we could and went straight to Luc and Riley's house to find you and Lily, but you weren't there."

Eden tried to work out what to say. "I—I...."

"The plague hit, Eden learned there was a cure in Cortez City, but she needed a guide to cross the Rim, and what do you know, but there I was, trying to drown myself in good whiskey in the bar she walked into. Your sweet sister mercilessly blackmailed me into being her guide, and so we broke into the city, stole the cure, found the Confederacy asshole who unleashed the plague, and worked out a deal with a general, giving him the Copperplate mining rights." Johnny yawned and stretched. "I think that's the short version, yeah?"

Both of them blinked at him.

"You missed the part where you put your fucking hands on my sister." Adam took a dangerous step toward the bed, but Eden darted between them again.

"And you missed the part where I put my hands all over him. Hello? I'm over thirty. You do not make my decisions for me. Jesus, Adam, if you start a fight I will throw you out of my home. Johnny's a guest. My guest. And yes, we're sleeping together. Get over it. I'm a big girl."

Adam froze, and then turned toward her incredulously. "I *built* this fucking house. You can't throw me out."

"You put the deed in my name when you walked out—"

"I seem to remember the story a little differently. I was forced to leave when this bastard"—Adam stabbed a finger toward Johnny—"shot me in the chest, and you took the amulet off to save my life."

"I thought we'd gotten past all of that?" Johnny arched a brow, joking lightly. "When I saved your ass in Rust City. Twice."

Eden glared at him, knowing he liked to lighten the mood whenever things got serious. "Not. Helping."

He held his hands up in surrender. "Sorry, my love."

"*Love?*" The word sounded like it got caught in Adam's throat—or up under a rib.

An amused chuckle sounded behind them. Mia leaned against the doorframe, her arms folded just under her breasts and her legs crossed. "Eden, have you been drinking? This is very much outside the rules."

Eden turned toward her sister-in-law. "Ha. Ha." Mia often mocked her for coloring inside the lines. "It was a stressful time. Johnny got under my skin before I even knew it."

Warm arms enveloped her from behind, and Johnny rested his chin on his shoulder. "I'm here to stay, McClain, so you'd better get used to me."

"Like hell I will."

Eden's heart fell. She adored her brother. But if he forced her to choose.... The mere thought of it sent her pulse racing.

"You said we were friends," Johnny protested.

"I didn't say we were friends." Adam was turning an alarming shade of red. "I said we weren't enemies anymore."

"*Adam,*" Mia called, locking eyes with him. "Why don't you walk it off? This is not fair to Eden. This is clearly her choice and once you've calmed down, I'm sure you'll be able to accept it too. Stop being a dick."

There was some serious eyeballing going on between them, and Mia arched both brows. If there was anyone who could rein Adam in, it was Mia.

Adam glared between them all, his nostrils flaring. "Fine," he snarled, and then he stomped out the door, slamming it behind him.

Johnny cursed under his breath, looking at her guiltily. "You okay, angel?"

*I'm not sure.* She wrapped her arms around herself. She knew Adam was only worried about her. Ever since the mess with Cane, Adam had been overprotective. At least he was aware of it. Most of the time.

Johnny sighed, bending to kiss her cheek. "I'll handle him."

"I'm not sure that's a good idea right now."

He cupped her face in his hands. "If it's making you unhappy, then McClain will get over it. He'll have to. And I'll be on my best behavior with him." His expression softened. "You always take on the weight of the world, angel. I know this will eat away at you, so I'll deal with it. You shouldn't have to worry about us. McClain and I are fucking adults. We can sort it out. Because we both love you, and neither of us wants to hurt you."

He pressed a kiss to her forehead. Then stepped back and nodded politely toward Mia.

"Long time, Mia. You look well."

Adam's wife smiled. "You and Eden McClain? Were you *trying* to push Adam's buttons?"

"Frankly, what's going on between Eden and me has nothing to do with McClain," Johnny replied, pausing to open the door. "I'll go talk to him."

Boots echoed on the veranda as he vanished.

"Sorry," Mia said.

"You didn't do anything." She crossed to her sister-in-law and hugged her. "I missed you."

Mia hugged her back. "And your brother missed you too. He's just having a moment of shock." A wry smile curved her lips as she drew back. "The second he received your letter he went into a panic. Thought he was going to arrive home and find bodies everywhere, so he's been pushing us across the Wasteland. He's been worried sick about you, only to walk into this. You know how he handles stress."

"As well as he handles women," she said with a sigh. Her voice grew small. "Do you think—"

"He'll be fine with it, Eden. He loves you very much and all he wants is to see you happy." The other woman's smile grew big. "And judging from everything I've seen, Johnny Colton makes you happy, am I right?"

A flush of relief went through her. She hadn't had a chance to share her good fortune with anyone. Maggie had been too busy dealing with the repercussions post-plague, and baby Tommy had colic, so Riley hadn't been getting enough sleep to sit and have a cup of tea with her. She needed to share with someone. She needed friends. A hug. Laughter. And someone who wouldn't judge her for the choices she'd made, like the council had.

A warm glow suffused her. "Very. I can't explain it, but I'm so happy. He makes me feel.... It's—" She had no words.

Mia threaded her arm through Eden's. "Good. I want to hear everything. All the juicy details you're not going to tell your brother...."

Johnny found McClain chopping wood out the back of the house. There was a small courtyard planted with an overgrown cumquat tree and packed with overgrown weeds. Eden's green thumb was as evident as her cooking skills.

Still, there was a serenity here he hadn't expected, if one didn't count a pissed-off older brother setting a log on the splitting block.

McClain's gray-green gaze flickered over him, his lips thinning, and then he drove the ax down into the log he had set up. It didn't merely crack or split; both pieces flew apart like they'd been shot from a catapult.

"Do I dare come any closer?" Johnny called, pausing a few yards away. "Or wait until you put the ax down?"

"I distinctly recall saying we were even when we parted ways at Rust City." McClain pointed a finger toward him. "You messing with my sister again? Unforgivable—"

"I'm not messing with her." Anger rose to choke him, the warg cutting him up inside like it had goddamned claws. *Easy.* Sarcasm had always been a defense mechanism, and he'd given in to it inside Eden's room with disastrous consequences for the woman he loved. He had to fix this. Maybe drop his shields a little. He scraped his hand across the back of his neck.

"I love her, McClain. She's the one good thing that's ever happened to me and I would fucking die for that woman. But here's the thing... she loves you too. And you and I being at odds? That's going to cut her heart out of her chest. I won't do that. And if you love your sister, then neither will you."

McClain lowered the head of the ax to the ground, always a good sign. "You love my sister."

It wasn't a question.

He crossed his arms over his chest. "More than anything in this world. I'm going to marry her, McClain. One day. And I would like to have your permission to ask her, when it comes time. You're the only family she has. It would be important to her. I'm pretty sure she'd like it if you gave her away too."

"*Motherfucker.*" McClain tossed the ax aside with a curse. "You're actually serious about this."

He grinned. "I'm going to be the father of her children. Brother."

"Why?" McClain demanded hoarsely. "Why her? I can't help but think—"

"This has something to do with you?" Johnny quirked a brow. "That's either astoundingly arrogant, or rather dismissive of your sister's charms. McClain, she's incredible. Eden's smart, she's stubborn, she's determined.... Sometimes when I look at her I know there's not a damned thing that can stop her when she sets her mind to something. Your sister crossed a brutal desert packed full of wargs to bring a cure back for those she loved, regardless of the risk to herself. When we got to Cortez City, she outsmarted two of the most powerful men in this hell-forsaken world. And then, after all was said and done, she arm wrestled the council of Absolution and the Confederacy into making a deal to get me out of there, all without killing a single soul." His voice dropped. "I know... I will never clear my slate. I know why you doubt me—trust me, I understand where you're coming from. But the question isn't why would I fall in love with your sister, it's why would she fall in love with me?"

He still wasn't sure he had an answer to that, though it was getting easier to believe it.

McClain chewed over the words, suspicion slowly turning to grudging acceptance in his eyes. "My sister's not an idiot. If she sees something good in you, then it must be there." He sighed. "Hell. Even *I* might have been warming up to you last year. I jumped off a fucking four-story building with you."

"We survived."

McClain slowly tipped his head. "You saved my life. You saved Mia. I was two minutes away from maybe offering you a place back in Haven when you stole my bag and took off. I won't pretend we don't have to sit down and talk about the past, but... you're not as bad as I once thought you were."

"Don't choke on it. I'd hate to have to tell Eden if you went down like this."

McClain sighed. "Word of advice. Don't put her up on a pedestal. I love my sister, but she's not perfect, and this won't survive if you think she is."

"You think you're telling me something I don't know? She can't cook for shit, and I know who's going to be doing the housework around here. She can hold a mean grudge, and she doesn't like swearing. I mean, who the fuck doesn't like swearing? I also have the feeling I'm going to be looking at lists for the rest of my life, but she might have to compromise there, because I don't do lists."

*I didn't do forever either.*

*Until now.* He rubbed a hand over the back of his neck.

McClain glowered. "You'll protect her?"

"With my life," he said fervently.

"And you'll never betray her?"

"I'd rather cut off my own hand. I'll love her, McClain, until the day I die. I'll remind her to eat when she gets lost in her thought processes, I'll help her set up her new clinic in Haven, I'll try to ignore the fact she snores like a train—"

"Good luck with that." The first flicker of a smile crossed McClain's hard mouth.

"I'll even put up with her overbearing, arrogant older brother, and that's almost a deal breaker."

The smile died and McClain stared at him flatly for a long moment. Then he sighed. "I'll accept this on one condition...."

"Which is?"

McClain hefted the ax. "You don't ever call me 'brother' again."

Johnny grinned. *No promises.* "So about her hand in marriage...?"

"Don't push your luck." McClain picked up the ax, resting it on his shoulder.

# epilogue



*Three months later...*

Butterflies raced through Eden's abdomen, leaving her slightly breathless.

"I just don't see what all the rush is about," Adam grouched.

"What's the point in waiting?" she asked. "There's not a single doubt in my mind about this, and Johnny *did* ask." The day he'd produced a ring for her was possibly the second happiest of her life, only slightly behind the day she'd rescued him from the Confederacy. Eden glanced down, staring at the plain gold band. "I can't believe I'm getting married."

"I can't believe you're getting married either. This collar's too tight," Adam complained, tugging at it.

Eden examined the buttons, smoothing the collar against his tanned skin. "It's fine. Leave it alone. You look very handsome in your shirt and jeans, and I'm sure Mia will drag you off somewhere to show you how much she appreciates it later."

"And you look stunning." He sighed. "I admit it. You're glowing. You're going to be the most beautiful bride."

*There might be a reason for that....*

"You're okay with this?" she asked softly.

Adam brushed one of her curls off her face, his expression implacable. "Eden, Colton asked me for your hand in marriage every day for the last three months. I'm okay with it. I finally gave in last week when he hinted he'd prefer if his children had his last name too, and you guys were maybe thinking about getting started on that."

Her hands splayed across her abdomen instinctively. "Uh, about that...."

Adam's gaze sharpened. "Edie?"

Another breathless shiver of nervous excitement went through her. It had been their little secret for the past two months, and she'd been worried how Adam would take this. "You're going to be an uncle... in about six months' time."

Apparently there'd been a little side effect from that night in Shadow Rock, if she had her timing correct. Blame it on the kaga. Although she'd had her birth control booster a couple of months before, she'd forgotten about the effect of the antibiotics.

The color drained out of his cheeks.

"Adam?" she asked sharply, a fist of anxiety lodging in her throat. She'd hoped he'd be pleased. "I'm happy. Please be happy for me—"

Adam dragged her into a tight hug, thumping her back. "I am happy for you," he choked out. "You just took me by surprise."

"Squeezing... too... tight...."

He let her go, and Eden smiled up at him tremulously. Adam brushed a tear from his eye.

"Jeez, big guy," she teased, poking him in the ribs. "Anyone would think you were the one pumped full of hormones at the moment."

"Something in my eye."

"Yeah, yeah."

"We might be adding to our family in the near future too," he admitted.

Her heart swelled. "Mia's—"

"No." Adam shook his head. "Mia was raised by a foster family who took her in when she was little. She strongly believes there are too many orphaned children out here in the Wastelands who need parents. It's a hard world. And I had a hand in raising Lily for a few years. They were some of the best years of my life, so... we've been discussing adoption."

Eden gave a cry of delight and squeezed her arms around him. "That's perfect. You'd be a great father."

He cleared his throat. "Speaking of perfect, we'd better get you out there before your groom starts to get nervous and thinks I've kidnapped you."

Eden smuggled a smile as she drew back. "You're starting to like him."

"Am not."

"Are too," she said.

Adam rested his hands on her shoulders, his gray-green eyes gleaming suspiciously. "You've always been my baby sister, and to see you today like this.... Mom and Dad would have been so proud, and I know—" The word came out choked. "*Shit.*"

He turned away, scrubbing at his mouth.

"Adam?"

He promptly held out his arm, waving her away. Couldn't get the words out right now.

She leaned up and kissed his cheek, accepting his arm. "Thank you," she whispered. "For all you've done for me over the years. And thank you for being here for me today."

He offered her his arm again.

The door banged open, and Riley stuck her head through. "What the hell are you guys doing in here?" She narrowed her brown eyes on Adam. "If you try and make a run for it with her, I will track you down and drag her back. Bridesmaid promise."

"Can everyone just relax?" he growled. "We're coming. I just needed a moment to say goodbye to my sister."

"We're living three houses down from you," Eden protested. They'd stayed at Absolution for the first month, before she grew tired of people staring at the warg in their midst. Some things never changed. Lucky for her, most of her family lived in Haven. It hadn't been a difficult decision at all. "I'm not going anywhere."

"No, you're not," he said, escorting her toward the door. "But now you'll officially belong to him."

"Oh God," Riley muttered. "You haven't changed a bit, McClain. You are so old-fashioned."

"Have you ever thought maybe it's the other way around?" Eden added. "Maybe I'm doing this for Johnny, so he feels like he belongs to me?"

Adam looked at her sharply.

"Johnny doesn't have a family," Eden pointed out. "I want him to be mine, and to feel welcome in my world. It's been hard for him. He's never spent much time around people, and he hates his past so much it creates a little bit of a wall between him and others. But now they'll be his people too. Maybe it will help him feel like this is his home."

Adam sighed. "If he starts calling me his brother—"

"I know."

Adam gave a curt nod. "Let's do this then."

Riley winked and held open the door for her.

Smoothing her green cotton dress of nonexistent wrinkles with one hand, Eden let Adam escort her out into the garden behind his house in Haven. Those butterflies were back.

Guests turned as they made their way out onto the veranda, and Eden bloomed into a smile when she saw all of her family and friends waiting for her. CJ winked at her as she passed him. Lily wore a white dress that Eden had taken in for her, and scattered a handful of wildflowers like desert sand verbena and arnica across the sandy gravel.

And there...

Waiting for her at the end of the narrow tunnel of people....

Her smile widened until it almost split her cheeks as Johnny heard the guests start to shuffle, and turned, unable to help himself. Their eyes met, and all of Eden's nerves died away as she met those dark, slightly cynical eyes. The self-deprecating cynicism he usually wore was gone. Instead, his mouth softened as he caught a glimpse of her, and she was pretty sure Johnny Colton stopped breathing for a second.

His gaze caressed every inch of her, as if he simply couldn't believe this was about to happen.

Eden joined him in front of the gorgeous red oleander that was in full bloom. A string of pretty lanterns hung above them, and she remembered them from Maggie's cousin's wedding a few years ago.

"You look...."

"I know. Riley found this dress for me in one of her trunks." She bit her lower lip shyly.

"It's not the dress," Johnny murmured, shooting her the sultry smile that did so much damage to her insides.

"You look pretty damn good too."

Black shirt, black jeans, his hat slung low over his face, and his jaw clean-shaven. Months ago he'd have looked like a dangerous outlaw in this getup, but the smile softened him. Life had softened him.

He looked happy.

"*Language*," he chided, and Eden smacked his arm.

"You're a bad influence on me."

"You need a bit of bad in you, angel. Helps keep you grounded." He leaned closer to her ear, his voice dropping. "*Eres la luz de mi vida y tienes mi corazón en tus manos para siempre.*"

*Oh, God.* He was using his sexy bedtime voice, knowing the impact it had on her. "Behave, *mi diablo.*"

"You don't even know what I said." His smile held all manner of sin. He was slowly teaching her his mother's language, though she found it difficult to concentrate considering he whispered Spanish words in her ear when he made love to her.

"Tell me later."

"I will."

Her unconscious mind had begun to associate the language with sexy times, and all their lessons ended up going off tangent.

Not that that was a bad thing.

"Ready?" he whispered.

"Let's do this."

Eden could scarcely take her eyes off him as the priest started the ceremony. She held his hands as the words washed over her, said what she had to, and smiled until her cheeks hurt.

Then Johnny slid a wedding ring on her finger, and people started clapping.

"You may now kiss the bride," the priest called.

Eden grabbed his shirt by the collar and lifted her face to his as Johnny cupped the back of her skull with his hand. Their mouths met, Johnny's feet braced apart and his body towering over her. A deeper kiss than she might have expected in front of her family—and brother—but as cheers lit the air, she found she didn't care.

Everything was perfect and Eden could finally cross off all items on her happiness list, and add one more.

*Surrounded by everyone she loved. Check.*

*Married to Johnny Colton. Check.*

*Having his baby. Check.*

*A new Spanish phrase to learn tonight—to be crossed off the second she managed to get some privacy....*

*Consider it checked.*

# THE END

# CLASH OF STORMS

## BOOK THREE: LEGENDS OF THE STORM
### COMING 2018

**The old eddas speak of *dreki*—fabled creatures who haunt the depths of Iceland's volcanoes and steal away fair maidens.**

The Blackfrost is a name both feared and reviled within the *dreki* clan that rules Iceland. When Malin joins forces with Sirius to help rescue the princess she loves, she has no idea of the journey ahead of her. This dark prince watches her every move, and protects her from those who might harm her—but is there something more to the look in Sirius's eyes?

*A dark prince. An unsuitable mate. Can this villain become her hero?*

Malin is a nobody in the *dreki* world. A servant far beneath him. And though Sirius's kiss burns through her like lightning, he's keeping far too many secrets for her to trust him....

But when Sirius sacrifices himself at her bequest, does Malin have the strength to save him from a fate worse than death? And can she ever give this wicked prince her heart?

*Want to know more about Clash of Storms? Make sure you sign up to my newsletter at www.becmcmaster.com to be the first to know its release date, read exclusive excerpts, and see cover reveals.*

*Dear Readers,*

*Thank you so much for reading* The Hero Within! *If you enjoyed it, please consider leaving a review online.*

*Burned Lands has always been a fun place to play. It started all those years ago when I set out to create a post-apocalyptic, action-fuelled trilogy featuring three cursed heroes. The only problem? Luc Wade—who was supposed to be the villain in book one—decided, nope, he's the hero. And Adam McClain, being the one who'd ruined Luc's life, graciously stepped aside in order to seek out his own HEA. But there was one more hero out there, always waiting for his own turn, and* The Hero Within *was finally time for Johnny Colton to shine.*

*Villain. Unrepentant charmer. Bartholomew Cane's right-hand man, yeah? Or not. I loved delving into Colton's psyche and unearthing a man who's done a wealth of bad things in his life. I always knew the reasons why—and the part Eden played in his downfall—so there is a particularly enjoyable feeling about finally closing out a chapter and getting to reveal all.*

*The Burned Lands are a dark place but I like to think there's hope and love there, and happy-ever-after's, and I promise the three couples are done with rabid reivers, wargs and Confederacy militias. I strongly suspect Luc and Colton are going to form a firm friendship, and conspire to make McClain's life hell. Colton's going to have many long years of calling McClain "brother".*

*It's one thing to write the darned book, and another thing to create something worth reading. I couldn't have done it without a lot of help from these amazing people:*

*I owe huge thanks to my editor Olivia from Hot Tree Editing for her work in making sure everything is in its right place; to my cover artists from Damonza.com who consistently hit it out of the park; and Marisa Wesley and Allyson Gottlieb from Cover Me*

*Darling for the print formatting. To Kylie Griffin and Jennie Kew, as always, who are the best support team any writer could dream of; and the Central Victorian Writers group for keeping me sane and celebrating the small goals with all those chocolates! Special thanks to my family, and to my other half—my very own beta hero, Byron—who understood the deadline rush, and always cheers me on from the sidelines.*

*Last, not least, to all of my readers who support me on this journey, and have been crazy vocal about their love for the London Steampunk series, and anything else I write! You guys make all the late nights, blood, sweat and tears worth it. I hope you enjoy this crazy little detour into a post-apocalyptic world!*

*Cheers,*
*Bec McMaster*

# ABOUT THE AUTHOR

BEC MCMASTER is a writer, a dreamer, and a travel addict. If she's not sitting in front of the computer, she's probably plotting her next overseas trip, and plans to see the whole world, whether it's by paper, plane, or imagination. She grew up on a steady diet of '80s fantasy movies like *Ladyhawke*, *Labyrinth*, and *The Princess Bride*, and loves creating epic, fantasy-based romances with heroes and heroines who must defeat all the odds to have their HEA. She lives in Australia with her very own hero, where she can be found creating the dark and dangerous worlds of the London Steampunk, Dark Arts, Legends of The Storm, or Burned Lands series, where even the darkest hero can find love.

For news on new releases, cover reveals, contests, and special promotions, join her mailing list at www.becmcmaster.com